Omnipotent

Jim Eves

1st WORLD
PUBLISHING

Omnipotent

Jim Eves

© Jim Eves 2008

Published by 1stWorld Publishing
P.O. Box 2211, Fairfield, IA 52556
tel: 641-209-5000 • fax: 866-440 5234
web: www.1stworldpublishing.com

Second Edition

LCCN: 2008941456
SoftCover ISBN: 978-1-4218-9045-6
HardCover ISBN: 978-1-4218-9044-9
eBook ISBN: 978-1-4218-9046-3

To *Bru,* who prevailed on me to keep writing when the words would not flow. Without her encouragement, this book would never have been written.

PART ONE
THE PROLOG

Introduction

Anton, Kelbeck Jr. and Joel Sampson had very little in common. Anton, a professor, taught at The University of California at San Diego, while Joel worked as a computer programmer at the Miramar Marine Corps Air Station.

Anton, a 65-year-old, quiet, studious man, spent his time fully engrossed in his research project. He found the classes he taught an encroachment on his time, keeping him away from his project. A sedentary man, he had no athletic ability at all. His wife was of a similar temperament and they had no children to disrupt the tranquility of their lives.

Joel, a 40-year-old, frustrated athlete, released his pent-up energy by running. He worked conscientiously at his job, but it was just a job; when his shift ended, he left his work at the office. He was a divorced man with no children and no current attachment. His life centered on his running.

They had one thing in common: both were first-generation Americans with foreign-born parents. Before I describe how they met and what ensued, I will tell you some details of their family history, which will help you understand the forces that drove these two men.

Chapter One

In the spring of 1938 when Adolph Hitler executed the "Anschluss" or union of Austria with Germany, Professor Kelbeck's father, Anton Senior, taught as a professor at the University of Vienna. He watched from his office window as the Brown and Black Shirt Nazis rounded up hundreds of Jewish men and women, including many of his family, and forced them to get down on their hands and knees to scrub graffiti off the sidewalks. He felt sick to his stomach with fear. Fear for himself; fear for his wife Sofia; fear for his family; and fear for all his Hebrew friends. The fear numbed his brain as well as his body.

When he noticed the Gestapo going through the university personnel records, he knew he had to do something quickly. He must shake off his fear and act now before they came for him. He could not help his family or friends, but he must save Sofia. The next day, with the help of one of his students, the son of a border guard, he and Sofia crossed into Italy. They each carried one suitcase containing clothes and jewelry.

They were hidden by professional associates in Italy while they applied for visas to go to the United States. After several months, a man contacted Anton claiming to be a colonel in the United States Army. He knew of Anton's reputation as a physicist and offered him a position at the California Institute of Technology to work under Theodore Von Kaman at the Guggenheim Laboratory in Pasadena, California. Anton accepted. When he told Sofia, they embraced, crying on each other's shoulders. The relief they felt was tempered by regret that they could not help others. A large weight had been lifted off their backs. They now had a safe future to look forward to. Two days later they had American visas and tickets for a train to Lisbon and a boat to New York.

They arrived in New York in July 1938 on a hot and humid summer's day wearing Austrian winter clothes and were met by a man representing the Institute. From New York they travelled by train to California where once again an emissary met them at the station and transported them to a hotel. Next morning the emissary drove Professor Kelbeck Senior to the Guggenheim Laboratory. He was immediately put to work, with John Parsons and Edward Forman, on jet propulsion research.

He then found the Army connection. General Henry "Hap" Arnold had contracted with the Guggenheim Laboratory to develop a jet-assisted take-off system to enable large bombers to take off from small Pacific Island airfields.

With the help of the institute, Anton's parents found a house in Pasadena and tried to assimilate into an American lifestyle. Being a shy, retiring couple, they made few friends. For the next seven years they were content to be by themselves with their books and their religion. All Anton's efforts to gather information about his relatives failed. The letters he sent them disappeared into a void; it seemed like they had fallen off the edge of the world.

Things changed in 1945, an extremely eventful year in their lives. In January they bought a house in Pasadena; in February, much to their surprise, Sofia discovered that she was pregnant; in May the war in Europe ended; in June Anton returned to Vienna on a fruitless search for his relatives; in July they applied for American citizenship; in August the war in the Pacific ended; in September they were granted citizenship; and in October Anton Junior was born.

In the years after World War II, anti-Semitism prevailed in the United States, but probably because of the large number of Jews in the Hollywood movie industry, this part of Los Angeles County was more enlightened than most areas. There were still plenty of anti-Semitic jokes and Anton could not join the exclusive county clubs, but these things were not a problem for them, they did not move in those circles.

Anton Junior was a tall, uncoordinated A+ student, what we would call today a "nerd." He spent most of his time reading in his favorite place, the library. Anton's studiousness created some problems. Fortunately, his size kept the bullies at bay most of the time. He would do homework for some of the bigger boys. In return, they would defend him from the others. He did homework for classes he wasn't taking just by reading the textbooks. He enjoyed doing this; he learned more this way.

He had no real friends, being a shy, lonely boy. In spite of all the knowledge he gathered, he did not know how to talk to people, especially girls. At first this made him very unhappy, and he would cry himself to sleep at night. Gradually he came to terms with it; his books provided solace. He just shut out the world.

In high school he felt that the curriculum did not go deep enough in the subjects he was interested in: biology, chemistry, physics, and mathematics. He still spent most of his time at the library and ninety percent of his reading was nonfiction. He graduated before the age seventeen with a full scholarship to UCLA in nearby Westwood.

He started college in 1962, a year after President Kennedy sent the first Green Berets into South Vietnam on a "Peace Keeping Mission." The mission developed into a war that didn't end until 1973 when the last American left Vietnam after fifty thousand Americans had died. He enrolled at UCLA just as James Meredith tried to become the first Negro to enroll at the University of Mississippi, which led to President Johnson's Civil Rights bill in 1964. The American youth, and some not so young, were taking to the streets to protest many worthy causes and some not so worthy. It was the days of hippies, yippies, flower children, Haight-Ashbury, pot, civil rights, and bra and draft card burning.

While all that was going on, Anton used the library for studying. When a million people marched on Washington, he studied in the library. When President Kennedy was assassinated, he studied in the library. When the first Selma march became "Bloody Sunday," he studied in the library. When the 1965 Voting Rights Act was passed, he studied in the library. When ten thousand young protesters arrived in Chicago, carrying just their backpacks, to be met by twenty three thousand police and National Guard's men, he studied in the library. He missed the Watts riots, the death of Malcolm X, and the speakers on the UCLA campus protesting the war.

He obtained two bachelors degrees in physics and biology in four years and for a short time considered becoming a doctor. He then realized he wanted to do pure research like his father, so he studied for a master's degree and a doctor of philosophy in Biochemical engineering.

In the fall of 1968 during the last year of his doctorate, he noticed that a young female freshman spent as much time as he did in the library. She was about 6' tall, very slim, and appeared not to have many friends. At least he never saw her with anyone. Anton himself was 6'4" and had never spoken to a woman before unless she spoke to him first, and then he would break off the conversation as quickly as possible. He could not help looking at this girl. Something about her made him think of her as a kindred soul.

One day she came up to him thinking he was a professor, and with a slight stammer, asked him if he could help her find a certain book. He told her he was a student but knew where the book was, leading her to it. Suddenly he found himself asking her if she would like to go for a cup of coffee and to his surprise she said yes. Her name was Mary Polanski; their going for coffee became a regular thing after their evening library sessions and he began helping her with her studies.

This went on for about six months and they became very comfortable in each other's company, but neither of them attempted to take their relationship to the next level. A major problem was her Catholic religion. Finally, Anton graduated and took a position at the University of California at San Diego, mainly because the University had research contracts with the Department of Defense in the area he was interested in.

Anton's career as a research scientist blossomed as the years passed. His reputation enabled him to acquire contacts with private industry as well as the military. In 2000 he won a bid to do research into the aging process for American Pharmaceutical Corporation. This became his obsession.

Chapter Two

Mary Polanski's parents owned a house on 190th street in Torrance, across the street from the Mobil Oil Refinery. Some days the smell of the refinery filled the air, some days it was hardly noticeable, but it was always there. You got used to it. Mary's father, Leo, worked as a field mechanic at the refinery, and her two older brothers as laborers. Leo adored his boys but had no time for his daughter.

From an early age the brothers teased her unmercifully. They called her ugly and stupid. They pinched and hit her when the parents were not looking. Leo said they were just being boys. Mary became a scared, introverted child who developed a stammer. She cried a lot and clung to her mother's skirts while in the house.

Mary's mother, Magdalene, was a large woman who would box the boys ears when they deserved it and would stand up to Leo. He would rant and rave, but he never struck her and she would have her way. Magdalene practiced her religion by going to Mass three or four times a week, taking Mary with her. Mary loved the church; it was quiet and peaceful and got her away from Leo and her brothers.

Mary, a gental girl, liked to help people any way she could, whether it was babysitting, running errands, or helping around the church. On Mondays, Magdalene helped count the weekend collections with five to ten other ladies. Mary went with her, and by the time she was 10, the ladies let her help out if they were shorthanded. Soon she became a regular counter. The priest and the other ladies loved her; she felt wanted for the first time. At that time she wanted to be a nun, but later she thought social service work would be her calling.

She did very well at school. This proved to her that her brothers were wrong about her being stupid. So maybe they were wrong about other things, such as her being ugly. She still stammered at home and at school, but at the church her stammer seemed to disappear.

At the end of tenth grade she asked her mother if she could go to college. Her father said absolutely no, he could not afford it, but her mother talked to the priest and he arranged for the church to give her a scholarship. Mary was accepted at UCLA but the scholarship only covered tuition and books. This meant that she had to drive to and from UCLA each day. Magdalene bought her a 1960 Buick Skylark and to Mary's surprise, her brothers would work on it to keep it running.

When the time came to start college, Mary wondered if she had made a mistake. She was terrified of the thought of all she had to do. Her brothers told her she would fail and should quit now. This goading gave her the strength to go the first day. To her surprise she found that she handled it very well. The classes were hard but manageable. The other students were friendly, although her stammering hindered her from making friends. The drive to school offered the biggest challenge.

Getting to Westwood in the morning took a miserable one-hour drive. Coming home in the late afternoon took a lot longer. She started going to the library after classes until the traffic cleared, enabling her to study and complete her homework in peace and quiet. Staying late had an additional benefit. Her brothers started work at 6 a.m., so by the time she got home they had gone to bed, and she got up in the morning after 6 a.m., so she only saw them on weekends.

Her liaisons with Anton occurred during the last six months of her freshman year; by the time she graduated he was a distant memory.

Following graduation, she took a position with the Los Angeles County Public Social Services Department. She liked the work, but the pay was not very good and her case load was too high. After about a year, one of her coworkers obtained a position with the San Diego County Public Social Services Department. She told Mary that the pay was better and the work load manageable. Mary submitted an application, was accepted, and moved to San Diego. She shared a three-bedroom apartment with her friend and another coworker. Finally she had friends with whom she shared a common interest. By now her stammering was a thing of the past.

One evening, while the three girls waited for a table at Applebee's, Anton Kelbeck walked in. Surprised to see her, Anton immediately felt the old attraction for her. After a few minutes' hesitation he went over to her to say hello. Mary stood up, clasped his hand, and greeted him warmly. This broke down his shyness, and soon they were chatting about old times and new situations.

When the hostess called Mary's table, Anton gave her his business card with his phone numbers on it. Later, as Anton ate, Mary stopped at his table on her way out and gave him her business card with her home phone number and address on it.

Soon they dated regularly. They would dine out, go to plays, piano recitals, or events at the colleges—always just enjoying being together. If she came to the small house he had purchased, it would be a quiet evening with a simple meal, and sitting together listening to music or watching television. It took two months for him to pluck up the courage to kiss her and four months before he confessed his love for her. It took a great effort for him to overcome his fear of being rejected. To his great delight, she told him she loved him too.

One Saturday morning they drove to Torrance to meet her family. Her mother hid her dismay when she discovered that Anton was Jewish. She could see how happy he made Mary as her joy glowed in her eyes. Her father and brothers behaved badly as usual and made no attempt to hide their antagonism. Her mother kept them in their place and Anton handled the situation like a gentleman.

After a few hours they left and drove to Pasadena. Anton's parents were equally dismayed at the religious difference, but treated Mary with polite civility. They stayed the night with his parents, then drove back to San Diego after breakfast.

On the journey back they sat in silence most of the way. The trip had brought their religious problem to a head. They had been avoiding it for six months, but now they had to face it. At Anton's house they sat looking at one another for a while until finally Anton broke the silence. "I care about you more than I care about religion. I don't want to lose you; in fact,

I want to marry you. There must be a solution."

Mary came to him and they embraced. "I feel the same. What can we do?"

"Well, we can't have a Jewish or a Catholic wedding. We'll have to find another way to marry."

"I don't want to just go to a registry office," said Mary.

"Okay. How about one of those garden weddings where there is an official but nonreligious ceremony with guests and a reception afterwards." Mary liked this idea and they spent some time discussing the details.

Mary discussed the situation with her priest who advised strongly against marrying outside of the Catholic religion, telling her she would no longer be able to take communion.

"Could I attend services?"

"Of course."

Anton talked to his rabbi and received the same strong recommendation against marrying out of his faith. When he asked if there would be any repercussion after the wedding, he was told of course not, and your wife will be very welcome at our synagogue. They decided to go ahead with their plans.

They made out a guest list and were both surprised at how many friends they really did have. They invited both families and were pleased when everybody came. The wedding took place on a beautiful summer's day. Everything went off like clockwork. Even her brothers behaved themselves. In fact, they flirted and danced with Mary's friends, who seemed to like them. When the brothers left they said they had had a great time.

The Kelbecks purchased a larger home and settled down to married life. Although they didn't use contraceptives, Mary did not get pregnant. Neither of them seemed to mind; they both had their work and each other. It was enough.

Chapter Three

oel Sampson's father, Robert, was born in August 1934 on Victoria Dock Road, Borough of West Ham, London, England. His parents were poor, honest, working-class people, struggling to make it through the depression.

They had met in 1912 while working at Tate and Lyle's syrup factory. His father had come to London from a farm in Essex to look for work, and his mother, the youngest of seven daughters, came from a Cockney family of costermongers. They wheeled their wheelbarrows through the streets of London selling their wares. By 1931 Robert's parents had five children, three boys and two girls, were unemployed, and renting part of a three-story house near London's Victoria Docks. They had no inside toilet, just an outhouse, and the older boys slept in a shed at the bottom of the garden.

Robert's mother, Helen, had a stall at the end of the road selling ribbons, lace, needles, and threads. Anything the local people needed to make and or mend their clothes. His father, Joseph, worked as a stevedore and each morning he went to the docks looking for work. The loading boss came to the gates looking for a few workers and after a melee the last men standing got the work. Joseph stood 5'6" tall and weighed 140 pounds and although a very strong man for his size, he rarely got any work.

He took a job as a boiler scaler, working inside the large merchant ship boilers removing the scale built up when hard water is turned into steam. The work was very hard and the fumes from the scale rotted the workers' lungs, a condition he suffered from for the rest of his life.

After a year of this, he took a job as a stoker on a merchant marine ship going to New Zealand. The work was hard, the hours long, and he missed his wife and family. He arrived back in England in early 1933, determined not to go to sea again. After a few months of fighting for work on the docks, he obtained a job at the Ford Motor Company plant in Dagenham, Essex. This entailed a bicycle ride of fifteen miles each way in all kinds of weather—rain, sleet, snow, and occasionally hot sunshine—wearing the clothes he had to work in.

A year later Joseph did something that, in those days for a man of his background, was a very brave thing: he purchased a house. He managed to put a small down payment on a house in Dagenham. It had a small front garden that he filled with flowers and a larger back garden in which the frustrated farmer in him planted apple and pear trees, and cultivated vegetables, strawberries, and gooseberries. Two months after Robert's birth, the whole family moved to Dagenham.

Robert's eldest brother, George, a 21-year-old married man, rented a house across the street. The rest of the family moved into Joseph's house, which had two regular size bedrooms and a "box" room that was big enough for a single bed and a small chest of drawers. Robert shared that single bed with number three brother, John, until he was 5 years, when John got married and moved. The two girls, Ellen and Joyce, shared the second bedroom and the second eldest brother, Fred, slept on a bed sofa in the living room.

Robert had a happy childhood even though it included World War II. During the German blitzkrieg of London, the family slept in an air raid shelter dug into his father's vegetable patch in the back garden. In the morning after an air raid, Robert and his friends searched for shrapnel, pieces of metal from exploded bombs. If they found hot pieces, they knew they were from the previous night's air raid.

The British government took a lot of the unused land away from its owners for the duration of the war, and gave it to anyone who would cultivate it. These "allotments" measured 100 feet by 25 feet and some were located in a field behind the houses one street away from Robert's family. Joseph farmed two allotments in addition to working all day and acting as a fire warden at night.

A shortage of food created the need for a rationing law. Everyone owned a ration book with coupons for all items in short supply. This included all dairy products, meat, and even clothing. The butter allowance consisted of two ounces a week per person, so everyone used margarine. Joseph added a chicken run and rabbit hutches to the bottom of his garden, and bred chickens and rabbits. There always seemed to be a homemade incubator in the dining room with baby chicks in it, waiting to grow big enough to return to the run. The family always had plenty of eggs, chicken and rabbit meat, and all the vegetables they could eat.

Robert was a good student without the advantage of help from his uneducated family. In 1945 England, you had to pass an examination called "The Scholarship" to go to high school. At age 11 Robert passed this exam and became the first member of his family to go to high school. He graduated third in his class at age 16, and obtained a position as an apprentice tool designer at the Ford plant.

The terms of the apprenticeship required that he would go to school one day a week and work four 8-hour days plus 5 hours on Saturday. He got paid the equivalent of $9.00 a week.

Fords had many apprentices, but he soon realized that only he and one other took the schooling seriously. The other was a young man three years older than he, named Doug Westbrook.

During the Korean War of the early fifties Britain had a military conscription system requiring young men to serve two years at age 18. You could get deferments to complete your education, but then you had to fulfill your commitment. At age 21 Doug Westbrook went off to complete his military service. He returned after spending two years in the Air Force as a switchboard operator, having forgotten most of what he had spent a five-year apprenticeship learning.

Robert could see himself in this position in another year. His office manager had told him stories about how he had volunteered for the Air Force, then the Navy, and then the Army, at the beginning of World War II, and nobody could take him because tool design was a reserved occupation. Robert knew he had a problem. He could waste two years of his life in military service, then later if a war occurred, he would not be allowed to serve in the military.

When his time came to register, he tried to get into the Air Force as a pilot but was told that if he enlisted for three years, he *might* get a pilot's slot. As soon as his apprenticeship was complete, Robert boarded a boat bound for Canada and a job with Avro Aircraft Company.

In 1959 Robert obtained his visa and crossed the border to work for Hamilton Standard at Windsor Locks, Connecticut. These were "The Glory Years" of aviation, with good engineers in great demand. Robert decided to become a contract engineer. He moved from company to company following the government contracts, ending up in December 1968 at Ryan Aeronautical Company in San Diego, California, where his life was about to take a drastic change.

Over the years, Robert Sampson had learned to play bridge. He had a regular partner and they liked to go to duplicate bridge tournaments. At one tournament they played against two women. One, named Ruth, caught his eye. She was very attractive, with a vivacious personality. Two weeks later he met her again at a local bridge club and managed to stutter out an invitation to go out for dinner. To his surprise she accepted, and his life would never be the same again.

Joel's mother, Ruth, was six years younger than his father, being born in March 1941 in Springvale, Maine. Ruth's father, Albert, the son of a wealthy Englishman named George Wilby, immigrated to America in 1875 at age 25. George's father, Frederick, owned textile mills in Bradford, West Yorkshire, then "The Woolen Center of the World." When Frederick left the larger portion of his fortune to his eldest son, the younger son George Wilby took his young bride, Elisabeth, and his limited assets and settled in Springvale. He purchased the local grocery store with living quarters attached to the back. The three-story building included ten apartments that he rented out.

The couple had two sons, George Junior and Albert, and a 1-year-old daughter Katherine, when in 1901 George Senior died. Elisabeth continued to run the grocery store until she was 75, when Albert took over. His older brother had moved to Florida and had no interest in the business.

Albert, now 36 years old, had married a beautiful French Canadian girl named Annette Douce who had come from Quebec Provence as a 4-year-old in 1904. They had three children, two boys and a girl, when they moved into the store's apartment, and had one more girl before Ruth arrived. The store's apartment had two small bedrooms, so some of the children slept in one of the upstairs rental apartments.

Ruth, a slim, gangly, girl, overcame her self-consciousness by becoming the class clown. She had an easygoing nature, always telling jokes, and playing pranks; she became the "leader of the pack." One summer when a group of the teenage girls were working as maids at a local motel, she organized a strike to get all the girls more money. The owner had to give in as they were the only "maids" available.

Some of her friends came from less affluent families, so she often "treated" other girls when they couldn't afford to go with the group. When going out to eat with her parents, she insisted on taking a friend with her. She cemented friendships that lasted her throughout her life, constantly keeping in touch with the girls she went to school with.

When Ruth graduated from high school she decided there was nothing for her in Springvale, so she went to live with her sister in Arlington, Virginia. At 5'10" tall and 115 pounds, she considered herself unattractive. Wearing glasses did not alleviate this opinion. Her self-consciousness and lack of confidence made her think that she would have trouble finding a husband. So when she met a young Marine stationed at Quantico name Steven Cauldwell, his attentions overwhelmed her. After a whirlwind romance, they were married.

Ruth wanted to have children right away; she felt this would give her added security. Although they tried, the children did not come along. When the Vietnam War heated up, Steve's battalion moved to Camp Pendleton, California, and in 1964 the Cauldwells purchased a house in Chula Vista. Ruth's outgoing personality attracted people and she made lots of friends. Steve served two tours of duty in Vietnam; the second began shortly before the Tet offensive of January 1968.

Steve worked in the Motor Pool at the Marine Firebase at Khe Sanh. He died when the Motor Pool received a direct hit from a rocket. Thirty four hundred allied and thirty two thousand enemy soldiers died during the Tet offensive, but only one death shattered Ruth's life. She spent two months grieving while living with her mother in Maine. Finally she decided to pick up the pieces and return to California. She had many friends in Chula Vista and they formed a very caring support group. She returned to her job at The May Company; her salary along with her Marine pension enabled her to just get by.

Ruth had many men interested in her, but she dated rarely, usually with Marine friends of Steve. She didn't want any romantic entanglements. Steve's memory still haunted her. She could never explain why she agreed to go out with Robert. The next day Ruth regretted having said yes when he asked her, and nearly called him to cancel, but her girlfriends urged her to go. She decided one date would not hurt. Robert behaved as only a gentleman would, his wit and charm broke down her fears, and she had a good time. When he asked to see her again, she found herself saying yes.

Robert and Ruth had a lot in common: bridge, music, dancing, and so much more. They dated often and soon liking one another turned to a deep, caring love. Over the next six months they became inseparable. They spent all their time together, traveling to bridge tournaments in other cities, even going on a cruise. Finally, Robert asked Ruth to move in with him. After a lot of discussion, she said no.

Robert decided the time had come for him to give up contract work and settle down to a permanent job. He surveyed the market and found a position with Northrop Corporation in Hawthorne, California. Before he accepted the job, he took Ruth to the Ruth's Chris restaurant on Harbor Drive and after a delicious meal, he proposed to her. He knelt down at the table and offered her the ring he had purchased. This time with tears in her eyes she said yes.

They were married and purchased a house in Torrance six miles from the Northrop plant. One year later Joel arrived on the scene.

Chapter Four

oel Sampson had a very happy childhood. His doting parents provided a secure environment in a fairly affluent household. His father rose to a senior management position at Northrop and earned a high salary. As an only child, Joel reaped the benefits of this.

His parents spent a lot of time with Joel and bought him educational toys at an early age. He could read and write before he entered kindergarten, but his strongest subject was mathematics. When he started school they encouraged him in everything he did and attended all the activities he engaged in.

Robert, an avid sports fan, didn't want Joel to play football for fear of injury, but he coached little league baseball and youth soccer, so that they could experience sports together. Joel had average athletic ability, but his memories of sports are happy ones.

Starting when he was 6 years old, Robert would take him to see the Dodgers play at Chavez Ravine. He would buy the Union Oil Dodger ticket package of six home games at $1.50 a piece for unassigned seats on the upper level. They would drive to the ball park early, park near the Union Oil station close to the exit, and walk in from there. His father said this made it easier to get out of the parking lot after the game.

Robert Sampson was a little under 6' tall, and 180 pounds, but to Joel he was a giant. He would have to run to keep up with him, and as they climbed the stairs his father would take both his hands in one of his and swing him up the stairs two at a time. They got there ninety minutes early so that they could get front row seats up there with the Gods. Although the players looked like toy soldiers from their seats, the view across the ravine was magnificent. Once seated, they would get cokes and hot dogs, and watch batting practice. Joel was in seventh heaven.

School work did not come easy for Joel. He had to work very hard to maintain his grade levels at As and Bs. He delighted in the mysteries of mathematics; when computers became prevalent he knew he had found his calling. With his SAT scores in the thirteen hundreds, many colleges accepted his applications, he chose the University of Southern California (USC).

Instead of just paying for Joel's education Robert gave him an annual allowance. This was enough to pay for tuition, books, and off-campus housing, with a little extra. Joel had to manage this money. To pay for additional activities, Joel obtained a job at a pizza parlor near the campus. He would come home most weekends, bringing friends. He also brought his laundry for Ruth to do.

He graduated from USC with bachelors degree in engineering and a master's degree in computer sciences. At 24 years old he went to work for Hughes Engineering, in El Segundo, as a systems designer on spacecraft guidance systems. He still lived with his parents in their house in Torrance.

His big interest was running. He would run at least one ten-kilometer race each month and do thirty training miles a week. He trained to fulfill his ambition of running a marathon.

Joel had a hard time making friends; he didn't seem to fit in. When a group of guys he worked with invited him to go on a four-day skiing trip to Mammoth, he decided for once not to say no, but to go along and see if he could enjoy it.

The group consisted of six men, so they needed to take two cars. Joel volunteered to drive as he had the big Ford station wagon that had been his mother's car. One of the other guys had a Cadillac, so he offered to drive too. They planned to stay at the Mammoth Lodge.

The village of Mammoth Lakes is over three hundred miles from El Segundo, north on Highway 395. If they left work early on Wednesday afternoon, they could make it there before 11. It would take two hours to get through the L.A. rush hour traffic, then another five hours on Highway 395, which was not a freeway. On the night before Thanksgiving, the roads would be packed, it being the first big ski weekend of the winter. The bumper-to-bumper traffic made the trip worse than Joel had expected. It was after midnight before he finally got into bed.

The next morning they had breakfast and took to the slopes before 8 a.m. Joel had limited skiing ability so, as a novice, had a hard time keeping up with the other guys. When they moved from the intermediate slope to the more difficult slopes, Joel left them and went back to the beginner's slopes. He realized that he had made a mistake in coming on this trip, and he had three more days of this. By noon he'd had enough, so he headed back to the lodge.

He went to his room and changed out of his ski clothes, and then headed for the coffee shop. After a good lunch, he did not feel like going back to his room so he decided to wander around the lodge.

Just off the main lobby he found a large room with a massive fireplace in the middle of one wall, a giant TV screen in the corner, and a number of couches and armchairs grouped in front of them. A movie played on the TV screen; seated on one of the couches watching it he saw a young woman with her leg in a cast.

He studied the woman for a while. She looked about his age, with long reddish-blonde hair that nestled gently on her shoulders. She wore a lavender-colored, long-sleeved, high-necked sweater and a mauve pleated skirt that came down below her knees. She seemed of average height with a trim, well-developed figure. The cast started just below the knee and ended up in the middle of her foot, which rested on the coffee table.

Joel's shy nature made him nervous around girls, especially pretty ones, and this one made him catch his breath. Before he realized what he was doing, he went over and sat next to her. She looked at him as he sat down and said, "Hi," and then turned her attention back to the movie. Joel sat there silently for a while, afraid to say anything in case she snubbed him, then encourage by the "hi," he asked "Did you break your leg today?"

"First run down the slope. We only got here last night, so I'm stuck here for three days with a broken shinbone."

"How did it happen?"

"I'm not a very good skier and I was on too steep a slope. I couldn't stop, so I turned to the right and hit a tree. The break was clean but I am going to be in a cast for six weeks. I would go home but I came with three other girls in their car. Even if it was my car I couldn't drive."

Joel found her easy to talk to. He had never felt this way with a girl before. He just asked a few questions and she did most of the talking. She seemed glad of the company.

Her name was Beth Langdon; she lived in Lakewood, which is about fifteen miles east of Torrance, just north of Long Beach. She worked for the Rockwell Space Division in Downey as a secretary.

He told her he worked for Hughes, also in aerospace engineering, and they talked for a while about their work and the companies they worked for. Suddenly Joel was telling her about himself, something he rarely did. He found her very easy to talk to. The movie was forgotten and they talked all afternoon like they were old friends. Finally Joel asked, "What are you doing for dinner?"

"My girlfriends are going to a restaurant in town where there is lots of action. I really didn't want to go there in the first place; now I guess I'll just order room service. "

"Why don't we try the restaurant here?" said Joel, "It looks pretty nice."

"What about your friends?"

"Oh! They'll probably go where your friends are going and I'm not really into that stuff."

Joel made a reservation for 7 o'clock, and then helped Beth get to the elevator and up to her room.

Leaving her at the door, he returned to his room to get ready for dinner. He was back knocking on her door at a quarter to 7 to help her down to the restaurant. By 7 they were seated in a corner booth ordering cocktails. As the evening wore on, he realized that he would rather be with this girl than skiing with his friends.

"Why don't I drive you home tomorrow?" He said.

"Don't you want to ski some more?"

"No, I've had enough of that."

"What about your friends?"

"We have two cars—they will all fit into the other one. I'll tell them later tonight, and we can leave early tomorrow; the trip will be easier going back on Friday."

So the next morning, after a good breakfast, they were on the road by 8 o'clock. The drive home went much faster. In fact, it went too fast. He played cassettes and found that they liked the same music; they talked about every subject they could think of. She told him all about herself.

Beth was born in 1972 at St. Ann's Catholic Hospital in Columbus, Ohio. Her father worked for North American Aviation as a design engineer and was transferred to the Los Angeles Division when she was 2 years old. When North American Aviation became Rockwell Corporation, he moved to the Space Division, where he still works. Beth had two brothers and two sisters, all younger than her. She helped raise them after her mother decided to work outside the house when the youngest was 5 years old. Beth loved children; she started babysitting at age 11 and would have done it seven days a week if she could have.

She had finished high school but didn't go to college. Her father got her a job at Rockwell as a clerk and she had worked her way up to being a secretary. She was now 23 years old with no serious boyfriends. By the time they arrived at Beth's house they knew a lot about one another, and Joel knew enough to know he really liked this woman.

"Will you go out with me?" he asked.

"With a broken leg?"

"You do fine on crutches and I promise not to take you dancing."

She laughed and said, "Yes."

They dated steadily for about a year before they decided to get married. During this time, their sexual experiences amounted to hugs and kisses but very little petting. Eventually Beth allowed Joel to fondle her breasts, but she would not let him touch her between her legs. She insisted that they waited until the wedding before their lovemaking went any farther. Joel went along with this; he loved this beautiful woman and would do anything for her.

Both families were delighted when they announced their wedding plans, for they had a lot in common, both being in the aerospace industry. The wedding was a small affair as neither had many friends and their families were small.

Their problems started on their wedding night. Beth insisted that the lights be turned off. Joel easily had an erection—after all he had waited for this for a year. Because of their inexperience, Joel had great difficulty penetrating her very restricted vaginal canal. After several futile attempts, he prematurely ejaculated. They lay there hugging one another until Joel fell asleep.

Beth felt relief that he had stopped. The whole experience had been unpleasant and painful. She longed with all her heart to have children, so she knew she had to submit to intercourse, but she hated the thought of it. She loved Joel and he tried to be gentle, but the feeling in her stomach would not go away.

A few hours later Joel awoke and wanted to try again. She submitted by laying rigidly on her back as this time he succeeded in penetrating her. Once he ejaculated, she pulled away from him, turned her back to him, and went to sleep with Joel cuddling her in the spoon position.

In spite of their sexual problem, the marriage was very happy at first, but this didn't last long. Joel transferred to the Hughes plant in Fullerton, so they bought a house there. They settled down to a quiet life, but Joel still liked to do his daily runs. Beth began to resent this and asked him to stop. His life turned into endless evenings of television and inactivity. Beth had never been an active person and she was contented to stay at home. She lived for her home, and waited anxiously for the day when missing her period announced her pregnancy; motherhood was her goal.

Their sex life didn't improve. Beth just lay there and let Joel perform the act. She refused to participate actively for fear of prolonging the act. A year went by and still no pregnancy. Beth insisted that they both be tested for sterility; When Joel's tests showed a low sperm count, she was devastated. Beth would not even discuss adoption—she wanted her own child.

So began the endless rounds of fertility clinics and artificial insemination doctors until they realized it was pulling them apart. Finally Beth asked Joel for a divorce. The parting was amicable as Joel realized Beth was not for him. Six months later, Beth remarried and now has three children.

It is now time to tell you what brought Anton and Joel together.

PART TWO
THE MACHINE

Chapter One

It was a typical day for late May in southern California. The sky above the University of California at San Diego was azure blue, but the late afternoon clouds were beginning to roll in off the ocean.

If you stood on the tennis court side of North Point Lane, you could smell the ozone, feel the gentle breeze, and see the Pacific Ocean over the tree tops, its cold dark blue stretching to infinity. From the other side of the lane, you looked down onto the oval running tracks, nine numbered lanes of dark red.

To the southeast, blocked from view by Warren College, stood the University of California at San Diego (UCSD) Medical Center perched on a mesa like the Parthenon on the Acropolis. The view below was not the Agora of ancient Athens, but the rush hour traffic on Route 5. The Science Research Park, home to Professor Kelbeck's Laboratory, hid behind the Hospital Cancer Center.

It was the time of day when students, carrying their books in backpacks, rode bicycles or walked from classrooms to living quarters located on numerous cul-de-sacs running off the Campus Loop.

Professor Kelbeck sat on the top step of the concrete bleachers that bordered the west side of the track and watched the lone runner. The man looked to be fortyish and was running laps at about a seven-minute mile pace. Maybe this will be the one. He had spent many an afternoon looking for the person he needed for his research project.

Joel Sampson neared the end of his five-mile run. He tried to do this distance four times a week. On Sundays he did the long run, at least ten miles. This kept him in shape to run the ten-kilometer road races that he entered about once a month.

Seeing the UCSD Tritons logo at the end of the track, Joel finished his run by sprinting the last fifty yards. He fell heavily to the grassy infield, gasping to catch his breath. Why did he continue to do this he asked himself? It never became any easier. The fitter he got, the faster he ran, and so he always finished in the same exhausted condition. Today had not been an easy run. Some days he could hardly drag himself around the track; each step was an effort. Other days he seemed to float around the track, his feet barely touching the ground. He got to recognize this as what they called "runner's high." What made the runner's high come he did not know, but he always looked forward to the next one and its intoxicating feeling.

After a few minutes he got up and slowly climbed the two-foot high concrete steps towards the men's locker room still breathing heavily from the exertion. He passed the man on the top step, and they nodded a brief greeting.

The locker room, a low building built next to the parking strip on North Point Lane, contained two sections, men's and women's. The 25 by 35 foot concrete locker room was cold and uninviting, except when full of students showering. It then had damp warmth and rang with the excitement of youth.

Joel entered the almost empty room and went to a locker in the center aisle that held his clothes. He noticed that the man had followed him and now stood behind him. He noticed two unusual things about his follower. First he was an elderly man, completely gray and slightly overweight, not the usual type seen in a locker room. Secondly, a fully dressed man usually carries an equipment bag when going to or from a locker.

Joel turned to face his visitor.

"Good evening. I am Professor Kelbeck, the head of the Biophysics Department of the University."

Joel shook the professor's offered hand saying, "Good evening. Is there anything wrong?"

"No! No! I was just wondering if you could spare me about an hour of your time this evening, after you have showered and dressed."

"Why sure, but what's this all about?"

"Why don't you come to my office later, we can talk better there," the professor said. "I will wait for you and you can follow me there so I can show you where to park and how to get to my office."

Joel stripped off his running gear and stepped into the shower. Here we go again, he thought. Joel had been running at the University three of four nights a week for the last six months. Prior to that he had run at a junior college near where he lived. The problem there had been that all the lockers were assigned to students and the only safe place he could find to leave his clothes was the faculty changing room. At first nobody had said anything because he looked too old to be a student, so they assumed he was a member of the faculty. After a few weeks they realized he wasn't and he was asked politely by the football coach to stop using the college facilities.

Joel finished dressing and met the professor at the parking area on North Point Lane. They drove separately to the Science Research Park, and he followed Kelbeck to his office.

The office contained a large cherry wood desk with a red leather swivel chair. You could not see the top of the desk because of the multitude of papers and books covering it. The walls were lined with bookcases that were completely full. The rest of the room was in the same state of disarray as the desk. Every article of furniture had papers or open books piled upon it.

Kelbeck removed the books from one chair saying, "Sit here," and then sat down behind his desk. "I guess you are wondering why I asked you to come here. Before I tell you I would like you to answer a couple of questions for me."

Joel nodded his agreement.

"Your name is Joel Sampson. You're 38 years old and you are not a student of the University. Do you have any serious illnesses?"

"Now wait a minute, how do you know all that?"

"Please be patient and I will explain everything."

Joel thought about this for a while; this definitely had nothing to do with him using the track facilities, so he decided to go along. Anyway, he was curious to know where all this was leading. "I broke my nose playing soccer, and I still have trouble with my sinuses in wet weather, but apart from that I'm pretty healthy."

Professor Kelbeck stared at Joel for a long while as if he was struggling with a decision. Finally he said, "I have had a background check done on you because I want to make you a proposition. My information tells me that you are an honest and reliable person, so I am going to take a chance. Before I tell you anything, I want your word that whether you accept my proposition or not you will never tell anyone what I am about to tell you."

"If it's not illegal or immoral, you have my word."

"For years I have been doing research work in the area of ageing. What causes aging and is there anything we can do about it. After many years with little success, I began to examine the basic atoms that make up the molecules, the smallest part of any substance, including all parts of the human body." The professor paused for a while, then continued. "An atom consists of an electron cloud and a nucleus made up of protons and neutrons. The protons and neutrons contain quarks that are typically bonded in pairs or triplets. Quarks come in several varieties that form tight bonds, held together by what is known as the strong force. The strong force gets stronger the further the quarks are apart. As the electronic field in an atom deteriorates, the quarks move closer together and cause aging. Are you following me?"

"A little. I took physics in college."

"I have been experimenting with a method of regenerating the electronic field of the atoms with a high-energy charge that forces the quarks apart and restores the atoms to their original level, thereby reversing the aging process. After many years of frustration, I managed to build a machine that reversed the wear in inanimate objects."

Joel stared at the professor, fascinated

"American Pharmaceutical Corporation heard about my work and gave me a sizable research grant to experiment on small living things. I started with insects and built up until I finally had success with rats. I have built a machine that appears to reverse the aging in rats."

"What does American Pharmaceuticals think of this?"

"That's my dilemma; I haven't told them how far I have progressed. I'm afraid if I succeed they will abuse the use of such a machine. It should be used for the improvement of life for all people, not just the powerful and wealthy. I want to see if I can really help people get healthier before I decide what to do with it."

"What are you planning to do, and where do I come in?"

"I have built a full-size machine that can be used on a human being, and I need someone to try it out on."

Joel stared at him in amazement. "You must be crazy to think that I would let you try this thing on me."

"Before you answer, let me give some more information on the process. It would help if I show you the machine; it's in my lab on this floor."

They walked down the hall to a door that was controlled by a security keypad. Kelbeck punched in the code and opened the door. It led into a small anteroom. "I set this lab up as a "clean room" when I started the particle bombardment, but it's not needed anymore. I keep it as a clean room for security reasons. It's a good reason to keep people out of here."

They went through the second door into a 20-foot square room that had a large piece of equipment along the back wall that looked like something out of a science fiction movie. In front of it was the machine. Kelbeck explained to Joel what he was looking at.

The machine was like a large recliner, with a semicylindrical section hinged to one side that could be closed to encase the occupant of the recliner completely. Coming from the equipment on the wall to the recliner was a tapered tube that attached to the head of the recliner. The head was like a crown that fitted over the scull, the feet fitted into a one-piece boot. There was a groove in either side in which the subject could lay his arms with the hands enclosed in metallic gloves.

"This is my second-generation Machine. The first one was just big enough to hold a large rat. I started with twenty-four rats, twelve males and twelve females. I caged them all together and soon eleven females were pregnant. I discovered that one male was sterile and one female had a blocked uterus. I then started caging the males and females separately."

"I obtained twelve more females and divided all of them into two groups. The control group A that received no treatment consisted of six males, six pregnant females, and six non-pregnant females. The group B receiving treatment consisted of the rest of the rats including the sterile male and the defective female. They were all given a complete physical before we started and detailed records were kept.

"All rats were put through a series of tests every day, which included maze negotiation, treadmill rotation, plus other tests. The B group also received treatments that started at a low level once a day and increased over a period of three months to a high level four times a day. The results were astounding. Even in the beginning at low levels of treatment, group B showed much more improvement than group A. Then at the high levels the advances were phenomenal.

"Group B rats negotiated increasingly more difficult mazes with ease. They generated ten times as much energy on the treadmill, and they grew bigger and stronger. The babies from group B were also bigger, stronger, and much healthier. The sterile male rat sired a baby and the female with the blocked uterus got pregnant. There were a couple of negative effects. The rats became more aggressive and I had to cage them separately, and two rats died when we increased the treatment levels too fast. I backed down and increased levels at a much slower rate. Then I had no more troubles.

"I know now that I have the treatment levels under control. I had this machine manufactured in pieces and assembled it myself. Nobody knows of its existence. I've used it on a limited number of animals including a chimpanzee with good success. I am now ready to try it on a human."

Joel was enthralled with what he was hearing. Although the technical aspects were way over his head, the idea of retarding aging was an exciting one.

"Why don't you get a volunteer from your students? I'm sure you would find one easily enough."

"I thought of that but there are a number of problems. A young person would not have aged enough for the result to be easily evaluated, it would be very difficult to maintain the secrecy I want, and we would probably need permission of parents. Also, I don't want American Pharmaceuticals to know until I have some results."

"I need someone who is older, is in good health, has a strong heart, and will maintain the secrecy. I've been watching you work out for a few weeks now; I got your name from your equipment bag, and ran a background check on you. Providing you pass the physical, I think I have found my man."

"Well I'm not your man, this looks too dangerous to me. I may not have a good life, but I would like to keep what I have."

"I will take every precaution. If you decide to do it, I would do a complete physical workup on you first to make sure there are no surprises. The physical is extensive, to ensure that you are in perfect health, and I would start the machine at very low levels and measure the effects constantly. Don't give me your final answer now; think it over and let me know in a few days.

Chapter Two

With this Joel left the professor and drove home with his head buzzing with thoughts about what he had just heard. That night Joel didn't sleep much; he tossed and turned thinking about the proposition. After a while he tried to get his dilemma out of his thoughts.

Still unable to sleep, Joel got up at about 2 a.m., and started a data file in his computer. He listed all the information he remembered from what Kelbeck had told him. He organized it into groups such as "Technical," "Personal," "Risks," and "Benefits." He read and reread the data. When he went back to bed sleep still evaded him.

It was not unusual for Joel to have sleepless nights; problems with his current work assignment kept him awake. Joel worked as a computer programmer for a small company called Inventory Management System. They had a contract with the Defense Department to develop an inventory management computer system for the Miramar Marine Corps Air Station. The contract represented sixty percent of the company's income, and Joel as the lead designer on the project needed to solve the programming problems.

The Station's equipment was housed in numerous facilities, some large, some small, throughout a very large area, approximately three miles wide by over ten miles long. Joel designed the system with little difficulty, but needed to make it a lot more efficient and cost-effective.

His company had leased some office space in the Micro Skills.Com building on Miramar Road, across from the golf course on the north edge of the Station. It was about six miles from the UCSD campus, convenient for running after work.

The next day he could not concentrate on the job. The lack of sleep made him groggy and he could not stop thinking about Kelbeck's project. He decided to do what he often did when he had a problem, go run.

He left work at 3 and drove to the University, changed into his running gear, and got out on the track. As he ran, Joel thought about his parents. He thought about them a lot.

Joel really missed his parents; they were killed in an automobile accident in 2002. They were driving east on Highway 40 heading from Barstow to Laughlin with another couple when they came to a section of the freeway under construction. One side was being worked on, so the other side was being used as a two-lane highway with one lane in each direction and no divider barrier. They were doing sixty miles an hour when a driver going west fell asleep, crossed the center line, and caused a head-on collision. The car behind them could not stop, so their car was compressed to half its length. Even seat belts and air bags could not save them.

By the time Joel had finished his run, he was rationalizing why he should accept the professor's invitation. The Professor would be very careful; he could quit any time; it might improve his ten-kilometer time; if it worked he would live longer; etc. He decided to tell the Professor he would take the physical and go from there.

Anton could not contain his delight. He asked Joel to take the next day off work. When Joel nodded his agreement, he said, "I have all the medical equipment in my lab. I bought it with some of the grant money. I knew I would need it for evaluations. Come in tomorrow and I will do the physical here. It includes MRI and ultrasonic scans of your brain, heart, lungs, and internal organs, an EKG, and a colonoscopy. At least, thought Joel, he'd get a great physical examination out of the deal.

The next day after completing the physical, Anton reviewed the results. He told Joel, "I can see no anomalies; you have passed with no problems at all."

They agreed to start the sessions immediately. "We will start the levels low, 5% capacity for fifteen minutes once a day for one week, then I will check your vital signs again, especially the EKG. Later I will set up some standards to check you for improvements in your performance."

Joel was strapped loosely in the machine.

"The computer keeps a record of every time the machine is used so that we will be able to check back to see the level and duration of every session."

The equipment started up with a low hum. Joel closed his eyes and tried to relax. It seemed like no time and the fifteen minutes were up.

"How do you feel?"

"No different. Was the machine working?"

"Yes, we will do it again tomorrow."

For a week, Joel received a daily treatment in the machine for fifteen minutes, and felt like nothing had happened. On three of the nights he ran his two miles afterwards and felt really loose.

On Saturday morning, before his five-mile run, he decided to do a fast one mile first. He did this about once a month. A year ago he could do a six-minute mile, the last time he struggled to a six-minute five-second mile. It seemed harder to maintain the level of effort every month. He would set off at a fast pace for the first two laps, then he would try to hold the pace for as long as he could. Today he finished the third lap, still holding on to a good clip. To his amazement, with a struggle, he held on for most of the forth lap. He clicked his stop watch as he collapsed, gasping on the center grass, and took a few minutes to catch his breath. When he looked at the time on his watch it said five minutes and fifty-eight seconds. He pumped his fist in delight—all his training was paying off.

Sunday's ten-mile run seemed easier too. After a couple of miles, he could feel the runner's high setting in. Sunday night he slept well, arriving at work on Monday feeling ready to tackle anything. He was still working on the Miramar Station inventory problem. He had spent some time Sunday thinking about it and had a few ideas he wanted to pursue. He called his team together, outlined the new approach he wanted them to investigate, and entered the outline into his computer. They worked all day on the new approach and it seemed to be very promising. His team was enthusiastic about it.

Monday night he returned to the laboratory. Anton wanted to continue 5% capacity for fifteen minutes. Joel said, "As I'm not feeling anything why not try 10% for ten minutes, and if I still don't feel anything, add another five minutes." They discussed this back and forth, and finally Anton agreed. After checking his vital signs, Anton strapped Joel in the machine. After ten minutes, Joel still did not feel anything, so Anton agreed to another five minutes. After twelve minutes Joel could feel a slight tingling in his arms and legs. After fourteen minutes he was feeling warm. When Anton unstrapped him from the machine, he told him of his feelings. Anton insisted he lie down and once more checked his vital signs. The vitals were all normal, but Anton made Joel promise to go home and rest for the remainder of the evening.

The next day at work, Joel called his team together and injected some new ideas he had into his instruction of the previous day. One member of the team said, "We've been working on this for two months. Why didn't you give us this approach before?"

"I've just thought of it," said Joel. Later Joel was thinking about this. Since he started the sessions on the machine, he ran the mile in five fifty-eight and had new ideas for his project. Could there be some connection?

That evening he told Anton of the improvement he had noticed. The Professor was intrigued.

"We need to set up the standards now, I thought it was too soon, but now I think you're ready. Here is my plan. Every Saturday I will meet you at the track at 8 a.m. We will check your time for a mile. Every Wednesday after your session we will go to the weight room and lift weights. To check the mental improvements, here are three books I want you to read and tell me how much you understand."

Joel read the titles of the books: *Biochemical Electronics, Advanced Physics,* and *Gray's Anatomy.* "I won't understand these."

"Well, try them and see if they get clearer in a few weeks."

They continued the sessions at 10% for fifteen minutes, and on Wednesday they went to the weight room to set standards for Joel. They decided two exercises were enough: the bench press and the leg curl. Joel managed 150 pounds on the bench press and 100 pounds with the leg curl.

That Saturday they met at the track. Joel gave Anton the stopwatch and started to run the mile. He planned to run three laps at his usual first lap pace, and then try to go faster for the last lap. After three laps, Joel still felt fresh and found no difficulty picking up the pace a little, so when he finished he still had a little to spare.

"I could have done better," he said to Anton

"Better! You ran it in five minutes forty-seven seconds—that is an eleven-second improvement."

They returned to the lab to discuss this new development. Joel believed that his improved times had to be the result of the sessions on the machine. He even understood some of the information in the books Anton had given him to read.

"Are you going to inform American Pharmaceuticals?"

"Not yet. We need a lot more supportive data. We will continue the sessions for a few weeks, then reevaluate the situation. Here are some more books for you."

Joel read the book titles: *Advanced Miniature Micro Processing Circuitry, Quantum Physics* and *Atomic Engines,* and *The Neural Nervous System of the Human Body.*

The next week they increased the machine levels to 15% for fifteen minutes and the week after to 20% for twenty minutes. The results continued to impress them. By the third week Joel could speed read a book a day with full subject retention. He went to the library for more advanced texts. In terms of physical improvements, he pressed 190 pounds; leg curled 130 pounds and ran the mile in five minutes and twenty seconds.

Chapter Three

On the Monday evening of the fifth week of treatments, they sat in Anton's office to discuss their progress. Joel started talking about how they could reduce the size of the machine by using miniaturized electronic microcircuitry and advanced computer processors, when he noticed that the Professor seemed disturbed.

"What's wrong?" Joel asked.

Anton thought for quite a while. "We have made a lot of process, but now I think it is time to talk about how we guard against this discovery being misused. If this falls into the hands of the wrong people, they will use it to generate an army of super soldiers, or sell regeneration to the super rich, or enslave a large portion of the world populace. Who knows what evil uses they could devise for the machine? I feel like the men who developed the atomic bomb must have felt. We must continue to keep it a secret, and we need to move the machine out of the lab."

"Do you want to move it to your home?"

"No. I don't want even my wife to know about the machine. She would worry. Could we use your apartment?"

"I'm renting a two bedroom, and I use one bedroom as an office. I could move to a three bedroom and we could build the machine in the third bedroom. You could have your own key and come and go as you please."

"You would do that for me?"

"I feel like it's my project too now, and I have a few ideas we should discuss."

They then got into a discussion on reducing the size of the power unit and control system as well as making the recliner and encasements much smaller. They made some rough sketches and circuit designs and finished up agreeing that Anton would start work on the new design the next day while Joel would look for a new apartment.

They suspended sessions on the machine until the new design was complete, with Joel spending as much time at the lab as he could helping Anton with the new approach. To Anton's amazement, Joel's help substantially improved the design. He had studied Anton's log books and notes so that he really understood the concept of the machine. He suggested simplifications and improvements that made the design much smaller with greater power. The new design required ordering quite a bit of new miniaturized equipment, and then salvaging the rest from the old machine.

While they waited for the new supplies, they restarted Joel's sessions on the old machine. Three weeks later, they received the last of their orders. Joel now pressed 240 pounds, curled 150 pounds and ran the mile in five minutes flat. Now they began stripping down the old machine.

Anton began to feel that Joel knew more about his age-retarding process that he did. Joel's mental improvements far outstripped the physical improvements. He wondered if he had created a monster, but Joel's personality did not seem to change. He was the same pleasant person, respectful, and deferred to Anton's leadership. They spent so much time together working closely on the project that a bond developed between them. Anton saw Joel as the son he never had, and Joel saw Anton as the father he had lost.

Joel moved into his new apartment, leaving one bedroom empty for the machine. They had all the new parts delivered to his new address. They moved most of the usable parts from the old machine in the trunk of Joel's car, then rented a U Haul for the last few large pieces. They cleaned up the lab, leaving no traces of the old machine. Three days later with the assembly process complete, they were ready for the trial run.

Anton decided to use a chimpanzee for the first run of the new machine. He obtained a male chimpanzee from the same source he had used before. He drove the animal over to Joel's apartment in his car. They sedated the chimpanzee and placed him in the machine. After five minutes at 10% Anton checked its vital signs and everything seemed to be okay. They ran the machine at 10%, 15% and 20% for five minutes with one-hour intervals with no apparent effect on the chimp. Then Anton strapped Joel in the machine for ten minutes at 10%, after which they called it a day.

After a week of 10% for ten minutes, their tests showed that Joel's physical capabilities had not changed at all. They tried fifteen percent for fifteen minutes for a week, and the physicals went down a little. Finally after another week of twenty percent for twenty minutes, they knew they had a problem. Joel now pressed 230 pounds, curled 140 pounds and ran the mile in five minutes ten seconds.

Joel still worked full time, so Anton spent all his time reviewing the design to try to find the problem. The next Saturday, Joel and Anton worked together on the design at the apartment. After four hours of reviewing their drawings, they decided that there was nothing wrong with the design, so they started checking every step of the assembly. Finally, when checking the flow of current across each circuit board, Joel found one that had an unusually high intermittent resistance that restricted the flow of current in a vital area. The cause was a poorly soldered terminal that created a loose connection. Anton took the circuit board back to his clean room and fixed the problem. Anton wanted a trial run with a chimpanzee again, but Joel argued that they had wasted enough time and wanted to get right back into the machine. Anton finally agreed and Sunday morning they started a week of ten percent for ten minutes.

A week later the test results were back to their previous levels and after another week of fifteen percent for fifteen minutes, Joel pressed 250 pounds, curled 160 pounds and ran the mile in four minutes, fifty five seconds. Another benefit came to light; Joel only needed five hours sleep each night to be fully rested. He spent the extra waking hours reading voraciously.

Anton decided the time had come to sit down and document their long-term goals for the machine. Joel agreed, so on Sunday they tried to list all the possible uses, outcomes, and consequences. They both agreed that they must maintain the secrecy; revealing their results would cause a media fervor that would swamp them. With three billion people in the world, it would be impossible to give everyone the benefit of the machine. If they set up centers to process people through the machine, how would they select who got first priority? There could be riots as people tried to get treatments. They would still have the problem of American Pharmaceuticals claiming ownership of the process.

Joel suggested that in addition to helping individual people, they should think of some way for Joel to use his new abilities to help a large number of people. Anton thought this a good idea, but wondered how. They ended the meeting leaving this as the subject of another meeting.

Anton wanted to try the machine on himself, but Joel insisted that he have a complete physical first, and then they would start at a very low level. He knew that Anton had had heart problems in the past.

Driving home from work the next day, Joel was thinking about the changes that had occurred in his life over the past few months. They were all for the better, and he had Anton to thank for this. He resolved to do his best to see that Anton's dreams for his invention came true.

Arriving home he saw Anton's car parked in front of the building and the light on in the machine room. Anton usually came over after Joel had eaten, but tonight he had come early. Entering the room, he saw Anton lying rigidly in the machine. He rushed to his side and shook him with no response. He checked for a pulse, but could find none. Joel fell to his knees with tears rolling down his cheeks. "Oh no!" he cried. It was like losing a parent all over again.

He knelt there for a while, with his upper body draped across the corpse. Finally he got up and walked into his office to call 911. As he picked up the phone, he thought about what was about to happen, and before he finished dialing, he replaced the receiver on the phone. If he explained what had happened, the machine would become public knowledge, just what Anton didn't want. He had no claim on the machine, so the American Pharmaceutical Company would take possession. He could not let this happen. He sat there thinking for a while until he had come up with a plan.

Mary Kelbeck would assume Anton was working late, as he often did, so he had a few hours. He waited until 10 p.m., and then with Anton's arm draped over his shoulder he "walked" him down to Anton's car. Nobody saw them. He placed Anton in the front seat and drove him to the lab; if the police stopped him he would say that he was taking Anton to the emergency room. At this time of night the Science Research Park was empty and Joel had no problem getting Anton up to his office unseen. He placed him in his chair behind his desk and gently laid his head forward. It looked like he'd had a heart attack while sitting there. Joel knew the coroner would establish the time of death, he just hoped that no one had been in Anton's office between then and now.

Next day Joel called Mary. He told her that he had heard of Anton's tragic death and would like to attend the funeral. Mary Kelbeck gave him the details of the funeral, and he went to the synagogue for the services. During the shivah he went to the Kelbeck house and finally got a chance to talk to Mary alone. He told her that he had not known Anton very long but he had liked and admired him immensely, so if there was anything she needed—help settling his affairs, a sounding board, or even financial help,—she should call him. He gave her his card and left.

Chapter Four

oel continued to give himself daily treatments in the machine. He rigged up a handheld button switch that enabled him to set the time and intensity level on the machine, then strap himself in. If his finger let go of the button, the machine would switch off. He increased the levels slowly to 60 percent for thirty minutes over the next month and found he could press 350 pounds, curl 210 pounds, and run a mile in under four minutes. The increases in physical capability had slowed to where the weekly change was insignificant, but his mental abilities continued to show startling improvements. He now only needed three hours sleep a night. His eyesight had improved to where he no longer needed his glasses. In fact, sometimes he felt like he could see right through the pages of a book.

Joel could speed read complex technical books, with complete comprehension, at a rate of three hundred pages an hour. The subjects of nuclear physics and force fields fascinated him. He felt he could build a miniaturized nuclear engine powerful enough to create a strong force field.

He also read books on levitation. At home he experimented with this phenomenon, and found he could slide a pin across a smooth surface just by concentrating on it with his mind. At first the slight movement he achieved exhausted him. After more sessions on the machine, he could move larger objects with ease and raise small objects off the table.

Another area he studied was martial arts. He read books on karate, jiu jitsu, tai chi, taekwondo, and kung fu. He practiced the moves at home as best he could, but knew he would have to go to an expert to practice the skills. Joel had seen a martial arts studio on Governor Street in University City, which was between the UCSD campus and his apartment. He decided to visit it next Saturday.

The studio covered two stores in a strip mall. Through the tinted window he could make out a class in progress. He entered the door to the extreme left, and found himself in a narrow hallway. To his right he could look over a waist-high wall. On the other side of the wall, a large room, about 30-feet square, contained four 12-feet 6-six inch thick pads, with a 3-foot gap between each pad.

The class consisted of eight students on each mat, ranging in age from about 7 to 12, paired off by size rather than age. All the students wore the traditional white robes, but each group sported a different colored belt. Each mat had a separate instructor watching the students practicing karate skills. A fifth man seemed to be overseeing the whole activity. The four instructors looked to be in their late twenties, but the fifth one was older. Joel estimated his age as about 40, but because of his great condition he was probably older.

The hallway ended at a small empty office; to the right of that, behind the workout room, Joel could see into a storage room. Joel stood at the end of the low wall near the office and watched the student practice. He recognized a lot of the moves from the books he had read. The students, although very serious, seemed to be enjoying themselves. The two largest boys began to fight violently, instead of just practicing their moves. The senior instructor pulled them apart and gave them a lecture on how karate was for self-defense not for aggression.

Having looked up the schedule of classes on the Internet and knowing this one ended at 10;45, Joel had arrived at 10:40. Finally the older man came over to his office and Joel followed him in. Offering his hand, the man said, "My name is Tom Bracher. May I help you?"

"I am interested in learning martial arts," said Joel.

"Which one?"

"I'm not sure. I see you cover most of them."

"Yes, we offer classes in judo, karate, kung fu, and taekwondo."

"What are your qualifications?"

"Why do you ask?" Tom seemed a little upset.

"I want to be sure you know what you are doing."

Tom looked at Joel for a while, then said, "I was on the 1980 United States Judo team; I was a professional kickboxer for ten years; I have a black belt in karate; and I am working with the 2008 Taekwondo Olympic team."

Joel maintained eye contact with Tom. "That's impressive," he said. "Do you give private lessons?"

"Only the first evaluation is private, after that it's group classes as you see here."

"How much do you charge for lessons?"

"A hundred and fifty dollars a month. You can come as many times a month as you wish, as long as you come to a class that is teaching at your level. Now, I am busy, do you want to enroll?" Tom walked away and sat behind his desk.

"Are you open on Sundays?"

"No!"

"Would you give me a private lesson tomorrow?"

"I don't work on Sundays."

"I'll pay you five hundred dollars an hour, with a two-hour minimum, paid in advance."

Tom came back and stood in front of Joel, "You are wasting my time."

Joel pulled out a wad of money from his pocket, counted out ten $100 bills, and laid them on the desk. Tom stared at the money.

"What do you hope to achieve in two hours?"

"I have learned all the moves from the books I read. I need an expert to demonstrate them for me and point out my errors."

"You can't learn martial art from a book."

"Humor me," said Joel, "if it doesn't work out you'll be a thousand dollars richer and you'll never see me again."

Tom stared at the money. He picked it up and said, "Be here tomorrow at 9 sharp. I'll wait five minutes for you, then I'm gone."

"Do you have robes I can borrow?" asked Joel.

"Yes."

"Okay, I'll see you at nine."

Next morning, at five minutes to 9, when Tom arrived, Joel was waiting for him. As they entered the studio, Tom said, "I'm sorry if I was curt with you yesterday, but I still think you're wasting your time and mine."

"If you tell me that again in two hours I'll go away and you can forget you ever saw me."

"Okay," said Tom. "Show me what you think you know."

Joel performed a number of karate moves that he had learned from the books.

"Not bad," said Tom grudgingly. "Now go through them again slowly."

As Joel did, Tom pointed out flaws in his stance, balance, and execution of the moves. Tom was very impressed by how quickly Joel mastered the moves.

After thirty minutes Tom said, "Let's practice the falls. I'll throw you and show you how to fall then, you throw me to get a better feel for the moves."

They did this for a while, then Joel said, "Can we fight for real, where you don't let me throw you?"

"We're not ready for that yet," said Tom. Joel insisted on trying, so Tom decided to teach Joel a lesson. They faced off and Joel made a move, but Tom threw him to the mat. This happened four times. On the fifth try, Tom found himself flat on his back with Joel standing over him.

After that, Joel won every move until Tom said, "You've convinced me. You must have had extensive training to be this good. Is this a practical joke? Did Sam Donaldson send you here?"

Joel said, "Can we try taekwondo now?"

"You are serious, aren't you? Yes, lets go."

For the next two hours Tom taught Joel all he knew and by noon Joel was winning every bout. Tom would not believe he had never tried these disciplines before, and was amazed not only at his ability, but the speed at which he could execute the moves. His reflexes were phenomenal.

As the men changed their clothes, Tom said, "You're not going to tell me what this is all about, are you?"

"No, but I will assure you I will not use my abilities for illegal purposes." He then handed Tom five more $100 bills, shook his hand and left.

Chapter Five

That afternoon, after his daily treatment, he sat down to plan his next move. If he was to execute Anton's plan for helping people, he needed to find a source of funding. His salary would surely not cover the cost, and if he was working full time, he could not be working on the plan.

He considered all methods of obtaining money,—the stock market, real estate, owning a business, all too slow. He certainly couldn't steal. Gambling! Maybe this was a possibility. Joel spent Monday evening at the library reading all the books he could find on gambling. From what he read, the consensus seemed to be that blackjack gave the lowest percentage to the casino, and with money management and card counting, the odds could be in the bettor's favor.

Surely with his new powers he could beat the house. In the next two hours he committed to memory the contents of five books on blackjack, ignoring all information that did not seem logical to him. He now knew, for any combination of cards, when to stand, hit, split, and double down. Combining this with knowing every card left in the deck should give him the edge he needed.

Joel's project at work was going so well that his boss was agreeable to him taking a week's vacation, so on Friday evening he took a cab to San Diego Airport with $500 in his wallet. Here he had his first setback. All the flights to Las Vegas were full; he hadn't given a thought to booking a flight. He may have a brilliant mind, but he was not very "street smart."

He was seventeenth on a standby list of other travelers. Six gave up in the first two hours, and the others were absorbed in ones and twos until at 10:15 p.m., tired and slightly discouraged, he finally got on a flight. The time had not been a complete waste; he had made a couple of calls to the local Las Vegas reservation agency and managed to get a room at one of the small motels and book a rental car at McCarran Airport. He would get good night's sleep, then begin his gambling at one of the casinos on The Strip.

The next morning he drove to Caesar's Palace, parked in the parking structure behind the hotel, and walked into the casino. Another surprise awaited him. The minimums on the blackjack tables were $25 and $50, with just a couple of $15 that were full. He asked a man standing around watching the gaming, where were the $5 tables. The man laughed and said. "You have to go downtown, or across to the west side of the Highway 15 for those."

"Where's downtown?" asked Joel.

"It's way north on Las Vegas Boulevard. The 15 is closer. Just go west on Flamingo and you'll find them."

Flamingo Boulevard is right next to Caesar's Palace, so Joel was soon crossing the freeway. He passed Rio Suites and stopped at The Golden Slipper. Entering the casino, he found that the table minimums were $5, $10, $15, and $25. The $5 tables were full, but after a short wait a woman left one table and he got a seat. The dealer was holding the cards, but the deck seemed thick. Then Joel realized it was a double deck. Nothing was the way he thought it would be. Still, he thought, he could count cards for two decks, so he started to play.

Bud Martin studied the new player at his table. Every once in a while one like this would come along. Face serious, eyes intense, and fingers nervous. They devoured the spots on each card as it was played, and you could almost hear the numbers click into place in their heads. When would they learn? For every gimmick they came up with, the house had a countermeasure, cold, unemotional, automatic. He was a $5 bettor and playing well; he seemed to know the game.

The method he was using was an old one, the progressive method. He would increase his bet if he won, from $5 to $10 then $15 and $20, then revert to his $5 bet if he lost. This gave the bettor a chance against the house if he hit a good streak, but if he played too long the house percentage would wear him down. Bud also noticed that occasionally he would not stick to his system and would bet $5 when he should bet higher and jump from $5 to $25. Like all the rest, Bud thought, he didn't have the patience to stick to the correct sequence.

After about an hour of playing, Bud began to realize that this one might be different. Either he was very lucky, or something was going on that Bud hadn't noticed. If he bet $5 when he should bet higher, he invariably lost. Conversely, when he jumped to a higher bet, he usually won. By now this $5 bettor was up $900. Then Bud spotted the answer; he only deviated from his system when the deck in Bud's hand was small. A card counter, and a good one at that. This guy was memorizing every card that had gone and only bet big when the odds were in his favor.

On the next deal, Bud still had about a full deck left in his hand when Joel carefully and nervously counted out $100 and placed it in the box. Bud stared at Joel for a few seconds, then with a flick of his free hand signaled for the pit boss.

Sandra watched Carney, the pit boss, walk slowly towards Bud's table. Someone was in trouble, for whenever Carney walked to a table, in his slow hesitant gait, it meant trouble. She had watched it brewing for the past hour. First Carney walks up and down behind a dealer, which means someone is winning steadily. Then he retires to his high stool at one end, and sits staring at the dealer's back with those piercing grey blue eyes.

What did she care? She had enough troubles of her own. So the bettor seemed like a regular guy, he was a $5 bettor, and she hated $5 bettors with a passion. They sat there, ordering their free booze like they owned the place, and if they got a blackjack she might get a $1 tip instead of 50 cents. She liked the $25 and up bettors; when they were winning the tips were really worth having. She would fix on her work smile, as she delivered their drinks and cleaned their ashtrays. She had all the right equipment to go with the smile, and if they were breathing they noticed.

This had always been her problem, they noticed. She had used her smile, and her body, like a weapon since she was 15, but it wasn't until two of the high school football team persuaded her to walk home across the fields after a school dance that she found the weapon could backfire. She had asked for it, she knew. She had even liked it, after the initial shock and pain, but since then she had made sure that the guy was of her choosing and the affair on her terms.

This is what made her current problem so bad. Cy Richards was over 50, fat, and bald, and the thought of being with him turned her stomach. Still, when the manager of the casino expressed a desire to "date," you could only stall so long. She would hate to give up this job. Her bank account was just beginning to get healthy again. There was no alternative; at her last break he had told her to come to his office after her shift ended. Instead, she would pick up her paycheck, and then head out of town.

Joel also watched the pit boss walk towards him. He had been intent on watching the cards, oblivious to all that was going on around him. This sudden turn of events had taken him completely by surprise. Carney reached the table and the dealer, said, "Shuffle."

"You can't shuffle," said Joel. "You have a full deck left."

"You're counting," said Carney.

"Sure, I'm counting. What's wrong with that?"

"We don't like counters around here. Shuffle!"

The dealer shuffled the cards while Joel sat there stunned. If he couldn't raise his bets, how could he take advantages of the odds when they were in his favor?

The dealer broke into his thoughts. "Want a card?" While he was thinking, the cards had been dealt.

"Deal me out," said Joel said, reaching for his $100 chip.

"The bet stays," said Carney laying his hand across Joel's. "The cards have been dealt."

Joel looked at Carney, then at the dealer, and finally at the Jack of Spades in front of the dealer. Slowly he picked up his cards; the first was a king. Good! The second was a deuce, twelve, a bad hand. With a jack showing, he should hit his twelve.

He stared at the dealer's hole card wondering what to do. The whole card was a six, he was sure of it. He could see the outline of the pips through the back of the card; it was the Six of Diamonds. Sixteen! The dealer would have to hit the worst hand possible. "I'll stand," said Joel. The dealer flipped over his hole card, the Six of Diamonds. Although Joel had been positive about the hole card, he still could not believe he had been right. The dealer turned over the top card on the deck, a ten, twenty-six he had busted. If Joel had hit he would have had twenty-two, a losing hand.

Joel collected his money and decided to try again. He placed $25 in the box and received a nine and a seven, but the dealer had an ace up. He called insurance. Joel stared at the whole card; yes, there it was again—not very clear—but definitely a queen. Blackjack!

"I'll take insurance."

The dealer turned over the queen and Joel saved half his bet. On the next deal, Joel was dealt seventeen and the dealer had a nine. He could see that the hole card was a king, so if the dealer had nineteen he might as well hit. Why not? He had a losing hand anyway.

"Hit me."

"Are you sure, you have seventeen?"

"Yes." Up came a three for twenty, A winning hand.

"Let me see those cards," said Carney as he handed the dealer two new decks. For the next hour, Joel won steadily. He started off with a $25 bet, then $50, and finally $100 bets. Carney changed dealers twice, before changing the table from a hand-held two-deck, to a six-deck shoe, which makes card counting impossible. Joel found that the shoe helped him. The dealer would pull the next card to be dealt out of the shoe a little, enabling Joel to see its back. Now, in addition to knowing the dealer's hole card he knew the next card coming up, so he knew if he wanted it or not. He could see that the best seat to see the shoe was third base, the last seat to be dealt, and resolved to sit in this seat next time he played. Finally, when Joel was up $6,000, Carney closed the table and told Joel he had played enough for today.

"You can't do that," said Joel. "I have money and I'm ready to play."

"Go play craps, or roulette, maybe tomorrow we will let you play black-jack again."

Joel noticed that Carney now had a bouncer standing either side of him, so he decided that he should not push the issue and headed for the cashier's window. From there he headed for the restrooms, to freshen up before he moved to another casino, to start all over again. Next place he would play it differently; he would be ready for them.

Chapter Six

Sandra watched Joel walk off in the direction of the men's room, thinking, there was a man she would really like to know well. She quickly dragged her mind back to her own problems, for she knew she had to move fast. She changed into her street clothes in record time and headed for the personnel office. The secretary handed her a pay envelope, saying, "Mr. Richards asked me to remind you to go to his office." Sandra nodded and walked away in the direction of his office. As soon as she was out of the secretary's sight, she changed direction and headed for the parking lot.

Outside she felt a little easier, but as she turned the corner to go down the side of the building she almost ran into two men. She recognized them immediately. They were Leon and Sam, Cy Richard's personal bodyguards.

"Where are you going, honey?" Leon said. He was a big man, at least 6' 3", 250 pounds and blond, whereas Sam was 6', about 190 pounds, and dark.

"Get out of my way, you big lug, or I'll scream." She heard the click of the knife opening before she saw the blade in his hand.

"I wouldn't do that, honey," said Leon as Sam grabbed her arms from behind.

At this very moment, Joel rounded the corner of the building, heading for his car. "What's going on here?" he said, sounding very naïve in his surprise. It was very obvious what was going on.

"You'll keep on moving if you know what's good for you." Leon made no attempt to hide the knife. They stood staring at one another for a few moments, then Leon started to move forward slowly. The movement of Joel's foot was a blur as he kicked Leon in the crotch. The knife clattered to the ground as Leon's hands moved to the painful area and he instinctively bent forward. Joel's leg moved again and this time his knee buried itself in Leon's throat. As Joel turned, Sam pushed Sandra aside and swung at him. Joel moved his head slightly, and as the punch slid over his shoulder he sank his fist hard into Sam stomach. Sam fell to his knees, trying to breathe and vomit at the same time. Joel brought both fists down hard on the back of his neck.

"Run and call the police," Joel said to Sandra, "I'll watch these two."

"No! If we wait around here for the police, Cy Richards will get us for sure."

"Who's Cy Richards?"

"Never mind, now. I'll tell you in the car. We've got to get away from here as soon as we can."

They hurried down the side of the hotel and across the parking lot to Sandra's car. As they drove to her apartment, she explained her situation to Joel, who was not fully convinced and still wanted to call the police, but Sandra was adamant. "While we wait for the police, Cy's people will get us."

"Why are you so afraid of them?"

"My roommate, Susan, was Cy's last girlfriend, and she told him she wanted out. The next thing I know she disappears, leaving all her belongings in our apartment. She has no family, and the police could not trace her, but I know she would never leave without telling me. I'm leaving for L.A. as soon as I can."

They reached her apartment and Joel helped her pack all her belongings and some of Susan's into her car. As he was closing the trunk, he realized he didn't even know her name.

"By the way my name is Joel Sampson, what's yours?"

"Sandra Lee," she replied.

"How can I get in touch with you in L.A.?" He asked.

"I don't know where I'll be. Give me your phone number and I'll call you."

He gave her his phone number and she hurriedly climbed into her car. With a wave goodbye drove off in the direction of the freeway to Los Angeles.

As Joel watched her drive away, he decided to hang around to see if her apprehension was justified. He crossed the street and walked half a block to a drug store on the corner. Here he waited, leaning against the stone blocks that divided the two front windows of the store and watched the front of the apartment house. Within five minutes of starting his vigil, a car pulled up in front of the building; and Leon, Sam, and two other men got out. One man hurried to the rear of the building, while the other three entered the front. Joel slipped into the drug store and watched through the window. Three minutes later all four men came out of the building, jumped into the car, and sped off in the direction of the casino. So Sandra was right, mused Joel, the situation was going to require a lot of deep thought.

He hailed a passing cab and had it take him back to the casino parking lot. During the drive he made one vital decision: these people were not going to drive him out of Vegas until he had the money he came for. He picked up his car and drove to his motel. Once in his room he lay on his back on the bed with his hands behind his head and closed his eyes. He had to come up with a plan.

He maintained that position for fifteen minutes without moving, then swinging his legs over the side of the bed he reached for the telephone directory. In the Yellow Pages under "T" he located the theatrical supply retail stores, and called one named Star Theatrical Supplies for information. He drove to their location on Valley View Boulevard and went in. For $55 he bought a kit with makeup and a book entitled *Professional Theatrical Makeup Made Easy*. The book explained all the steps required to obtain certain desired effects with makeup. In addition, he bought three wigs; three types of facial hair; cheek, nose, and teeth inserts. Next he went to the mall and bought a money belt at a luggage store.

Returning to his motel, he settled his account, telling them he would be leaving in two hours. Back in his room he changed his appearance radically. He then drove to The Bellagio and checked in. With his $6000 winnings;

he could now afford to stay anywhere he wanted to. Safely in his room, he proceeded to practice using the makeup kit until after about three hours he had memorized the steps required to produce five completely different appearances. Now he felt that after a hearty meal and a good night's sleep, he was ready to resume his gambling.

The next morning Joel drove to The Mandalay Bay at Hacienda on the south end of The Strip wearing one of his disguises. He found a $25 table where the third-base seat was open, sat down, and bought $500 worth of chips. He placed a $25 chip in the box and received his cards, a five and a seven—twelve—a bad hand. The dealer had an eight showing. He stared at the back of the dealer's hole card and slowly he felt he saw the impressions of an eight the dealer had sixteen.

"Do you want a card?" The dealer's voice brought Joel back to the game. Joel then looked at the shoe and saw that the next card was a five; this would give the dealer twenty-one; he had to take it to stop the dealer getting it.

"Yes, hit me." The dealer gave him the five. Joel said. "I'll stand." The dealer then turned over his hole card—an eight—hit it with the seven to bust.

After that, Joel won about twice as many hands as he lost, and gradually increased his bet to $50, $75, $100, and finally $150. He made no sudden changes in his bet, and at $150 he bet that amount on every hand. This way nobody would think he was card counting; it would seem like luck, and he attracted no attention. When he had won a little over $5000 he left the table, cashed in his chips, went to the men's room, put the money in his money belt, and moved to the next casino. It had taken him about one hour and fifteen minutes to win that much, so he decided to limit his time at any one casino to one hour maximum.

He moved up the strip going to Excalibur, New York New York, MGM Grand, Monte Carlo, Paris, and Barbary Coast, until he had $45,000 and a nearly full money belt. He had skipped Bellagio's because he was staying there. He drove to the nearest Wells Fargo Bank, opened an account, and deposited $50,000, keeping a $1,000 of his original winnings for expenses. It was now 3 p.m. and hunger pains made him stop for a late lunch. After lunch he went back to his hotel and spent an hour around the pool.

At 6 p.m. he was on the move again, driving to Caesar's Palace. In the evening the heavy bettors came out, so nobody noticed him. He started at

$100 and worked up to $300 a bet. Again, he won two of every three bets he made, and in an hour he had $12,000. With the cash in his money belt, he moved on next stop was the Flamingo, then Harrah's, Mirage (where he had dinner), Venetian, and Treasure Island. By now his money belt was full. He was heading back to Bellagio, when he decided to make one last stop at Casino Royale. He played for about an hour, and at 2 a.m., he decided to call it a day. As his money belt was full, he asked the cashier for an envelope, and put the money in his jacket inside pocket. It had been a long day, but Joel did not feel tired. Since he had started the treatments his energy level had been very high.

He returned to his hotel room. As he unlocked the door, he felt two hands in his back push him violently into the room, sending him sprawling on the floor. Joel rolled over onto his back and came to his feet with fists clenched, but the man who was closing the door behind him with his foot had a gun in his hand. That brought Joel up short.

"Okay, let's have the envelope in your inside pocket."

"What envelope?"

"Don't act coy with me, I was watching you at the Casino Royale, I don't know how you do it, but you sure are the luckiest guy I ever saw." Joel had a terrible sinking feeling in his stomach as he stared at the gunman in disbelief. The people you met in this town were unbelievable. He was going to have to keep his eyes open in the future and watch the people around him.

"The envelope, repeated the gunman. Hand it over."

"What if I don't?"

"I could always take it off your body but I would rather not because I think you may be able to win some more money for me."

"You know I'm not in this alone," said Joel. "I have a partner, who'll be coming through that door any minute now."

"What are you trying to pull? Do you think this is my first heist? Now give me the envelope." Joel reached slowly inside his jacket, thinking, If only I could divert his attention for a moment. Looking past the gunman's shoulder, Joel noticed the lamp on the table by the door, and remembering his experiments with levitation at home, he concentrated on the lamp.

"Put the envelope on the bed and move back," said the gunman. Joel did as he was told, still concentrating on the lamp. The gunman moved towards the bed when suddenly—Crash! The lamp toppled off the table. The gunman swung around and Joel leaped forward, hitting him squarely in the back and sending him sprawling on the floor. With a swift movement of his foot, he kicked the gun across the room.

"Now," said Joel, "I'm going to show you why you're gonna to leave me alone in the future."

The gunman got to his feet, and noticed that Joel had not picked up the gun. A grin spread across his face. He was two inches taller than Joel and thirty pounds heavier, so as Joel moved towards him he took up a very professional stance and came to meet him. The two men met in the middle of the room. Joel evaded the man's punch and gave him two sharp raps on the nose with his left. This made the gunman mad and he swung hard with his right, which Joel let slide over his shoulder and then hit him in the stomach. The blow was not too hard; Joel did not want to end the fight with one punch, he intended to make sure this man didn't come back for more. He then proceeded to punish him with jabs and hooks until he dropped to his knees with both hands over his face.

"Now get out of here," said Joel. "If I ever see your face again I'll pick up from where we left off." The man scampered out of the room, leaving Joel with his money intact and the new owner of a Smith and Wesson 38-caliber handgun.

From then on Joel's stay in Vegas ran smoothly. He gambled for two more days using all five of his disguises and winning $100,000 a day. This time he put all the money in one bank account; he had special plans for it. On Wednesday he was on a plane flying back to San Diego, with $3,000 in cash in his pocket.

Thursday morning Joel called a number of financial planning companies. After discussing what he wanted with each, he selected one and went to meet with its representative at his office. He opened a trust account in Mary Kelbeck's name, instructed the planner to invest it for maximum growth, and send $5000 a month to her, starting with a check that day. He placed $300,000 in the account. The man told him that amount would only last about three years. He said not to worry, he would be adding to the account soon.

Joel then went to a private investigator and hired him to go see Mary. He instructed the investigator to tell Mary that he represented an insurance company with which Anton had a policy that upon his death became a trust. She would receive $5,000 a month for the rest of her life. The check would come from a financial planning company that managed the trust.

Joel gave notice to his employer, and immediately restarted the sessions on the machine. He set the controls at sixty percent for half an hour and had two sessions a day. Once again the improvements were more mental than physical, although he could now run the mile in four minutes and twenty seconds, bench press 350 pounds, and leg curl 200 pounds. He kept practicing the levitation, and was able to move larger and heavier objects.

Joel spent a lot of time at the University library speed reading technical books. He never checked any of them out because he could read a book in thirty minutes with full comprehension. The subjects included philosophy, psychology, biology, internal medicine, surgery, computer sciences, chemistry, mechanics, metallurgy, quantum physics, and others. His favorite was nuclear sciences, especially the design of nuclear engines to produce energy. Joel learned a lot, but he also found that in most texts he saw conclusions that were flawed, and he could devise improved approaches.

In nuclear engine design he felt that he could greatly reduce the size, which was one of the major problems. He decided to design a miniaturized engine of his own. Another area he found fascinating was force fields. Some work had been done with this but the energy required to produce force fields like the ones on the fictional starship *Enterprise*, was not available for a practical application. He wondered if he could combine a miniaturized nuclear engine with an advanced force field design. In between his daily sessions and two more trips to Las Vegas, he spent his time working on this project.

Joel finally found that he could not learn any more from reading. He had absorbed all the present level of knowledge. From now on he needed to use his brain to free think and advance technology far beyond the current state of the art. He would create concepts that were hundreds of years ahead of today's capabilities. His creations would be used to benefit as many people as he could reach.

PART THREE
SILVER RANCH

Chapter One

ne Monday morning in late July he received the call from Sandra Lee. She was in Los Angeles working as a secretary under a different name. She had seen Leon coming into her office building and had managed to slip out the back without him seeing her, and called from a gas station. Joel thought for a while, then said, "go to the Beverly Hills Hilton Hotel, check in as Mr. and Mrs. Sampson, get a suite, and tell them your husband will be checking in soon." He then got $10,000 from the bank and drove to Los Angeles.

Checking in at the Hilton, he joined Sandra in her room. She was terrified. "If they can track me here they can find me anywhere. I didn't know what to do. You were the only one I could call."

"You did the right thing. Don't worry I will help you. Let's go find Leon." They drove to her apartment in Joel's car and he cruised by with Sandra scrunched down in her seat. Leon was parked a block away watching the front of the building. Joel drove past him, then parked.

Leon was so intent on watching for Sandra that he didn't see Joel approach from behind, open the back door, and slip in behind the driver's seat. As Leon started to turn his head in surprise, Joel reached across and wrapped his arm around Leon's throat, pinning his head against the headrest. "Do as I tell you or I'll snap your neck."

"Who are you? What do you want?" Leon croaked.

"Don't you remember me from the parking lot?" If Joel's throat hold wasn't making him go red, Leon would have paled as he remembered. "Using two fingers only, hand your gun over to me." As Leon reached for his gun, Joel tightened his arm around Leon's throat. "Be sensible" he said. Leon meekly handed over his gun. Joel released the safety on the gun, pressed the barrel into the back of Leon head, and removed his arm from around Leon's throat. "Now we're going up to Sandra's apartment. Remember I have the gun. I can beat you in a fight, and I can run faster than you."

They both got out of the car. Sandra apprehensively joined them and they walked to her apartment. Once inside, Joel emptied the bullets out of the gun.

"What are you doing?" cried Sandra.

"Leon needs to understand what a serious situation he is in." As he said that, Leon charged at him, head down, trying to ram him in the stomach. Joel moved slightly to the side. As Leon went by him, he brought both fists down on the back of his neck. Leon slowly got to his feet. Seeing that Joel was just standing there looking at him, he took a boxing stance.

For the next five minutes Joel toyed with Leon; he hit him at will with light blows, while Leon lumbered around without landing one blow. Joel would slap his face with both forehand and backhand tweak his nose, and generally embarrass him. Finally he let Leon get him in a bear hug, which he easily broke. Then bear hugging Leon, he lifted him of his feet and crushed him until he was gasping for breath. Putting him down, Joel asked "Have you had enough yet?" When Leon nodded, Joel told him to sit down.

"Now you're gonna tell me anything I want to know, or else I'll send Sandra out of the apartment and start to really work on you." Leon sat there sullenly. "Why are you here?" No answer. Thwack! Joel slapped him across the face.

"If I talk to you, Cy will kill me."

"Cy will never know that you talked to me, and if you don't I will cripple you and you will wish you were dead. So, why are you here?"

"I am supposed to bring her back," he said gesturing towards Sandra. "Nobody runs out on Cy and gets away with it."

"How did you find her?"

"Cy put the word out on the streets with a photo and a reward."

"Why does he want her?"

"He will use her then sent her where all the other girls go."

Joel thought for a moment about Sandra's roommate. "Like Susan?" he asked?

"Yes," Leon answered. Joel's guess had paid off.

"Where is that?" A look of terror came into Leon's eyes. He realized that he had let something slip.

"I can't tell you that."

"Sandra," Joel said, "why don't you go back to work and leave me alone with Leon? I don't want you to hear him scream when I break his legs. I'll crush the bones and he will be crippled for life. You wouldn't mind that, would you? After all, he's probably crippled a few people in his time."

"Okay," said Sandra moving towards the door.

"No!" said Leon. "I'll tell you but you must promise that Cy will never know who told you."

"When I'm finished with Cy he won't be thinking about who told me— he will be lucky if he is still alive. Now, where is Susan?"

Leon told them there was a place called Silver Ranch that was like the Chicken Ranch brothel in Pahrump, only the girls working there had no choice. Cy handpicked girls who had no family to initiate a search for them. He would make them his girlfriend for a while, then sent them to the Ranch when he tired of them. He has about ten girls at the Ranch, and allowed influential friends or trusted employees to go there, in return for favors. When he found a new girl, he would sell one of the others to white slavers from China.

The Ranch is about sixty miles north of Las Vegas, up Highway 93, off a road going east through Meadow Valley towards Elgin. Five miles down this road is a dirt track, and about a mile down this is the Ranch.

Joel told Leon he was going to let him go, but if he saw him again he would kill him, and if Cy Richards came after him he would tell him who gave him information. "You had better move back east, and find another job," he said.

Joel suggested to Sandra that they go back to the Hilton and make use of the suite; after all, he had to pay for it, so they might as well use it. Once there, they ordered dinner from room service and discussed their plans. Joel wanted Sandra to move into a motel near his apartment in San Diego, where she would be safe while he investigated Leon's story. She would have none of this, saying, "I want to go with you. I'm sure I can be of help." Finally he gave in and they agreed that she would go into work next morning, tell them she had a family emergency and needed time off, then they would go look at the Silver Ranch.

When it was time to go to bed Joel said, "I'll sleep on the sofa." She was surprised; she felt sure he would come on to her—in fact she was disappointed that he didn't. Still, he insisted on sleeping on the sofa.

Next morning, Tuesday, they were at a sporting goods store by 8 o'clock, where Joel purchased equipment he thought he might need, including a large backpack, binoculars, a telescope, and a portable cooler. By 9:30 they had taken Interstate 10 east to Interstate 15, and headed north to Las Vegas. They arrived at McCarran Airport by 3 p.m. Joel checked the rental places until he found a four-wheel drive Jeep Commander for rent. He left his car in airport parking, and then got back on Interstate 15 heading north. The road gently climbed up Apex Mountain, with Lake Mead to the right. By 5 o'clock they arrived at Exit 64 on Highway 15 at the Route 93 intersection. The only sign of life there came from a number of large trucks lined up about a hundred yards north east of the intersection, at a landfill dump site.

Joel had expected to find a motel and a restaurant nearby. He didn't want to arrive at the Ranch at night. He wanted to reconnoiter in the daylight. Hiding his disappointment, he drove back towards Las Vegas to find a motel. They got off at Lamb Boulevard and drove west one mile to a Comfort Inn. Joel said they would get some rest and start out early next morning. He got one room with two double beds and they went across the street to Carmen's Carniceria to have Mexican food for dinner.

Over dinner, they opened up to one another. Joel told her he was divorced and working in San Diego She told him she was an orphan; her parents had died in a car crash when she was 9, and she was raised by her aunt in Spokane, Washington. Her aunt had her own family, and made it obvious that Sandra was a burden, so as soon as she was 18, she left without telling them where she was going and headed for Las Vegas. Joel told her how his parents died and they empathized with one another. Joel decided he liked this girl and by the end of the evening they were friends. Again Joel made no attempt to sleep with her, getting into the bed nearest the door, saying good night, and going to sleep.

On Wednesday morning they checked out of the motel, filled the cooler with bottles of water and sandwiches, and drove north on Highway 93. To the east was the Maopa Maopa River Indian Reservation and to the west the Desert National Wildlife Range. Further west was the Nellis Air Force Range that includes the Nevada Test Range and Site 51, where it was rumored that the aliens from the Roswell UFO were interned. The terrain on both sides consisted of shrub and small cactus plants. They passed the Apex Power Station on the left, then drove through a range of low hills. After about thirty-one miles, they passed Highway 138 and entered Lincoln County. A few miles further, just past another range of hills, they saw a wide, well-kept unpaved road heading east.

Joel drove slowly down the dirt track, around the back of the second range of hills, until he could see the Ranch, hidden from Highway 93. He turned off into the desert shrub looking for a place where he could reconnoiter the ranch. The terrain rose gently to the north as Joel circled around the ranch, keeping well away. He came to a rise in the desert floor like a small mesa and parked the Jeep behind it. He got his backpack out of the SUV, and climbing covertly to the top of the mesa, lay flat on his stomach looking down at the ranch. Taking his binoculars out of the backpack, he surveyed the complex below him.

There was an 8-foot high, quarter-mile square block wall around the perimeter with a 6-foot chain-link fence inside it. There was a 10-foot space between the wall and the fence. In this space he could see six Rottweilers. In the center of the compound was a two-story building that looked like a small L-shaped hotel. Leon had told him that the long leg of the L, which looked about one 100-feet long, contained the girls' bedrooms upstairs and a lounge downstairs. The short leg, about 60-feet long, had the guards' bedrooms upstairs and the kitchen downstairs with the "Madame's" office and quarters at the far end.

In the middle of the south wall was the only entrance to the compound. It was like an air lock. A car could come through the outer gate in the wall into a space and the outer gate would close, trapping the car between the wall and the fence. There was a guard shack to one side filling the space between the wall and the fence; the guard would identify the occupants before opening the inner gate in the fence. Beside the guard shack was a large kennel for the dogs, accessible from the guard shack.

The binoculars were 10x power so he could not see much detail from a quarter of a mile away. Joel slithered back down the mesa and retrieved a telescope from the car. It was 50x power and would show much more detail. Back on the mesa he studied the main building. From his position he was in line with the corner of the L-shape. The drapes on the windows were open and he could see women in the upper bedrooms just lounging around. In the office was a woman who looked to be about 50 years old sitting at a desk talking on the telephone. The kitchen area appeared to be empty. Between the kitchen and the lounge was a dining room, also empty. In the lounge, two men were playing cards.

Joel made a detailed sketch of the compound, then settled down to watch. It was 10 o'clock and the sun was getting higher in the south; he was glad he had thought to bring a hat and plenty of water. Soon the two men came out the main entrance of the house and started smoking. Cy Richards must be a non-smoker thought Joel, no smoking in the house. At 10:30, the woman from the office carried a flask from the house to the shack, and quickly returned. At noon, the two men from the lounge came out of the house, walked to the shack, and the two original guards returned to the house. They went upstairs to the bedrooms and the drapes were drawn; must be their time to sleep.

Sandra, who had become bored a long time before and had been sitting in the shade of the car reading, brought him some fresh, cool water. "How's it going?"

"Apart from the heat, okay."

"How long are you going to stay here?"

"Until I get a feeling for their routine."

At 12:30 two men he hadn't seen before appeared in the lounge; they must have been sleeping in the morning. Joel watched all afternoon. The routine never varied: smoking breaks, coffee breaks, and playing cards. At 4 o'clock the two men in the lounge relieved the two in the guard shack and one of them fed the dogs.

He wrote down his observations. He had identified six men and a woman moving freely about the grounds. The men worked the gates in four-hour shifts, four hours on, eight hours off, then four hours on.

During the eight hours off they would sleep for four hours and be on call the other four. The dogs were fed at 4 p.m. and probably at 8 a.m. in the morning when the guards changed shift. He also noticed that the dogs barked when any desert critters approached the wall and the guards would yell at them but not go to see why they were barking. It seemed they must have gotten tired of false alarms. There did not seem to be many customers coming and going. It was Tuesday; maybe the weekends were busier.

As Joel watched, he formulated his plan to enter the facility. He would need some ground beef, sleeping pills, a grappling hook, wire cutters, lengths of rope, duct tape, latex gloves, and a sharp knife. He could get all these things easily, except the sleeping pills. After the 4 o'clock shift change he decided he had seen enough. He returned to the car and told Sandra his problem with the sleeping pills. She said she knew a girl in Vegas who could always get barbiturate tablets from her supplier for the right price.

Chapter Two

They drove back to Las Vegas, and checked into a motel away from The Strip. Joel paid for one night in cash, then he went out to get the supplies he needed while Sandra called her friend on her cell phone. When he got back, she told him she had arranged for him to meet her friend Laura, at a bar at 9 o'clock; she would have one hundred barbiturate tablets for $500. Sandra could not go with him in case someone spotted her and passed the information on to Cy Richards. Sandra described her friend to him, and said she would be wearing a red top and black pants.

Joel parked two blocks away from the bar, and at 9 p.m. sharp, he walked into the bar, spotting a woman in a red top with a low front trimmed in lace, wearing tight-fitting black pants. She looked like a hooker. When he asked her, she said she was Laura and told him to go out to the alley in back of the bar, where she would pass the stuff to him. Joel was immediately wary; Laura was too nervous even for a drug sale.

A tall black man followed them out. Joel turned to face him keeping his back to the wall.

"Do you have the cash, man?" said the black man.

"Show me the merchandise," Joel responded. The man produced a bottle containing about one hundred tablets, the label read "Pentobarbital."

"That will be $800."

"Laura said $500."

"The price went up."

Just then two more men came out of the back door of the bar; one was holding a gun. Joel grabbed the bottle of barbiturates and hit the black man, who went down hard.

"Don't shoot unless you have to," said the man without the gun, "It's Sandra we want."

They were both bigger than Joel and they came at him confident that they had the advantage. Moving sideways, Joel grabbed the gunman's arm. As he twisted it up his back, he heard he the bone snap.Quickly turning to the other man, he knocked him out with one punch.

Laura stood there stunned; before she could move, Joel grabbed her by the throat and slammed her against the wall, saying, "Some friend you are." She slid to a sitting position on the ground. "If you move, you'll get some more."

The gunman was sitting nursing his arm and babbling. Joel picked up the gun and turned his attention to the black man. Quickly going through his pockets he found two more bottles and six neatly folded packets. These he transferred to his own pockets.

Joel picked Laura up, holding her off her feet. "You go back into the bar and if anyone asks you what happened, you say you don't know. You brought me out here and went straight back in. If you say anything else, I'll come looking for you." With this Joel walked rapidly down the alley and back to the Jeep. Driving away, he thought about this new vicious side of him and worried that his newfound power was corrupting him. He rationalized that so far he had only hurt bad guys who deserved it and he was protecting good people. He would have to wait and see what he did when a basically good person upset him.

Back at the motel he told Sandra all that had transpired. She was shocked at Laura's part in it and felt that she must have been coerced. He asked her if she could tell if the barbiturates were the real thing.

"I've taken barbiturates before. Let me see them." He gave her the bottle and she tipped a couple into her hand.

"Yes, they seem real, the color and size are right." He showed her the six packets he had taken from the black man. "This is heroin," she said.

"Are you sure?"

"Yes!" He looked at her quizzically, but didn't ask any more questions. It was none of his business how she knew it was heroin. "Let's get out of this motel before they trace us here."

They drove north on Interstate 15, back to the Comfort Inn, and got a room. Once inside, he told Sandra to crush about a hundred tablets on the table and separate the powder into six piles. While she was doing this, he opened the cooler, took out six re-sealable bags of ground beef, and laid them on the table. He opened one of them, took out the beef, and mixed one pile of the barbiturates in with the meat. Sandra opened a second bag and started helping him.

"What are your plans for tomorrow?" she asked him.

"I want to get back to the ranch at about a quarter to 4, observe until midnight to confirm their schedule, and then I'm going in. I think you should stay here at the motel." Sandra would have none of this.

"We're in this together. You are going to need me."

"What are you going to do?"

"If you get caught I can go for help, and if you succeed I can come in and get the girls to trust you." Joel finally relented, seeing some wisdom in what she said.

"Okay, let's go and get some dinner."

Joel called the motel office and the clerk recommended a nearby Italian restaurant that turned out to be very nice. On the way to the restaurant Joel noticed the brightness of the half moon and hoped the light would not be a problem the next night at the ranch.

Over some bruchetta, veal cacciatore, and a bottle Riesling, they continued to become better acquainted. Sandra told him. "I don't remember my parents at all, but I remember the anger. A 6-year-old should never be that angry. I blamed my parents for leaving me. I would lay awake at night hating them, and crying because I missed them. I was sullen and disobedient both at home and at school, wouldn't do homework, glad that I got bad grades. I did participate in sports, my one outlet, and they had a dance class at school, which got me my only good grade. My aunt tried her hardest to help me, but could not cope—I was a hellion. She had even paid for me to take dancing lessons."

"At 13 I went to the police station and asked to see the accident report.

The sergeant on the desk told me to go away they didn't have time to look up records for everybody that came in. A Lieutenant Barker overheard our conversation as he entered the station. He took me to his office, found the file, read it first, and then let me read it. A drunk driver had run a red light and broadsided my parents. They did not have a chance. Driving below the speed limit through a green light, they couldn't do anything to stop the tragedy. Five people died, including the drunk driver."

"After that, I realized my parents were not at fault, and slowly came around until my grades improved—so did my relationship with Aunt Jessica. At 18 I graduated and left to try to make it as a dancer in Las Vegas, but the talent was not there. I began to see the reality of things, and had planned to go back to Spokane when my present problems started. I can't go back to Spokane until I'm sure my problems will not follow. I can't let anything to happen to my aunt and her family."

The wine began to show its effects by the time they got back to the motel. Sandra said, "I'm afraid of what might happen tomorrow."

"Would you please hold me?"

Joel told her, "I can't get involved in a long-term relationship because of commitments I have in San Diego. That is why I am keeping my distance. It would not be fair to you."

"We can have the next few days then, I'll go to Spokane."

Joel put some music on the motel radio. As they held one another and swayed to the music, Joel felt himself letting the tension of the past few days evaporate, and with the smell of her perfume filling his senses, started to slowly undress her. For her part, Sandra started to undress Joel, and soon they clung to each other with their bare bodies entwined. For a long time they kissed and caressed until at last Joel picked her up, gently laid her on the bed, and stretched himself out on top of her. He slowly entered her and soon the passion of the moment overtook them and they were locked in a wild frenzy of lovemaking.

They slept in each other arms, awaking in the middle of the night for a repeat performance. They both slept until 10 a.m., then they lay in bed talking until hunger made them think of breakfast. After a communal shower, where they found that the ardor of the previous night had not been sated, they ate breakfast at a coffee shop. They spent a couple of hours lounging around the motel pool, talking about everything, and nothing, but avoiding their plans for the evening.

Chapter Three

At 3 o'clock they set out for the ranch, arriving at their previous parking spot behind the mesa, at 3:45. They lay on top of the mesa side by side studying the compound. At first Joel used the binoculars while Sandra trained the telescope on the upstairs bedrooms used by the girls. She wanted to see if she could recognize anyone. She was rewarded by glimpses of Susan and two other girls she knew—girls that Cy had told them had "given up dancing and gone home."

At 4 o'clock guards in the shack changed and the dogs were in the shack, and fed. The evening dragged on and Joel was happy to see that there were no visitors, but when the moon came up he felt dismayed to see how much it lit up the desert. Now using the telescope, Joel watched the madame go to bed, and then, two of the men go to the guard shack at midnight. The two returning men went up to bed, while the two men who had been sleeping, entered the lounge. He waited thirty minutes more, and saw that the two men in the lounge were also sleeping, one in a recliner and the other on a couch.

It was time to begin the assault. Joel took Sandra in his arms. "I'll call you when I can. When I say to drive the Jeep to the front gate, you come on in. Everything will be okay. If I say drive the truck to the front gate or anything weird, you get in the car and drive away as fast as you can. Do you understand me?"

"I'll go for help," said Sandra.

"No! Who can you trust? You just go back to Spokane."

She nodded, so he kissed her and left to the sound of her whispering, "Be careful."

Joel put on a pair of latex gloves to avoid leaving fingerprints. Wearing the backpack with the meat in it and carrying the grappling hook, he stealthily approached the north wall of the compound, the one opposite the guard shack. The dogs started to bark as he crouched in the shadow cast by the wall. He heard a man shouting at the dogs, and they quieted down. He took the one-pound balls of ground beef out of the plastic bags, and threw them one by one over the wall. He waited about a minute between throwing each ball of meat, hoping this would enable each dog to get its share. Then he sat there waiting for fifteen minutes.

He threw the grappling hook over the top of the wall and waited to see if the dogs started barking. Nothing! Pulling himself up to the top of the wall, he peered over, and could see all six of the dogs lying on their sides lifeless. He hoped the dose of barbiturates in the meat hadn't killed them. He reversed the grappling hook and rappelled down the inside of the wall. Keeping a low profile and hugging the wall, he made his way to the kennel side of the guard shack.

Joel noticed that the door was severely marked where the dogs had been scratching at it, and this gave him an idea. Standing by the hinge of the door, so that he would be behind it as it opened, he scratched on the door with his knife. He heard a curse from inside, and a voice shouted, "Get away from that door." He continued to scratch until finally the door opened and a guard came out still yelling. As he cleared the door, Joel pole-axed him with one blow, caught his body, and lowered him to the ground. Relieving him of his gun, Joel quickly entered the kennel and peeked into the guard shack.

The second guard walked towards the door to see what was going on. Joel closed the gap between them and pressed the nozzle of the gun into his neck saying, "Be quiet."

"You fire and the whole house will be roused," said the guard.

"You yell and they'll be roused, so I'll fire." The guard, who was a much bigger man, sensed there was an impasse, so he grabbed Joel in a bear hug.

Joel stamped hard on the man's foot and at the same time brought his head up sharply under the guard's chin. The bear hug was broken, so Joel stepped back, then hit the guard hard in the stomach. He went down on his knees, gasping for air, and Joel hit him over the head with the butt of the gun.

Joel carried the first guard into the shack. Using the rope and tape from his backpack, he tied their arms behind their backs, their feet together, and put duct tape across their mouths. Then, bending their legs up behind their backs, tied their feet to their arms. Trussed up like chickens, they were unable to move. Joel then searched the shack and the kennel looking for anything useful. In the kennel he found a large bottle of chloroform and wads of cotton batting. They must use this on the dogs for some reason. Both items went into his backpack.

He found a baseball cap and a jacket belonging to one of the men. Putting these on, he was ready to tackle the main house. Before leaving the shack, Joel call Sandra to let her know everything was going according to plan, and again she entreated him to be careful. He slipped out of the shack door and headed for the house, walking boldly across the compound until reaching the office end of the house. He slipped into the bushes along the side of the house, and keeping below the window level, made his way towards the front door.

Once again his luck held. As Joel crouched in the bushes beside the door, getting his next move clear in his mind, the door opened and out came one of the men. The man paused at the top of the three steps leading up to the door, then slowly descended to the bottom. He looked in Joel's direction and took a packet of cigarettes out of his pocket, but the bushes hid Joel. Then, turning his head in the other direction, to shelter the match from the wind, he started to light his cigarette.

Joel soaked some cotton batting in chloroform, moved silently behind the man, knocked the cigarette out of his mouth, and clamped the batting over his mouth. The man struggled briefly and then went limp. Joel dragged him into the bushes, took off his coat, and trussed him up like the other two guards. He added some more chloroform to the batting, and was ready to go into the house. Entering the front door, he found himself in a 20-foot square tiled entryway with the open door of the lounge across from him.

Quietly crossing to the lounge door, he looked in and saw the fourth guard lying on the couch with his eyes closed. He noted that the carpet covering the lounge floor would deaden his footsteps. He crossed to the couch, placed the batting over the guard's mouth, and placing his knee in the man's stomach pushed down with all his weight. The man resisted violently, but Joel held him down. The struggle lasted less than a minute. Joel trussed up this guard and placed him behind the couch, out of sight. He then brought the man that he had left in the bushes, into the lounge, and dumped him on top of his partner.

Joel looked around the lounge. The 30-foot wide by 80-foot long room had a 12-foot ceiling. Large picture windows covered both the left side and the far end. A large HD television filled the wall on the right side, with couches and love seat placed for watching. A 25-foot long, well-stocked bar, almost filled the fourth wall; at the far end he saw a small tiled dancing area with a complete sound system. A door in the left wall near the bar led to the entryway.

Joel returned to the entryway. The stairway to the second floor went up to the left, with a door to the right of the staircase. He went through this door and found it led to a hallway. Off the hallway to the right a door opened into a triple garage with three vehicles in it. The door to the left led to a 25-foot square dinning room, with a door and a serving hatch at one end. The door at the end opened into the kitchen. In the middle of the dining room sat a fifteen foot square table, big enough to seat twenty people. Further along the hallway another door led into the kitchen. The hallway ended with a door into the office, which was locked. Retracing his steps to the entryway, Joel cautiously climbed the stairs to the second floor.

The staircase went up six stairs to a small landing, then came back in the opposite direction for six more stairs to another landing, then finally back again for the last six stairs. At the top, off to the left, he found a long corridor going down the middle of the long side of the L-shaped building. There were five doors on each side of the corridor. The design of these doors allowed them to open inwards so that the occupant could not burst it from the inside. To the right the corridor ran down the short side of the building with three doors off to the right side and one door at the very end.

Moving down the corridor to the right, he carefully opened the first door. There was nobody in the room. It contained two single beds, two chess of drawers and two small desks. The beds had been slept in but remained unmade. In one corner he saw another door. Crossing to this, he peered in and found an empty bathroom.

Back in the corridor he moved to the second door. This room was identical, except there was a man sleeping in one of the beds. He snored so loudly that Joel could understand why the men didn't share a room with the man they were on duty with.

He closed the door gently. He wanted to make sure he found the last guard before he went any farther. With things going so well, he didn't want any surprises. Joel carefully opened the third door. Once again it was an identical room with a man sleeping in one of the beds. This time the snoring was not so loud. Closing the door gently behind him, Joel took his backpack off and took out the chloroform. He added more to the batting, then approached the bed.

He suddenly realized that the snoring had stopped and the guard was coming out of the bed at him. He ducked in time and took the first punch on the top of his head. He heard the man curse. Joel rolled to one side and as he looked up, saw a foot aimed at his head. Grabbing it, he twisted violently, sending his assailant crashing to the floor. Jumping to his feet, Joel grabbed his arm and struck him hard on the jaw, rendering him unconscious.

Joel hurried to the door to see if the commotion had awakened the last guard, only to see him coming through the door with a gun in his hand. "What the hell's going on in here? Who the hell are you?"

Joel backed up a step, staring at the gun. The man was looking passed him at his friend on the floor. Joel concentrated and willed the gun to move sideways. To his amazement, it did. As soon as it had moved enough so that it was not aimed at him, he stepped forward and hit the man hard. The gun fired, but the bullet went off to the right as the last bad guy bit the dust.

He picked up the gun and moved into the hall in time to see a middle-aged woman in a dressing gown coming down the hall. He pointed the gun at her and waved her into the room. "What am I going to do with you?" Joel said.

Joel told her, "Go into the bathroom, close the door, and stay there until I tell you to come out. If you do as I say, I won't hurt you." She did as he told her. Once she was gone Joel put the gun away and tied up both men the way he had the others. He then called Sandra and told her to bring the Jeep around to the front gate. She said, "I was worried, I heard a shot."

"I'm okay. I'll see you soon."

He went to the bathroom door to find it locked. "Open the door!" No answer. With one kick he busted the lock. The woman was cowering in the corner, obviously scared. "Who are you?"

"I'll tell you that later. Come out. I won't hurt you," He took her downstairs, where she saw two other guards behind the sofa, and then, prodding her with the gun, followed her to the guard shack. Seeing the last of the guards tied up, she knew he was in complete control of the compound.

Chapter Four

"Open the outer gate," Joel told the woman. She obeyed. After Sandra drove in, he said, "Close the outer gate and open the inner one." Sandra came into the shack and hugged him, then turned to look at the woman.

"I know you. I've seen you at the casino The girls told me you were a dancer in the seventies, Rachel, isn't it?"

"Hi Sandra," said the woman.

"Drive the car to the house," said Joel. "We'll follow you." After Sandra was gone, Rachel closed the inner gate and they walked back to the house.

"Which room is Susan in?" Joel asked Rachel. The three of them went upstairs. Rachel retrieved some keys from her bedroom and took them to the second door on the left in the main corridor. "Open the door," Joel ordered.

The room contained comfortable-looking king-sized bed, a small dresser, and not much else. The heavy bars on the windows filled the frame. One wall had two doors, one closed, probably a closet; through the open door Joel could see a bathroom. The arrangement benefited the customer more than the occupant.

Sandra went in. Susan was sitting on the bed with a fearful look in her eyes.

When she saw Sandra, she rushed into her arms. "Have they got you too?"

"No! No!" Said Sandra. "We're here to rescue you."

"I heard a gun go off."

Sandra spent a few minutes explaining the situation.

"Let's get the rest of the girls and we can tell them all together."

"Give Sandra the keys," Joel said to Rachel, and she did. "You and Susan free the other girls and we will meet in the lounge."

Keeping Rachel with him, Joel went to the bedroom where the two guards were, picked one up, and took him downstairs. Rachel was amazed that an average-sized man could carry such a big man with ease. What kind of man was this? Keeping Rachel with him, he went back upstairs for the other guard.

By this time all the girls were assembled in the lounge. Joel was introduced to them, but they all regarded him with suspicion. Who could blame them. Six of them looked scared and timid, the other two, Belle and Pat, looked hard as nails.

"Sandra, take six ladies into the dining room and get me seven chairs please," said Joel. When they left Joel dragged the two guards, who were now conscious, out from behind the couch. After the girls brought the chairs in, Joel lined them up along one wall. Untying the rope binding their hands to their legs, Joel sat the four guards on chairs with their hands over the back. He then tied their arms and legs to the chair.

"Watch her," Joel said to Sandra pointing at Rachel. "I'm going to get the other guards." He made two trips to the guard shack and soon all six guards were sitting in the lounge. He then tied Rachel to the seventh chair. "Now, ladies, tell me, did any of these fine gentlemen abuse you?" They all started to talk at once. "Whoa! Hold on," said Joel. "Let me put it another way. Who was the worst?"

"Lennie," they all said in chorus, pointing to the biggest guard, who must have weighed at least 250 pounds. Joel walked behind Lennie's chair, picked him and the chair up as if they were a sack of feathers, carried it to the tiled dance floor, and set him down at one end facing them.

As he walked back, he said, "I don't want to get blood on the carpet when we start the fun and games. Who's the next worse?" The women pointed out Mitch, Ron, and then Wade.

When he had four guards lined up on the dance floor, the girls all agreed that the last two, John and Pete, had treated them gently, even though they had partaken of their favors. The bigger of the two, John, had a fight with Lennie to try to stop the brutality, but Lennie had won. These two he left where they were.

"How about Rachel?" The consensus was that she had tried to control the guards, but when she reported them to Richards he sided with the guards. His rule was as long as they didn't leave any bad marks, anything was okay. "Give me the key to your office," Joel said to Rachel. After she did, Joel collected all the weapons he had confiscated, took them down the hall to the office, and locked them all, except one gun, in there.

Upon returning, he took Sandra aside. "It's 2 a.m. Why don't you and the ladies go upstairs and get some sleep?"

"I want to stay with you."

"We can't both sleep at the same time. I will require about two hours of sleep later, so I will need you rested."

Sandra reluctantly agreed. Joel told all the girls to go with Sandra. "You'll be sleeping behind an unlocked door for a change."

"What are you going to do?" asked Belle.

"I'm going to interrogate these men and it might get bloody."

"I want to watch" said Belle. "I can sleep later."

"Me too," said Pat.

"Anybody else?" said Joel. There was no answer. "Okay, you two can stay."

The rest of the women left the lounge, heading for bed. Joel turned his attention to his four victims. Lennie, Mitch, and Ron looked at him defiantly, but Wade was obviously shaken.

Joel decided that Wade was the weak link of the four. He said, "I don't want to waste a lot of time on this, so I'm going to show you how serious I am." Joel handed the gun to Belle and said, "Don't interfere unless I am unconscious." He walked up to Lennie and undid the ropes around his legs, then told Pat to go behind Lennie, untie his hands, and get out of the way.

"Are you serious?" she asked.

"Yes, trust me, do as I say."

Pat reluctantly did as he asked.

A big grin spread across Lennie's face as he came out of the chair and rushed Joel, swinging a right hook. Joel grabbed his arm, bent over, and flipped Lennie high over his back. He landed with a loud thud on his face. Lennie got up gingerly to see Joel standing there waiting for him. This time he approached Joel carefully and suddenly locked him in a bear hug. Joel let him squeeze for a while, then placing his hands on Lennie's shoulders he slowly pushed him away until the bear hug was broken. Lennie realized he was in trouble. Joel now started boxing Lennie, hitting him in the face at will, until his face was a bloody mess. Then, Joel beat him about the body until he collapsed on the floor. The room was deathly silent; nobody could believe what they had just witnessed.

Belle walked up to Lennie and started kicking him as he lay on the floor. Pat joined her. Finally, Joel had to move them away. He took the gun from Belle and made them both sit on one of the couches. Joel tied Lennie back to his chair, and made sure that the bonds of all four guards were secure.

He moved in front of Mitch and said, "Mitch, are you ready to answer my questions?" Mitch didn't answer, so Joel knelt down and started to untie his legs.

"Okay, okay, what do you want to know?"

"Tell me about the Chinese white slavers."

"I don't know any thing about them."

"Then you're no good to me conscious, are you?" Once again Joel knelt down.

"I do know a little. The girl is given enough drugs to keep her quiet for about twenty-four hours. She is packed in a coffin, then Ron and Wade take the box to Morro Bay."

Joel moved down one chair to Ron. "Now, Ron, tell me more." Again silence, and Joel knelt down.

"The box has special lining so that the girl is not hurt, and the coffin has air holes," Ron blurted out.

"What happens in Morro Bay?"

Silence from Ron. Thwack! Joel hit him so hard across the face that his head jerked sideways and a red imprint of a hand started to appear on his face. "I could ask Wade these questions, but then I wouldn't need you any more. I want you to tell me all you know without me asking questions. I will hit you every time you stop, until I think I know all that you know."

"Let me have a go at him," said Belle. "I know a trick or two—some of them he taught me."

"There you are, Ron, if I'm not happy with what you tell me, I'll turn you over to the ladies."

Ron told them that Cy had a 50 foot power cruiser at the Redondo Beach Marina and a full-time skipper to take care of it. Cy would instruct the skipper to cruise alone to Morro Bay, docking at the harbor by 6 p.m. on the evening of a delivery. He and Wade would drive a hearse, with the coffin in it, to Morro Bay, where they'd loaded it on to Richards' cruiser. The three of them would then meet a Chinese freighter about twenty miles off the coast. The freighter, on its way back to China having loaded up in San Pedro, wanted to be well away from Los Angeles before taking the coffin on board. The coffin was never opened before it was loaded onto the freighter, as the Chinese knew that Richards would not double cross them. His predecessor had, and Cy knew what had happen to him. The Chinese would lower a hoist and take the coffin off the cruiser, without him or Wade going on board.

"How do the Chinese pay for the girl?"

"A five kilo package of heroin is lowered down from the freighter after the girl is on board."

"When is the next delivery?"

"Belle was due to be shipped out in Saturday night."

"How long does it take to drive to Morro Bay?"

"About eight hours. We would rendezvous with the freighter at one a.m."

Satisfied that he had enough information for now, Joel told Belle and Pat to go to bed. After they left, Joel went to the kitchen, took off his bloody latex gloves, made a sandwich, being careful not to leave any fingerprints, and returned to the lounge to eat it. Finished eating, he settled back in a recliner.

For the next five hours he sat, letting his mind race. First, he finalized the plans for his trip to Morro Bay, storing that away. Then, he worked on plans for his miniature atomic-powered engine and force field generator. Then his mind turned to how he was going to use Anton's machine to benefit as many people as he could. The five kilos of heroin had triggered the thought that if he drastically reduced the supplies of illegal drugs, that would benefit millions of people—not only the poor soul that used drugs but the peripheral people, parents, spouses, and children.

Chapter Five

Upstairs, Belle and Pat decided to share a room; they'd had enough of being alone. As they lay in bed Pat said, "What do you think of this Joel? Do you think we can trust him?"

"He's a man, isn't he? When could you ever trust a man? They'll all screw you in the end." As she continued talking, Belle realized Pat had gone to sleep. Pat never had trouble sleeping. Not being too smart, she didn't worry about problems. They didn't bother her.

She lay there thinking about Pat's question. Belle's whole life was a dichotomy. On the one hand, she hated men, but on the other hand, she loved sex. Her mother had died just after her eighth birthday. She and her father became very close; some nights she even slept in his bed.

His lack of education didn't enable him to earn much money, so they lived in a two-bedroom apartment in the poorer section of Buffalo, near the chemical plant where he worked. She had a happy childhood, doing okay in academics at school, and excelling in sports, where she played volleyball and basketball. This all came to an end shortly before her sixteenth birthday.

She came home from winning a basketball game and they hugged, as they often did, when he suddenly kissed her on the lips inappropriately. She pushed him away and he apologized, but later he came up behind her and slipping his arms around her, fondled her breasts. Belle loved her father dearly and didn't want to offend him. The next night he gently and lovingly took her virginity. At first she enjoyed the sex and because she loved her father, told herself to just accept the situation.

Soon she realized this must stop and told her father she would not sleep with him again. He got upset and cried until she felt sorry for him. They wound up in bed again.

Her grades had dropped to where it looked like she would be held back a grade. One day after class, her math teacher, Mr. Max Jenson, asked her to stay back after class. As he talked to her about her bad grades, she burst into tears. As Belle cried Jenson pressed her for an explanation and soon she told him the whole story.

He told her she must tell the authorities, but Belle said no, she couldn't send her father to jail. Max made her promise to come to him if she changed her mind. Three days later, on a Friday, her father came home late at night with a friend. Both of them had been drinking heavily and her father made her sleep with his friend.

When the friend had left and her father fell asleep, Belle took a taxi to Mr. Jenson's house across town in a nicer part of Buffalo. Max Jenson, a 38-year-old bachelor, let her spend the night in his spare room. The next morning Belle still didn't want to report her father to the authorities. She was desolated and could not think for herself. They went back to her home to collect all her belongings and Max told him, "If you make any attempt to contact your daughter again, I will report you to the police."

Max told Belle, "You can stay with me until we figure out what to do, but no one must know. They wouldn't understand. I'll drive you to Billington Street, just a mile from school, and you can take public transport from there. If one of us has to stay late for any reason, you can take a bus home."

Two weeks later she still lived with Max. The arrangement worked well. Belle would cook and clean in return for food and lodging. He didn't have a steady girlfriend, but if Max had visitors, Belle would be out or lock herself in her room until they left. Max visited her father and told him Belle was living with a married couple he knew. If he sent $1000 a month to Max for her expenses, they would not report him, but he must never try to see her again. Max opened a bank account for Belle and put the money in it each month. She used it for clothes and personal expenses.

After a while, Belle began to enjoy life again. Max helped her with her schoolwork and soon her grades exceeded her best levels ever. She told her friends she lived with an aunt across town, but still used her father's address to stay at the same school. They had a few hairy moments, but on the whole life went on smoothly. She didn't go out with school friends too often because her heart told her she loved Max, and they spent a lot of time together.

After six months they finally consummated their relationship and Belle's life needed nothing more. They lived this way for a year until Belle graduated. Although the subject had never been discussed, she expected them to get married once the school problem no longer existed. To her surprise and dismay once she found a job, Max asked her to find an apartment and move out.

In her mind she had always dreamed of a honeymoon in Las Vegas, so when she realized Max meant what he said, she packed up all her possessions and headed for Nevada. That resulted in her working as a cocktail waitress at the Silver Slipper and a head-on collision with Cy Richards. So getting back to Pat's question, "Did she trust Joel?" In a pig's eye.

At 6:30 a.m. Sandra came into the lounge. She and Joel went into the kitchen, where they could embrace in private. Joel kissed her deep and hard, then soft and gentle.

"I needed that," said Sandra.

Still holding her in his arms, Joel said, "I'm going to get some sleep now. Awake me at 9. Do you want me to wake Belle to help you?"

"No, I'll be okay. You go sleep. I changed the sheets in Rachel's room, use that."

At 8:45 Joel awoke by himself. He put on a clean pair of latex gloves, then stealthily went down the stairs. He found Belle and Pat in the lounge taunting the guards, and Sandra and the rest of the girls in the kitchen and dining rooms preparing food.

"Oh there you are," said Sandra. "I was giving you an extra thirty minutes while we finish getting breakfast." He went to her and hugged her.

"Thank you, I'm refreshed now. I don't need much sleep."

"Why don't you wait in the lounge? We won't be long."

He took the gun from her and went into the lounge. Belle and Pat were still annoying the four bullies. He made no attempt to stop them; the men deserved it and they were doing no serious harm. Soon Sandra came in to announce that breakfast was ready. Holding the gun loosely in his hand, Joel had the girls untie John, Pete, and Rachel, then he checked the bonds of the other four. He told Rachel, John, and Pete to precede him across the entryway into the dinning room, where the table was piled high with food.

When they were out of earshot of the other four guards, Joel said to John, Pete, and Rachel, "You three can help me or not, I don't care. If you co-operate, I promise you will get out of this alive, but if you give me any trouble, you'll join the other four. You three sit on the far side of the table against the wall." Joel sat in the middle of the kitchen end of the table with Sandra, and Susan, and the other girls used the other two sides.

The food consisted of tureens of cereals, scrambled eggs, bacon, sausages, hash brown potatoes, and toast, with thermos jugs of orange juice, milk, and coffee. They all sat down and started to eat. When they were finished, Joel said, "We need to discuss what you ladies want to do. Let's go around the table, starting with you Rita."

"I don't know," said Rita. "I don't want to go back to the life I had before, but I certainly don't want to go back to Michigan."

"Well, I do," said June. "I want to get out of here as fast as I can and go home to Indiana."

"Not me," said Mary. "It would have been okay here if we were free to come and go and someone controlled the sadists. I might go and see if they have openings at the Chicken Ranch."

They continued around the table. Two girls wanted to go home; the rest seemed to agree with Mary, except a couple who were reluctant to admit it. Joel said, "I hope you'll all stay here for a couple of days, I have some ideas that would result in you all having some cash to plan your future with. Anybody have a problem with this?" No one answered. Joel looked at each girl individually, then said, "I'll take that to mean we are in agreement."

"Tell me, Rachel, who owns this property?"

"Cy Richards. He has it incorporated, but he's the only owner. The grant deed is in his safe—I've seen it. He left it here in case the authorities searched his office or home and found the deed. He wanted as few people as possible to know about this place."

"What else does he have in his safe?"

"Well, I know he has information about his offshore bank accounts; he bragged about it one time when he was drunk, and he has quite a bit of cash."

"How much cash?"

"I don't know, but a lot of one hundred dollar bills."

"Do you know the combination?"

"No, only he knows that."

"Does anybody know a lawyer who will help us and keep his mouth shut?"

There was a brief silence, then Pete said. "Can I say something?"

"Sure speak up."

"I'd like to join in with you. I was not happy with what I was doing here, but once you work for Richards it's hard to quit. I think John and Rachel feel the same—we have discussed this before."

"Okay, you're in, but I won't be able to trust you until you prove your sincerity."

"Well," said Pete, "I know a lawyer that Richards cheated on a big deal, and then threatened his family to keep him quiet. He would probably help you if his name was kept out of it."

"That sounds great. What's his name?"

"Jack Sullivan," said Pete.

"Okay, we'll try him."

"Here's my plan," said Joel. "I'll get Cy Richards to sign over the ownership of this corporation to the ten girls as joint owners and the lawyer will take care of the paperwork. Then you can use it as you see fit, open up your own Chicken Ranch if you want to. Rachel, John, and Ron can work for you and we'll get a trustworthy accountant to take care of the books. Or, you can sell the property and share the profits. You'll all share in the contents of the safe."

John said, "You'll have to kill Richards if you do that, or he'll kill us all. Will you kill him?"

"No," said Joel. "I have a better idea. He'll be our next shipment to China."

Slowly that sank in, and then everybody around the table laughed.

"Rachel, how do we get Richards out here to visit us, preferable alone?"

"Well, he usually comes out when we're ready to ship a girl, but Leon or Sam will be with him."

"I don't want to wait that long. What if you said Belle was sick—would he come out or just sent a doctor?"

"He never pays for a doctor. He would come out himself, especially if I said she was really bad."

"Let you and I go to your office. Sandra, keep everybody here." Rachel unlocked the door. Once inside, Joel said to Rachel, "Tell me why I should trust you?"

She thought for a while, then said, "Cy keeps me here all the time, I'm as much a prisoner as the girls. I've been thinking of trying to escape for some time, but haven't had the opportunity, or the nerve, to do it. This is my chance for a new life."

Joel studied her face and somehow he knew she was telling him the truth. "How about John and Pete?"

"We are friends and I told them how I feel. They said they feel the same, but other people who left Richards disappeared without a trace."

"What do you think about the lawyer?"

"I heard that story. Cy thought it was funny. He sent Leon to visit the guy's wife while he was at work. Leon scared the life out of her. I think he'll help you if you ask him the right way."

"Show me the safe."

"It's under the left side of the desk, Cy figured the desk was too heavy for one person to move; he has a special dolly he uses to move it."

Joel walked over the desk, lifted the left end, and moved it aside. The safe was exposed. He placed the desk back over the safe. "What can we say is wrong with Belle?"

Rachel thought a while. "How about stomach pains that seem like appendicitis? I'll tell him we might have to send a different girl—that should get him out here."

"Let's call him now."

"No, he would suspect something if I called him before noon."

They went back into the dining room. Joel spoke to Ron and Pete. "I'm going to trust you on Rachel's say so. Are there phones in your bedrooms?"

"No."

"Then I want your cell phones and I don't want you near a phone for the next week, okay?" They both agreed. "Susan, would you please collect the seven cell phones? Nobody is to use them until this caper is over. Belle, you watch John and Rachel." He gave Belle the gun. "Pete, you, me, and Sandra are going to call that lawyer." They went to the office. Pete looked up the lawyer's phone number, then sat behind the desk and dialed the number. Joel got on the extension.

The lawyer came on the line and Pete said, "Hi Jack, this is Pete Fargo." There was a long pause, then Pete said, "Don't hang up, Jack, you know I didn't like what Richards did to you."

"What do you want?"

"There's a guy here I want you to listen to, you might be interested in what he has to say."

"Hi Jack, my name is Joel Sampson and I'm having problems with Cy Richards. I need the help of a lawyer to take him down."

"I don't want to get involved with those people again."

"What if I can promise you that nobody will know about your small involvement?"

"How small an involvement?"

"We need someone to process the documents for a property transfer."

"Is it in the State of Nevada?"

"Yes."

"What if Richards finds out?"

"He won't be around to find out."

"How are you going to do that?"

"Do you really want to know?"

"No, I guess I really don't."

"There's ten thousand dollars in it for you."

"I don't want your money, just get Richards. How do we work this?"

"Well, Jack, if you can bring to us all the documents needed to transfer a piece of real estate, showing where Richards has to sign, I will get them back to you with the signed grant deed."

"How about the notarization?"

"If I supply the witnesses, can you get it notarized?"

"It's possible."

"Don't tell anybody about this; the fewer people who know the better."

"Of course not—the three of us knowing is two too many. Where do you want me to bring the documents?"

"There is a Comfort Inn on Lamb Boulevard off Highway 15, north of Las Vegas. A woman named Sandra will meet you there in an hour. She will be driving a Jeep Commander. Give her the papers, then go away and forget about them until Sandra or Pete return them to you. Someone bringing the documents to you will prove that you will never have to fear Richards again."

"Okay, said Jack, "but give me ninety minutes. I have to pull the documents together."

"That's settled, then Thanks Jack." Joel hung up and turned to Sandra. "You okay with this—can you do it for me."

"I've come this far—I think I can handle it."

"It's nine thirty, if you leave at ten fifteen you should be back before we call Richards at twelve thirty."

They went back into the dining room. Joel got the gun back from Belle and collected all the cell phones. He then unplugged all the house phones and locked them all in the office, putting the keys in his pocket. "Now let's talk about the plan so that you all understand. Rachel, Pete, and John, I am going to tie you three up again, so that the other four don't know you are working with us. Don't agree to help me in front of them. It will cover you if something goes wrong. When Richards arrives, I will gag all seven of you. I will then get Richards to sign the documents and open the safe. After that, we will put him in the coffin and Wade and I will take him to Morro Bay."

"What are you going to do with the other four?" asked Belle?

"I don't know yet, but they can't do much harm with Richards gone. We will cross that bridge when we come to it. For now, I guess we should feed them. After I tie up our friends, you girls can feed them where they sit."

They all went into the lounge and Joel tied up Rachel, Pete, and John loosely. The women had a lot of fun feeding the four guards. They made it as painful as they could and got more food over their faces and clothes than they did in their mouths. The guards probably would have rather gone hungry. Joel finally stopped them, but left the men in the mess the women had made.

While the women were having fun with the guards, Sandra left to go meet the lawyer. She took the Jeep. Susan went to the gates to let her out and close the gates behind her. By 12:15 she was back bringing a folder containing the documents. Joel had her put them on the desk in the office.

Chapter Six

At 12:30 Joel untied Rachel and asked Sandra to join them in the office. "Now, Rachel, remember don't ask Richards to come out here. Let it be his idea. Just tell him that Belle is sick. If he wants to talk to anyone else, make it Pete or John. The others are sleeping or on the gate."

"I use the name 'Mary' when I call Cy. Nobody at the hotel knows about the ranch or me being here."

"Where do they think 'Mary' is?"

"I don't know, Cy never told me."

"Okay," said Joel, 'Mary' it is."

Rachel picked up the phone and dialed the number, with Joel listening on the extension.

"Hello," said a woman's voice.

"This is Mary. Can I speak to Cy?"

"Just a minute—hey Cy, it's Mary."

"Okay, I'm coming." Cy picked up the phone. "Mary, what's up, Honey?"

"Belle is sick."

"What's wrong with her?"

"She has stomach pains—I think it might be appendicitis."

"Will she be ready to go in two days?"

"I doubt it. She needs a doctor."

"Who else can we send?"

"That's up to you, I guess."

"I'd better come on up. I'll see you in about two hours, but I got to be back here by seven. Rachel hung up the phone. "Will he tell anyone where he is going?" asked Joel.

"Probably not. He keeps things close to the vest, he doesn't trust anybody."

"John and I will be on the gate when he gets here."

"He will have Leon or Sam with him."

"I doubt if it will be Leon, and it will be nice to see Sam again."

"You know them?"

"Oh yes, we have met before, haven't we Sandra?"

Sandra smiled. "Yes" and I'm sure it won't be Leon, and I don't think Cy is going to make his seven o'clock appointment."

Back in the lounge, Joel tied Rachel to the chair again. Turning to Wade, he asked more questions about the delivery of a coffin to the Chinese. After a little persuasion, Wade opened up and talked freely. The hand off took place at 1 a.m. on a Sunday and the safety code was a flashing SOS. No flashing light warned them that something was wrong and the freighter would not stop.

By 2 o'clock some of the women were getting a little edgy. Joel asked them to go to their rooms until he had Richards secure and he would call them. Joel then gave a gun to Sandra and asked her if she would be okay watching the men.

Belle said, "I'll see that they behave."

"You keep away from them or you will forfeit your share of whatever we get." He then untied John, who protested that he was not going to help him.

Joel put on Wayne's coat, and carrying his backpack with the chloroform and batting inside, left the building. As they walked to the main gate,

Joel said. "When the car is in between the fences, you go out and get Sam to roll down his window. I'll come out push you aside and take it from there."

They waited in the guard shack. Richard's limousine didn't arrive until 3:45 and by this time John was getting nervous. As he let the car through the wall, Joel asked, "Are you going to be okay?"

He said. "Yes, now that they are here I feel better."

As John went out and tapped on Sam's window, Joel added chloroform to the batting. He knew this was the crucial moment. Would John betray him and warn the men in the car? As Sam rolled down his window, Joel came out of the shack, pushed John aside, and with his left hand reached in through the window, placing the batting over Sam's face and jamming his head back against the headrest. While Sam struggled in vain, Joel pointed the gun in his right hand at Cy.

"Keep your hands where I can see them."

"Who the hell are you?" Said Cy.

Joel didn't answer. He just opened the back door, reached in with his left hand, and lifted Cy out of the car, sending him sprawling in the dirt. Grabbing Cy by the scruff of his neck, Joel lifted him off the ground and slammed him face first against the limo. He searched Cy, found him to be unarmed, and pushed him back into the limo. Pointing the gun at John, Joel said, "Move Sam over and you drive." Then he climbed in the back with Cy.

John did as he was told, and when Cy started to protest again, Joel jammed the gun into his neck roughly, telling him to shut up. Once back at the house, Joel took Cy and John into the lounge, tied them to chairs beside the others on the dance floor. While he went back to the limo to get Sam, he sent Belle upstairs to bring the other girls down. When they were all assembled, he asked them if Sam had ever abused any of them. Once again he got a chorus of yeses. "He was as bad as Lennie."

Slapping Sam's face roughly until he was awake, Joel said to Cy, "I want you to watch carefully. You need to understand how ruthless I can be and what a serious situation you are in." He waved Sam to the center of the dance floor and gave the gun to Sandra. "Now, Sam here is your chance. let's see what you can do."

Joel walked up to Sam and jabbed him on the nose.

"If I hit you, she will shoot me," said Sam.

"No, she won't, but by the time I'm finished with you you'll wish she had." He jabbed Sam again. This time Sam suddenly swung a haymaker at Joel's head, which waved in front of his face as he leaned back. "That's better," said Joel as he gave Sam three lightning jabs to the face that started Sam's nose bleeding.

For the next few minutes, Joel beat Sam about the face until both eyes were closed and his cheeks were bleeding; then he worked on his body until he finally collapsed to his knees and fell flat on his face. Joel picked him up like he weighed nothing and placed him on a chair. Taking some rope from his backpack, Joel tied Sam to the chair.

Walking over to Richards' chair, Joel stood in front of him. "It's your turn now; let's see what you're made of." Joel untied Richards saying, "We're going into your office for a conference." Leaving Sandra to keep an eye on the others, he prodded Richards in the direction of the office. "Please try to escape. I would love to work you over before we talk."

On the way down the hallway, Joel ushered Richards into the kitchen. Picking up a small butcher's cleaver, he said, "I might need this." In the office he tied Richards to the desk chair. Lifting the desk out of the way to expose the floor safe, he asked for the combination. Richards had a look of terror on his face, but said nothing.

Joel placed Richards' left hand on the arm of the chair with his pinky on top separated from the rest of his fingers. He picked up the meat cleave and placed the blade against the top of the pinky, drawing a little blood. "Now, one more time—what is the combination?"

"You wouldn't dare." Whack! The cleaver came down and chopped the finger off at the second joint. Richards screamed.

Joel got an elastic band out of the desk and using some Kleenex, stopped the flow of blood. He then selected the second finger and placed it on the arm of the chair. "What was that combination?" he asked. "Three turns to the left to forty-five, two turns to the right to sixty-three, one full turn right to twenty-two then back to eighty-one," stammered Richards.

"You sure that's right? If the safe doesn't open you'll be missing two fingers when I ask again."

"It's right! It's right."

Joel knelt down at the safe and used the combination. The safe opened.

Ah…I see you've decided to be sensible. You might get out of this alive." Examining the contents of the safe, he took out the grant deed to the ranch.

Joel opened the folder on the desk and took out the documents the lawyer had prepared. Untying Richards' right hand, Joel placed a pen in front of him and said, "Sign these where they are highlighted." As he hesitated, Joel picked up the cleaver and moved around to Richards' left hand.

"Okay. I'll sign, but this is under duress and won't stand up in a court of law."

"Maybe, but we'll worry about that later; at least it will cause you problems."

Richards signed all the documents. Joel put them back in the folder, left them on the desk, and they went back to the lounge. He asked Rachel if there was a first aid kit. "Yes, it's in the kitchen."

"Susan, would you go get it, and bring it here? See if you can patch up Richards' hand." Once Richards was patched up and tied to his chair, Joel was ready for the next phase.

Joel gathered all the team in the dining room. It included Pete, John, and all the ladies. The atmosphere was very tense. Everyone seemed nervous, except for Belle and Pat; they seemed to be enjoying the situation. Sandra said what the other girls were thinking; "Are you sure you're doing the right thing? We've crossed over the line into an illegal situation."

"You're right," Joel replied, "but would any of you feel safe if I release Richards now?"

Nobody answered.

"Anyone who wants to leave now can go. I won't force you to stay—that would turn me into Cy Richards. I will give you a thousand dollars each and drive you into Las Vegas. But I must ask you not to go to the police unless you feel you absolutely have to. If you stay, you'll get a share of Richards' fortune and, if necessary, I'll take responsibility for everything. I'll say that I forced you all to stay."

"How much money do you think Richards has?" Susan asked.

"He once boasted that he has two million dollars in his offshore account," said Rachel.

"The codes are in his safe," said Joel. "I would see that each of you gets an equal share. It could be over two hundred thousand dollars each."

"How much would you take?"

"Nothing. I'm already a wealthy man. I don't need your money."

"Does anyone want to leave?" Joel let this sink in for a while, and then looked at each girl individually until he got a nod. "Okay. That's settled, but if you change your mind let me know; my offer to drive you to Vegas still stands."

To Pete, John, and Rachel, he said, "I am going to trust you three, because after seeing what I am capable of, I don't think you want me for an enemy."

"Do we get a share of the money?" Pete asked.

"No, but you could share in the ranch and its new business. How you cooperate in the next few days will influence that."

"Now, down to business. Sandra, you take the real estate documents to Jack Sullivan this evening. It should only take a couple of hours. Ask him how soon he can get the documents recorded."

Susan asked, "Can I go with her?"

Joel looked at Sandra who nodded. "She'll be company on the ride."

"Okay, but don't go anyplace where you might be seen and recognized."

"Wade and I will take Richards to the Chinese boat. If we leave at two on Saturday afternoon, we'll be back by nine a.m. Sunday. The five men in the lounge will not be untied for any reason. They will be fed and taken to the bathroom by me before I leave and if they want to go again before I get back they do it where they sit. Is that understood? They'll try to trick you, so don't even take their gags off. If they appear sick, it can wait till I get back. Sandra will be in charge while I am gone. If anyone gives her a problem, they will answer to me when I get back."

"Now let's see, it's five thirty now. If you ladies could get us all a meal we can all relax and enjoy a quiet evening."

"I'll be in my room," said Laura. "I couldn't be in the lounge with those five staring at me."

"After we've eaten, you can feed them, and then I'll move them," said Joel. "Then, we can use the lounge in comfort. I will have to use seven of the lockable rooms. Tonight Sandra and I will use Rachel's room; that will leave the guards' rooms, and three other rooms for you. If you ladies can't sort out the sleeping arrangements yourselves, I will assign rooms."

"We'll take care of it," said Belle. "We slept two to a room last night, so it won't be a problem." With that resolved, Sandra asked Cate and Lucie, to help her with dinner and they headed for the kitchen.

Joel went into the lounge and asked the men if anyone needed to go to the bathroom. They all nodded yes. He said, "I'll take you one at a time and stay with you. Please try something when it's your turn, because I enjoyed working on Lennie and Sam so much I would like another chance." So one by one he untied them and walked them to the bathroom. After he was finished, Joel said, "Well, I'm disappointed in all of you; I was looking forward to showing you the errors of your ways."

They ate a dinner of steaks and baked potatoes and the girls had fun feeding the captives. Joel carried Cy, tied to his chair, upstairs to put him in one of the girl's bedrooms. He left him there behind a locked door, still tied to the chair. Joel repeated this process with four of the guards and Sam, leaving Rachel, Pete, and John until last. These three he untied, escorted to a room each, and locked them in.

Sandra and Susan left to take the documents to Sullivan. The rest of the team settled down in the lounge. Joel went into the office and sat behind the desk. The design of the atomic engine filled his mind. He needed to put it down on paper, and then he could start building it. The events of the last few days had interrupted his plans; he needed to complete this activity, and get back to fulfilling Anton's dream.

After Sandra and Susan returned, he and Sandra watched some television, then, went to bed. Once again they were alone in a bedroom. They repeated the wonderful night they had spent in the motel, the only difference being that Joel checked on the prisoners three times. After he had his three hours' sleep, he lay there, mentally working on the design of his force field generator.

Chapter Seven

Next morning after breakfast, Joel examined the coffin in the garage. It had thick padding on all surfaces, with a one-inch diameter hole bored through the wood and padding at the foot end. The panel at the head end was two pieces of wood, with a small fan in a recess between them. The fan, a battery-operated unit, pulled air out of the coffin through another one-inch diameter hole. The hearse looked authentic and in good condition. A Dodge Caravan van, and a Lincoln Town Car rounded out the trio of vehicles.

At 1 o'clock Joel took a tray of food upstairs to the room Cy was in. He untied Cy's hands, uncovered his mouth, and told him to eat. When Cy finished eating, Joel retied his hands in front of him, untied his feet, and told him to follow him downstairs.

Cy started telling Joel what would happen to him when he was released. Joel slapped him hard across the face. This put an end to his ranting.

Downstairs, Joel took him to the bathroom. When he finished, his hands were retied in front of him, and fresh tape placed across his mouth. Joel told Cy to lie down on the sofa, and while he held him down, Belle injected Cy with the drugs meant for her.

Joel carried his limp body out to the garage, placed him in the coffin, closed the lid, and locked it. Pete and John helped him move the coffin into the hearse. A check of the hearse showed the oil level and tire pressures to be okay. Behind the visor, he found the keys. The engine started right up; the fuel gauge showed a full tank.

Joel then supervised each of the other five men being fed. He took them to the bathroom individually, leaving Wade until last. With four of them safely back in their rooms and tied to their chairs, he took Wade downstairs for a chat.

"If you do exactly what I tell you, I'll release you in a couple of days. If you don't do what I tell you, I won't kill you, but you will wish that I had."

"I'll cooperate. I'll do anything you say. I didn't want to be part of this, but I couldn't get out once I was in."

While Pete and John guarded Wade, Joel took Sandra into the office to say goodbye. He held her in his arms and they kissed.

She told him of her fear, both for him and in her ability to control the situation while he was gone.

Joel assured her she could handle it and gave her a small pistol, saying, "I've locked all the other guns in the safe. Keep this hidden, but handy, and don't use it unless you are in danger."

Sandra made him promise to call her when they got to Morro Bay.

"I don't want to wake you up."

"Who's going to sleep? I won't, not until I know you're on you way back."

They kissed some more before returning to the lounge.

Joel gathered everybody together, and once again told them that Sandra was in charge in his absence and warned them to support her, or face his wrath. Then, after hugging Sandra once more, he and Wade went to the garage and climbed into the hearse.

The land mass between the ranch and Morro Bay is some of the most desolate and rugged country in the United States. It encompassed large portions of the Mojave Desert, including Death Valley National Park; the Sierra Nevada Mountains, crowned by Mount Whitney at 14,494 feet, the tallest American mountain outside Alaska; numerous smaller mountain ranges; and the produce-rich San Joaquin Valley.

Large areas of this country contained United States military bases, including the huge aforementioned Nellis Air Force Training Range, Fort

Irwin National Training Center, China Lake Naval Weapons Center, and Edwards Air Force Base, from where Chuck Yeager became the first man to reach the edge of space.

As the crow flies, the distance to Moro Bay measured about four hundred miles west—southwest, but by road the shortest distance was five hundred miles. Instead of heading west, they started out south—southeast, on Highway 93 to get to Interstate 15. This road headed south through Las Vegas to the Nevada border. Crossing into California and San Bernardino County, the largest county in California, they climbed the Ivanpah Mountains to 4,726 feet. The cool air here contrasted to the heat of the desert. The relief was fleeting as they descended through Halloran Pass to Baker, where the tallest thermometer in the world showed the temperature to be 110 degrees.

From Baker, the road turned west, through towns with names like Zzyzx and Yermo; with the Mojave River to the left, they entered Barstow, the railroad hub of the west. From Barstow they picked up Highway 58, heading west to Bakersfield. After thirty-six miles, they crossed Highway 395 at the Four Corners and entered Boron in Kern County. They continued on towards Mojave.

The remnants of the famous Twenty Mule Team Road paralleled the highway to the south. This is part of the road, that between 1883 and 1889, the 100-foot long, twenty-mule teams carried over twenty million pounds of borax from Furnace Creek in the middle of the Mojave Desert, to the railway station at Mojave.

From Mojave, Highway 48 climbed northwest to 4000 feet through the Tehachapi Mountains to Highway 99 in Bakersfield. One mile north on 99, Highway 58 continued west through the Temblor Mountains, entered San Luis Obispo County, and crossed the Carrizo Plain to Santa Margarita. Here, they turned south on Highway101; with the Pacific Ocean to their right, they drove to San Luis Obispo. Turning northwest, they followed Highway 1 to Morro Bay. Leaving highway 1 on Morro Bay Boulevard, heading west to Front Street, they turned north until it became Embarcadero Road, and continued on to the pier.

They arrived at midnight. All of Morro Bay slept peacefully. Joel parked in a parking lot near the pier and called Sandra to let her know they had arrived. She had no problems to report at her end. She said, "I miss you. I will not sleep until you call after the delivery; please hurry back."

Wade pointed out Cy's Cruiser moored at the pier.

"How do you get the coffin to the boat?" Joel asked Wade.

"There is a gurney on the boat; we use that."

"Introduce me to the captain as Bob."

Leaving the hearse securely locked, they walked onto the pier, and out to the Cruiser. Wade went on board and rapped on the cabin door. A man came out, looked at Joel, and said, "What happened to Ron?"

"Nothing. Cy decided to send Bob."

"Why?"

"Cy doesn't give me reasons. If you want to know ask him."

They went below decks and found the folding gurney strapped to one of the forward bunks. Wade and Joel carried it back to the hearse, making as little noise as possible. There they unfolded the gurney, moved the coffin out onto it, and carefully wheeled it back to the boat. Once on board, Joel felt better; it would be difficult to explain the coffin to a nosy police officer.

The captain started the engines as Wade slipped the moorings, and then smoothly backed out of the slip. He slowly cruised towards the opening in the breakwater, but once through, opened up the throttle, heading out to sea. He set a course due west and as large as the boat, was the speed caused the prow to rise out of the water. The Cruiser took forty minutes to reach twenty miles out. The captain eased back on the throttle, settling the boat back down into the ocean. A three-quarter moon lit the clear sky. Off to the south, Joel could see a freighter, outlined against the horizon, as it plowed through the calm ocean.

The captain set a course to intercept the freighter, and fifteen minutes later Wade went out on deck and flashed the SOS message. The freighter hove to as the Cruiser pulled alongside. Suddenly Wade became enveloped in a bright light. The Chinese man behind the spotlight, recognized Wade and hailed him in pigeon English.

"Do you have the cargo?"

"Yes," replied Wade.

A hoist descended from the freighter's loading crane. They swiftly attached the loops, one over each end of the coffin. The coffin rose into the air. The hoist came back down with a bundle on it. As Wade retrieved the bundle, they pulled away and headed back to shore. The transfer took less than five minutes.

While the captain steered the cruiser, Joel took the package from Wade and moved to a corner of the stern hidden from the wheelhouse. Silencing Wade's protests with a glare, he cut open the package and poured the loose heroin into the wake of the boat.

They left the captain to take care of the boat, and walked off the pier. By 2 a.m. the hearse pulled out of the parking lot to begin the long journey back to the ranch.

Joel called Sandra, and told her she could go to sleep now. She sounded drowsy; he suspected he had woken her up. The trip going east took thirty minutes less because of the very light traffic at this time on a Sunday morning. Back at the ranch, Joel locked Wade in his room, and with his promise not to try to escape, he left him untied. He then joined Sandra, in Rachel's room.

Chapter Eight

Monday morning Joel and the ten women sat around the dining room table to discuss their future. First of all, Joel announced, the safe contained $360,000. Each girl, including Sandra, would receive $30,000, and the rest would be kept for initial operating expenses. It would pay salaries until business picked up. "I don't deserve a share," protested Sandra.

"Yes you do," Belle said, "if it wasn't for you, we would still be slaves."

Joel handed each girl a thick envelope.

"I also have the codes for the offshore banks. There appears to be about two million dollars in them." Some of the girls gasped; the others just smiled. "My cell phone number is 555-341-2784. Each of you should open up a checking account and call to give me the routing number and account number. I will transfer one-tenth of the money to each of you. The phone number will be good for two weeks only."

"That's two hundred thousand dollars each," said Belle. "I can quit working."

"That, and the profits from the ranch, could give you a modest income for the rest of your lives." The girls sat there stunned, but Joel pushed on.

The next order of business was for the nine new owners of the ranch to decide if Rachel, John, and Pete would be given an interest in the business. The girls had a lot to say on the subject, some for, and some against. Joel suggested they set up ten shares with each girl owning one share and the tenth share to be divided evenly between Rachel, John, and Pete. There seem to be a lot of support for this idea, so Joel called for a secret ballot. He gave each girl a slip of paper and asked them to write yes or no on it. Eight girls voted yes and one voted no. When Joel announced this, Lacie said. "I voted no, but I will change my vote to make it unanimous, but only if you change the name of the ranch."

The other girls laughed. "How about Freedom Ranch?" said Belle. They all seemed to like this, so the Richards Ranch became the Freedom Ranch.

"You'll have to find new girls. I'm sure you ladies won't stay here."

"Oh, I don't know," said Belle. After a good vacation I might come back. That way I can keep an eye on things."

"Well," said Joel, "I suggest you hire Rachel to manage the ranch for you." The girls, some of them still a state of shock, nodded their okay.

With this settled, Joel brought the three new partners to the table, and told them of the decisions concerning their shares and Rachel's position, but not about the money. Pete said, "I think that is very fair." The other two nodded in agreement.

"Everyone would get a weekly salary and at the end of their fiscal year a distribution would be made to each share. You can carry on from here. Sandra and I will be leaving after I take care of the men upstairs."

Joel went up to Wade's room and tied his hands behind his back. Going to the other four rooms, he untied their legs and made the five men walk downstairs with their hands tied behind them. He ordered them outside into the compound. All the girls came out to watch. He told the men, "Drive the hearse into Las Vegas and do what you want with it. Don't ever come back to this ranch or interfere with any of these ladies. If you do, there is no place you could hide from me. I will find you and kill you."

He untied Wade's hands, and told him to untie the others. The men rubbed their wrists slowly, then Lennie, Ron, Sam, and Mitch advanced on him menacingly.

"We'll show you who's leaving," Lennie said.

"I hoped you would do this. I'm going to make sure you do as I just told you." With lightning speed, Joel moved sideways next to Ron and kicked him in the knee, then Mitch in the groin. Both men went down, leaving Sam and Lennie standing. Joel backed off a little, and as the two men came at him, kicked Sam in the head, caught Lennie's fist as he swung and pummeled him to the ground, unconscious. The other three men rose again and with a series of karate kicks and chops, Joel soon had three more unconscious on the ground.

He told Wade to back the hearse out of the garage, and unceremoniously threw each man into the back. With parting advice to Wade to move away from Las Vegas and disappear, he watched the hearse leave the compound.

Joel collected all the gear he had brought with him and loaded it into the Jeep. He and Sandra then said goodbye to the new owners of the ranch, climbed into the Jeep, and drove away.

"Where do you want me to take you, after we drop off the Jeep?"

"I have to go back to Los Angeles to quit my job and pack up my things, then I'm going back to Spokane."

They exchanged cars at McCarran Airport and started the three hundred mile journey to L.A. in silence. Outside of Barstow they stopped for lunch at Peggy Sue's, a fifties dinner that specialized in good home-cooked food.

As they ate Sandra asked Joel, "Can we spend a few more days together before we part?"

"How about three nights at the Beverly Hills Hilton?" replied Joel. "We can make love at night and play tourist during the day." Sandra's smile gave Joel his answer.

Joel fulfilled his promise to Sandra, but at night after he slept the three hours he needed, he would lay there, his brain working on his miniature atomic engine problem. Thursday he drove Sandra to her apartment, and then headed back to San Diego. He had been gone ten days, a long time to be away from his project.

Over the next week Joel received bank account and routing numbers from all ten women. He transferred $200,000 to each bank. This left a small amount in each of Cy's overseas accounts so that they would not close. He then disposed of the cell phone, a prepaid untraceable type.

PART FOUR

STARTING ANTON'S PROJECTS

Chapter One

As soon as he arrived home Joel check his abilities. He pressed 340 pounds, curled 200 pounds, and ran the mile in four minutes and four seconds, all slightly worse than a week ago. He still only needed three hours sleep each night. Joel resumed the daily session on the age-reversing machine. He had been up to sixty percent of maximum power for thirty minutes, before Sandra had called. He started again at that level then, over a three week period, gradually increasing to seventy percent, but remaining at thirty minutes. He decided to do two sessions a day at this level for a while. He could now press 400 pounds curl 240 pounds and run the mile in three minutes fifty two seconds. In addition, he could float a 10-pound weight up to the ceiling using his psychokinetic abilities of telekinesis and levitation. His X-ray vision also improved; he saw through increasing thick objects.

He called Rachel after a week for a progress report. The girls had received their money, and each one wanted to thank him personally. After two weeks, he called again, and Rachel told him they had opened for business, doing very well for the first week. He gave her a new untraceable cell phone number, so that she could call him if she needed him.

During this time, Joel also worked diligently, fifteen to twenty hours a day, on his projects. The miniature nuclear engine occupied the majority of his time, but he also worked on the force field project. When he could not work on either of these because he was waiting on information or parts, he gathered information on the United States drug problem, or practiced levitation.

Joel could not find a manufacturer to produce the parts he needed, so he decided to acquire his own workshop. His needs included a clean room for the electronic and computer components, a lead-lined plutonium storage room, a machine shop capable of making miniature parts, and a test facility. He found a small electron component manufacturing facility for sale, because the owner had lost his government contract.

The down payment for the purchase took a lot of Joel's capital. This brought his financial position in danger. He realized he had to show taxable income, to justify his spending, or the IRS would be after him. His Las Vegas winnings, so far, had been under $1,000 at each sitting, therefore not taxed. From then on, when he made his weekly trips to gamble, he stayed at one casino until he had won $100,000. When he cashed this in, they made him fill out a form and pay twenty percent federal tax. Joel obtained a pilot's license and purchased a Cessna 206, for flying to and from Las Vegas.

In addition, he invested in the stock market. He found that his ability to read information about a company rapidly and his keen analytical mind enabled him to select stocks that went up in price, even in a down market. Soon he had a net worth of over $2,000,000, all declarable income. Joel visited the financial planning company and added $500,000 to Mary Kelbeck's account. Joel then opened an offshore account in the Cayman Islands, depositing $500,000.

The workshop Joel purchased measured 40 feet by 45 feet. It contained a 20-foot square clean room, a 10- by 20-foot storage room, a 25- by 30-foot machine shop, a 10 by 20 design office, and a 10 by 25-foot office. He converted the design office into the test facility with soundproof walls, upgraded the clean room to a lower dust particle level, and built a 10-foot square lead-lined plutonium storage room at one end of the office. The plutonium room contained an enclosure, where gloved pincers facilitated the handling of the plutonium without exposure. Built into one wall was a very sensitive Geiger counter.

When the contractor finished building the lead-lined room, Joel covered the office side of the wall containing the door, with bookcases. The bookcase covering the door, swung open, to reveal the entrance. The machine shop required upgrading. Joel bought machines capable of making extremely tiny components. His atomic engine needed to be small enough to hold in one hand.

Now he had to find a source for obtaining a small amount of plutonium. It had to be Pu 238 plutonium, which is not fissile, and has a half-life of 88,000 years, with alpha decay. This plutonium is used in pacemakers, and spacecraft, as an electrical power source. It is not on the International Atomic Energy Authority list of banned materials. To Joel's surprise, Pu 238 is available commercially.

Joel had finished the design of the atomic engine, so using his machine shop, he manufactured all the components he could not purchase. After assembling the engine, he ordered one kilo gram of Pu 238, enough to generate maximum energy for about three years. In the plutonium room, he placed a small amount of plutonium inside the engine's lead-lined compartment. The engine ran and produced electrical power. Its performance did not satisfy Joel, so he worked on it twenty hours a day for a week until it reached maximum power.

He had designed a device that would convert energy to a force field, but it needed an enormous amount of energy. The devise consisted of an annular tube, which projected two fields of ions, one negative, the other positive, across the inner circle. If enough electrical energy could be transmitted through the two ionic fields, any object coming into contact with the ions would be repelled. The question was, would the atomic engine generate enough energy, to produce a force field that would resist penetration?

In the test facility, he had constructed a 6-foot diameter steel frame, containing a 1-inch diameter force field generating tube. The atomic engine resided in the base connected to the tube.

Joel ran the engine at twenty-five percent of power, then, threw a baseball at the center of the frame. The ball went through, but lost a lot of momentum, and dropped before hitting the far wall. Increasing the power to fifty percent, the ball still penetrated, but immediately dropped to the floor. At seventy percent the ball bounced off the force field. Joel placed a linear measuring device against the back side of the force field. It registered a quarter of an inch deflection, when the ball was thrown again.

Joel increased the power to one hundred percent, and the ball bounced off the force field without any deflection at all. Joel continued his testing.

He found that a bullet would lose its momentum, but could still penetrate the force field. He increased the amount of plutonium in the engine, until at triple the original amount, and at one hundred percent power, a bullet bounced off the force field, without deflecting the measuring device.

Joel then constructed a titanium belt that clamped around his waist. At the back of the belt he mounted the atomic engine. From each side of the belt, a bar extended 12 inches. The bars supported two 6-foot long hollow vertical beams. At the top and bottom of the beams, Joel mounted two 3-feet diameter force field rings. The power ran from the engine, around the belt, through the bars, along the vertical beams, and energized the force field vertically, from the top ring, to the bottom ring.

This provided a 3-foot diameter protection frame around him that could not be penetrated. He could walk inside the frame, but it was unwieldy, and would look ridiculous out in public. It needed work to miniaturize it. To switch the force field on or off, he used an electronic switch similar to those used to open car doors. Instead of having a clicker, he used his mental powers to activate the switch.

Joel found it increasingly difficult to keep his activities a secret. He had numerous visits from sales reps, trying to find out whether they could sell him their products, asking what his business was. Also, the other small businessmen, in the complex he shared tried to find out what he was doing. He decided to duplicate his facility in a remote area. He planned to keep this workshop and the apartment as his addresses of record, but find a remote location to build a second home.

Joel purchased five hundred acres of land halfway between Victorville and Barstow, ten miles northwest of Highway 15. The terrain's elevation averaged 2,700 feet, on a reasonably flat plateau. He had a 4,000 square foot, single-story home, built in the middle of the property. The house had a full basement, 2,000 square feet of which became his new workshop. The new workshop contained every thing the old one did, including a lead-lined plutonium storage room. The rest of the basement consisted of additional living quarters, with storage for a month's food supply, and a weight lifting room. Surrounding the entrance to the basement, Joel built a force field, so that nobody could enter, unless he switched it off. Also in the basement, he built the latest redesign of the age-retarding machine. He had reduced its size considerably, using miniaturized components, and a nuclear engine for power. The head gear looked like large ear phones, the foot connections like foot warmers, and the hands just rested on a metal armrest.

Down the middle of the property, Joel had constructed a 2,500-foot long runway, so that he could fly his Cessna in. With the airfield as its axis, Joel had built a compound around his house and airfield. The circular compound had a wall all around, with an electronic gate where the dirt road entered his property. The 6-foot high block wall, had a 10-inch wide, 20-inch deep, concrete trench at it's inside base. In the trench, Joel constructed a 9-inch diameter force field projector, aimed so that it created a dome over the airfield and house. The circular dome enclosed the middle fifty, of his five hundred acres of land.

Joel then designed and constructed an atomic engine, big enough to power the force field. This, he buried against the inside of the wall, half way around from the gate. It supplied enough power to provide a protective cover over his compound. To switch his force fields on and off, Joel designed a switch that he could activate using his brain to send radio frequency signals. Its operation was similar to a television remote control; he called it his "mind-controlled switch."

On the far side of the landing strip from the house, but inside the dome, Joel constructed a 30- by 60-foot, one room building, with a 20-foot ceiling. The building had one entry door, with an airlock, so that you entered from the outside into the airlock, then through a second door into the main room. In the center of this room he placed a large conference table that seated twenty people. Next to the airlock, he built a nuclear engine, which projected a force field around the inside walls of the room, so that, when activated, it prevented anyone from entering or leaving. He would use this building to detain people as he needed to; he thought of it as his brig.

Joel had the buildings, the wall, and the landing strip all build by a construction company. The atomic engines, and all the force field components, he manufactured and assembled himself.

Joel still exercised every day. The distance around his five hundred acres measured about four miles. He would run the distance twice at a five-minute mile pace, then, lift weights for an hour. He followed this with thirty minutes on the machine. He would work on his project until 3 a.m., sleep for three hours, and start running as the sun came up. His mental abilities astounded him. If he concentrated on a person's mind strong enough, he could get flashes of his or her thoughts.

During the six months it took to build the protection device, and construct the compound, Joel began to feel the loneliness of his life. A number of times he went different places seeking female companionship. He found his efforts difficult, boring, and unsuccessful. After two months, he went to visit Rachel and his friends at the Freedom Ranch. He spent a week there, relaxing, spending time with John, Ron, and the girls. They were the closest thing he had to friends.

He had sexual relations with some of the women at the ranch, not as professionals, but by asking for their permission and receiving it. They all knew there could be no long-term relationship. He treated them tenderly, and with affection, which they returned, making it a pleasant experience for all.

He returned home to work on his projects, still unfulfilled in his quest for companionship. A month later he decided to visit Sandra in Spokane. She had used her money to buy a dance studio, with a little apartment attached, and taught all kinds of dancing. She had three teachers working for her, two of them girls she knew in Las Vegas, and they taught, ballet, modern, tap, and hip hop. They spent three happy days together, but they both knew it would lead nowhere; they each had their own lives to live.

Chapter Two

oel also spent time investigating the drug industry. He loitered in areas in San Diego, where drugs were sold. He watched transactions, followed dealers home, followed the dealers to their suppliers, and finally found the location of a major distributor, a Colombian named Carlos Ramirez. This man lived in a luxury high-rise in La Jolla.

Joel sat in his car watching the building, trying to think of a way to get inside. If he used force, some innocent party might get hurt, or worse, killed. Suddenly, his car door opened, and a gun pressed against his temple.

"Get out of the car."

A large Latino man stood connected to the other end of the gun. Joel slowly eased himself out of the car.

"Into the Lincoln," said the man.

Joel obliged, his mind racing. He had under-estimated their security system.

Climbing into the back of the Lincoln, Joel asked, "What is this all about?"

"Shut up," said the gunman.

The driver, an equally large man, pulled the car away from the curb, heading along Torrey Pines Road. They made no attempt to blindfold Joel, so he figured this would be a one-way trip. They turned east on La Jolla Village Road, then along Miramar Road, an area he knew well. The car turned into a small manufacturing complex and drove through an open door of one of the buildings.

The 30-foot by 40-foot room they entered had four lines of tables across the far end. On the tables sat stacks of boxes of small baggies, spaced 6 feet apart, with a chair in front of each stack. They all got out of the car, and with the driver in front and the gunman behind, walked passed the tables and entered an office. Sitting behind a huge desk was Carlos Ramirez staring at him, a smirk on his face.

"We know you're not a cop, so who are you, and why are you following me?"

Joel remained silent, but in his mind he analyzed the situation: three men, but so far only one gun. The gunman must be his primary target. Carlos solved his problem for him. "Felix, Jose, the man has lost his tongue, loosen it up for him," he said in Spanish.

Felix put the gun in his belt, then he and Jose advanced on Joel. Felix aimed a blow at Joel's midriff. Avoiding the punch, Joel grabbed Felix by the belt and shirt front, lifted him off his feet, and threw him at Jose. Turning his attention to Carlos, Joel pushed the desk hard, jamming Carlos against the wall. Moving back to Felix, Joel hit him once in the face. He went down pole-axed. Taking the gun from Felix's belt, he hit Jose across the head with the butt.

Pointing the gun at Carlos, Joel pulled the heavy desk away from the wall with one hand. Carlos bent over, clutching his stomach, "You've broken my ribs."

"Good, I'm gonna to break a lot more before I'm finished."

Picking Carlos up, Joel threw him into a corner, ordering him to face the wall. When he obeyed, Joel tucked the gun in his belt and looked for something to tie up the two thugs. In a closet, he found a collection of men's clothing, including some ties. He used two ties to bind Felix and Jose's hands behind their backs, and their belts to strap their legs together.

Walking over to Carlos, Joel picked him up by the scruff of his neck, stood him with his back against the wall, and said, "Where do you keep the heroin?"

No answer. "Okay." Joel took hold of his little finger on his left hand, and bent it backwards until it snapped. "How many fingers do I break before you tell me?" He took hold of the second finger on the left hand.

"Okay! Okay!" screamed Carlos, "I'll show you." He led Joel out of the office, into the room next door. This room contained a large safe.

"There, in the safe."

"Open it."

Carlos hesitated. Joel reached out and grabbed his hand.

"Okay."

"Unlock it but don't open it."

Carlos unlocked the safe and stepped back.

"Turn and face the wall," said Joel. Carlos obeyed. Joel opened the safe door, and there on top of six packages of heroin, he saw a gun. He now had two guns. To keep his hands free, he tucked both guns in his belt. Keeping one eye on Carlos, he took one package of heroin out of the safe and placed it on top. Standing with the safe between him and Carlos, Joel tore a corner off the package. Glancing over his shoulder, Carlos said, "Be careful with that, it's worth a lot of money."

Joel deliberately spilt some on the floor. With a snarl, Carlos launched himself at Joel. Joel evaded his rush, brought the base of his right palm up under Carlos's chin sharply, lifting him off his feet and laying him flat on his back. He dragged Carlos across the floor to the safe. Lifted him onto his feet with one hand, he made him take the rest of the packages out of the safe.

With Carlos carrying the heroin, Joel pushed him out into the corridor, along the hall, and through a door marked restroom. Once inside, Joel said, "Open the packages, and pour the heroin down the toilet."

"I will not."

Joel slammed Carlos against the wall with his forearm across Carlos's throat and grabbed the small finger of his right hand, saying, "One last chance."

"Okay, okay," said Carlos.

Joel stood watching, while Carlos poured six kilos of heroin down the toilet and flush.

"You know you're a dead man."

"Well, do a better job of it than you did this time."

Joel hit Carlos and left him unconscious on the bathroom floor. He returned to the office to get the keys for the Lincoln from the driver's pocket, then drove back to his own car.

This experience highlighted his vulnerability. With all his intelligence, and physical capabilities, he still lacked street smarts. To make a dent in the drug trade, first he had to stay alive. Loading the few remaining things he needed from his apartment and the workshop on his Cessna, he filed a flight plan for San Francisco, then flew to his compound. He switched on the force field; if they did find him, he would be safe.

Joel's first priority must be to redesign the force field suit to make it practical. He strapped himself in the machine at fifty percent power and stayed there for one hour, thinking. This made his mind race. By the time he left the machine, he had a design in his head for sending the ion fields along a surface so that they would follow the surface as it changed direction.

Joel rebuilt the belt to accommodate this free flow force field concept. He added a feature that would put an electrical charge on the outer surface of the suit. The intensity could be varied, using a thought-operated control switch. He acquired a mannequin, attached the belt to its waist and turned the belt on. The force fields followed the contours of the human shape until they joined together to form a complete enclosure of the mannequin, like an invisible space suit. The force field circulated outside of the half-inch thick titanium belt protecting it, and stayed a half-inch away from the skin surface. Joel used nuclear power, and miniaturization, to include an air filtration system inside the force field. This kept the air in the half inch space fresh enough to breathe.

He now had to test it. Outside, behind his house, he built a barricade; from behind this, he fired a gun at the mannequin. The bullets bounced off. Next he exploded three sticks of dynamite next to his dummy. It blew the dummy over, but left it unscathed. Finally, he purchased a junker car and drove it at the dummy, running over it. The car sustained damage to it front bumper, and under carriage, but the mannequin remained unscathed.

Joel could not put it off any longer; he had to try the suit on himself.

He took off all his clothes and clamped the belt around his waist, thinking, I'll switch it off immediately, if there is a problem. He used his mind to initiate the force field flow. He felt no sensation at all. He tried to put his clothes back on, but some would not fit because of the half-inch space. All that would fit were tee shirts and shorts. His shoes were way too small, but he didn't need them—the suit protected his feet.

Joel tried to walk, then run. The belt moved with him. He ran the length of the runway as fast as he could; still no problem. He picked up a rock and threw it. The force field kept the rock a half-inch from his fingers, making the throwing action awkward. He would need practice to get used to this.

Joel calculated that the extra half-inch around his waist increased his pant size from a 32 to a 36. He drove to the nearest mall, and purchased some extra large shirts and size 36 pants. Returning home, he put on a shirt and pants over the belt, with a regular pair of sneakers. When he turned on the belt, the force field billowed out the shirt and pants, but went over the outside of the sneakers. It made him half an inch taller, but looked okay in the mirror. All this took two days, and he was now ready to tackle the drug trade.

Joel realized that to combat the drug dealers, he would have to be as ruthless as they were. He would be hurting people, maybe even killing some of them. Did he have the stomach for this? It bothered him a lot; would the results allay his conscience? He decided that if he had to harm a few bad people, to help a lot of innocent ones, he could justify this in his mind.

How should he begin? The data on the Internet gave a very confused picture. Where did the blame lay: Colombia, Afghanistan, the CIA? He would have to work up to them. First, he would try to help some people in need. He would start in Watts. If he could walk the streets of Watts, this would validate his "suit," but first he needed to collect a few things from his San Diego apartment.

Wearing the suit, Joel flew to San Diego to see if his apartment was under surveillance. He walked up to his front door and two men followed him.

Chapter Three

Brian Hallows hated stakeouts. He had been on this one for three days; at least he caught the day shift, 8 a.m. to 8 p.m. sitting in a car with Jack Gonzalez, their only break being when one of them went for coffee or lunch. At least he could tolerate Jack's company; he might have been paired with Manny West—that would have been unbearable.

Bess didn't like the twelve-hour shift any more than he did, stuck alone with three small children. As much as she loved them, she needed a break now and then. He had to admit the overtime pay helped pacify Bess. Their house, though in a good neighborhood, needed a lot of work. This would help pay for remodeling the kitchen.

The subject of the stakeout had assaulted Carlos Ramirez; Brian would've given him a medal, but instead he had to arrest him. Ramirez had given them the name and address of their quarry, so why hadn't they taken care of him themselves? That surprised Brian. The bad guys usually took care of their own dirty work.

They knew Ramirez controlled the drug traffic in the San Diego area, but couldn't prove it. Sometimes Brian thought Ramirez had someone high up on his payroll; he kept slipping through their clutches. Like the time they had a solid tip that a drug shipment would be coming into San Diego.

They had the harbor staked out, but the boat suddenly changed course and went into San Pedro. Brian felt sure someone had tipped them off.

Jack tapped him on the arm and pointed, a man fitting the description of the assailant was entering the front of the apartment block. They got out of the car and followed him in, catching up with him as he unlocked the door and entered his apartment. Brian had a warrant for Joel's arrest, so he could enter the apartment legally. He flashed his badge, saying, "Joel Sampson, you are under arrest for the assault of Carlos Ramirez." Then he started to read him his rights. While he did this, Jack pulled one of Joel's arms behind his back and tried to put handcuffs on him.

"Hey look at this," said Jack. "The handcuffs won't fit; he has something around his wrists." As Brian moved forward to see, Joel grabbed him by the jacket lapels, swung around, and pushed him into Jack. Both men toppled backwards over the coffee table behind them. Joel reached inside Brian's jacket and removed the gun from his shoulder holster. The two police officers got to their feet, facing the revolver pointing at them.

"You'd better give me that back," said Brian. "You're only wanted for simple assault right now; you shoot a police officer, and nothing can save you."

"Then you had better make sure I don't shoot one of you. Put your handcuffs on the coffee table." They spent a few minutes in a staring contest, then seeing that Joel's eyes did not waver, they both put their cuffs on the table. "Now, you," said Joel, pointing at Jack, "Put your gun on the table, then handcuff your partners hands behind his back." Jack did as he was told. "Now put handcuffs on one of your wrists." Jack did this. "Both of you, into the kitchen." The three men walked into the kitchen with both policemen looking for an opportunity to disarm Joel.

Waving the gun at Jack, Joel said, "Loop one arm through your partner's." Jack moved as though to do this, then suddenly swung the handcuffed hand and hit Joel across the face as hard as he could with the loose handcuff. Joel didn't even flinch. While the men stared in disbelief, Joel grabbed Jack's arm and twisted it up his back, while holding Brian by his arm. He then looped Jack's hand through Brian's arms, threaded the loose cuff through the refrigerator door handle and snapped it on Jack's wrist. Both men were now locked to the refrigerator door, with their hands behind their backs.

Joel put duct tape over their mouths, saying, "You should be able to work this loose and call for help. I'll leave the handcuff keys on the table, but I'll put your guns in the refrigerator, incase some undesirables answer your call. By the way, if you want to find where Ramirez keeps his drugs, he has a diluting activity in a warehouse of Miramar Boulevard." Joel gave them the address.

Joel collected the things he had come for, then, left the apartment, leaving the door unlocked. He drove to the San Diego airport, filed a flight plan for San Francisco, and flew to his compound.

Joel strapped himself in the machine for three hours at fifty percent power. He needed to spend time thinking about what he wanted to accomplish with his powers. He thought about the hopelessness of the human condition. Happiness, everybody's goal, eluded most of the world's population. Even the affluent living with constant pressures, the drive to make money or achieve fame, had little time for real happiness. Their children lived in the shadow of the parents' accomplishments, which they strove to equal or exceed. The percentage of happy people among the rich was surely higher than the poor and definitely higher than the oppressed.

Some people barely have the basic needs of air, water, and food, and knew nothing of Maslow's five levels of happiness. For those past level one who were comfortable enough, level two ("Am I safe enough?") created a problem. These people must be the focus of his efforts, moving them to level three ("Am I part of a group"—can I achieve the feeling of belonging?) Then maybe he could move many people to level four, where they obtain recognition for their achievements. Maybe a few would reach level five, self-actualization, reaching their highest potential.

He would start in the United States, helping to improve the everyday living of poor people, by providing safety and education.

Joel exited the machine determined to help as many people as he could move to level three and live without fear. He would start in an area where people had the basic of life, but lived in fear, and Watts came to mind.

Three days after his encounter with Carlos Ramirez, Joel flew his Cessna into the Compton airport. He rented a car, drove to 103rd Street in Watts, and parked. He switched on the "suit" as he walked to a housing project, called Richardson Gardens, which had over one thousand apartments. He passed lots of people, on the streets, or sitting on their porches. They all stared at him as he passed.

Reaching Richardson Gardens, he saw that the fence around it had a spiked top, curved inwards, as though to keep the tenants in rather than predators out. Entering through the gate, he encountered a woman arguing with two young men. She looked in about her mid-thirties and the two men in their early twenties. He listened to their conversation. She told them to stay away from her son, Arnell; he didn't want to be in the Cripps. They told her they would decide what her son wanted, not her; if they told him to join he would, or suffer the consequences. Just then one of the men noticed Joel.

"What are you doing here, Whitey?"

The woman turned and said to Joel, with concern in her voice, "You'd better git fast."

The two men turned their attention to Joel as he said, "You should show more respect for the lady." They stopped when they realized Joel hadn't tried to run.

"I'll show you respect," said the smaller of the two as he pulled a switch blade out of his pocket and flicked it open. He lunged at Joel, who let the knife slide under his arm. Then clamping the assailant's arm against his body, he bent it up until a snap told him the arm had broken. The larger man swung at Joel's head; he evaded the blow and kicked the man in the crotch. The man went down on his knees, clutching the offended body part.

Joel turned to the woman and said, "I would like to help you. Is there somewhere we can talk?"

"I don't want anything to do with you. Their friends will be here soon and they will blame me."

"Don't worry. I will protect you."

"If you don't leave now you'll be dead; you can't even protect yourself."

Just then four more young men arrived on the scene. The smallest of them had a gun in his hand. "I don't believe it," he said, "Whitey's really here. You two let this guy get the better of you."

"He surprised us, Tye," said the man with the broken arm.

"Well we have some surprises for him." To the woman he said, "Tanisha, you've caused trouble for the last time. You're both coming with us." He prodded Joel with the gun and with two men in front and four behind, Joel decided a confrontation here might harm the woman, so he meekly went with them. They turned into a street lined with two-storied four-unit apartments.

In the middle of the block they entered one that looked, from the outside, like all the others, old and rundown. Inside, the downstairs had been remodeled. The left half consisted of one large room with a bar and entertainment center at one end and a staircase going up from the front door. A ceramic-tiled area dominated the center of the floor, surrounded by sofas and recliners against the walls, making it look like a party room. In the center of the right-side wall, a door led into the right half of the building. Through the open door, Joel saw a kitchen at the back and an office in the front. He couldn't see anyone in that half of the ground floor.

Around the bar, ten other people, four men and six young women, stood talking. Silence fell on the room as they entered. Their abductors pushed Joel and Tanisha into the center of the room. Suddenly Joel lifted Tanisha off her feet and pushed her through the door to the kitchen and closed it behind her. He turned with his back to the door, and faced the Cripps. He now stared at five guns.

Tye laughed. "What good do you think that'll do? If she got away, we would soon pick her up again. Bro, we have Whitey here to entertain us tonight."

"Your right," said Joel. "But you might not like the way this ends."

"Wow, you got guts, but we'll soon change that. Rashid, spill a little of his blood—not too much he has a long day ahead of him."

The largest man in the room, at 6'6" and 250 pounds, approached Joel. He tried to put a bear hug on Joel, who hit him hard in the midriff, knocking all the wind out of him. Joel then picked up Rashid and threw him at Tye, knocking him over and pinning him under the big man's weight. This stunned everyone in the room. Then four guns pointed at him

To the gunmen, Joel said, "I'm only going to say this once; if you fire those guns at me, the bullets will bounce straight back and hit the shooter."

One gunman said, "Well, let's find out. How about a bullet in the leg?" He fired his gun. The bullet hit Joel in the left leg and ricocheted. The gunman fell to the floor screaming, with a bullet in his leg. The room went very quiet.

By this time, Tye had pushed Rashid off him and regained his feet. "What's going on? Who are you?"

'Superman, without the cape. Do you want any more proof."

"Tie him to a chair."

The six unscathed men rushed at Joel, who went into action; in less than a minute, all six men strewed the floor. Joel collected all their guns and knives, and ushered everyone to the bar end of the room, away from the door. He took the guns to the other end of the room, emptied all the bullets out, and piled them in a corner. When he turned around, one of the men had gone behind the bar and was pointing an Uzi at him.

Holding his arms out to the side, Joel said, "Go ahead! You'll probably kill all the people in this room except me. I'll make sure the first bullet ricochets back and hits you."

"Devern, put a single shot in his shoulder," said Tye. The man fired and the bullet ricocheted back, hitting the gunman in the shoulder.

Tye stood there staring in disbelief. Who was this man? All his plans would be ruined. He had just convinced Diego Ramerez that he could take over the leadership of the Cripps from the current leader Kory. This man could spoil everything just as he had reached his goal. As a child he'd taken a back seat to the big guys. Only by being smarter, and more ruthless, had he overcome his size handicap. He started out, at age 10, killing cats and dogs in front of the other kids, and graduated to cutting some of his enemies, with a switch blade knife he's stolen. After that, the big guys became his gang, and they would beat up anyone who opposed him.

He killed for the first time at age 14. This made him a leader of his age group and a member of the Cripps. Now at 23, and number two man in the gang, he was about to oust Kory and be the new leader. He could not let this man stop him; he had to get Diego to send men down here to deal with this guy. Tye made a break for the door.

Joel intercepted him, picked him up, and threw him across the room. "The next person who tries to leave this room will finish up in the hospital."

Joel retrieved the Uzi, unloaded it, and added it to the pile. He refaced the group of Cripps, all watching his every move. Pointing at the next largest man in the room, Joel said, "Come here." When the man stood in front of him, Joel stretched his arms out to the side and said, "I'm sure you've beaten lots of people. To show you how hopeless your position is, I want you to hit me anywhere you like, as hard as you can."

Suddenly the man hit him, with all his might, in the stomach. His knuckles broke with a sickening cracking sound.

"You won't be beating anyone with that hand for a while."

Joel returned to the pile of weapons and picked up a knife. Pointing to a smaller man, he said, "This is your knife—come here." Reluctantly, the man approached him. He gave man the knife. "Stick it in me."

The little man smiled, then with an upward thrust drove the knife towards Joel's heart. The knife snapped at the hilt and the blade bounced back, cutting his hand. "Is everyone convinced?" Nobody said a word as Joel looked at them one at a time.

Finally Tye said, "What do you want from us?"

"I want to improve the lives of the people living in this area. I will use all of you to help me do this."

"And if we don't help, but try to stop you?"

"I am prepared to kill all of those who oppose me. To prove I am capable of killing, I could select one of you now, to die. If I select someone, it will be you," Joel said, pointing at Tye. "Would you like me to do that?" Nobody answered his question.

"You have three choices: you can leave this area and never come back, you can oppose me and end up crippled or dead, or you can start a new life by helping me. If you decide to stay, you can live your lives peacefully your own way, or you can work for me. If you work for me, I will pay you a living wage to go to college, learn a trade, or just do odd jobs for me. It will be your choice. There will be no drugs, minimal booze, but a chance at a decent life."

Chapter Four

oel walked to the kitchen door, opened it and called to Tanisha to come out.

When Joel had pushed Tanisha into the kitchen, she had stumbled and landed face down on the floor. She lay there for a while, trying to contain her fear. It seemed like she had been afraid all her life. As a child, seeking comfort in the crowd, walking to and from school; as a teenager trying to avoid the boys, until finally she was cornered and raped. Her mother couldn't help her, working two jobs and trying to raise Tanisha, and her two brothers left no energy for fighting the world. She never knew her father. He left before her first birthday.

Tanisha had been a precocious child. Although her poor and uneducated family did little to help her, she spent hours in front of the television watching *Sesame Street, Captain Kangaroo,* and other children's educational programs. At age 4 her aunt Maisie gave her a children's A-B-C book, which became her prized possession. By the time she went to kindergarten she not only knew the alphabet and her numbers, she could read her precious book.

Her kindergarten teacher, 25-year-old Ms. Brewster, with her master's degree and a brand new teaching credential, still had enthusiasm for her job. The class consisted of some with learning disabilities, some who did not want to be at school and disrupted the class, some who obediently listened to her lessons, and Tanisha. Tanisha absorbed everything Ms. Brewster gave her and came back for more. Tanisha's only had an IQ of about 120, but her desire to learn set her apart from the other students. Ms. Brewster saw her potential and gave her additional books to read.

The teacher protected her from the bullies in the classroom, but on the playground they teased her unmercifully because she wanted to learn and called her "teacher's pet." She would often go home in tears, but got little sympathy and no help.

As she moved through grade school, she tried to hide her need to learn, while still tying to fulfill it. While the rich schools built gymnasiums and swimming pools, the poor school struggled to buy books and supplies. The well-used books the school gave Tanisha sometimes had pages missing or were so dirty she could not read them. She would swap with other kids to find the missing pages.

The teachers, for the most part, had given up on teaching. To teach in Watts meant you could not get a teaching job elsewhere, so the quality was low to start with. The disruptions in class and the implied threats of violence brought the standard even lower. To have all D and E grades would reflect on the teachers, so they graded on a scale. The best student got an A and so on down the scale. This allowed Tanisha to become an A student while learning at a C level.

The meeker children would move in packs, giving themselves a false sense of security going to and from school. This did not stop the harassment; the bullies had formed gangs and delighted in terrorizing the weaker children. At age 14, as Tanisha walked home from a football game, two gang members pulled her into an alley and raped her. She did not tell anybody, but after this she stayed away from situations where this could happen again.

She graduated at the top of her class, but the high school diploma still only got her jobs, cleaning homes, or work in kitchens. Then along came Shaquil. He decided she would be his woman, so she had to live with him. She didn't know what scared her more, the beatings or his idea of lovemaking. Shaquil was gunned down in a drive-by shooting three years ago, leaving her with two boys and a girl. She had felt guilty because of feeling relieved when Shaquil died. The eldest son, 15-year-old Arnell, had reached the age where he became fresh bait for the gangs. His father had been a Cripps, so they figured they owned him.

Lying there, she began to wonder why they hadn't come into the kitchen to get her. She could only imagine what they had done to the white man. He must have been crazy to come to Watts. She looked around her. The kitchen looked like it came out of a magazine. A huge refrigerator, the latest model stove, a walk-in pantry, and no roaches. She fought a constant losing battle with the roaches. She could see into the office. A large desk dominated the room. A safe, three file cabinets, and three chairs made up the rest of the furniture. All the windows had thick vertical bars.

She got up and slowly walked to the door. She pressed her ear against it, just in time to hear a shot. This made her jump back, but the scream she heard didn't sound like the white man. Back at the door she listened to the white man telling them what they had to do. She heard everything from the initial shot on. Finally, the door opened, and the white man stood there.

"I'm Joel. Come on out, Tanisha, there's nothing to be afraid of."

Tanisha walked timidly into the party room. All the Cripps sat at the bar end of the room, looking very subdued. "Did you hear what I told these people?" Joel asked. She nodded. "I would like you to be a key part of my organization. Are you interested?

"What would I have to do?"

"I want to help the people who live in Richardson Gardens, by improving their lives. I won't give them money, but we can educate them so they can earn a decent living. You would tell me what needs to be done, and I will supply the money to do it. I will give you some of my ideas, but you will be in charge of what to do. I want to set up a child care center, so that the mothers can work, then train them so that they can get good jobs —also, provide the opportunity for anyone who wants to go to college."

"Could we fumigate my apartment?"

Joel laughed. we'll fumigate all the buildings in Richardson Gardens and anywhere else you say."

"You have that much money?"

"You come up with worthwhile projects and I'll supply the money. Is there a community leader who has been trying to help people?"

Tanisha thought for a while. "Parson Branch tries to help but his resources are limited. The Cripps destroys everything he tries to do. He's not afraid of them, but it's frustrating."

"Would he come here if you called him?"

"I'm sure he would."

"Okay, then call him. Say you'll explain why, when he gets here."

Tanisha went into the office to call the parson. Joel turned his attention back to the Cripps. "Who wants to help voluntarily, who wants a new life? At first no one moved, then one girl said, "Can you protect us?"

"You saw what I can do. I want to help gang members as well, but if I have to destroy them to help the others, I will. If you want to help, move to the right." She did, then slowly one by one the other five girls and the four wounded men followed her, leaving the others to the left. Slowly four more men joined the volunteers, leaving Tye and the knife man at the left end of the bar. He pointed at the first girl to raise her hand. "What's your name?"

"Tywanna."

"Okay, Tywanna, do you know where there's a first aid kit? We have four men who need attention."

"It's in the kitchen."

"Go get it, and you girls help these men as best you can." As the girls worked on the wounded, Tanisha returned from the office.

"Parson Branch is on his way."

At that moment the front door opened and a man walked in. He looked around the room and said, "Tye what's going on here."

"Kory," said Tye, "Whitey's holding us prisoner."

Kory pulled out a gun and pointed it at Joel.

"Tye, you had better warn him what'll happen if he shoots me."

"You warn him yourself," said Tye.

Joel stared at Kory, concentrating on the gun. Slowly Kory's hand pointed up to the ceiling, then turned so that the gun pointed at Kory's mouth. "You had better drop the gun before it goes off."

Kory tried to pull his gun hand down with his left hand, but it would not budge. He dropped the gun, and his hand suddenly fell to his side. Joel picked up the gun and ordered Kory to join the others at the bar. Pointing at the man with the busted hand, he said, "What's your name?"

"Shaun."

"Okay, Shaun, you tell Kory what's been happening here. Don't leave out the opportunity to go to college and help the community." Just then, Parson Branch entered. "Wait a minute, Shaun, I want the parson to hear this."

Tanisha introduced Parson Branch to Joel, explaining that he wanted to help and had a lot of money for projects. The parson appeared skeptical, but agreed to listen. Shaun started to recount the events of the morning. To Joel's surprise, Shaun spoke quite well; he left out the jive talk, using clear plain English. Joel added a point or two, but in all Shaun explained the situation very well. When he finished, Joel asked him if he had graduated from high school.

"Yes." Said Shaun.

"Why didn't you go to college?"

"Gang pressure."

"Would you like to go now? Are you willing to trust me and take a chance?"

"I've been hoping for an opportunity to get away from the gang, but it takes money."

"Well, I have the money and I need your help." Shaun just nodded his head. "Do you know if any of the others feel the same as you?"

Shaun looked at his friends for a while. "I've talked to Rashid, Devern, and Jamaal about this. They seem to feel the same.

Joel looked at these men. "Is that correct?"

"Can you protect us from Kory's bosses? They'll be coming after you," said Rashid.

"I won't wait for that. I'm going after them first."

Kory Williams had listened to all that Shaun had said. It sounded unbelievable, but all around him he could see evidence that supported it. The white man had total control, four people looked injured, and Tye kept his mouth shut. Maybe he could use this situation to his advantage. His meeting with Diego had not gone well. They wanted to replace him with Tye, but Tye's violent streak made them nervous. Diego only killed out of necessity, Tye killed for pleasure. As soon as they found a suitable replacement, his term as leader ended. Kory knew they considered him too soft. All the killing made him sick, but you didn't tell Diego you wanted out. The only way out came with a pine box.

His entry into the Cripps, at age 16, began against his will. Once he accepted that, he could not say no, he made the most of it. His size kept him out of trouble most of the time, and when he had to, he handled himself well, but avoided killing anyone. Being seven years older than Tye, he had a leadership roll before Tye came along. The people ahead of him died from gang violence, one by one, until he rose to the top. For the last three years he had looked for a way out, but the opportunity had not presented itself. One leader before him had walked away. His body washed up on the shore north of Malibu. Could this man possibly stand up to Diego? The risk might be worth it—he had to do something soon.

Parson Branch and Kory spoke at the same time.

"What do you want from me?" said Parson Branch.

"Can I speak to you in private?" said Kory.

"Just a minute please, both of you. Shaun, you and Rashid see that nobody leaves; we're going into the office. Call me if anyone gives you a problem. Parson, Kory, and Tanisha, let us go into the office."

In the office Joel asked Kory what he wanted to say.

"I've been in the Cripps since I was sixteen, and I've worked my way up because I had no choice. You did as you were told or took your punishment. I'm 32 now and have been looking for a way out for a while. This appears to be my chance."

Joel asked Branch, "Do you believe him?"

"Yes, Kory and I have talked about this a few times. He has been a stabilizing force, keeping people like Tye in check."

"Okay, I'm going to trust you. I will protect you, but be assured I have the power to be ruthless. If you cross me, you will die."

"Parson, I want your help. I promise you I will not harm anyone who is innocent or basically well meaning. Only the very wicked will need to fear me."

Branch looked Joel in the eyes for a while trying to size him up. He seemed to make a decision. "I will help you, unless, I see that your cure is worse than the disease. If this happens, I will fight you."

"Good, just the answer I would expect. Now tell me your opinion of Tanisha. I want to put her in charge with your guidance. Can she handle it."

Both Branch and Tanisha looked at him in surprise.

"Tanisha is an intelligent, brave woman. She has had a rough life, but has stood up to the Cripps. She will do anything to protect her children. With the right help, she can do anything you want."

"How about Tywanna?"

Tanisha spoke up. "She is the daughter of a friend of mine; she also wants to leave the Cripps. She is quite bright, but needs to go back to school." The Parson nodded his agreement.

"Tanisha, will you be my representative, in charge of everything?" Tanisha nodded. "We'll discuss your salary in private later; it'll be a lot more than you currently earn. Kory, you and Tywanna will be her assistants, and Parson, you'll be her advisor." As the Parson nodded, Joel said. "Let us go upstairs."

As they crossed the recreation room, Joel noticed that Rashid had tied up Tye. The rest of them sat watching a movie on television.

"Can we leave now?" asked Tywanna.

"Give me half an hour and I will settle with all of you."

Upstairs Joel found a corridor going down the middle of the building. To the left was a master bedroom with a bathroom. Kory said, "I sleep in there."

Two doors on the right side opened into two smaller bedrooms.

"Rashid and Rafael sleep there," offered Kory.

"Who is Rafael?"

"The little guy with the knife," said Tanisha.

Just before the corridor turned to the right, there was a bathroom on the left and past that a door opened into another master bedroom suite.

"Tye sleeps there," said Kory.

Around the corner, Joel saw two more doors on the right leading to two more bedrooms, with a Jack and Jill bathroom between them. Finally, at the bottom of the corridor a door led to a living room, with a small kitchen at the back.

"I designed this floor like this," said Kory. "It gives me somewhere to get away from the mob downstairs. Nobody comes in this living room without my permission."

Joel said, "You are going to lose a lot of your privileges in exchange for your freedom. Tanisha is in charge—now you work for her. I expect you to be her strong right arm; play your cards right and I will take care of you later. Tanisha, would you consider moving into this building with your children, if I made it safe for you?"

"Not if Tye and Rafael are living here."

"Don't worry about them; they'll both be gone in a few days."

Returning to the bend in the corridor, Joel said, "Kory, have a very sturdy door with two dead bolts built here, so that everything down the side corridor and Tye's master bedroom is behind the door. That will make a nice apartment for Tanisha and her family. You and Rashid can stay where you are and provide protection for her. I will use Rafael's room. I want Tye and Rafael out of here once we are finished with them. Keep them tied up in one of the bedrooms until I tell you to release them. Kory, is there seven thousand dollars in the safe?

"There's a lot more than that."

"When we go downstairs go get me seven thousand and bring it in the big room. Now, let's go see what's going on down there."

Downstairs Joel faced the six female and ten male gang members. "You all now work for the Richardson Gardens Restoration Corporation, except for Tye and Rafael. You will be paid four hundred dollars a week to start, more as you prove your worth. If you go to college, all your expenses will be paid; other trade school classes will be available. Tanisha is president of the corporation; she will assign you to projects once she gets organized. Rashid and Shaun, your job is to guard Tanisha; you will go with her where ever she goes. Kory is the vice president working for Tanisha. Tywanna, you will help Tanisha in the office. Anyone who gives Tanisha a bad time will answer to me."

"What are you going to do with us?" asked Tye.

"I thought of taking you with me in my airplane and dropping you out over the desert. Parson Branch convinced me to think that over. If you don't cause trouble, I'll let you go in a few days. Give us trouble, and out of the airplane you go."

Kory had returned from the office. "Give them each four hundred dollars. You will get another four hundred each every Friday from Tanisha. I want you all to report to Tanisha, here at 9 a.m. tomorrow. Rashid and Shaun, guard Tye and Rafael, the rest of you can leave." They all filed quietly out the door; the whole thing was too new for them. Tomorrow they would come back wondering if today really happened or if they dreamt it. Tywanna stayed behind. She came up to Joel nervously.

"Can I ask you a question?"

"Fire away," said Joel.

"I want to go to college. How can I do that and work in the office?"

"Once you enroll in college, the office work will be scheduled around your availability. I want you to get a good education and become a key person in our corporation."

Tywanna face lit up and she turned and left. She couldn't believe her luck; one minute she is a virtual prisoner of the gang, and then suddenly a whole new life opens up before her. Would it be snatched away from her tomorrow? She could only pray that it wouldn't. She had always gone along with whatever happened, afraid to have hopes of her own. Her mother had told her, "Don't have dreams, then you won't be disappointed when they don't come true." Even so, she had wanted to go to college. She only hoped she had good enough grades for it. She knew she could have done better at school, but what for? The others didn't work for grades, and she always wanted to be one of the "in crowd."

Office work, bookkeeping—she would love that. For the first time, that she could remember, her future looked bright. If only this Joel guy could deliver what he promised. Why should she trust a white man, or any man? They were all the same; all they wanted was to get into her pants. But what did she have to lose.

She had angered Tye by being the first to move to the right; he would never forgive her for that. When she first joined the Cripps, Tye had made her his woman. He treated her gently at first, and then wanted her to do more perverse things. Finally, he made her sleep with other men, and they treated her like trash.

She had always liked Tanisha; working with her would be easy. She must just relax and see what develops. But she knew she wouldn't sleep much tonight.

Chapter Five

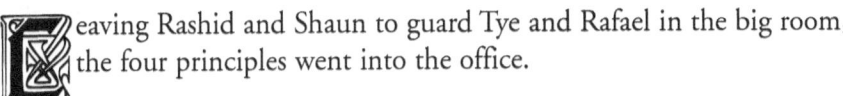eaving Rashid and Shaun to guard Tye and Rafael in the big room, the four principles went into the office.

"Parson, how much involvement do you want in the corporation?" asked Joel.

"Officially, none; unofficially, as much as you need me. I think your goals overlap mine."

Okay, you will be Tanisha's advisor. Come up with projects between you, and I'll tell you if I can fund them. I want to hire as many people as we can from within the Hood and only go outside for special expertise. My top priority is education, especially teaching people a trade. Tanisha, work on getting as many students into college, and setting up classes for others. We can use the big room as a classroom, and maybe rent the church hall for another classroom. Buy whatever you need."

Joel saw that Tanisha was taking notes. This gave him confidence that she could do the job. "Find a lawyer to set up a corporation with the three of you as officers, Tanisha as president. Kory, how much cash is still in the safe?"

"About one hundred thousand dollars," said Kory.

Both Tanisha and the parson gasped.

"Tanisha, use that money as you need, keep a record of all expenditures. Have Tywanna start a set of books. When you have the incorporation papers, take the money to the bank and open an account for the corporation, with you as the only signatory. Have Kory, Rashid, and Shaun escort you. I will deposit another million in the account once it is open, then more as we need it."

"You have that kind of money?" asked Branch.

"Yes, and we will fund some of your programs, such as your soup kitchen, with Tanisha's approval. Hire some of the local people to help you; we will pick-up the payroll. There will be a lot of drug users needing help when we shut down sales of illegal drugs in this area. Parson, you should set up a rehab center to help them. We will co-operate with the Head Start, Sage Center, and Community Services people."

"Kory, you will be in charge of security; your number one project is to protect Tanisha. Someone must be with her at all times. We will expand your involvement once I eliminate the danger from your ex-bosses. Now open the safe."

Kory hesitated.

"Either you are with us, or not, which is it?" Kory moved over to the safe and opened it. "It's your safe, Tanisha. What's in it?"

Tanisha moved to the safe. "Nine stacks of one hundred dollar bills…" She counted one stack, "with hundred bills in each stack, and one with only thirty one hundred dollar bills."

"That's the one I took seven thousand dollars from. Here is the six hundred I had left." He offered the money to Joel.

"You keep that as your salary, from next Friday on you'll get eight hundred a week."

Tanisha continued the inventory. "Ten packages of what looks like drugs."

"Each packages contains one hundred, one-ounce packets of heroin, each worth fifty dollars," said Kory.

"Parson, will you flush all that down the sink?" Joel said, as Kory gasped. "No, on second thought, let Kory do it, while you watch. Kory, you live in a new world now, you had better adjust fast."

"I'm sorry, I'll do it, but it's hard flushing fifty thousand dollars down the drain." Both men went into the kitchen.

"Okay, Tanisha, what's next?"

"An accounting book with a list of names—it appears to be the users. Two guns, a grant deed for this building, and a bank book in Kory's name, with a little over ten thousand dollars in it."

Joel looked at the accounting book; it contained purchases as well as sales. A Diego Ramirez supplied their drug. Could he be related to Carlos? The book showed two addresses for him, one in Santa Monica, the other in Beverly Hills. As Joel stored the addresses away in his mind, the two men returned to the office.

"Parson, I'll give you this ledger. It contains the names of users. They will need your help. Kory, you take the guns and collect all those in the big room. Find a safe place for them. Also, here is your bank book. I'm going to let you keep the money in this account. Are there any questions"?

"How will we get in touch with you?" asked Branch.

"Tanisha will have my number. I will deal through her."

"Kory, you take Tye and Rafael upstairs, tie them up, and leave them in one of the bedrooms. Then tell Rashid and Shaun what's going on. Then get to work on adding a door in the corridor. Parson, do you have any more questions?"

When neither man said anything, Joel continued. "Now I want to talk to Tanisha alone." The two men left the office. "How do you feel, Tanisha?"

"I'm in shock, I'm not sure I can handle this."

"You can. Just don't try to do it all yourself. Your job is to delegate. Let others do the work. Use the Parson and me when you want advice."

"What if I get into trouble, and they won't let me talk to you?"

"Give me your cell phone number; I'll call you daily for a while. If you are being coerced just say you need a car for Tywanna. That'll be our code for trouble, and I will come a quickly as I can. I should never be more than two hours away."

"What if they won't let me talk to you?"

"Then I'll come immediately." He gave her a piece of paper. "That's the combination to the safe. Take one thousand dollars for your first week's salary. We will increase that, if you work out in this job, and I'm sure you will. Once Kory puts the door in upstairs and I take care of the suppliers, we will kick Tye out and you can move into the apartment. I'm going to say goodbye to Kory, then I'm leaving."

Joel shook hands with Tanisha, and went upstairs to find Kory. He found two men tied up in one of the small bedrooms and his three helpers in the living room. "Is everything okay?"

"Yes, but we were discussing what the reaction of Ramirez will be."

"Is he your only supplier?"

"Yes, he runs all the drugs in the area," said Kory.

"Is there anyone else we should worry about?"

"Well, all the Hoods around us will try to move in when they find out we have stopped selling drugs."

"They will all be getting visits from me in the next few days. That should take care of them. Tell me about the two addresses for Ramirez."

"The one in Santa Monica is a warehouse where he stores the merchandise; the other is where he lives. Both are heavily guarded with alarms and armed men. The warehouse also has guard dogs."

"I'm going to pay a visit to the warehouse now. Give me your cell number; I'll call you when I'm finished there so you will know where you stand." Kory gave him the cell phone number.

"Aren't you going to write it down?"

"No need to. I remember everything I hear."

Chapter Six

oel left the building, walked to his car, and drove to the airport. He retrieved some maps from his Cessna, and while he ate a late lunch in the airport restaurant, he checked the addresses. Joel decided to walk to the warehouse from the Santa Monica airport. He then filed a flight plan and flew to Santa Monica. Soon he stood across the street from his destination. He planned to destroy all the drugs in this building. He didn't want the police involved, so his actions had to be stealthy. The less gunfire the better.

The warehouse looked to be 50 feet wide by 150 feet long, located on the end of a block of similar units. A Chevrolet Caprice and a Honda Accord sat in the front parking lot. The front entrance led into an office area with the window blinds drawn so that you could not see in. At the back a large pull-up garage door admitted delivery vehicles. Joel decided on a frontal assault. He switched on his suit, then crossed the road and turned the door handle to find it locked. He knocked on the door.

A large Hispanic-looking man opened the door about a foot, and said in an accented voice, "Whatever you're selling, we don't want any."

Joel pushed hard on the door and the man staggered back cursing. Joel entered the office, closed the door behind him, and moving closer to the man, hit him hard on the side of his head. He fell to the ground unconscious.

A second man seated at a table, with playing cards on it, started to rise, reaching for his gun. Joel grabbed the edge of the table, lifted it up, and used it as a battering ram to pin the man against the wall. Throwing the table aside, he rendered this man unconscious with one blow. The office contained packing materials. Joel used some duck tape to bind the men, wrapping it around their hands and feet, and gagging them.

Moving to the door to the back area, he opened it a crack to see if the commotion had attracted any attention. Nothing seemed to be stirring. Opening the door wide, he stepped through. He heard a thud as a man to the right of the door hit him on top of his head with the butt of his gun. On the left side of the door, stood a man holding back two large dogs on leashes. Joel hit the man to the right, and turned to face the danger on his left.

As the man released the dogs, Joel activated the electrical charge on the outside of his suit. The dogs leaped at him, going for his throat. Their paws contacted the electrical charge and they fell back yelping. The man urged them to attack again, but after getting a second shock they kept their distance. The man pulled a gun out of his belt and pointed it at Joel. "Who are you?" he asked.

Joel raised his hands as he stared at the gun. Slowly the man's hand turned until the gun pointed directly into his mouth. Like Kory, he tried to pull his right hand down with his left hand, but it would not budge. The gun clattered to the floor. As Joel moved towards him, the man hit him hard on the chin. With a scream, he hugged his bruised knuckles. The dogs still kept their distance.

Joel switched off the electrical current, grabbed the man by the throat, and lifted him off the ground. The man struggled, but only succeeded in throttling himself more.

"If you behave yourself, I'll let you live," Joel said. Putting him down, Joel picked up the gun, and made him bind the third man. He asked "What's your name?"

The man didn't answer. Joel picked him up by the throat again and let a little current run around the outside of the suit.

The man screamed, "Mario! Mario!"

"Okay, Mario, where are the drugs?"

"What drugs?"

Joel reached for his throat again.

"I can't tell you, Diego would kill me."

"After I have dealt with the drugs, I will let you take me to Diego as your prisoner, and we will see who is going to do the killing."

In the warehouse Joel could see fifty, 6-foot cube crates, stacked two crates high in five rows, by five deep. Each row had a 5-foot wide aisleway between the crates. Mario led Joel down the second aisle to the third crate, and using a crowbar pried off the front of the crate. Joel hefted one of the hundred packages inside; it felt like 2 pounds, or a kilo. "How much is this worth on the street?" asked Joel.

"That's pure heroin, when cut four to one with flour you will get one hundred and twenty, one-ounce packets. At fifty dollars an ounce, that's six million dollars."

Joel didn't want to flush 220 pounds of heroin into the sewers. The result might be an environmental disaster—he couldn't take that chance. He asked Mario where they kept the flour. There he found eight, 100-pound sacks of flour. He emptied three in one corner of the warehouse and put the heroin in the sacks. He and Mario carried the sacks out front to the Caprice and put them in the trunk. With Joel beside him, Mario drove the Caprice to the airport, where they loaded the sacks onto the Cessna.

Joel filed a round-trip flight plan out of Santa Monica, and with Mario onboard flew east to the Soda Mountains just west of Baker. Putting the aircraft on autopilot he slit open each bag of heroin and emptied the contents out of the window. Mario behaved himself; even if he could over-power Joel, who would fly the plane? Returning to Santa Monica, Joel refueled the Cessna before he parked it.

Once back in the Caprice, he told Mario to drive him to Beverly Hills. Diego Ramirez's home stood near the top of Hillcrest Road in The Trousdale Estates, with a panoramic view looking south over the whole of Los Angeles County. They drove north on Interstate 405, turned west on Sunset Boulevard to Hillcrest Road, and climbed north into the Hollywood Hills. The trees lining the roads changed from palm trees to deciduous as they climbed. As they neared the top, Mario turned into the Ramirez's estate. Mario informed him that the security systems made it an impregnable fortress. The gated property had two armed men at the gate, an electronic surveillance system, and men patrolling the grounds with dogs.

Joel's suit seemed to work very well, so he decided to use a frontal attack. He told Mario to drive into the estate and offer Joel to Diego as his prisoner. He warned Mario about bullets fired at him being ricocheted back at the shooter before giving him the gun. Mario thought Joel crazy, but this might get him off the hook with Diego later.

They drove up to the gates. The guard, seeing Mario, let them in. The grounds were spacious and immaculate. A long driveway led to a circular parking area in front of the front door. The ranch-style house must have been at least 10,000 square feet with a six-car garage. They parked, walked to the front door, and another guard let them into a huge foyer.

Joel could see a hallway going straight ahead, double doors to the right, and a much larger set of double doors to the left. Seeing the gun in Mario's hand, the door man asked, "What's going on?"

Mario didn't answer his question, but said, "Where is Diego?"

"In the living room."

The guard knocked on the doors to the left, and hearing a response, opened the doors. He followed as Mario ushered Joel into the living room, where they saw three men sitting talking. The man who appeared to be Diego said in Spanish, "What are you doing here, Mario? Is everything okay at the warehouse?"

Mario proceeded to tell them the whole story, adding that after they landed at Santa Monica, he wrestled the gun from Joel and brought him here. Diego came out of his seat in a rage and got face to face with Joel. "You destroyed six million dollars worth of heroin? You are going to suffer for this. Ernesto, Rolando, tie him to a chair."

The other two men in the room moved until they stood one either side of Joel. They tried to grab his arms, but could only get a half-inch away from them. They pulled but could not move him, or even his arms. Joel just stood there. Rolando pulled a gun. "Go sit in that chair," he said.

"Don't fire that gun; the bullet will ricochet and hit you," said Joel in Spanish. Silence filled the air, then everyone laughed.

"Shoot him in the leg," said Diego. "Don't kill him. He's not getting off that easy." Rolando moved away from Joel, then fired at his leg. The bullet ricocheted back and hit Rolando in the thigh. He screamed and fell heavily backward and landed seated on the sofa. The silence was now deafening. The three other men attacked, but Joel soon rendered them unconscious.

He turned back to Diego, who now held a gun. He held his arms out to the side and said, "Go ahead, shoot me."

Diego looked at Rolando sitting on the sofa, and threw the gun at Joel. It bounced off him. "Are you the man Carlos told me about?"

"Ah, Carlos," said Joel. "Yes I must visit him again. I hear he's been looking for me." Joel approached Diego, grabbed him by the throat, and lifted him off the ground. The more Diego struggled the more it choked him. "I have one question for you. Do you want to live?" Putting Diego back on his feet, but still holding his throat loosely, he said, "I want an answer."

"Yes," Diego gasped.

Joel released him. "If you do every thing I tell you to, I will let you go back to Colombia to tell your partners about me. If not, I will kill you, and send one of you men back there with the news." Diego stared at him in silence, then tried to run. Joel caught him easily and dragged him into the kitchen, found a butcher's chopping knife, and said, "Where is your office?" Diego led him across the foyer to the other double doors, and used a key to unlock them. Joel took the key from him.

The office contained the usual furniture, desk, chairs, file cabinet, and safe. "Open the safe." Diego didn't move. Joel forced Diego into an arm chair, jammed his head against the back with his left elbow, and sprayed his right hand on the arm of the chair. As he raised the chopper, he said, "I can send you home with or without fingers—it is up to you."

"Okay, I'll open it."

Joel searched the safe. "I don't see your overseas bank account. Where do you keep that information?"

"I don't have one."

Joel jammed him in the chair again and raised the chopper.

"You wouldn't dare."

Swoosh! The knife came down and Diego's right pinky dropped to the floor. Diego's screams brought three more guards running into the room with guns drawn. "Shoot him!" yelled Diego.

Three shots rang out, and three men fell to the floor with gunshot wounds. Joel examined the three men; one died as he got to him. The other two had shoulder wounds. Joel had known that eventually someone would get killed. He rationalized that these men had killed many times, so he had little sympathy for them.

Joel propped the two wounded men up against the wall, and dragging Diego with him, went into the living room and brought Rolando into the office. He locked the doors. Now he could keep an eye on all of them. He jammed Diego back in the armchair, spread his right hand on the arm, and raised the chopper. "Now that bank account—where is the information I want?"

"Okay, okay," said Diego. There's a floor safe."

"Where?"

"In the corner. A square of carpet pulls up. It's underneath that."

Joel raised the chopper again. "What's the combination?" Diego told him. Joel took a box of Kleenex off the desk, gave it to Diego, and told him to stop the blood flowing from his finger.

Moving to the safe, Joel opened it, and removed the offshore bank account information. He whistled as he read it. The account had over $50,000,000 in it. He sat down at the desk, picked up the phone, and called Diego's bank. Using the routing and account numbers, he transferred all but $100 from Diego's account to his own Cayman Island account.

Joel spent the next thirty minutes going through the contents of both safes. In the overt one he found maps of Colombia, the country, two states, and three local maps. Ledgers in this safe showed Diego's major customers. He committed the names to memory; Kory would know them. In the covert safe he found documents that referred to two different addresses, one in each of the two states. He located the addresses on two of the local maps. He put the maps and ledgers in a briefcase lying on the desk.

He told Diego, "Go back to Colombia. If you come looking for me, I will kill you. I'm only leaving you alive to deliver a message to you boss. Tell him he can come looking for me if he likes, but if he waits a while I will come visit him."

Joel picked up the briefcase and left the house. He drove the Caprice down to the gate. A guard came out of the shack, pointing a gun at him. He got out of the car, and as he walked towards the guard, he made the gun turn until it pointed into the guard's mouth. From inside the shack the second guard took a shot at Joel. The bullet bounced back, hitting the second guard in the shoulder. Joel made the first guard open the gate, got back into the Caprice, and drove away.

On the way to the airport he called Kory and told him that Diego had been taken care of. He left the Caprice at Santa Monica Airport and flew back to his compound near Barstow, closing the force field after he landed. He arrived home at 8 p.m., twelve hours after he had left that morning. He had accomplished a lot in one day. He had plenty of energy left, so he decided to spend some time planning the next steps. He strapped himself into the machine and set the controls for seventy percent for thirty minutes.

Chapter Seven

While in the machine, Joel's mind ran rampant. The thoughts and ideas came with the speed of a computer, and he stored them for future use. One group of thoughts covered what to do about the other gangs surrounding Watts. Another covered how to spread his work to other cities. A third concerned going to Colombia and other sources of street drugs.

A lot of his ideas concerned advanced technology hundreds of years ahead of today's. One idea that kept pushing to the forefront tackled the need for faster transportation, for better utilization of his time. This idea revolved around a transporter similar to the one on *Star Trek*.

Leaving the machine, Joel found that he felt completely refreshed. The sessions replaced any need for sleep, and he found that after each session he could read people's minds better.

He went to his workshop and constructed a second force field suit belt. It could only be turned on and off by his thought process. This would preclude any misuse if it fell into somebody's hands. Next, he built a smaller, lower-powered, age-retarding machine. He wanted to install this in his room, at the headquarters building in Watts. If he could use it on Tanisha, she would be a lot more valuable to him.

Joel decided to visit Carlo Ramirez again. He flew to San Diego, took a taxi to his apartment to pick up his car, and drove to La Jolla. He entered the high-rise that Carlos lived in, found the manager's apartment, and knocked on the door. The manager told him Carlos lived in apartment 1010, but he would have to call him to let him know Joel was coming up. When he got out of the elevator on the tenth floor, two men awaited him with drawn guns. They escorted him to apartment 1010 and they all went in.

Carlos met them as they entered the living room. He had a splint on his pinkie. "It's the crazy man! We meet again. I've been searching for you," he said in Spanish.

"Have you talked to your brother Diego lately?" Joel replied in the same language.

"I don't believe all that stuff he told Papa; he's just making excuses for losing all that heroin."

"What excuses did you make?"

Carlos's face darkened with anger. "You are gonna pay for that. Shoot him in the knees."

Joel turned to the gunmen. "Before you shoot I must warn you that what Diego reported is true—the bullets will bounce back and hit you." One gunman laughed and shot Joel in the knee, then fell to the floor clutching his own knee. The other gunman picked up a chair and hit Joel as hard as he could over the head. The chair shattered but had no effect. Joel struck each of the gunmen once, rendering them unconscious. To Carlos he said, "I want you to return to Colombia with Diego, confirm what he tells them, and tell your Cartel that the United States is off limits to them."

"Now where is your latest shipment of heroin?"

"You destroyed all the heroin we had."

Joel could see he lied. "How many of your fingers will I have to chop off before you stop lying to me?" Carlos did not reply. Joel grabbed him by the throat, carried him into the kitchen, and asked, "Where do you keep your knives?" Carlos's face took on a blue hue, so Joel dropped him on the floor and continued to search the kitchen drawers, finally finding a carving knife.

"Okay," croaked Carlos. "It's in the safe." They went into the master bedroom, and in the closet Joel found a large safe.

He nicked Carlos on the chin with the knife saying, "Open it." Carlos knelt in front of the safe, opened it, pulling out a gun. He pointed the gun at Joel, who laughed, then Carlos meekly gave the gun to Joel.

"I should really kill you for all the grief you have caused to so many people. If I send you back to Colombia, maybe "Papa" will do it for me. Tell "Papa" I'm coming after him soon." Joel struck Carlos on the chin, leaving him on the closet floor. He retrieved three kilos of heroin from the safe. He found a shopping bag in the kitchen, put the heroin in it, and left the apartment.

Flying out of San Diego, he headed west out over the Pacific Ocean. With the airplane on autopilot he slit open the packets of heroin, and let the powder float down to the water. Turning east-north east he flew back to his compound. Joel spent another thirty minutes in the machine.

After lunch, Joel loaded the small crate containing the parts of the new age-retarding machine into the Cessna, along with the second belt, a spare pair of size thirty-six pants, and an extra large shirt, He then flew to the Compton airport and rented a place to park his Cessna in a hangar. He got a car from Hertz, transferred all the cargo from the airplane to the car, switched on his suit, and drove to Watts. He entered the Richardson Gardens Restoration Corporation headquarters building to find Tanisha hard at work. She had all the people from the previous day there, waiting as she handed out their assignments. He heard Tywanna talking to the pest control people, Kory had a crew upstairs working on the door, and Shaun worked on a list of the staff's educational preferences.

Carrying the crate up to his room, he closed the door, opened the crate, and assembled the machine. It looked like a recliner. Then he went to see Tanisha.

She told him a lawyer would have the incorporation papers in two days; Kory had convinced him of the urgency. Joel didn't want to know how Kory had convinced him. He told Tanisha he had all the money she would need—all she had to do was spend it wisely. Next, Joel told Kory to let Rashid handle the door project; he needed his help.

He told Kory, without going into a lot of details, what had transpired at Diego Ramirez's house. "He won't be bothering us for a while. We can release our prisoners." Joel told Kory the name of Ramirez's customers. Kory knew them all. "I will visit them. I want you to come with me." Kory showed his apprehension. "You can't be hurt, but they will kill me. He took

Kory into his bedroom showed him the belt and the over sizeclothes, and told him to put them on. When he did, Joel switched the belt on and said, "I'm not going to tell you how it works, but now you can't be harmed." A smile spread over Kory's face. "Let's go," he said.

They went into the bedroom containing Tye and Rafael. As Kory untied them, Joel said, "I'm letting you both go. If you cause me any trouble at all I will put you in my airplane, fly out over the ocean, and drop you off. My advice to you is to leave this area. You can go see your friend Ramirez, but I don't think you will get a good reception from him. He is probably packing for his trip back top Colombia." Joel escorted them out of the building and watched them drive away in Tye's car.

Joel asked Kory if he had an old clunker of a car they could use, preferably one that could not be traced back to them. He didn't want to get his rental car damaged. Kory said he had just the thing, a large Chevy they used to cruise through other gangs' turf. "Great," said Joel, "you drive. Let's go visit Parson Branch first."

They found Branch in the parsonage working in his office. "You busy?" asked Joel.

"I'm just working on my shopping list for the Soup Kitchen."

"This should make it easier." Joel handed him a check for $100,000. "It's for the Soup Kitchen and to help the drug addicts get rehabilitation, Set up our own program; bring in a few experts, but use local people as much as you can. Give me an accounting of how you spend it and I will give you another check."

"This is very generous. How can I ever repay you?"

"Well now you mention it, there are two things. First, I need a contact in each of these eight towns to do for me there what you are doing here." The list contained the following towns: Bell, Lennox, Inglewood, Maywood, South Gate, Vernon, Walnut Park, and Willowbrook. "You don't have to tell them too much, just that I have money to assist them."

"This will be easy. We have a meeting of all the local clergymen as a sort of support group. What's the second thing?"

"I need contacts in other major cities to do our work there—Chicago, New York, Boston, and others."

"We keep in touch with people in other cities. I should be able to work on that."

"Thank you. I'll appreciate all the help you can give me. Now Kory and I must be on our way, we have work to do."

Back in the car, Joel told Kory to drive to Inglewood. On the way he asked about the Inglewood gang, who led them, did he have a second in command. He told Kory he wanted to take at least the two top leaders from each gang in the eight towns on Diego list to his compound for interrogation. If the third top man had a lot of influence, they needed to take him too. Kory told him that in Inglewood, Vernon, and Walnut Park, they needed the top three. Joel told Kory to stay in the car when they got there. If they saw Kory they would head for Watts to get their leaders back. Kory said he had a ski mask in the car. Joel didn't ask him what he used it for, but told him to wear it but still stay in the car.

In Inglewood, Kory drove to where the gang hung out and pointed out the three men he needed. Joel decided to use a frontal attack. These men would not call the police to fight their battles. Who would believe that one man attacked ten gang members and kidnapped three of them? Their pride would not let them admit it.

Joel walked up to the leader and said, "Josh Manchester, I want you to come with me." He grabbed Josh's arm and pulled him towards the car. The ten men attacked him and in a matter of seconds they all lay unconscious on the ground. Joel disarmed the three men he needed, then loaded them into the trunk of the Chevy, telling Kory to drive to the Compton airport. On the way there, Joel struggled with how much he would tell Kory. Could he trust him? Would he betray him after seeing the power Joel possessed? He decided he needed someone, and Kory seemed dedicated to his cause. He started to trust him by turning off both force field suits.

Kory drove into the hangar and they loaded the three men into the Cessna. Joel told Kory to get into the airplane. Kory hesitated; he had heard what Joel had told Tye about dropping him off over the ocean. Joel realized trust was a two-way street. "Get in," he said. "I promise you will be safe." On the way there, Joel told Kory about his compound, but only what he thought he needed to know. At the compound, with Joel carrying two men and Kory one, they took their prisoners to the Brig.

As they left Kory said, "What's to stop them leaving when they awake?" Joel handed him a pickaxe, and they went back inside. Joel switched on the internal force field and told Kory to try to leave the building. "I don't want to damage the walls," said Kory.

"Be my guest. Do all the damage you can."

Kory used the pickaxe on different places on all four walls, then finally the door, without making any impression at all. "I'm convinced. Let's go."

They flew back to Compton and resumed the prisoner gathering in Bell, Maywood, Lennox, South Gate, Vernon, Walnut Park, and finally Willowbrook. Joel switched on his and Kory's suits, and "thought on" the brig force field each time they took prisoners in. The previous prisoners had recovered and tried to attack them, unsuccessfully.

Before the last trip to the compound, Joel told Kory, "I'll call you tomorrow when I need help, but now it's important that you go back to Watts and help Tanisha. I need to know that you will do what I ask of you and keep your mouth shut." Kory tried hard to hide his disappointment. He said, "I will do as you ask, but watch out for Ernesto Lecarno from Vernon. He is a sadistic killer who will never give in to you."

Joel used his thoughts to switch off Kory's belt and told him to keep it for now. He wouldn't be able to switch it on, as it didn't have a switch, and he would need it when they returned the gang members. He then took the last of the prisoners to his compound.

With his seventeen prisoners safely locked up, Joel took them seventeen loaves of bread and seventeen large bottles of water, and left them for the night to stew over their fate.

Joel called Parson Branch, and asked him to arrange a meeting with his friends from the seven Hoods that he had prisoners from. He did not tell him about the prisoners. Branch said, "I've already contacted the key people and have arranged the meeting for the day after tomorrow."

This fit in perfectly with Joel's plans. "Good work, Branch, I hope they are as co-operative as you. Tell them the meeting is at the Cripps house in Watts. Kory will pick them up in a minibus and guarantee their safety. I want them to meet Tanisha, and see what we are doing there." Joel then called Kory, told him to get the seven names and addresses from Branch, and have them there by 10 a.m.

Next, Joel had a session on the machine, then worked until 3 a.m. on his latest project. He had decided that if he had to travel back and forth to the East Coast, he needed a faster method of transportation than his Cessna. Again, the problem revolved around a source of energy that produced enough power to activate the transporter. If, in his nuclear engine, he used hydrogen atoms, as they did in the hydrogen bomb, he could increase the energy released by a hundred-fold.

Joel slept for three hours, did his morning exercises, had another session on the machine, ate breakfast, and went to face his prisoners. He switched on the suit before he entered the airlock.

They must have been planning what to do the night before, for when he entered the brig, they attacked him en masse. Luckily, he had thought to close the force field as soon as he passed through the door, for as sixteen of them descended upon him, one tried to slip past him and out the door. Joel activated the electrical current on the outside of his suit, and they all retreated quickly. He surveyed them as they surrounded him. They all showed signs of combat, cuts, bruises, and a few black eyes. There must have been quite a battle, before they called a truce and decided to work together against the common foe.

"I want you to sit around the table; we have things to discuss. Sit with your friends from your Hood."

"And what if we don't?" asked one man.

Joel looked at the man who had spoken. Their eyes locked and he tried to read his thoughts. The hatred and venom that came through shocked him until he had to look away. "You must be Ernesto Lecarno."

The man smiled. "If you've heard of me you know you've made a big mistake."

"To answer your question, if you don't obey me I will give you electric shock treatments until you do. If I can't get you to do as I ask, I will kill you and move on to the next man. I am going to start with you."

Before Ernesto could move, Joel grabbed him, slung him over his shoulder, and dumped him in a chair at the table. He placed his hands on Ernesto's shoulders, and every time he tried to rise out of the chair, gave him a shock. After four shocks Ernesto sat still, but as soon as Joel moved away from him, he got up and ran around to the opposite side of the table.

Joel moved until he faced Ernesto across the table, then with a standing leap jumped up on top of the table, bounced immediately across the other side the table, landing on top of Ernesto. He picked Ernesto up like a sack of potatoes, hurled his body twenty feet down the room, where it thudded into the wall and dropped lifeless on the floor. Joel turned to face the other prisoners and said to the second in command from Vernon, "What's your name?"

"Jodam."

"Do you want to be next?" There followed a few moment of silence, then Jodam walked over to the table and sat down. One by one the rest of them followed, until sixteen seats at the table had occupants.

Joel told them what he had done to Diego Ramirez and that he had returned to Colombia. Diego would not be supplying their drugs anymore. Joel then outlined what he had initiated in Watts, explaining Tanisha's, Kory's, and Parson Branch's roles, without naming them. "I intend to do the same in each of your Hoods. You each have choices. You can oppose me, and I promise you, I will kill, or cripple you. You can move out of the Hood and not come back. You can live peacefully in the Hood, and I will not bother you, or you can join me. Whatever you have done in the past is forgiven; you start with a clean sheet with me. Help me change things, and together we will give your people a good life. Of course, you could go to the authorities. They probably would not believe you, and if they did, I would definitely have to kill you."

There followed a lengthy discussion around the table. They showed a great reluctance to give up the power they had enjoyed for years. Joel picked up Ernesto's body, dumped it on the table, and said, "Your power has already gone. How many of you do I have to kill before you realize that?" He looked each one in the eyes, until they broke off the eye contact. "I want your help, but I will do it without you. I will pay you a living wage if you join our organization. Who will help? Raise your hand." Slowly one after another the hands went up. "I can see in your eyes that some of you aren't convinced. You think you will get me later, but if you shoot at me the bullet will bounce back and hit you. So I have one more demonstration for you."

Joel told one of them to bring his chair to one end of the room. He gave the man a gun and said, "Shoot me, but hold the chair in front of you when you do." The man grinned, and then with the chair seat covering his chest, he fired the gun at Joel. The force of the bullet hitting the chair made him stagger backwards. Joel took the gun away from the man. "I will be coming to each of your Hoods in the next few days to help you convince the rest of your gang to join us."

The look of defiance in their eyes changed to a look of resignation. They all remained silent for a long time, as Joel stared them down, one by one. Finally one man asked, "What will be our role in the new order?"

"You will support and protect whomever is selected to be the leader in your Hood."

"Can we be the leaders?"

"If you are smart enough, and willing to work hard to develop the skills, yes, you can be the leaders. I will pay for any education you want to get, and if it is business management, you can be a leader."

The questions continued for a while, then, when they finally dried up, Joel said, "I will take each of you back to your own Hood now, but I must blindfold you first." He called Kory and told him to meet him at the Compton airport, wearing the belt. Then, he put four blindfolded men in his Cessna and flew to Compton. There he activated Kory's belt and told him to drive them home. It took four trips to get all the gang members back to Compton. Joel told Kory to meet him back at the Compton airport after he had delivered the last ones home.

He flew back to the compound, loaded Ernesto's body on the Cessna, and dropped it out of the airplane over McGorman Peak in the Kelso Dunes Wilderness Area. He met Kory at the Compton airport. After deactivating Kory's belt, they went for lunch. Over lunch, Kory told him that the incorporation papers had been recorded and a bank account opened. They had completed the work on the upstairs door and Tanisha had started to move in. He said that Tanisha had too much work. Joel called Tanisha and told her to hire an experienced person as temporary help to train some of the Hood people to help her. She agreed to do that. He got the account and routing numbers for the bank account from her, so that he could deposit more money in it.

Chapter Eight

Back at the compound he worked on the transporter until 3 a.m., again making considerable progress. The next morning he arrived in Watts by 8:30, switched on his belt, and spent an hour and a half helping Tanisha before Parson Branch and his friends arrived. She asked, "Can I hire two of my friends to help? They are both very capable—they just need an opportunity."

"You could do anything you want just get the job done. One objective is to hire as many Hood people as you can, starting with those with capabilities, while we trained the rest. I want you to find a replacement for yourself here in Watts. I need you to be my co-coordinator. I will send you to other Hoods to help their leaders get started and make sure they understand our objectives."

When the community leaders arrived, Tanisha and Kory sat in on the meeting. Joel let Parson Branch explain to them the objectives of the Restoration Corporation, nullifying the gangs, training their people, including sending to college those who wanted to go, and finding them jobs. He told them that Joel had sufficient finances to do the same in their Hood. They asked about the Cripps and Kory explained how they fit in as protectors and aides. One man, Clarence Hunter, who ran a soup kitchen in Vernon, seemed to be the most vocal. He said, "Lecarno will not let them do this in their Hood."

Joel said, "I have already talked to Ernesto. He agreed to leave the area and I will have the new gang leader come to you tomorrow, to pledge his support for this activity."

Hunter laughed. "You're wasting our time—that will never happen."

"All I ask," said Joel, "Is when they do come to you, find me the right person to do what Tanisha is doing here. It must be someone from your Hood—it could even be a gang member. We want local people to do most of the work. We will train them and pay them while they learn."

They all expressed concern about the chances of Joel's plan succeeding. Branch got them to agree to find the right person, but said they would not do anything more until the gangs agreed to support the project. The meeting ended and Kory took the men home. Joel went with them, and after they dropped off the last man, he switched on Kory's belt and told him to go to the gang headquarters in Vernon.

Jodam met them at the entrance. "I'm having a hard time convincing them to cooperate. I told them what happened, but they don't believe me; they think I killed Ernesto to take over the gang."

Joel entered the building and the gang surrounded him threateningly. He looked into the eyes of each man one at a time, sizing them up. One man had the cold raw killer look that he had seen in Ernesto's eyes. With a sudden move, he grabbed him by the throat and lifted him off the ground. The rest of the gang closed in on him, pounding at his body. They beat their knuckles raw without making an impression on him. When they tried to pry his fingers away from the man's throat, they could not budge them. One man hit him with a baseball bat, with no effect. Finally, another man pulled out a gun and fired at Joel. The bullet ricocheted and the man went down with a bullet in his shoulder. This had a sobering effect on all of them. They backed off, uncertain what to do.

"Which of you would like me for an enemy?" He walked up to the biggest man in the room. "Would you like me for an enemy? Answer me."

"Nuh-no."

Joel looked around the room. "You all have the same three choices I give everybody. Join me, keep out of our way, or take a one-way plane ride with me out over the ocean. He went back to the man he had been choking. You only have two choices: you leave the southern California area, or you get a one-way plane ride. I'll check back with Jodam in a couple of days and you had better be gone. The rest of you have a chance to start a new life. You'll be starting from scratch; your past will be forgotten. Jodam, if you have any more trouble call Kory—he knows how to get in touch with me. If anything happens to Jodam, you will all suffer."

Joel, Kory, and Jodam went outside. To Jodam, Joel said,"Go see Clarence Hunter, tell him I sent you. You two must work together now. I want you to collaborate on picking me someone to head up the training program for your Hood, preferably a woman. Have her contact Tanisha and we will fund her activities."

As Kory drove Joel back to the Compton airport, he said. "We are going to have trouble with Tye. He's making threats and once he builds up enough courage, there's no telling what he'll do."

"You return to Watts. Keep an eye on Tye. I'll come tomorrow and talk to him." Joel flew to the compound. During the flight he thought about the past few days. He had started some worthwhile projects, but he had killed one man and threatened to kill several more. There had to be a better way.

Back home he strapped himself in the machine, set it at sixty percent, and remained there thinking for two hours. Thinking about a problem while in the machine accelerated his ability to find a solution. Climbing out of the machine, he knew what to do. The few times that Joel had locked minds with people like Ernesto, he sensed that he could influence their thoughts. He would force a conditioned reaction similar to the Pavlovian theories, by putting them in a hypnotic state. He would practice his new approach on Tye tomorrow.

Today he had to work on his transportation system. The first concept Joel had considered followed the principles of the *Star Trek* transporter. He felt he could build the transporter—that was not the problem. Finding enough power to activate it, accurately landing in a three-dimensional space, and getting back to the compound were the problems. The first two he knew he could solve in time, but he would need a transporter everywhere he went, to send him back. Even if he had a transporter in major locations like New York, or Chicago, he would still have to use conventional methods to travel about, once he arrived there.

Joel's next concept consisted of a backpack power unit with a nuclear engine. The powerful engine could project an object weighing about 200 pounds at up to ten thousand miles an hour. Of course a man couldn't survive at these speeds, unless encased in a protective force field. He designed a complex belt that was a three-inch square hollow titanium tube, fitted around his waist. Inside the square tube he packed a nuclear force field generator, a heat reduction unit, and an oxygen generating system. On the outside of the belt at the back he attached a nuclear rocket engine. The belt would generate a force field three inches from his body, protecting him from the elements. It also supplied oxygen and kept him cool, while the rocket engine would propel him to wherever he wanted to go. Joel started work on building his transporter immediately.

The next morning Joel flew to Compton, where Kory met him. "I had Shaun and Rashid take Tye and Rafael to headquarters; we will meet them there," said Kory.

Arriving at the building, Joel told Kory, "You watch Rafael while I talk to Tye upstairs in Tanisha's living room."

When they got there, Tye faced Joel with a belligerent look on his face. They locked eyes and Tye tried to stare Joel down. Gradually Joel got control of Tye's mind until he had him in a hypnotic state.

Joel told Tye, "You have a terrible pain in your stomach. It is so bad you can't stand up."

Tye dropped to his knees, clutching his stomach and moaning in pain. Joel left him that way for about a minute, then said, "The pain has gone away but you will remember how bad it hurt."

Tye stopped moaning, but stayed lying on the floor, still in a hypnotic state.

"Can you hear me?"

Tye nodded.

"Then listen carefully. Everytime you think of harming Tanisha or any of her people, or doing something to impede our project, the bad pains in your stomach will return until those thoughts go away. Do you understand?"

Tye nodded again.

"Stand up."

When Tye stood up, Joel looking deep into his eyes, and said, "You will awaken and not remember anything."

They went down stairs to the meeting room, where Kory and Tanisha stood talking. Tye looked at Tanisha for a while, then, fell to his knees clutching his stomach and moaning. Within a minute he recovered and got back on his feet. Joel took Rafael upstairs and indoctrinated him the same way. Bringing Rafael downstairs he told him and Tye that they could leave. They both looked relieved as they hurried out the door.

Joel then told Kory and Tanisha what he had done. He wanted them to understand what was going on when Tye had dropped to his knees moaning. "I would like to hypnotize both of you in a positive way, so that you each have more confidence in your ability to do what has to be done."

Tanisha said, "I agree if Kory is present while you do it."

Kory said, "That sounds like a good idea. I'll do it if Tanisha is present."

Joel hypnotizes them one at a time. He told them while they were under that they had the ability to do anything they wanted successfully and when they woke up they would be stronger, happier, and more relaxed. Tanisha went back to work in the office and Joel sat talking with Kory.

"What is that recliner in your room upstairs?" said Kory.

"Come on up, and I will show you."

In Joel's room, he had Kory sit in the machine. Looking into his eyes, Joel hypnotized Kory. He placed the headgear over his head, put his feet in the boots, and laid his arms on the armrests. Joel set the machine at thirty percent power for thirty minutes, and watching him carefully for signs of discomfort, talked to him for all of the half hour. Joel talked about his plans for the corporation, where he saw Kory fitting into it, how he could make himself more useful, and what books he should read. He then gave Kory lessons on philosophy, psychology, people management, and financial management. He hoped that hearing all this while in the machine would make a lot of it stick. After he switched the machine off, he took off the headgear, and told Kory he had just sat down in the recliner. He then awakened him. They discussed how comfortable the recliner was and Joel said he would use it to relax when he visited.

They went back downstairs and Kory said he had things to do, so Joel went into the office to talk to Tanisha. He asked her, "Would you like to see my recliner?"

"Yes, I wondered what you used it for." They went upstairs and Joel repeated the same procedure with Tanisha as he had with Kory. He felt if he could give each one of them thirty minutes a week on the machine they would be very valuable assets to him. Joel liked Tanisha; her intelligence and dedication demonstrated a strong character. Maybe after a few sessions on the machine and with them working closely together, this could be the relationship he needed.

The three of them went out for lunch, and Joel got to know both of them a lot better. After lunch Joel asked Kory to drive him to the other Hoods so that he could meet with each of the gangs. With their belts switched on, they set out to make the rounds. At each Hood, Joel met with the same resistance as at Vernon. This time he handled it differently. After showing off his powers to get their attention, he talked to each gang member privately. The real bad asses he used the pain in the stomach treatment on; the wavering ones, he hypnotized to brainwash them into supporting the project; and the ones who showed a willingness to help, he talked to about the opportunities for education and employment. They finished up revisiting Vernon, where he gave that gang the same treatment.

The next stop took them to Parson Branch's church. Joel needed to talk to the parson about contacts in other cities, and he wanted Kory to be in on the conversation. He told Branch, "I need someone in each city to oversee the activities in their jurisdiction, but I don't want them to build a bureaucracy. I want the people in the Hoods to be trained and paid to do all the work."

"I know just the man in Chicago, but I will have to scout around to find the right person in other cities. I'm sure my contacts will find the right people. Give me your email address and I will send you the information as I get it." Joel gave Branch the address.

"Kory, I need you to identify as many gangs as you can in the southern California area; we must reach out to all of them."

"I know most of them. Let me make a list, then I can check it to see how complete it is."

"Make out a plan for you and me to visit all of them."

Joel had Kory take him back to the airport. On the way Joel said, "I wanted you in that meeting because when we get organized in other cities, I want to be able to send you there to check up on how they run things. You should enroll in a correspondence school, and take business classes."

"I've been thinking of going back to school. Maybe correspondence classes are a good way to do it."

Joel spent the next two days working on his transporter. He built a prototype and tested it by flying around the desert at slow speeds. He made modifications to the steering and the air-conditioning. When its performance satisfied him, he climbed to ten thousand feet at a speed of five hundred miles an hour and flew for thirty minutes, in a wide circle, finishing up back over his compound. Encountering zero problems, Joel climbed to sixty thousand feet and traveled east, gradually increased the speed to five thousand miles per hour. He slowed down and descended to see if his navigation system had taken him where he had planned. Below him he saw Flagstaff, exactly where he expected to be. The transporter had taken him two hundred and eighty miles in fifteen minutes. The ascent and decent had taken a lot of that time; at this rate he could travel to New York in less than one hour. Joel knew he would not be picked up on radar an object the size of a man was too small, especially traveling at five thousand miles per hour.

During these two days, Joel received an email from Branch with the name of a contact in Chicago, Brian Jefferson. Branch had called Jefferson, discussed Joel's objectives with him, telling him to expect a visit. Joel called Jefferson and set up an appointment for the next morning. That night at 3 a.m. Joel used the transporter to go to Chicago. Arriving at 7 a.m. Chicago time, he rented an apartment to use as a base of operations. Leaving his transporter there, but wearing the two protective belts, he arrived on time for his 9 o'clock meeting.

Joel introduced himself to Jefferson, and explained how he had recruited the gangs in southern California to help in his education programs. He didn't mention the violent way he had done it.

Jefferson said, "I've been trying to do that here for years, but with inadequate funding and gang resistance, I haven't made much progress."

"If I get the gangs to co-operate and supply the funding, will you work for me as my Chicago area overseer? I don't want to build a large organization. I want the people who live in the Hoods trained to do what needs to be done, and get paid for it."

"You won't be safe in the Hoods, and they won't listen to you."

"Let me worry about that. Do you know a gang leader who is ready to leave the gang life?"

Jefferson thought for a while. "There is one man, Javis Diaz. We talked once about how the gangs could be used as a force for good, but he is too afraid to make the break."

"Could you arrange a meeting with him for me?"

"When and where?"

"Here and now."

"Let me try his cell phone." Jefferson dialed a number and waited a few seconds. "Hi, Javis, can you talk?" After a short pause. "I have a man here who wants to talk to you. I think he's worth listening to. He has money he wants to spend helping people." He listened for a while. "Okay, my place in one hour. See you then." Jefferson closed his cell phone. "He's coming. I hope you are for real. If you're not, I will lose a lot of credibility."

"Don't worry, you will be happy with what is about to happen. One thing, though, when he gets here I want to talk to him alone. Do you have a room we can use?"

"Now, wait a minute, what do you want to say to him that I can't hear?"

"I'm going to convince him to take me into the Hood. You introduce us, then leave. I don't want you coming to the Hood with us. As you said, it's too dangerous. Once I've convinced the gangs to help us, you can go into the Hoods safely."

"I thought I was going to be a partner in this?"

"You will be once I have defanged the gangs. Until then, it's better to keep you out of it, in case I fail. Then there will be no fallout on you." Jefferson saw the sense in this, so he showed Joel to a conference room and they sat there talking until Javis arrived.

Chapter Nine

Brian Jefferson first opened his eyes with a silver spoon firmly planted in his mouth. His father, the CEO of a billion dollar corporation, finally had the son he desired after having three daughters. His mother, who came from old money, shared her husband's delight. Brian benefited from every possible advantage they could think of. They enrolled him in Yale, his father's alma mater, at birth, and he went to the best private schools.

He did nothing to disappoint them. His grades put him in the top ten percent of his class, and he participated in all sports. In fact, his love of sports caused him great frustration because his abilities failed to reach up to his ambitions. At football he wanted to play quarterback, but he got no playing time behind two better than he was. He switched to wide receiver, but still didn't start, but at least got to play.

Graduating from college with a masters degree in business, he went to work for his father, in the human relations department. Brian chose this assignment himself because he liked to work with people. In spite of his indoctrination into a position of wealth and power, Brian did not like the cutthroat pursuit of profit. In company conflicts, he found himself siding with the workers.

Brian knew he differed from his peers. For all his intelligence and education, he found himself mentally arguing against their assumption of superiority and lack of social conscience. After being rebuffed for expressing his opinions, he learned to keep these thoughts to himself.

A local charity, soliciting for an organization trying to feed Chicago's homeless, requested a contribution from his company. He father objected to the amount he gave to them and a heated argument ensued.

Brian decided to go to work for the charity as a fund solicitor. His father refused to grant him an allowance, but Brian had a trust left to him by his maternal grandmother that gave him $50,000 a year. By reducing his standard of living, he managed to make this suffice. His success with the charity gave him the fulfillment his life needed. The doors of many wealthy people opened for him because of his social standing.

Jefferson discussed his organization with Joel. He solicited funding for people who ran ten soup kitchens throughout the city, with a counseling room attached to each. They would have to close two in a month for lack of funds.

"How many counselors do you have and who are you counseling?"

"We have five counselors, who give me two days a week free, so each facility gets a counselor for eight hours a week. The clients include street people, prostitutes, and just plain poor people."

"The three groups we must help. What's making you close two soup kitchens?"

"I can't afford the rent."

"How much a month is the rent on all ten kitchens?"

"Fifteen thousand dollars."

"How much would you have to pay a councelor to get more?"

"Thirty dollars an hour."

"I'll write you a check for thirty thousand dollars. Find five more councelors, have one at each kitchen for forty hours a week. This check will cover the rent and councelors for one month. When we are organized here I will pay those bills every month, until they are no longer needed." Joel wrote the check and handed it to Jefferson.

"Are you for real?"

"You'll find that out when the check clears."

When Javis Diaz arrived, Jefferson introduced them and left the room.

Left alone, the two men sized one another up. Joel looked deep into Javis eyes. He didn't see the hatred and anger of an Ernesto; instead, he saw resignation and disappointment. "What do you want from me?" asked Javis.

Joel answered him in Spanish, "I want to change your life, and make you a force for good, instead of evil."

"You want to get me killed, that's what you want."

"Take me back to your gang's home base, as your prisoner, and I will convince them to support our program."

"And what is your program?"

"To train, educate, and get jobs for all the unfortunate people out there —but only those that want to be trained. Anybody who wants to be left alone, we leave alone, as long as they don't interfere with us."

"You're crazy! I will just get you killed."

"Look into my eyes; you'll see I'm serious." They locked eyes and Joel slowly got control of Javis's mind, putting him in a trance. "You will take me to your gang, and when I convince them to help, you will support the program with all your heart and mind."

They said goodbye to Jefferson as they left, and Javis drove them to a rundown part of town, where all the advertising was in Spanish. Joel asked, "How many members are there in your gang?"

"Ten core members and about eight hangars on."

"I want all the core members there when I talk to them. I don't want to go through his twice."

"Jose is the one you have to convince, I'll make sure he is there. He's been trying to oust me for the last six months."

"Do you control all the drug sales in your Barrio?"

Joel could see the Javis struggled with this question. "Are you a narc?"

"No, but I am going to eliminate all the illegal drugs in Chicago."

"You are a dreamer. The Mob will eat you up for breakfast."

"Tell me the highest level Mob member you know and I will deal with him. After we finish with your gang, you will be a believer."

"His name is Paolo Di Canio. He controls all the drugs in Chicago."

"Give me his address and I will pay him a visit." Javis thought this man was loco, but he gave him the address anyway.

They stopped in front of a building with a marquee that read, "Puerto Rican Social Club," and went in. A large dance hall filled the downstairs, with a bar at one end and a stage at the other end. Upstairs over the bar they entered a large club room. Ten young men sat around, talking and drinking. They all wore at least one article of yellow clothing.

One man, of average build, wearing baggy, oversized pants hanging low on his hips and a yellow sweatshirt, approached them. He stared at them with piercing black eyes; Joel could see the hatred boiling over out of them. "What have you got for us now, Javis?"

"Hi Jose. I found this gringo outside. He says he wants to convert us."

"I want you to help..." Joel go no further; Jose backhanded him across the face, as hard as he could. "Yeowl!" yelled Jose, clutching his broken knuckles.

"You shouldn't have done that. Let me finish what I was saying." Jose pulled out a knife with his left hand and tried to jamb it into Joel's stomach. The knife snapped into two pieces.

"Kill him! Kill him!" yelled Jose. Joel switched on the electrical field on the outer surface of his suit as the gang members crowded in on him. They backed away quickly as they received a shock. One man pulled a gun.

"Before you fire that, I must warn you. The bullet will bounce back and hit you." The man hesitated.

"Shoot him, Jesus," shouted Jose.

"Why not hold a chair in front of you to be safe?" Jesus didn't know what to do.

"Shoot him, shoot him," repeated Jose. Jesus picked up a chair and, holding it with the seat protecting his chest, fired at Joel. The bullet ricocheted, hit the chair, and made Jesus stagger backwards. Jose pulled out his own gun, fired at Joel, and fell to the floor clutching his bleeding shoulder.

After that, Joel repeated the process he had used in Los Angeles. He talked to each man one on one, in a separate room, hypnotizing each one. The bad cases he gave the stomach pain treatment, the good ones he recruited for the program.

Over the next few days, with Javis wearing the second belt, they visited all the gangs in the Chicago area. Using the same tactics, Joel got them all to agree to support the program. His method worked, because he talked to them in a language they understood: violence. Then, after he hypnotized them, he held out the carrot of a better life. He could not achieve his goals by being Gary-Good-Guy.

When they finished, Joel retrieved the spare belt and Javis dropped him off at Jefferson's office. The check he had given Jefferson had cleared. Brian said, "I guess you are for real. I'll support you anyway I can." Joel asked him to look for a person in each district to lead its own education program. "We just need an intelligent person we can train. Get somebody from the Hood. They will have the people's trust."

Jefferson said, "The men who run the soup kitchens know all the local people. They will find us the right person."

"I also need a person like you in all the big cities. Can you make me a list of anyone you know who could help us?" Jefferson agreed to do this.

From Jefferson's office, Joel took a taxi to the Blackstone Hotel, on the corner of Michigan Avenue and Balboa Street, the address Javis had given him for Paolo Di Canio. He maintained a suite of rooms at the penthouse on the twenty-first floor. Joel decided he would use a frontal attack. Getting off the elevator, He found himself in a small foyer, about 20-feet square. He could see three doors, one on either side and one straight ahead. The one in front of him had Di Canio's name on the door.

He knocked on the door. The man who opened it stood 6'6" tall and weighed 250 pounds. He wore a dark blue suit and tie, with a red hand-kerchief in the breast pocket. Joel hit him hard in the chest with his shoulder, sending him sprawling in the entryway, and closed the door behind him. The man came to his feet quickly, but Joel hit him once on the chin, flooring him again. This time he stayed down immobile.

Two more men appeared in a doorway to the left. The first also wore a suit and tie. The other man wore a dress shirt, but no tie or jacket. Joel guessed he was Di Canio. The leading man pulled a gun from a shoulder holster and fire at Joel. The bullet ricocheted; hit the gunman in the heart, killing him instantly. Di Canio picked up the gun and pointed it at Joel.

"Don't shoot, Paolo," said Joel. "You saw what happened to your friend." Paolo hesitated.

"If you must shoot, please use a chair to protect your chest. I don't want you dead."

Paolo backed up carefully, keeping the gun trained on Joel, who followed him slowly. He backed through a door to the right, which led them into a dining room. "Are you wearing a bulletproof vest? I will shoot you in the head."

"A bulletproof vest would not make the bullet rebound. If you shoot me in the head, the bullet will hit you in the head." Paolo picked up a chair, held it low in front of his upper legs, and shot Joel in the thigh. The bullet ricocheted; it hit the chair so hard that Paolo dropped it. Joel advanced until he stood face to face with his adversary. Paolo reversed the gun in his hand and hit Joel hard across the head. The force of the blow knocked the gun out of Paolo's hand.

Joel looked deep into Paolo's eyes. He saw fear, confusion, and venom. He fought for control of Paolo's mind. He resisted with a great effort, but Joel's mind won the battle. Gradually, he put Paolo into a trance. "Do you have any drugs in the apartment?"

Paolo made one last effort to resist and lost. "Yes."

"Take me to them." He followed Paolo back through the entry, into the living room, across to a hallway with four doors, two to the left and two to the right. The first door to the right led to an office containing a safe. "Open the safe."

Paolo obeyed. Inside Joel found twenty small packets of heroin. He made Paolo take them to the bathroom and flush their contents down the toilet.

Returning to the office, he examined the other contents of the safe. He found financial ledgers with records of drug transactions, a bank book for a bank account in the Cayman Islands, and $100,000 in $100 bills. The ledgers had information on the sources of Di Canio's drugs. Some came from Mexico and the rest from Afghanistan. Joel tore the two pages out of the ledger and put them in his pocket. He saw a briefcase sitting on a chair; he emptied its contents on the floor and put the cash in it. Sitting at the desk, he called the offshore bank. The account had $157,000,000 and change in it. He transferred $157,000,000 to his own offshore account. He now had $200,000,000 in that account.

Turning his attention back to Paolo, Joel looked deeply into his eyes and made him feel the terrible pains in his stomach. Paolo fell to his knees in agony. Joel said, "Everytime you want to harm somebody, everytime you want to deal in illegal drugs, everytime you want to break the law, you will feel these terrible pains in your stomach. The pains will be so bad you will be unable to do anything until your evil thoughts go away. Now you will drive me to where you keep the rest of your drug supply."

Returning to the entryway, Joel revived the other bodyguard, hypnotized him, and gave him the same stomach pain treatment. The three of them left the apartment. Down in the lobby Di Canio ordered his limousine brought to the front entrance and with the bodyguard driving, they headed to the South Side of Chicago. South of 99th Street they came to Little Village, in South Lawndale. Joel recognized this as the Barrio where Javis had taken him the first day. They stopped in front of an ordinary-looking house. The three of them entered the house, and Joel found men and women in each of the three bedrooms, taking kilo bags of heroin, thinning them with flour, and making small packets like the ones Paolo had in his safe. Each room had two guards watching the Latinos package the heroin.

Joel told Paolo to have all the Latinos go home and the guards to go into the living room. One of the guards started to protest, but Paolo shut him up, and everybody obeyed him. Joel then took the guards one at a time into a bedroom, gave them the stomach pain treatment, and told them to leave. He found a suitcase in one room with the unopened bags of heroin in it. He had the bodyguard put the rest of the heroin in the suitcase and carry it out to the car. They drove back to the Blackstone Hotel. Still seated in the car, Joel told them they would remember everything that happened, except why they got the stomach pains. He told Paolo that he had agreed to loan Joel his limousine. He released them from their trances and they all exited the car. Joel got behind the wheel and drove away.

He left the car three blocks from his apartment. Back in his bedroom, he opened the suitcase, emptied all the bags so that the suitcase contained loose heroin, and then closed it. He put on the transporter belt, balanced the $100 bills on the top surface of the three-inch wide belt, and turned it on. Picking up the suitcase of heroin, he walked up the stairs to the roof of the building. Starting the engine he ascended to five thousand feet, cruised east to the center of Lake Michigan and descended to one thousand feet. Opening the suitcase, he spread all the powder over the surface of Lake Michigan, and dropped the suitcase. Ascending rapidly to sixty thousand feet, he headed west for California.

Back at his compound, Joel laid in the machine for two hours, planning his next move. He decided to visit the Ramirez family in Colombia. But first he transported to Watts to check on their progress. He stored the transporter in his room at the headquarters. In a meeting with Kory and Tanisha, Joel brought them up to date on the events in Chicago. He arranged for Kory to fly to Chicago the next day to meet with the gang leaders. Kory would show them how they could support their objectives. Tanisha would go to Chicago as soon as Jefferson had a list of team leaders for each Hood. She would help them set up programs similar those in Watts.

They briefed him on their progress so far. Tywanna has been accepted at UCLA for the next semester, Tanisha had enrolled at El Camino Community College for a business administration course, and Kory had started a correspondence course. One hundred and five people requested help to qualify for college. Forty-seven looked qualified; for the rest Tywanna had set up pre-requisite classes. They had completed the fumigation of all the Richardson Gardens buildings, and they planned to fumigate other houses as people requested this service. They had contracts with teachers for trade school classes, and classes in plumbing, auto repair, and carpentry starting the following Monday. Tanisha had contacted three large employers in the Los Angeles area to get people in their training programs, offering to pay half of their wages. Things seem to be really humming.

After the meeting Joel took, first Tanisha, then Kory, up to his room for a session on the machine. He would hypnotize them first, then plant suggestions about how they can improve themselves. He also gave them some of his knowledge to help in their work. The benefits they got from the machine showed in their increased performance and maturity. He had decided to assemble one machine in each major city and use it to improve the key people in his program, thereby benefiting much of the population.

Chapter Ten

oel continued his sessions on the machine. His head filled with ideas way ahead of the current level of technology. One idea in particular fascinated him. He really needed to be able to enter places occupied by innocent people without detection or harming them. He needed to be invisible.

The eye sees by light hitting an object and reflecting back into the eye. The eye can only pick up wavelengths in the 400- to 700-nanometer range. If he could add an ability to his protection suit, to absorb all light rays in this range, he would be invisible. He worked on this project at night.

Brian Jefferson, from Chicago, had emailed him the names of community activists in six other cities: New York, St Louis, Boston, Miami, Kansas City, and Oakland. Over the next two weeks, he spent three days in each city setting up local organizations paralleling those in Los Angeles and Chicago.

Once he had control of the gangs and had the leaders in place, Joel would find a suitable building in the ghetto or Barrio and buy it for the corporation. The building had to have multiple rooms, like a small apartment block or office complex. He would relocate the occupants by offering them two months' free rent in a similar facility. Then he would instruct the leaders to rehabilitate the property to meet their needs.

One requirement would be a bedroom for him to use when he visited. In this room he would construct another age-retarding recliner/machine for giving the selected leaders sessions to enhance their capabilities. Joel would hypnotize them, place them in the machine, and while their abilities were being improved, plant ideas in their heads about how to manage their piece of the corporation. This ensured the success of his project. Joel also would do spot checks from time to time and root out anyone trying to use the program for their own benefit.

He asked Kory, Tanisha, and Jefferson to find replacements for themselves, and then assigned them as coordinators. Kory would visit the ex-gang leaders to find out if they had any problems, Tanisha would do the same with the corporate leaders in each Hood, while Jefferson's made sure the money was spent wisely.

Kory reflected on the changes in his life since meeting Joel. He liked his new position in the organization. He felt a lot better about himself. He now performed positive and constructive tasks instead of negative and destructive ones. The talks with Joel in his room helped him a lot. He always seemed to be revived and more confident after each session.

The travelling to other cities appealed to him; he had always wanted to travel. He and Tanisha had agreed to travel together, for company and support. They talked a lot about how their lives had improved; she also felt so much better after her talks with Joel in his room. Kory found her very intelligent and attractive. He had known many women, but none seriously. What could he offer a woman? He didn't want the one-sided relationships of a gang member, where the woman obeyed submissively. He wanted a partnership with a woman he could talk to and plan their future together. With Tanisha he could have that kind of relationship, even though she was four years older than him.

On their third trip, three nights in San Francisco, they ate at a restaurant on the Embarcadero that had a small dance floor. After dinner and a bottle of wine, Kory asked Tanisha to dance. While holding her in his arms, he told her of his feelings for her, expecting to be rejected. To his surprise, she confessed that she had become very attracted to him. From then on their relationship developed into a romantic fairy tale, making them both happier than they ever thought they could be. They were both concerned about Joel's reaction to their romance, and after much discussion decided to be upfront and just tell him.

Three weeks after their wonderful night in San Francisco, when Joel made his weekly visit to Watts, they took him into the office and told him. Joel remained silent for about a minute while he struggled with his emotions. At first he felt anger, which he hoped didn't show on his face, as he overcame it. Next, he felt disappointment at the opportunity he had been too busy to pursue. Finally, there was joy as he saw the happiness in their faces. He forced a big smile to spread across his face, and he hugged them both in congratulations. "We won't get married for at least a year, but we thought you ought to know."

"Have you told Arnell?"

"Yes, he is delighted; he has worshiped Kory for years."

"You must have an engagement party here to announce it to all your friends!"

Later Joel thought about his reactions to their news. Maybe he hadn't lost his humanity; he could have vented his anger and lost two very good friends.

Chapter Eleven

Joel had long wanted to address the area of abuse. Spousal abuse, child abuse, sexual abuse, bullying, but especially pedophiles. Once again he would be addressing a huge problem and could probably only make a small dent in it, but anything he could do was worth the effort. He arranged a meeting with Tanisha and Kory; he needed to find someone to lead this effort. They would start a major advertising campaign to find abused people, then set up hotlines in each major population area to take the calls. He asked Tanisha to contact her counterpart in each city and ask each to identify one person in their organization with the ability to manage a program like this. Tanisha had shown a tremendous increase in capability, partially from the sessions on the machine and partly from her inherent ability. He looked upon her as his strong right hand.

"Arrange to fly the candidates to Los Angeles for a briefing on the program. While they attend the briefing, I will interview each and pick the best one to manage the overall program. The rest, if capable, will handle the activities in their own city. If the volume is large enough, they can hire people and set up boiler rooms to take the calls."

Two days later Tanisha called. "I've obtained rooms for all fifty people coming at the Hyatt airport hotel and rented a meeting room for tomorrow.

Joel asked, "Will you attend—can you spare the time?"

"Yes, I will help in any way I can. I feel this is a great project."

"Please get me a large suite, with a room for people to wait and a room for interviews, and schedule the candidates to come to this suite in five-minute intervals, starting at 7:30. You can talk to the next person in the waiting room while I am interviewing. We'll start the meeting at 2. Tell everybody they will be staying an extra day, and arrange for a bus to take them to Disneyland."

At 7:30 the next morning, the first candidate knocked on the door of his suite and Joel began the interviews. The young African American, who looked to be in his late twenties, wore a low-priced but neat suit and a tie. He looked very uncomfortable. Joel looked deep into the man's mind and evaluated him from the inside. He found a mind eager to learn, anxious to please, and ready to work hard to achieve both goals. While controlling his mind, Joel told the man to relax and be confident in his abilities. This took about three minutes, then he asked the man a few questions about himself.

Joel repeated this process fifty times until he had met with all the candidates. Half of them seemed capable of managing the project, but one young lady, Lisa Wilkins, stood out from all the rest. She hailed from New York, had a keen mind, and was determined to succeed. Two candidates, Nathan Hunter and Darlene Williams, seemed to lack the intelligence and drive, to even run their own district activities, but he didn't want to give up on them just yet.

At the 2 o'clock meeting, with Tanisha on the podium with him, Joel addressed the fifty young people. He told them, "The objective of the program is to find people who are being subjected to abuse, any kind of abuse. You will be in charge of activities in your district. There will be an overall manager to help and advise you, and you can also get help from the person who selected you for this job and from Tanisha, who you met this morning. The manager will contract with an advertising agency, and you will be given ads to place in newspapers and on billboards, asking people in trouble to call the abuse hotline. You will be answering the phones yourself; if the volume of calls gets high enough, you will be able to hire somebody to help you.

"Your objective is to get their name and address so that I can visit them. We will not give anybody money—that is not our intention. We will make lists of all the people calling, and I will take it from there. We can work with any other local agencies, such as abuse shelters and hotlines. It doesn't matter how we find the abused, as long as we find them. Are there any questions?"

"What are you going to do with the lists?"

"I will make sure the abuse stops."

"How will you do that?"

"I won't tell you that, except that it will be legal, and will not get you into trouble."

"When do we start?"

"The day after tomorrow, I'm sending you all to Disneyland tomorrow, complements of the Corporation. There will be a bus outside the hotel at 9 tomorrow—don't miss it. Now, everybody enjoy this evening and the trip tomorrow. You can all leave now, except Lisa Wilkins, Nathan Hunter, and Darlene Williams. Would you three stay behind."

As everybody filed out of the meeting room, Joel took Tanisha aside. "Lisa is the one I have selected to manage the program, reporting to you. What did you think of her?"

"An outstanding choice; she impressed me."

"The other two are marginal for the district leader position, so I want to talk to them some more. Would you please drive all three to Watts and I will meet you there?"

"Sure, I'll see you there."

Joel had spent half an hour with Kory getting up to speed on the program when Tanisha arrived back at headquarters. He left Nathan and Darlene with Tanisha and took Lisa up to his sitting room. There he offered her the position as manager. She took the news very calmly, thanked him for his confidence in her, and stated that she would do a good job for him. Joel then hypnotized her and had her sit in the machine for half an hour while he outlined all he wanted her to do. He could see the improvement she obtained from just half an hour in the machine, and vowed to give her more time when he visited her district.

Next, Joel brought Nathan up to his room. He wasted no time hypnotizing him and getting him in the machine. He gave Nathan a full hour, talking to him all the time. The improvement was substantial, and brought him up to an acceptable level. Joel repeated this process with Darlene, with the same result. He had Tanisha arrange for someone to drive them back to the hotel.

Joel gave some thought to the question he had been asked: "How will you stop the abuse?" He worked out a scenario in his mind and it went like this. Joel waits until the abuser is at home, then knocks on the door. He takes control of the mind of the person opening the door, and has that person invite him into the house. If it is the abused, he calms the person down and assures that person that he or she will never be abused again. If it is neither the abuser nor the abused, he will have the door opener take him to the abuser. Once in the presence of the abuser, Joel will hypnotize the person deeply, then tell that person if he or she ever thinks of abusing anyone again he or she will suffer sever stomach pains. He then tells the abused what he has done, so the abused understands what is going on.

Joel used this approach many times in the following months. The success of the hotlines exceeded expectations. The newspaper ads and billboards brought a lot of calls. With some it took two or three calls before the caller would give his or her name and address—and some never did.

He started out spending two days a week visiting the people on the lists provided him by his hotline teams. In one day he could handle at least thirty visits, especially if they were all in one city. At first there weren't that many, but after a month he had to increase it to three days a week. Most came from the big cities, but a surprising number came from rural areas. After four months the volume tapered off, and he went back to two days a week, then one day a week.

The other area of abuse he tackled was the pedophiles. He asked each district to obtain the list of registered pedophiles. There are over 370,000 names on the registered sexual predators database; if he visited fifty a day it would take over twenty years to see them all. Some of their offenses were as mild as Peeping Toms, so Joel had his people evaluate them and pick the worse for him to visit. With all the other things he had ongoing, this was the best he could do.

After sending the three candidates back to the hotel, Joel transported back to his compound.

Chapter Twelve

The next day Joel traveled to each city in his project, checking status and giving time on the machine to key individuals. He left at 5 a.m. to be on the East Coast before 8, and worked his way westward, ending in Watts. From there he headed home, arriving at about 3 p.m. When Joel descended to hover above his compound, he could see six police cars at his front gate. There were police officers trying to walk between his wall and the force field. Beside the gate, a hole had been blown in the wall.

Brian Hallows watched the object hovering above the desert enclave. He had been trying to locate Joel Sampson since their encounter in San Diego, but his heart wasn't in it. He knew Joel had gone out of his way not to hurt them, so he wasn't the usual thug. He had worked the duct tape off his mouth using the refrigerator door hinge, and after a few minutes of shouting, Joel's neighbor had uncuffed them, so the embarrassment was minimal. Besides, anyone who went after both Carlos and Diego Ramirez had a death wish; to still be living, he must be something special.

He knew Joel had flown out of Lindberg Field, but never arrived in San Francisco. He'd disappeared off the radar screen somewhere near Barstow. Then, when the Beverly Hills Police had called saying Diego Ramirez had filed a report claiming Joel had cut off his finger, Brian knew he had to get serious. He searched Joel's bank account and found that he had purchased land near Barstow, and then found the contractor who built the house on it.

Brian had tried to land on the airfield in a helicopter, only to encounter an obstruction covering it. When they drove up to the gate and tried to push it in, they found the obstruction impenetrable. They climbed over the wall, but still couldn't get in. They exploded three sticks of dynamite between the wall and the obstruction; this only blew a hole in the wall.

Brian had kicked the problem upstairs, and a high-level meeting had been called between the San Diego Police, the Beverly Hills Police, and the San Bernardino Sheriff's office. He had been waiting for two hours. He had never liked the desert, the heat, and the sand. A twenty-knot wind blew steadily, getting sand into everything, the car, his clothes, and especially his shoes. He couldn't wait to get back to San Diego and a cool ocean breeze.

The hovering object started to descend slowly, then suddenly all the officers between the wall and the obstruction jumped over the wall at the same time, and the object landed in front of the house.

Joel had surveyed the scene around his compound. Before he could land, he had to get the police off the force field. He switched on the electrical charge on the outside of the force field and all the police jumped back over the wall. He switched off the force field, landed, and switched the force field back on.

Joel walked up to the gate. He could see Brian Hallows on the other side. Brian held up a piece of paper with a phone number on it. Joel took out his cell phone and called the number. Brian answered.

"Unblock the gate and let us in."

"Why should I?"

"I have a warrant for your arrest."

"That's a reason for me not to open the gate."

"We will blast our way in and someone will get hurt."

"Go ahead. If you could, you would have done it by now."

"Let me come in alone and talk to you."

"Give your partner your gun, and have everybody back up one hundred yards, and I will let you in alone."

Brian held the phone down against his leg, and Joel could see him arguing with his partner. Finally, Jack took Brian's gun, and all the vehicles backed up a hundred yards. Brian walked up to the force field until he could touch it.

"Pull up your pants legs," said Joel

"Why?"

"I want to see if you have a back-up gun." Brian obeyed. "Now turn around—good you're clean. When I say 'now,' you have three seconds to walk in through the gate." Joel used his mind to turn off the force field. "Now." Brian walked in and Joel switched the force field back on.

Brian turned around and banged his fist on the force field. "How did you do that? I didn't see you touch anything."

"Maybe one day I'll tell you, but right now we have business to discuss. Let's walk up to the house."

"I'd rather talk right here."

"We need to go to the house; I have things to show you. I promise I won't harm you. I won't attack you, but if you attack me I'll defend myself."

Brian followed Joel into the house; he tensed when Joel picked up a baseball bat and a gun. Joel handed the bat to Brian and said, "Let's go out back"

"What's the gun for?"

"I'll show you; follow me."

Outside Joel gave Brian the unloaded gun, then said, "Hit me with the bat."

"I will not—you looking for a police brutality plea?"

Joel laughed. "Do you remember when Jack hit me with the handcuffs? Start lightly, then hit me harder."

Brian suddenly understood; he hit Joel lightly over the head. Then he hit him again harder. Finally, Brian hit Joel so hard he could feel the bat vibrate in his hands. "You're wearing some kind of protection."

Joel led Brian to the barricade he had built to shoot at the mannequin and gave him bullets for the gun. Walking ten feet in front of the barricade, he said, "Shoot me."

"I will not."

Joel held his left hand out to the side. "Please shoot at my hand, but stand well behind the barricade."

Reluctantly, Brian pointed the gun through the small hole, and fired at Joel's hand. The bullet ricocheted and buried itself in the wooden barrier.

"Now shoot at my heart." Brian did so, with the same result. "I needed to give you this demonstration so that you might understand my powers. You must keep your officers under control so that no one gets hurt."

"Who are you? Did you come from another planet?"

"No!" Joel said with a laugh. "I have just developed advanced technology. I will not harm any decent people like yourself, but I do intend to harm a lot of unsavory characters. Right now I intend to stop the flow of drugs into America. I read from your thoughts that there is a meeting going on in the San Bernardino's Sheriff's office, right now. I need to go there and talk to them. First, I will let you out of the gate."

Joel and Brian walked over to the gate. Brian called Jack and had him move everybody back again. Joel switched off the force field and let Brian out. As Brian walked out, Joel activated his transporter, climbed to a hundred feet, then closed the dome over the compound.

Heading a little west of due south, Joel arrived at the sheriff's headquarters in fifteen minutes. The building was easy to find; it had sheriff cruisers parked all around it. He landed in the back parking lot. A man in his forties got out of his car and approached him. Before he could ask questions, Joel took control of his mind. His thoughts informed Joel that he had been called in on his day off to attend a meeting about some guy in the desert. It had taken two hours to assemble the attendees, including the police chiefs of San Diego and Beverly Hills. As a lieutenant in charge of the SWAT team, his expertise fit their requirements.

Joel told him to take him to the meeting and, if asked, to introduce him as his counterpart from San Diego. They entered the building through the back door, climbed the stairs to the third floor, and entered a large corner conference room. Eight men sat at one end of a table big enough for twenty people. The San Bernardino sheriff sitting at the head of the table said, "Ah, John, there you are. I'm sorry to spoil your day off. Who's that with you?"

Before anyone could say another word, Joel took control of the minds of all nine people in the room. Seven of them had clear consciences, but two, one from San Diego and one from Beverly Hills, supplied information to the Ramirez brothers. He penetrated these two minds and told them that from now on they would perform their jobs diligently and any thoughts of helping criminals would cause severe stomach pains.

Joel told the nine law enforcement officials that he came from Washington to inform them that the compound belonged to the CIA. They had a covert operation in process, to reduce the amount of drugs coming into the United States. They would no longer tolerate the Ramirez brothers and their counterparts in other cities; they would be closed down. Joel must be left alone to do his assignment. Their activity in the desert must be discontinued immediately.

Joel transported back to his compound; all the police cars had disappeared.

PART FIVE

OTHER
COUNTRIES

Chapter One

nce back at his compound, Joel spent two hours in the machine, at seventy percent power. His mental capabilities had increased at a prolific rate. He could now get control of people's minds, so that they would do and say the thoughts he placed in their heads. He used this, along with the stomach pain punishment, to convert evil people to supporters of his objectives. He could also make them think of subjects he wanted information on, and therefore obtain all they knew. He decided he would use this ability to evaluate if a person was good or bad. If good, he would not penetrate any deeper into their personal thoughts.

He needed to prepare for his trip to Colombia. He decided to add a weapon to the transporter. He had developed a laser gun that could cut through any obstacle. He attached it to the top of the transporter belt so that it folded up against his chest. He also developed a fanny pack type of belt made out of titanium that fitted around the outside of the protection suit, but inside the transporter. He would use this to carry items like his checkbook.

Joel researched all the information he could find on Colombia, using the Internet and the library. He obtained maps of the Department of Valle del Cauca and the cities he expected to visit. He located the two addresses he obtained from Diego Ramirez on the maps: the first a city residence in

Cali, the second a county estate in the Upper Cauca Valley. He committed to memory all streets around the city address and all terrain around the rural address.

He found that the Ramirez brothers belonged to the Norte Del Valle Cartel, headed by Leon Montoyo and Juan Carlos Ramirez. They had started making cocaine from the coca plant, imported from Peru and Bolivia, then graduated to growing opium poppies and cannabis. When Peru and Bolivia started their coca eradication programs, the Cartel started growing its own coca plants.

The time had arrived for his quest to Colombia. At 8 a.m. on Monday morning, Joel put on the transporter, switched on the belt, started the engine, and ascended to sixty thousand feet. He set a course due south southeast for Cali, Valle Del Cauca, Colombia. The distance of thirty-five hundred miles took him one hour. As Valle Del Cauca is in the same time zone as New York, he arrived at noon, local time, and hovered above the City of Cali at an altitude of five hundred feet, reconnoitering the area. Locating the luxury condominium building Leon Montoyo lived in, he noted it had a flat roof, on which he landed gently. Joel switched off the transporter belt and switched on the protection belt, enabling him to use his hands. The transporter now looked like a personalized backpack.

Entering the stairwell, Joel descended to Montoyo's floor. The man answering the doorbell turned out to be a live-in servant, taking care of the home while the occupants visited their country estate. Joel returned to the roof, reactivated his transporter, and headed for the Upper Cauca Valley. Following the Cauca River, he found the small native village of Chibcha in the foothills of the Western Cordillera range of the Andes. The villagers are a mixture of mainly Mestizos, some Malattoes, and a few Chibchas Indians. Two miles past the village he spotted Montoyo's villa perched on a giant ledge protruding out of the side of the mountain, 200 feet above the river. In the valley below he saw a small airfield, with one landing strip, and a small hangar. It reminded him of his own airfield. In contrast to the unkempt dirt tracks leading from the village, the road from the airfield to the villa resembled a four-lane city highway, a monument to Montoyo's wealthy status.

Joel hovered 500 feet above the villa. The rectangular estate covered approximately two acres, with an 8-foot high wall surrounding it. The two-storey villa rested against the mountain and curved in an eighth of a circle arc,100-feet long and 40-foot wide, with the main entrance in the center. The gate in the wall opened at the left side of the property and the driveway circled around a large water fountain 40 feet from the front door. To the right, the ground terraced down to a recreation area. Joel could see a lap pool, a swimming pool, a tennis court, and a Jacuzzi. The far right corner of the wall had a tower resembling the guard tower of a prison. He could see two men and a machine gun in the tower, but the gun pointed outwards at the road coming up the mountain.

He landed in the driveway just outside the front door, switched off the transporter, but left the protection belt on. Two guards, who had been patrolling the grounds, ran up to him with guns drawn, as he rang the door bell. The man who opened the door, looked like the Major Domo. The two guards both started explaining that the gringo had dropped out of the sky. Joel said in Spanish, "I wish to see Leon Montoyo."

A voice behind the Major Domo said, "Who is it, Pedro?" Diego Ramirez appeared in view. "You!" he exclaimed in surprise. "I told them you were coming. Now they will believe me. Bring him in." A man prodded Joel with a gun and he entered large foyer. He could see a hallway leading down to the left and gigantic double doors to the right. Beyond them on either side, wide circular staircases curved up to the second floor, meeting in the middle.

They led him through the double doors into a living area that would be insulted to be called a living room. To his left stood a wall of glass that looked down the mountain, across the river, and over the endless valley below. The right side opened into the kitchen, dining room, and bar. At the far end, half of another wall of glass opened to allow access to a decorative patio overlooking the recreation area. All the people on the patio turned to look at him. The two elderly men he surmised were Leon and Juan Carlos, the two elderly ladies their wives. He recognized Carlos Junior, but the other two men and four women he did not know. One of the woman, attracted his attention; her beauty filled the room in a kind and gentle way.

"This is the gringo I told you about," said Diego

"That's him, Leon," said Carlos, coming to his feet.

"You have the audacity to come here. Now you are my prisoner; you will pay for what you did," said Leon.

"You have it wrong," said Joel. "You are all my prisoners." The guard behind him hit him on the back of the head with the butt of his Uzi. The blow had no effect on Joel. He turned, snatched the Uzi from the man, bent it across his knee, and threw it over the terraced hill into the pool.

"Kill him!" screamed Leon.

"No!" shouted Diego. But the second guard ignored him and fired the other Uzi. The bullets ricocheted off Joel, killing the guard and shattering the plate glass sliding door behind him. The gunfire brought three more armed guards running onto the patio, with their guns aimed at Joel.

"Don't shoot!" yelled Diego.

"No! Tie him to a chair," said Leon. The three guards converged on Joel, two grabbing his arms, the third wrapping his arm around Joel's neck. Using the mental switch, Joel turned on the electric current on the outer surface of his suit. The men recoiled screaming, then stood around him uncertain what to do.

"Now do you believe us?" said Carlos. "This man is a monster."

Joel said, "Leon, I want you to come with me to one of your bedrooms. I want a private talk with you. If you value the safety of your children and grandchildren, you will do as I say."

Leon looked around him at his family, and then led Joel into the villa, across the living area, through the foyer, down the hallway, to the master bedroom suite at the far end. Joel had no concern that the others might leave. Where would they go and what would they do?

Once alone, Leon stared at Joel defiantly. He had faced many adversities in his climb to the top of the Cartel and he had faced them without fear. He would not show this man any fear now. Joel returned his stare. Slowly, he penetrated Leon's mind, until he had him in a trance. First, he subjected him to the stomach pain treatment, and then he told him that he would cease all his illegal activities immediately and would command all the members of the Cartel to do the same.

"I will come back and visit anyone who disobeys this command. They probably will not survive a visit from me. Next, all farming of coca, opium poppies, and cannabis will cease. The fields will be given to the village to farm and profit from as a community, planting coffee or any other legitimate crop. Now I want you to send for the leaders of the village community, including at least one woman. I want to talk to them."

They returned to the patio. Leon gave one of the guards the names of five men and one woman, telling him to bring them to the villa immediately. While he waited for the villagers to arrive, Joel continued by taking each adult currently at the villa into the bedroom alone, for behavior modification. He started with Juan Carlos Ramirez. He needed to make sure they all followed Leon in their change of life style, and each one felt the penalty for non-compliance. They all showed belligerence until he hypnotized them, except two. A guard, Esteban Ortega, and Diego's sister, Elena, both exhibited a lot of compassion for the plight of the villagers.

Joel studied Elena for a while; after all her beauty caught his eye. At 5'6" tall and 130 pounds, she had a slim but full figure. Her oval face had perfect symmetry, with a small straight nose, piecing blue-green eyes, black eyebrows, and thick lush lashes. She had shoulder length hair. But her skin surpassed all the other features, with its blemish-free silky smoothness and a very light tan.

Reading her thoughts, he learned of a life of frustration and despair. At 18 she had enrolled in the University of Bogota to study for a degree in fine arts. Her father had forced her to live in his town house just outside of Ciudad Blanca, University City, on the edge of the Historical Center of Bogota, with a Dona as a constant companion. She fell in love with an idealist young man named Jorge Gaitan, grandson of the former mayor of Bogota, whose assassination during his second presidential campaign in 1948 led to massive riots, and ten years of political unrest called La Violencia.

They met while studying in the Ernesto Guhl Library, and would sit in the Plaza Che drinking coffee, underneath the Painting of Che Guevara that graced the façade of the university's main auditorium. He defied her father who forbade her to see him and died at the hands of a gang of her fathers thugs, with Che looking down at him. From then on she hated her father and everything he stood for. She lost herself in her studies and graduated with honors, obtaining a B.A. in fine arts with a minor in economics.

Her father tried to force her to marry one of his lieutenants. When she refused him, the man beat her, a serious mistake. Her father loved her in his way, so he personally killed the lieutenant. Now 30 years old and unmarried, she openly voiced her opposition to the violence in her family. This made her an outcast; she could not escape the family, but she would not marry without love.

The other exception, the guard, Esteban Ortega, did not transmit the same evil aura as the others when Joel evaluated his mind. He had been recruited from the village and forced to join the Cartel. He showed an above-average intelligence and great empathy for the villagers. Joel asked him to join in when he talked to the villagers.

The villagers arrived. Joel took each one of them into the bedroom for evaluation. Their thoughts revealed simple working people, whose fear cast a shadow over their lives. They wanted to be left alone to live their lives as simply as possible. The woman, Maria, had potentially high intelligence, but no education. He had an interesting conversation with her. She spoke openly about the villages problems.

The meeting took place in the dining room. The attendees were Leon, Juan Carlos, Diego, Carlos, Elena, Esteban, and the six villagers, the last seven showing their nervousness. Joel started the meeting by telling the first four that if they did not do as he asked, or impeded Esteban and the villagers in any way, he would eliminate them, and replace them with people who would co-operate.

To the villagers he said, "All the land now belongs to the village, to be farmed for the benefit of all the villagers; you can grow anything you want except opium poppies and cannabis. You seven will be the village council to start with, but in six months you will hold elections for the seven council seats. Elections will be held every two years. I will supply all the money you need for the first year; after that you should be self-supporting."

The villagers all looked a Leon. "Tell them that is what you want," said Joel.

Leon fell, face down on the table, clutching his stomach, moaning loudly. Everybody stared at him. Finally he gained control of himself and said, "This is my wish; you will do as this man says."

"Elena will be your advisor, she will open a bank account for the village and I will put money in it. Are you okay with that, Elena?"

"I will be very happy to help in any way I can."

"Good! I want you to upgrade the village school and arrange private college-level tutoring for Esteban and Maria here in Chibcha. Also take them to Cali; get them used to the city. I want them to be the village's interface with the outside world. Maria, I want you to call me once a week, to tell me if everything is okay. If I don't hear from you, I will come here to see if someone is preventing you from calling me. Do you understand?"

He handed Maria, Esteban, and Elena his card with his phone number on it.

"There is no telephone in the village. How will I call you?"

"Elena will bring you to the villa."

Juan Carlos started to say something, and then collapsed in his chair clutching his stomach.

"The men in this family must control their evil thoughts or there will be a few heart attacks," said Joel. "I will return tomorrow. If I do not see changes, heads will roll—literally. Your lives have changed, but at least for a while you still have lives. Any questions?"

Esteban asked, "What do you want me to do?"

"Take control. You saw my powers. The Cartel is finished. It will not oppose you. Convince the villagers all this is for real. Implement what I have asked for. Can you do that?"

"I will try."

"Good. I will see you tomorrow. Now, Leon, you and Juan will take me to your office."

Once again they crossed the foyer to the hallway, and entered the first door on the left. The furnishings in the office would have outclassed any corporate office in the United States. No expense had been spared. The opulent desk faced a large picture window, overlooking the valley. The padded desk chair could swivel around to a computer consol that contained every piece of the most up-to-date business equipment available. The pictures on the walls looked like original art, and the bar at one end replicated the one in the living area. At the other end, a conference table stood surrounded by six comfortable-looking chairs. The 18-inch square floor tile could be seen around the edges of two enormous Persian rugs.

"Where's your safe?"

There followed a brief silence, then both men fell to their knees clutching their stomachs.

Joel laughed. "You wouldn't lie to me would you?"

They showed him the safe behind one of the paintings, and he made them open it. Inside he found five different bank accounts, one in the

U.S.A., two in Colombia, and two in the Cayman Islands. Looking through them, Joel whistled. The deposits totaled over $2,000,000,000. This would finance his projects for quite a while. Sitting at the desk, he transferred $2,000,000,000 into his own account. The two men stood there stunned.

"I've left you half a million dollars; if you give me trouble or anything happens to Esteban, I'll come back and take that, as well as your lives.

Joel walked out to the driveway, activated his transporter, and flew home. He arrived at his compound by 2 p.m.; his trip only took six hours. He relaxed in the machine, with it running at sixty percent, while he planned what he wanted to do next. He now had $2,000,000,000; he could afford to add more cities to his restoration program.

Chapter Two

oel decided that the time had come to do something about the Iraq situation. He could not change the minds and hearts of the total Al Qaida population, but two things he could do. He would deprive them of their weapons, and neutralize their leaders by controlling their minds with his hypnotism. Fallujah would be a good place to start. As the crow flies, Barstow to Fallujah covered ten thousand miles, due east, crossing the United States, the Atlantic Ocean, and northern Africa. The Fallujah time zone is eleven hours ahead of California, but because Iraq does not use daylight savings time, it is only a ten-hour different in time. Because it takes two hours to get there he must leave home at 7 p.m., to arrive there at 8 a.m.

So one Sunday evening Joel strapped on his transporter, rose to sixty thousand feet, accelerated to five thousand miles an hour for two hours, and then descended to five hundred feet above Fallujah, arriving there at 8 a.m. Monday morning. The city, on the eastern bank of the Euphrates River in the Province of Al Anbar, lies forty-three miles west of Bagdad. Joel could see it justified its name of the "City of the Mosques"; he could see over one hundred of them. He could also see extensive damage to the city, including the mosques.

At the eastern edge of the city, on the Via Abu Ghuravb, the only road to Bagdad, Joel could see a U.S. Marine road block. The troops came from Camp Bahatia, formerly FOB Volturno, the Marine base two miles southeast of Fallujah. On the western side, on the edge of the Jotan district, he could see a group of twelve armed men entering the city from the direction of Al Habbaniyah. Dropping down, he landed in front of them, switched off his transporter, and left the protection belt on.

Taken by surprise, they immediately took cover in doorways and alleys. Joel spoke to them in Arabic. "Come out, I want to talk to you." Joel looked unarmed, so the leader told four men to go to him and bring him into an alley. The four men surrounded Joel and prodded him with their weapons, until he moved meekly into the alley.

"Iyad, his body feels as hard as a brick," said one of the men.

"Search him, Abu," said Iyad.

"I can't, His body is protected by something."

"Let me see."

Iyad approached Joel, and their eyes met. Joel penetrated Iyad's mind and took control of his actions.

"Abu, hit him over the head with your Uzi."

Abu did as ordered, and the Uzi bent under the impact. This startled the men. They crowded around Joel, prodding him with weapons, until he turned on the electric current. This caused them to move back, after receiving a shock. They raised their guns as though to shoot him.

Joel had Iyad tell them, "Do not shoot." Joel's objective wasn't to kill them.

"Let us take him back to camp," said Iyad. "We must show him to Salam; he will know what to do."

With Iyad leading, and most of the rest behind Joel, they headed west out of town, back down the road to Al Habbaniyah. A mile down the road they encountered the personnel carrier they had left hidden in a partially demolished building, and rode the rest of the way. As they left Fallujah, the Euphrates turns south, but after driving five miles the river had snaked back and met them again.

On the banks of the river they entered a small village. The village had only one street, with six dwellings on each side. It seemed to be peaceful enough, but after they entered, Joel realized it resembled a movie set.

Nothing was what it appeared to be. The shallow drafted river boats didn't fish the river, the fields had very little crops in them, and the artisans only pretended to produce wares. The village currently had twenty residents. He obtained this information from Iyad's mind.

The village functioned as an arms depot for the terrorists of the Sunni Wahabi sect, under the command of the Committee of the Faith. The front rooms of each dwelling looked normal, but all the back rooms contained weapons.

Iyad led Joel to a dwelling in the middle of the village; they entered, but the others stayed outside. Inside, four men sat on the floor talking. One rose as they came in. "Iyad back so soon? Did you complete your mission?"

"No, Salam. We captured this American, and I thought you should see him right away." Salam walked up to Joel, and they locked eyes. Salam had a stronger mind than Iyad, but not as strong as Joel's, who soon controlled his thoughts and actions.

"Everybody leave the house. Iyad, you wait outside the door." The three men and Iyad left closing the door behind them.

Joel told Salam, "If you even think of killing anyone again you will have such severe pains in you stomach that you will fall on your knees until the thoughts go away. Now, show me what you have in the back rooms."

One room contained rifles, Uzis, mines, and rocket launchers. The other room had ten vests with sixteen sticks of dynamite sewn between the inner and outer layers of fabric. Six other houses had similar caches of weapons; the others contained beds for eighteen people.

Using one of the houses for interviews, Joel had Salam send one terrorist at a time to him until he had spoken to all of them. Each one had volunteered for action; three teenage girls wanted to be suicide bombers. Nobody lasted more than three months, but the replacements kept coming in. He saw no conscience or remorse in any of them; just hatred and dedication. He told them all to go back to their communities and put their dedication to work rebuilding out of the rubble. If they felt like volunteering again, they would feel the stomach pains.

By the time he finished his interviews, he could smell enticing aromas filling the village. Salam invited him to lunch with them. Shorbat Rumman, made from lamb shanks and pomegranate juice, was the main course, followed by Hadgi Badah, cardamom cookies tasting of almonds and ginger.

Finally, all the ex-terrorists left the village, heading for their homes, leaving Joel alone with Salam. Salam lived in Fallujah, and Joel needed his help with the citizens there. Joel used their munitions to set charges in each of the six armories, then, using an electronic detonator, set them off from a safe distance. The village exploded in six simultaneous blasts that shook the earth. They drove off in the direction of Fallujah, trying to put as much distance between them and the wreckage, before someone came to investigate.

After about a mile they slowed down, and Joel started asking questions about the situation in Fallujah. Salam said, "Most of the people couldn't wait for the fighting to end, but he still had people who supported him."

"I want to talk to them, plus those leading the effort to rebuild."

Arriving in Fallujah, they went to the Muallimin district, and Salam introduced Joel to an Iraqi named Dahr Sabah. "What do you want?" Dahr said to Salam. "I told you I would turn you in to the Americans if I ever saw you again."

"Listen to this man; you will like what he has to say."

"I don't want to hear your propaganda. What is an American doing with the likes of you?"

"Let me tell you that," said Joel, and Dahr turned to face him. Looking into his eyes, Joel saw a different story from the others. Here he saw strength of character along with frustration, and a little despair. Joel took just enough control of Dahr's mind to make him receptive to what Joel told him. "I want to help you rebuild in Fallujah."

"I've heard what's going on with Iraq reconstruction efforts," Dahr said. "Millions of dollars being spent but none of it reaches us. What isn't lost to corruption and mismanagement goes to large projects, like water treatment plants, hospitals and schools. The largest amounts go to rebuilding the army and police forces. We need all those, but it doesn't help us in our daily lives. We need homes and jobs and money to buy food and clothes."

"That is exactly what we should do: rebuild houses, first your home, then your neighbors', and finally all the city. I will supply the funding, you will order the materials from your local stores. You will use only residents of Fallujah to do the work, I will pay their wages. Then they will have money to buy food and clothing, and all the money goes back into the economy of the town. We will rebuild schools, and mosques as well. You don't need any outsiders to tell you how to rebuild your city. Once we get Muallimin in the works, we will spread out and rebuild Jotan, Shurta, Muhandisin, and all the other districts."

"That will take a lot of money. Do you have that much—who is funding you?"

"You let me worry about the money, you get the people. Open a community development bank account. I will put twenty million dinar in it. You spend all that in one week on materials and salaries; if I like what you have done, I'll put fifty million dinar in the account. The faster you show results, the more money I will give you."

"How do I know you mean this?"

"What can you lose? Of course, if you take my twenty million dinar and do nothing, I'll come back and take it out of your hide." Joel said with a smile. "But I can tell you are an honorable man; we will have a successful partnership. Let's go to your bank right now so you can open a new account and I will transfer the money into it."

Dahr took Joel to his bank and opened an account. Joel did an electronic transfer from the corporation funds. When the bank clerk told Dahr the money was in the account, he shook Joel's hand saying, "You will not regret this. I will work diligently for you."

After depositing the money, Joel transported back to California. He arrived there at 5 a.m., just in time for a session on the machine and his daily morning exercise routine. If he had his two sessions a day in the machine he could go days without sleep.

Chapter Three

The next day, Tuesday, he planned to go to Afghanistan, so he worked on perfecting the languages. He spoke the Dari form of Persian well, but needed to practice Pashto, Turkmeni, and Uzbeki. He listened to tapes of each language while undergoing the session. This left about four hours for Joel to work on his latest technology project, invisibility. No work had been done in this field. Joel's ideas were breaking new ground a hundred years ahead of their time. He needed time to test his theories.

He had obtained 200,000 Afghani, from five different banks, for a total of 1,000,000 Afghani, and packed it in his titanium fanny pack, ready to go. He needed the money with him to give to the farmers, after he destroyed their poppy crops. The Afghanistan currency exchanged at the rate of 46 Afghani to 1 dollar. The average per capita income in Afghanistan stood at 46,000 Afghani per year. He would give them money to buy seeds for other crops. Wheat ranked second to opium, followed by melons, vegetables, rice, and cotton. Then he would get the drug traffickers off their backs.

Afghanistan is twelve and a half time zones ahead of California, but only eleven and a half hours because of daylight saving time, so to travel the 12,500 miles and get there at 8 a.m., he had to leave at 6 p.m. Joel arrived in northern Afghanistan, in the province of Badakhshan. He scouted up and down the province until he could see a poppy field below him, in the district of Jurm. The province had a sparse population of three thousand, living mainly in villages nestled in the poppy fields. The villages looked like the center of a spider's web, with the dirt tracks radiating out through the fields. The wider dirt roads connected the villages together.

He landed in the center of one of the villages, causing an instant commotion. The children crowded around him, while the women tried to pull them back. Finally an elderly, bearded man, wearing a turban, pushed his way through and the children fell silent, moving back out of respect. "He dropped out of the sky, Rohullah," said one of the women in Dari.

"What do you want?" asked Rohullah.

Joel locked eyes with the Afghani and took control of the man's mind. He read him as a proud man, struggling to keep his dignity in a changing world he didn't understand. He thought Joel came from the drug lords, and the hatred showed clearly.

"I want a meeting with all the farmers. Can you call them in from the fields?"

Rohullah nodded, then led Joel to a tall pole with a bell attached to the top, everybody followed. He instructed the biggest boy to ring the bell. The clear tones pealed out across the countryside, summoning thirty-five men, women, and teenagers, who drifted in by twos and threes, all asking, "What's wrong? Is there an emergency?" The average age in Afghanistan is 18, with less than three percent over 65. This group seemed to fit that demographic, with Rohullah, who looked to be 60, the eldest.

He introduced Joel to a man, saying, "This is Ahmad, our leader."

Joel looked deeply into Ahmad's eyes. He saw a strong man, frustrated by his inability to do better for his people. He loved his wife and children, but sometimes he felt like giving up the hard work and joining the drug traffickers. They had made him an offer again last week; he had come close to accepting, but could he face his son if he did? What did this man want of him?

Joel gained control of Ahmad's mind, and without verbalizing the words, told him that he was there to help.

"Let's go to the meeting room. Noora, take the children back to the school."

One of the women herded the children in one direction, aided by the other women and the female teenagers. All the males followed Ahmad and Joel to a large empty hut with barren floors. They sat down in a circle, leaving a gap opposite the door for Ahmad, Rohullah, and Joel. Joel counted twenty-four men, ranging in age from 15 to forty-five, plus Rohullah. Nobody in the forty-five to 60 range.

They all stared at him, making it easy for him to stare into each individual's eyes, one at a time, until he had command of all their minds. He felt this to be the best way; they would never understand what his goals were, but as long as he protected their interests he would have a clear conscience.

"I am going to destroy your poppy fields." A gasp of horror rang around the room. "I am going to pay you, so you will have money to live on and to buy seed. You can plant wheat, vegetables, or maize, whatever you want to."

"We can't do that! The drug lords will not let us—they will not let us buy seed, and they will take your money."

"I will take care of the drug lords."

"If you destroy our crops, the drug lord will come and kill you. They watch us all the time. Isf we do something they don't like, they punish us. How can you resist them?"

"Do you have any weapons?"

"We have one old pistol, a saber, and of course scythes."

"Bring them here."

"Khalid, go get them, Wazip, you help him," Ahmad ordered. Two of the older teenagers left the room. "How much money will you give us?"

"Two hundred thousand Afghanis to start with, more as you need it until you can support yourselves." Again a gasp went around the room; everybody started talking at once. From the conversation, Joel gathered they thought that a lot. "How long could you live on that?"

"We could live for months, but we will need to buy seed. How do we do that?"

"I will make arrangements for that."

Khalid and Wazip, returned with the weapons. The revolver looked like it would explode in your hand; the scythes could be very dangerous; the saber was a magnificent weapon. It had a long, wide, curved blade, with an ornate carved hilt, big enough for two hands. Joel held it in a fighting pose; he marveled at how great the balance felt.

"You must be very proud of this."

"It's a village heirloom—we cherish it."

"We had better use a scythe; I wouldn't want to damage this." He handed the saber to Ahmad. "Strike me with the scythe."

"Why would I want to harm you?"

"I'll do it," said one of the older men, rising to his feet.

"Abdul, why do you want to harm this man?"

"He asked us to, and if I kill him our problem will go away." Ahmad started to protest, but Joel moved to the center of the circle of men and said, "Let him."

Abdul picked up the scythe, and without hesitation, swung as hard as he could, striking the blade squarely across the back of Joel's neck. The force of the blow knocked the weapon out of Abdul's hand; it fell to the floor, landing at his feet.

"How can you survive a blow like that?" said Ahmad.

"The same way I will defeat the drug lord." Joel grabbed Abdul by the front of his tunic and stared into his eyes. "This man is a traitor; he is the one who tells your enemies what you are doing. Tell them, confess." With Joel controlling his mind, Abdul began babbling about how the traffickers paid him to report anything he saw in the village."

"Kill him!" the villager cried.

"No!" said Joel, "We will use him. Let him go."

"He will bring the killers back to our village."

"Then I will show you why you need not fear them anymore."

With Joel controlling their minds, they had no choice but to let him go. As he scurried away down the dirt road, Joel asked, "How long before the drug lord's men arrive."

"No more than two hours," said Ahmad.

Joel took 200,000 Afghani, a mixture of 50, and 500 Afghani notes, and handed them to Ahmad. "Put these in a safe place. I am going to eradicate the fields. Can we eat lunch when I return?"

Ahmad grinned broadly. "We will make you a feast."

"How far do your fields extend? I don't want to eradicate your neighbor's fields until I talk to them."

"We extend halfway to each village in all directions; there is a road that marks the boundaries."

"When I leave tonight, I want you to invite all your neighbors to a meeting tomorrow, here at 8 a.m."

Joel walked to the edge of the village, activated his transporter, rose to about ten feet, and using his laser gun started to eradicate the fields. He used a low-level beam that killed the poppy plants, without starting a fire; in this arid climate, a fire could get out of hand. After about an hour and a half, when Joel had eradicated eighty percent of the fields, he saw a cloud of dust approaching the village from the east. Ten men on horseback, riding hard, headed his way. Joel returned to the village to find its occupants panicking. He regained control of their minds, calmed them down, and told them to keep out of sight while he dealt with the intruders.

Joel retrieved the saber from Ahmad, walked to the eastern edge of the village, then twenty yards further down the road, and waited. The road ran straight and flat, so Joel could see the riders a mile away. He stood with the saber in front of him, arms out stretched, two hands on the hilt, blade pointing vertically down, touching the dirt.

The riders stopped fifty feet from him, not sure what to make of him. The leader told one man to move forward. "Shall I shoot him, Faisal?"

"Yes," said Faisal.

The rider stopped ten feet in front of Joel, raised his pistol, and shot Joel in the head. The bullet ricocheted and hit the rider between the eyes, pitching him backwards off the horse. He hit the ground with a loud thud. The horse panicked, reared up on its hind legs, then bolted passed Joel into the village. A second horseman fired his rifle at Joel with the same result, and two men lay dead on the road.

The leader sent a third rider charging at Joel, with saber raised above his head. Joel rose to seven feet of the ground, and using the back of his saber, unseated the rider. Returning to earth, Joel struck the man as he tried to rise, rendering him unconscious. Turning his attention back to his adversaries, he saw the seven remaining riders charging at him. Rising quickly to seven feet, he engaged them in a brief battle, resulting in seven more men lying unconscious on the road.

Ahmad and the villagers cautiously approached Joel from behind. "I knew Allah would send you to rescue us and smite the infidel."

"Can you tie up these men and take care of the horses? I'm going to finish eradicating the fields. I'll be about fifteen minutes."

"Leave them to us; I will put them in the meeting room."

Joel rose to about ten feet, then headed out to finish the fields. Ten minutes later he returned to smell great aromas emanating from an open fire in the center of the village. The menu included Murgh Kebabs, chicken with Tandori marinade, made from chili, ginger, garlic, and lemon; Nan bread; and Sheer Payra Fudge, made with corn syrup, pistachios, walnuts, and cardamom. Ahmad assured Joel they didn't eat like this very often; they had cooked this special feast to celebrate their good fortune. The meal was delicious.

Joel asked Ahmad, "Do you have a room where I can talk to each captive alone?"

"I will be honored if you will use my home."

"Bring them to me one at a time."

As each man came into the room, Joel hypnotized him and gave him the stomach pain treatment, then told him to go back to his home and live a good life. After the treatments they left the village on foot. He kept Faisal till last and told him, "You will take me back to your drug lord, as your prisoner.

Leaving eight horses for the villagers to keep, and Joel told Ahmad, "I'll be back tomorrow for our meeting." Joel and Faisal then rode off in an easterly direction.

As they rode, Joel asked about the drug lord. Faisal said, "He calls himself Mohammad, but I suspect he has taken that name for effect. He lives with his wife and children in a great house, inside a walled compound. He commands one hundred armed men, who lived in a barracks. His armor includes a tank; three personnel carriers; four jeeps, with machine guns mounted on them; numerous small arms in an armory; and a stable that used to have thirty horses. There is a processing laboratory in the compound. Mohammad buys the opium poppies from the farmers for a pittance, extracts the morphine, and chemically processes it into heroin, which he sells to traffickers for a large profit."

The flat, arable land began to climb into the foothills of a range of low mountains. Ahead, Joel could see the compound, with 8-foot high wall, and a turret at each corner. As they approached, the guards, seeing Faisal with only one unarmed man, opened the gates. They entered, dismounted, and a number of armed men followed behind them.

Joel could see a large western-style two-storey house at the back; in contrast, a mosque of traditional design stood next to it. A large man with a beard and turban, dressed to make himself look like the prophet, came down the steps from the front door of the house. "Where are the others, Faisal?"

"Two dead, the rest captured."

"Who did this?" roared Mohammad.

"This man."

"Alone?"

"Yes."

"Seize him! And take him to the cells."

The cells, thought Joel, this sounds interesting. He let two men grab his arms and drag him across the compound, towards the barracks. Mohammad followed. The building measured 200-feet long by 40-feet wide, and looked like it had been recently renovated. The drug profits paid to keep the troops happy. They entered a door on one end, leading to stairs going underground. At the bottom a corridor ran the length of the building with cells on either side. The cells had heavy doors with small barred windows and two enormous dead bolts, but only one dead bolt had a lock. At the far end of the corridor, a door opened into a 40-foot square room. If it hadn't been so tragic, Joel would have laughed. The room looked like the dungeon of a medieval castle, complete with torture equipment. The walls had chains hanging from them; in the center stood a rack, in one corner a metal bowl on a stand glowed with hot coals. One set of wall chains held an unconscious man.

Joel felt the anger rising inside of him. How many unfortunate people had suffered at the hands of these monsters? He activated the electricity in his suit and the two men holding him fell back with a scream. Turning to face his captors, he heard Mohammad say, "Close and bar the door. Don't let him out." Two of Mohammad's men stood in front of the door; the other four advanced upon him.

Joel decided not to make this a short fight; these men had to pay for what had been going on here. He left the electricity on at a low level, as he punched and kicked, with blows hard enough to hurt, but not knock them out. The two by the door joined in the fray, and they kept coming back for more, as Mohammad cajoled them into greater effort. Finally, eight badly beaten men lay on the floor. Joel caught Mohammad as he tried to open the door and gave him the same punishment.

Joel's anger subsided; he hadn't lost his temper like this since acquiring his powers. It had felt good, but he mustn't let it happen again. He could hear more men outside the bolted door. Reviving Mohammad, Joel stared into his eyes and took control of his mind. As he opened the door he had Mohammad order the men to go to their rooms in the barracks. Next he released the prisoner hanging from the wall and six others in cells.

Joel, Mohammad, and the seven prisoners went to the main house, with Mohammad carrying the semi-conscious man. His wife and four children, met them at the door. He had Mohammad order his servants to tend to the prisoner's wounds and to feed them all; he also told him to send his wife and children to their rooms.

They had to have a serious discussion. To eliminate Mohammad would leave a power void that some other tyrant would fill. Joel planned to use Mohammad to protect the villagers and to make the poppy eradication work. They went to his study. It contained the usual opulent furnishings, but the walls coverings differed. Mohammad liked intricate handwoven tapestries. Joel admired their beauty and felt the depth of the pile. He knew he was looking at something very special.

He examined Mohammad's bank books; again, the amounts astounded him. All the drug profiteers knew about offshore accounts: it must be taught in Trafficker 101. His wealth amounted to one billion and two hundred thousand dollars. Forbes list of billionaires did not include the drug world. Joel transferred a billion dollars to his own account. Putting Mohammad into an even deeper trance, Joel gave him the stomach pain treatment.

"You will also feel the pains if you fail to follow my instructions. You will now become the benefactor of all your villages, by supplying them with free seed to plant their crops, and protecting them from anything that threatens their happiness. You will invite them to pray at your mosque on the sabbath and preach all the peaceful laws of The Prophet and his Quran, including equality for women."

"How many villages do you command?"

"Eight."

"That's about three hundred people. Get word to each village tonight that they must send a representative to tomorrow's meeting, and they must do as I say."

"Okay. What about the traffickers? They visit me once a month, expecting supplies. They can be dangerous if I don't co-operate."

"When is their next visit?"

"Mustafa and three bodyguards will be here in three days."

"I will be here to take care of them. Have the seven prisoners driven home when they are fit enough. Now I want to talk to your soldiers."

Joel went to the barracks and interviewed each man alone. He found them to be the usual mixture, some just wanted to go home, others followed orders, but half of them enjoyed the work they did. He treated each one according to his degree of evil. Leaving the barracks, Joel activated the transporter and went home, arriving there at 6 a.m.

During his session on the machine, he worked on the light-absorbing modification to the protection suit. He had developed a device that absorbed light in the 400- to 700-nanometer range; now he needed to add it to the suit. By the end of the session he had all the details worked out in his head. He spent the rest of the day adding this capability to one of his back-up suits. He hadn't quite finished by 6 p.m., when he had to leave to get to the meeting in Afghanistan by 8 a.m. Wednesday.

When he arrived, fourteen representatives from the other seven villages awaited him. They held the meeting in the large room, but before they started Joel looked each one in the eyes and took control of their minds, to ensure their co-operation. The meeting took only an hour; he told them what he intended to do and gave each village 200,000 Afghani. They had been warned what to expect by Mohammad, so they reluctantly agreed, but nobody there expected Mohammad to keep his word once Joel left.

Joel spent the rest of the day eradicating fields of poppy plants. Afterwards, he visited Mohammad to check on the prisoners: six had been driven back to their villages; the seventh was still recovering. He talked to the man in Dari to make sure they were treating him well. He then transported back to California, arriving at 5 a.m. Wednesday.

Chapter Four

After a session on the machine, Joel did his morning exercises, before sleeping for three hours. After lunch he transported to Watts for an update on Restoration Corporation activities from Tanisha and Kory. They reminded him that their engagement party would be at the church hall that Saturday, and he promised to be there.

They now had ten major population areas, each with eight sub-areas, running smoothly. Tanisha had hired a certified accountant, full time, to oversee and train ten people selected from the Hood. Each one managed a major area, checking the validity of every request for money. The total budget exceeded $10,000,000 a month. Joel reviewed an overview of their programs. Because of the use of local people wherever possible, the achievements justified the expenses. He noted that the San Francisco region seemed less efficient than the others, so he decided to visit them, to give the leaders time on the machine and some hypnotic suggestions. He then, transferred $20,000,000 into the corporation bank account.

Upon completing his business in San Francisco, he returned to the compound, to spend time on his invisibility project. He called it his "Cloaker." He completed the modification of one suit. To test it, he transported to Colombia to check on Esteban. Arriving at the Ramirez villa, he activated the cloaking device, and walked around undetected. He chuckled when he heard that Leon Montoya had been sick with stomach pains, but the others seemed to be adjusting to their loss of power.

Joel switched off the Cloaker when he visited Esteban. Elena happened to be with him, so they had a three-way meeting. Elena had opened a bank account, with two signatures required, hers and Esteban's. Joel deposited 20,000,000 pesos ($10,000) in the account, telling Elena to keep account of all expenditures. "If you spend it wisely, there will be a lot more. I don't mind if you expand your activities to other villages. If someone gives you trouble, I will deal with them."

Elena said, "I thank God for your coming. It gives me a new life, and let's me do what I have wanted to do for years, help the villagers."

"Show me ways to educate, and help the deserving, and I will fund your programs. The money is there for the right projects." Joel lingered, talking to Elena. Esteban left them to get back to work, so they spent three pleasant hours, talking about their work, and about her ambitions. She had a good education, but the family refused to let her use it. Why should she work when they supplied her with everything she needed? They didn't understand her frustration and boredom. He enjoyed her company, and promised himself he would see more of her.

He couldn't even touch her, because his suit kept his fingers one half-inch away from everything. He would have to turn it off to make contact with her. He had decided never to turn his suit off in hostile territory—that would make him vulnerable, but in this case he was sorely tempted.

Joel returned to his compound, to work on upgrading his three spare suits. He had improved his nuclear engine to be more efficient and powerful. His force field would now withstand any weapon currently available. He added transporters and lasers to each suit, and Cloakers to the outside of both the suits and the transporters. He also updated the nuclear engine operating the dome over his compound.

Joel still tried to get two sessions a day in the machine. It got more difficult with all his travelling. He now only needed two hours a day sleep, so he would sleep in the machine, using an alarm to awaken him. During the other two-hour session he would work on problems. His levitation capabilities grew enormously. In addition to lifting heavy weights, he could raise himself off the ground. He could not fly yet, but could raise himself up to thirty feet in the air. It took all his concentration to levitate, but once up there he could hover while performing other tasks.

At 6 p.m. Thursday evening Joel transported to Afghanistan, arriving at 8 a.m. Friday. He saw the drug trafficker's Land Rover already in the compound. When Joel entered the dining room, Mustafa's agitation showed on his face. Mohammad's stalling only made him madder; he was demanding to see the merchandise as Joel walked in. The two bodyguards stood and pulled guns one pointed at Mohammad and the other at Joel. "Who the hell is this?" asked Mustafa.

Joel stared at the gun pointing at Mohammad; it moved up and around until it pointed into the man' own mouth. The second bodyguard shot Joel. The bullet hit his chest, rebounded, and the man went down, hit in the heart. The first gunman sat down hard in his chair, the gun still in his mouth. He could not move or drop it. Joel left him like that; he figured this man had terrorized a lot of people—let him find out how it felt.

Joel turned to Mustafa, took control of his mind, and told him to sit down. Then he calmly asked Mohammad to report on his activities. Mohammad looked at the man with the gun in his mouth; slowly his face relaxed, replacing tension with a smile. "You continue to amaze me. How do you do that?"

"You haven't seen half of what I can do. Have you had any stomach pains lately?" The smile left Mohammad's face. "Do the villagers have any seeds yet?"

"The first supply of vegetable seeds arrived and they have them; the other crops should be here in a week. The villagers have cleared their fields ready for planting."

"Good. Anything else to tell me?"

"I had a visit from Khalid. He heard about the destruction of the fields, and wanted to see it for himself. I now hear he is preparing to attack and take over my villages."

"How many other drug lords does this province have?"

"Three. I controlled the trade to the east through China, Khalid is north of me and controls the contacts through Tajikstan, and Wazip has the western route through Pakistan."

"Don't worry. I will visit both of them today and take care of that problem."

Joel transported north to visit Khalid. By the time he left him, he had the villagers clearing their fields ready for new crops, and Joel's bank account had received a sizable increase. A visit to Wazip, in the west produced the same results. By noon, Joel headed for Helmand province, leaving two more despots fighting stomach pains and wondering what had happened to them.

The situation in Helmand proved more difficult. The Sunni Muslim, Pashtun people, speak Pashto. The Taliban had regained a strong presence in this area, in spite of the NATO efforts. The farmers could grow their opium poppy crops and sell them, but the Taliban took a percentage off the top. Joel brainwashed the farmers into changing their crops from opium, but he had to work his way up through the ranks of the Taliban. The villagers told him who among them sympathized with the Taliban, and Joel made one of the collaborators lead him to the camp of the local leader. From there he worked up to Mohammed Omar Mullah, Emir of Afghanistan and head of the Taliban movement.

The Taliban is controlled by the Mullah and Mawlawi families. Joel knew that to control the mind of one man only would not stop the actions of the whole movement. He had Mohammed call a meeting of fifteen members of these two families, plus Mohammad Sharif, Minister of Interior Affairs. These men held key positions in the Taliban; such as Mohammad Hasan Mullah, Chairman of the Ruling Council; Abdul Kabir Mawlawi, First Deputy Council of Ministers; and Nanai Mawlawi, Habibullah Ershad Mawlawi, and Muhammad Hasan Rehmani Mullah, Field Commanders.

It took Mohammad Omar Mullah three days to get all these men in one room. They expressed great resistance to coming, because it gave NATO an opportunity to get them all at once. Mohammad prevailed, and finally, Monday morning, Joel faced them all. He found it a great challenge trying to control the minds of sixteen strong-willed people. The silence stretched into minutes as the battle of wills continued. Eventually, Joel had them all under his influence.

He started by administering the stomach pain treatment, to each one individually; he wanted to make sure it worked for all of them. Joel told them they now had a new purpose in life:s to make the lives of their people happier and more fulfilling. As Sunni Muslims, they must interpret the words of Abu I-Qasim Muhammad, The Prophet, as written in the

Qur'an, to mean live in peace and love thine enemies. Democracy must be looked upon as a goal for all of Islam.

They must start by sending all their troops home to their families with orders to live a peaceful life; then they must initiate peace talks with NATO. Leaving these men to carry out his instructions, Joel headed for Kabul and the NATO headquarters to see Four-Star General Dan McNeil.

Using his cloaking device, Joel infiltrated into the general's office. He studied the man as he waited until everyone left the room. McNeil showed signs of great stress; since he had taken over from the British General David Richards, things had gone from bad to worse. The Taliban activity had reached an all-time high, and his soldiers' death rate climbed daily. He had served in five foreign conflicts, including Vietnam, but this assignment drained him the most—maybe he was getting too old for this. He thought he'd seen his worse days when accused of covering up the deaths of two men, at the Bagram prison.

Finally, the room cleared and Joel could get control of the general's mind. He told him the Taliban would be asking for peace talks and he must respond in good faith, or suffer the stomach pains. He instructed him to pull the NATO troops back to give the Taliban time to start the peace process. Joel left him on the phone calling a staff meeting to pass on the new orders.

While Mohammed Omar Mullah arranged the meeting in Helmand, Joel had returned home. On Saturday evening he attended Kory and Tanisha's engagement party. Joel had told them to invite anybody they wanted to, from the people they interfaced with in other cities, at the corporation's expense. In addition to all their local friends, there were twenty couples from fifteen different cities. The upbeat atmosphere gave Joel a feeling of satisfaction, but also a feeling of loneliness. All the people talked about their new lives, and each had someone to share the excitement with. Even though everyone wanted to talk to him and thank him, he still felt like an outsider. He wished he had been able to bring Elena here.

As the reports of a peace initiative by the Taliban hit all news outlets,, Joel returned to Iraq for the next step there. Although eighty percent of the worlds' Moslem's are Sunni, in Iraq only thirty-five percent are. Half of the Iraqi Sunnis are Arabs and half Kurds. Over sixty percent of the population is Shiite, following the Shia branch of the Moslem religion. *Shia* means "follower," or "followers of the Prophet." Iran's Moslems are mainly Shia, but they support the the terrorists in Iraq. The Sunni believe that the Caliphs inherited the leadership of Islam from Muhammad, whereas the Shiites believe the Imams to be the divinely appointed successors.

Joel, using his Cloaker, infiltrated the office of the Shiite Prime Minister of Iraq, Nouri al-Maliki. Taking control of his mind, he instructed him to issue invitations to a closed-door meeting, in four days, to the following people: The Kurdish President of Iraq, Jalai Talabani, his son Qubad Talabani; Shiites Vice President Tariq al-Hashemi, Abdelaziz al-Hakin, his son Amman al-Hakin, Cleric Muqtada al-Sadr, and Grand Ayatollah Ali al-Sistani; and Sunni Vice President Adil Abdul Mahdi and Sheihk Harith al-Dhari. If Joel could get these nine men to work together for the common good, Iraq's problems would soon be solved.

While Nouri al-Maliki's staff prepared the invitations, Joel visited each one of the men personally, and privately, to ensure their attendance. He had trouble finding some of them two were out of Iraq and the Ayatollah slept with two bodyguards in his room. Before the day ended, Joel made sure they had all been conditioned to respond positively to the invitation.

He also visited Dahr Sabah in Fallujah, to check on the status there. The reconstruction projects were gaining momentum; work had started on ten homes, with forty people working on them. Reading Dahr's mind, Joel could tell that he spent every dinar wisely, with no corruption and the greatest efficiency. Joel put another 50,000,000 dinar in Dahr's bank account, telling him to hire many more people and start on a lot more houses. Before Joel left Fallujah, he asked Dahr for a contact in Mosul. He gave him the name of Abu Talib and recommended him highly. Dahr told Joel, "I will call Abu, tell him you will be visiting him, and explain what is being done in Fallujah." Joel then returned to his compound.

Chapter Five

The next day Joel visited the city of Mosul, the second largest city in Iraq. Its population used to be over two and a half million, but it is now less that one and a half million. They constitute a mixture, with Arabs being the majority and Kurds the next largest contingent. The people of Mosul are called Maslawi, and so is the language they speak. Maslawi is a Syrian dialect of Arabic. The city has sustained a lot of damage in the twenty-first century, first from the wars and then from all the terrorist violence and armed suppression. It looked like a ghost city.

His contact lived in the Al-Hadbaa' district of Mosul. Abu Talib, eyed the strange American with suspicion; he practiced his religion devoutly and knew in his heart that Allah could not be happy with all the innocent lives being sacrificed. But the Americans had not improved the situation. Each day it seemed to get worse. He prayed for a solution every day. Joel's appraisal of Abu showed another good man frustrated by circumstances beyond his control.

They talked for a while, feeling one another out. Joel asked Abu, "Could you organize a grass-roots group, to use local people to repair homes?"

"I'm sure I can, with the help of my friends, but how would we pay for it?"

"We will open a bank account, as I did for Dahr. How much do you need to hire some workers and get started?"

Abu hesitated, not knowing how much to ask for. "How about a million dinar? I could hire five men and start on two houses."

"I'll give you twenty million dinar. Hire all the men you need—try to do ten homes as soon as you can. If I'm happy with the way you spend the money, there will be a lot more. I'll need an accounting of the twenty million before you get more—just a list of wages and materials."

"That is very generous. When will I see you again?"

"In about a week. Changing the subject, could you tell me how I can contact Abula Shayma, the terrorist cell leader? I want to make sure he doesn't interfere with your activities."

Abu Talib regarded Joel with suspicion. "I don't know anything about the terrorists, but I heard that Taha Yassim might be able to contact them."

"Could you take me to Yassim?"

"I will point him out to you, but I don't want him to see us together."

Abu owned a beat-up 1995 Honda Civic. Joel took off his transporter pack and sat in the passenger's seat with the pack on his lap. They drove to the bank, where he deposited the money in Abu's account. Next they drove to the Al-Jadeeda district of Mosul. As they drove, Joel said, "Buy yourself a better car with the money I gave you. You will need it to conduct business for me. There is no reason you should not gain reasonable perks from our association."

"Thank you. I will be careful to spend your money wisely."

They reached Al-Jadeeda, and stopped on a street in an upscale residential area. Abu pointed to a house across the street—that was where Yassim lives. Joel got out and put his packback on. "Are you sure you will be safe?"

"Don't worry about me; I will see you in a week."

Abu drove away, and Joel crossed the street and knocked on the door of Yassim's house. A young man answered the door. From his mind, Joel read his name, Harb.

"I would like to talk to Tasa Yassim."

"What about?"

"I will tell that to him."

"I am Tasa Yassim."

"No you're not Harb. Is he here?"

There followed a lengthy silence.

"No!"

Once again Joel could read in Harb's mind that he lied. He pushed him over backwards, entered the house, and closed the door behind him. Harb came to his feet, fists clenched, but before he could take action, Joel took control of his mind, calmed him down, and ordered him to lead him to Yassim. A staircase went up to the right, and beside them a short, narrow hall led to a large room at the back.

One of the three men seated in the room, rose as he entered with Harb. He was Tasa Yassim, and he held a gun loosely in his hand. Not wanting to lose his terrorist contact to a ricocheting bullet, Joel took control of all the minds in the room. He ordered four of the men to go about their business and leave him alone with Yassim. They left without saying a word. Tasa's mind revealed a weak man, over his head in his relationship with the terrorist, just hanging on by his fingertips. The man had no character, just an overdose of greed and fear.

"Now Tasa, I'm looking for Abula Shayma. Can you take me to him?"

Tasa struggled internally, not wanting to answer, but he could not combat Joel's mind control. "He lives on the next street. I'll take you there."

They went out the back of Tasa's house through a small back garden, into the garden of the house behind, and up to the back door. Tasa banged on the door until it opened, revealing a woman covered from head to foot, with just her eyes showing. "We need to see Abula," said Tasa. Without saying a word, the woman turned and led them into a large back room similar to the one in Tasa's house. Leaving them there, she left the room, returning in less than a minute with Abula.

"Who is this Tasa? What do you want?"

Before Tasa could answer, Joel took command of Abula's mind. This man differed from both Abu Talib, and Tasa. He had Talib's strength, but used his religion for his own purposes. He had Yassim's greed, but not his weakness. He was the worst combination, a strong, greedy, religious fanatic with no conscience.

"I want a tour of your house, including the armory."

Abula tried to resist Joel, but the battle lasted only a few seconds.

"Okay, this way."

They walked down the corridor, through the kitchen, and into the larder. In the small room, Abula removed the rug, lifted the trap door in the floor, and descended a staircase. Thirty feet down, they entered a cellar, with concrete floor, walls, and, 10 feet above, a concrete ceiling. The ceiling supports were 12-inch square columns, on 10-foot spacing. The 30-feet wide by 60-feet long cellar went under both back gardens, with an exit in Tasa's house.

Weapons of every description filled the room. They included boxes of dynamite; racks of rifles, Uzis, and handguns; mines; rocket launchers; mortars; boxes of ammunition; and racks of dynamite-laden vests, for suicide bombers. Three men stood by the dynamite discussing the making of IEDs (Improvised Explosive Devices). They turned upon hearing Joel approach, and one pointed a gun at him.

"Don't shoot!" said the older man, with a voice of authority. "A stray bullet could start explosions."

The man's mind told Joel his name, Abdallah Husayn, the battalion commander. Joel had found one big fish and two more cell leaders. His luck held. He had found the arsenal for all of Abdullah's operations.

Controlling all their minds, Joel now had five terrorists in the cellar with him. He would give them the pain in the stomach treatment, but what to do with all these weapons? Then he realized the weapons were useless without ammunition.

Joel ordered Abdallah to suspend all his operations and bring all his cell leaders to the cellar by noon tomorrow; he would be here to meet them. Leaving them to make these arrangements, Joel went outside and activated his transporter. It was 2 p.m.—that made it nine a.m. in Colombia. If he left now he could have lunch with Elena. If he spend the afternoon with her, he could still be back home by 6 p.m.

When Joel arrived in Colombia, he found Elena in a well-constructed house in the village.

"I used some of your money to have the villagers build me an office here in the village. I can work out of here and sleep overnight in the back bedroom, if I don't feel like going home."

"What are you doing for a telephone?"

"It's funny you should ask. I asked Leon to get a line extended from his, with my own private number. He said no; then he had an attack of terrible stomach pains. The pains wouldn't go away until he called the telephone company to have a phone installed the next day."

"They did it that fast?"

"Yes, when Leon says jump, even the phone company asks "How high?" Did you have anything to do with the pains? I got that impression when Leon cursed you, and the pains got worse."

Joel laughed. "Yes, I used hypnotic suggestion. If you need anything for our project, ask any of the men. They will help or suffer the dreaded stomach pains."

Elena told him of her progress. "The school had been enlarged and supplies purchased. Three new teachers from Cali now teach all the city school system subjects, and a private tutor works with Maria and Esteban six hours a day, seven days a week. They are like sponges, absorbing every thing they are taught. The villagers work the fields, laughing and singing, and the children delight in their new school. It's all thanks to you."

Joel switched off his protective suit for the first time outside of his compound since he had perfected it. Taking hold of Elena's hand, he said in a soft voice, "What about you Elena, what are you getting out of all this?"

She looked at her hand in his and started to pull away. Stopping herself, she gripped his hand, and looked at his face, puzzled by this sudden show of affection. "I am fulfilling a lifetime dream, helping my people. I've always thought of them that way, my people. I don't want anything to spoil it." He understood her meaning; she wanted to be friends, but no more at this time. He would have to go slow, and see what developed.

"Let's have lunch," he said with a cheery voice.

"Why don't we eat with the children?" she replied. "I pay some senoras to cook lunch at the school. That way, we know the children get at least one good meal a day."

"Good idea. Let's go."

They reached the school in time to join the children, and teachers, in a meal of chicken enchiladas, rice, and refried beans. After lunch, Joel and Elena walked out to the nearest fields, and talked to some of the villagers. They crowded around him all talking at once. They spoke a dialect that mixed Spanish with their native Indian tongue, and it took him a while to understand it. By the time they left he could hold a conversation with them. They obviously adored Elena. This could not have happened in a few days; she must have shown them kindness in the past.

Returning to the village, they visited with Maria, Esteban, and their teacher, Raul. Joel appraised Raul, reading his thoughts. He decided that Elena had made a very wise choice. Raul's motive covered more than the excellent paycheck; he genuinely wanted to succeed with his two pupils. As with Elena, he would not go deeper into Raul's personal thoughts.

Joel and Elena returned to her office and sat there talking about everything, and nothing. They now felt comfortable with one another, and the afternoon passed rapidly. He hugged her goodbye, turned on his belt, strapped on the transporter, and headed for home.

Next day he entered Abula Shayma's cellar at noon Iraq time. Abdallah Husayn and his ten cell leaders stood around waiting for him. The seven Joel had not yet met wanted to know what they were doing there, saying it was too dangerous—the Americans could catch them all at once. When Joel entered, seven guns pointed at him. "Hold your fire," warned Abdallah, "You will blow us all up."

Joel took control of the new cell leaders' minds, as a mass hypnosis, then spent five minutes with each one evaluating them. Their beliefs fit into a similar pattern: rigid conviction that Allah wanted the holy war, a fight to the death, and democracy was the tool of the devil. He gave them all the stomach pain treatment, so that the thought of killing would bring the pain.

As a group he ordered them to move all the weapons in the cellar out to a location in the middle of the desert. Everything had to be there in forty-eight hours. Once they completed this task, they and all their men had to go back to their homes and live in peace. Joel left them planning how to accomplish this.

While in Mosul he visited Abu Tabil to find that work had started on two houses; then on to Fallujah to see Dahr Sabah; and finally to Bagdad, to find out the time and place for the meeting with the Moslem leaders. The meeting place would be the large conference room next to Nouri al-Maliki's office, in three days, at 10 a.m. Joel then went home to plan his biggest activity so far, a visit to the President of the United States.

Chapter Six

Joel lay reclined in the machine for three hours, with the power at eighty percent. He had to get this one right. He felt like he was gay, and about to come out of the closet. If this went wrong, there would be no turning back, with the whole world knowing about him. All his plans could go down the tube. He lay there thinking of Anton Kelbeck, Jr. Would Anton approve of what he had done so far? Joel hoped his progress met with Anton's approval, but he knew Anton wanted more, and so did he. He was ready.

At 8 o'clock the next morning, Washington time, Joel landed on the small lawn just south of the West Wing of the White House. He wore his protection suit with its cloaking device activated and over this his transporter, with its cloaking device. He stood quietly waiting to see if he had been detected. Nothing happened. He turned off the transporter but kept the cloaking device over the backpack.

He followed the concrete path, as it curved up to the Oval Office and under the roof extension, supported by marble Doric columns. Still undetected, he opened and entered through the Rose Garden door, into Karen Keller's office. Joel moved silently to an unused corner of the room as Karen looked up from her desk. Seeing no one enter, Karen, the president's personal secretary, called security, and a Marine guard quickly entered the room. With Karen following behind, the Marine checked outside. They searched for about five minutes, while Joel stood there virtually holding his breath. The Marine reported the incident, and a thorough search of the grounds began, using dogs and metal detectors. The Marine and Karen both returned to their workstations.

Joel moved passed Jared Weinstein, Special Assistant to the President, into the short hallway leading to the Oval Office. He stood in a recess next to the Oval Office door, waiting for it to open. He stood there for ten minutes, before he heard a buzz on Jared's desk. The presidential assistant rose and went into the Office. Joel slipped in behind him, moved silently to his left, past the grandfather clock, and stood in the recess of the window next to the clock. The President handed him some papers, and Jared left, closing the door behind him.

As Joel stood there he felt sure the President could hear his heart beat, it sounded like a drum to him. Joel looked at the President and concentrated on his mind. The thoughts came fast and furious—all the problems of the world filtering through one mind. How one man could handle such stress—it must be overwhelming. Slowly the President turned to face him. Joel had made contact with his mind and had taken control. Without Joel saying a word, the President picked up the phone and said, "Karen, I don't want to be disturbed for thirty minutes. Hold all my calls, and nobody is to come in."

"Mr. President, I will not harm you. I have a true story to tell you, I want you to listen carefully and remember all I tell you." Joel proceeded to tell him the story. He left out the machine and how he got his powers, but described the powers. He told him what he had done in Watts and other cities; he told of Colombia, Iraq, and Afghanistan. He told him he intended to go into China, Russia, and Africa. He told him of his next project, Congress. He asked him not to tell anyone about this visit no one would believe him; they would think he had a hallucination.

"I am telling you so that as events evolve, you can act with wisdom and knowledge. I want you to be open to peace initiatives, no matter how unlikely they seem or who is proposing them. For now, slow down the military action in Iraq and Afghanistan. Bring troops home. I will advise you if there is a problem."

"How will you advise me?"

"I will visit you like this."

"Using the cloaking device?"

"Yes."

"We could use that for our military."

"You don't get it yet, do you? There will be no need for the military when I am finished."

"No military! I'm glad I'm leaving."

"I will brief your successor when the time is right."

Joel boldly walked out of the Oval Office, through the Rose Garden door onto the South Lawn. He activated the transporter, and returned home.

He needed to do some research on the Congress, both House of Representatives and the Senate. The house had four hundred and thirty-five members. Each representative has an office; these offices are located in the Cannon Building, the Longworth Building, the Rayburn Building, and the Gerald R. Ford Building. The one hundred senators, have offices in the Russell Building, the Dirksen Building, and the Hart Building.

To visit each one of these men individually would take weeks—that would be if he could find them in their offices. There had to be a better way. He could go to the Capitol Building and brainwash them while Congress was in session. That had several problems. The chambers held very few politicians, unless there was a major bill to vote on. Even if he could close the public gallery, it would be impossible to close the press gallery without a major news furor.

What if he got the party leadership to call closed-door meetings? That would be four meetings: Senate and House for Democrats and Republicans. He would only have to visit and brainwash, eight to ten people to get them to call the meetings, then attend four meetings.

He selected the people he needed to visit. House Democrats: Speaker Nancy Pelosi, Majority Leader Steny Hoyer, Majority Whip James Clyburn; House Republicans: Minority Leader John Boehner and Minority Whip Roy Blunt; Senate Democrats: Majority Leader Harry Reid and Assistant Majority Leader Dick Durbin; Senate Republicans: Minority Leader John McKinney, and Minority Leader Pro Tempore Len Fasano.

Once again Joel arrived in Washington at 8 a.m. to spend the day visiting these people. He started with Nancy Pelosi. Using the cloaking device, he slipped into her office, waited until she was alone, and then, controlling her mind, had her tell her secretary to leave her alone for half an hour. He told her, "I want you to set up a meeting with all the House Democrats, so that I could talk to them. There must be total secrecy and security, with no one but the representatives in the room."

"We don't have a room big enough for all of them."

"What about a congressional hearing room?"

"That would hold half; you will need two meetings."

"Okay, two meetings for the House Democrats, two meetings for the House Republicans, and two meetings for the Senate, six meetings. Allowing forty-five minutes for each meeting, we can do it in one morning, from seven thirty to noon."

"When do you want this to happen?"

"As soon as possible. Can you do it in three days?"

"I can try, but you might not get everyone there."

"I must have ninety percent, Can you do that?"

"I'll try."

"Co-ordinate with John Boehner, Harry Reid, and John McKinney, but don't call them until this afternoon. Remember, total secrecy, no press. By this evening Steny Hoyer and James Clyburn will know what's going on; they will help you."

Joel left Pelosi's office, and proceeded to have the same conversation with John Boehner, Harry Reid, and John Mc Kinney. In the afternoon he tracked down the other congressmen on his list, and told them to support the effort of the leaders.

Chapter Seven

Returning to California, Joel spent extra time in the machine. Then he practiced self-levitation, and group hypnosis; he would be using both in the next few days. He worked on a change to his force field suit that enabled him to touch Elena with his bare hands. The design change added a narrow ring around each wrist that closed off the force field before it reached his hands, leaving them bare. The rings could be deactivated if he needed full protection.

He also worked on a two-person transporter. He designed a new, three-inch square, hollow tube, oval shaped, to fit around two people. The tube circumference adjusted to fit different-sized people. Joel flew face down; the second person would lie on Joel's back, also face down, with an inflatable cushion between them. The larger tube enabled him to upgrade the oxygen generator, and the air-conditioning system.

He called Elena and asked if he could visit her the next day. She seemed pleased to hear from him, so at 8 a.m. the next day he arrived at Elena's office. For the first time he could hold her hands in his. They talked about her projects and how well they seemed to be going. Then Joel asked her if she would like a ride in his new transporter. Elena was not a timid soul—she agreed readily—so Joel strapped them both in. He told her to tell him immediately if she wanted out, and with her assurances that she was comfortable, they started to ascend.

He climbed to a thousand feet, flew across the fields, above the workers, then turned and flew over the villa. She could see her family sitting out on the patio and the children swimming in the pool. She thought what useless, wasted lives they led. Joel returned to the village and landed. Elena was exhilarated. "Can we go farther?" she asked.

"Can you take the whole day off?"

"Why? What do you have in mind?"

"We could go to the United States; I will show you my home."

She hesitated—the idea thrilled her but could she trust Joel? "What time would we get back?"

"Anytime you want, but it's a two-hour flight each way, and if we stay there four hours, we would be back by five."

Okay, let's do it. I'll just go tell Maria and Esteban we're going. Do I need to bring anything?"

"No, we can get anything you need there."

The two-hour flight seemed to go by quickly. Once Elena got her breath back, after the rapid climb to 80 thousand feet and the acceleration to five thousand miles an hour, they talked the rest of the way. At that altitude they experienced no sensation of flight and the air-conditioning kept them very comfortable.

He told her some of his story, explaining how the belt worked, but leaving out the machine. Mainly he talked about the work in progress in Watts and the other cities. He mentioned Kory and Tanisha; she asked if she could meet them.

Once home Joel switched off his belt completely; he felt safe with Elena. The compound amazed Elena and she delighted in exploring the house. She thought it large, until he took her down to the basement, which doubled its size. He asked her, "Would you like to try on a belt?"

"Yes, I would love to." Joel attached the belt over her clothing. She walked around in it awkwardly, tried picking up a few small items.

"I don't think I would like to be in this all the time. I feel a little claustrophobic."

Joel removed the belt. As he tried to move around her to place the belt back in the storage cabinet, Elena moved sidewise and he accidently bumped into her. As she started to fall, Joel put his arms around her, caught her, and pulled her close to him. Her arms had gone around him automatically to save herself from falling. They stood there looking into one another's eyes for about twenty seconds, then Elena stiffened, pulled away, and turned her back to him. Joel felt a cold shiver go through him, as he stared at her nape. His hopes for this relationship shattered; he had thought she liked him, but apparently not.

Slowly Elena turned to face him. She closed the gap between them and placed her hand on his arm. "I'm sorry, that was childish of me, I do like you very much. Since you came into my life I have known nothing but joy and fulfillment. I'm not sure how deep my feelings are for you. Could we go a little slower and see what happens?"

Joel felt relief surge through his body. "Would it be okay if I hug you?" She came into his arms and they embraced. He whispered in her ear, "We will take all the time you need. Now, how would you like some lunch?"

"Can I have an American hamburger? Better still, a McDonald's hamburger?"

They transported to The Train Station in Barstow, the largest McDonald's in the world. When he transported into a public place, he used the cloaking device when landing. She couldn't believe all the different kinds of food available, and all the things for sale, even a liquor store. After the hamburger and a coffee ice cream, her favorite, for dessert, they transported to Watts.

Tanisha and Kory welcomed them. The headquarters bustled with activity. Tywanna worked on enrolling students of all ages for the next semester of college; Rashid had a group of people to match to jobs available; and Shawn was signing up applicants for the four trade school classes at the church hall. Tanisha showed Elena all the projects they had going, and how they kept track of them. Elena, obviously impressed, asked lots of questions; the two women hit it off from the start.

As they left the headquarters, Elena asked, "Can I buy a dress while I am here? I'll pay you for it, when next you come to visit me."

"We will buy you a whole wardrobe; you can leave some clothes here for the next time you visit."

"Where can we go?"

"I know just the place." Joel transported them to Redondo Beach, to the parking lot of Nordstrom's department store. Inside, Elena spent a pleasant hour going through all the clothes on display. She picked out three dresses, two pair of jeans, two tops, lingerie, a pair of Nike's, and a gift each for Maria and Esteban. Finally they paid for her selections. Joel adjusted the transporter belt, so that the purchases could lie on the cushion between them, and they returned to the compound.

After selecting the clothes to take back to Colombia, Elena put the rest in one of Joel's spare bedrooms. She said, "I feel a little tired now."

"I have just the thing for you." He showed her his recliner/machine. "Lay in this for half an hour and you will be completely rested." She looked a bit skeptical, but he had her sit in it with her feet in the stirrups, put the headphones on her, and told her to grip the armrests. He set it at thirty percent for half an hour.

"Wow! This is really relaxing." After saying that, she drifted off to sleep.

He sat there just looking at her for thirty minutes, unable to believe his good luck at finding her. When she awoke she went to the spare bedroom, and came out wearing a new top and jeans. She twirled to show him the new outfit. "That recliner really works. I've never felt so rested after such a sort nap."

They spent the next hour sitting on his patio, talking over a glass of wine. She sat beside him as they looked out over the barren landscape. When he took her hand in his, she squeezed it, and left it there.

As they transported back to Colombia, Elena reached around the air cushion, and clasped both his hands and they talked all the way. Once there, Joel was in no hurry to leave. They had a meal with Maria, Esteban, and their families. He felt like he could relax with these folks. He left at 9 o'clock, but because of the time difference, arrived home at 8 o'clock.

Chapter Eight

oel needed be in Iraq the next day, for his meeting with the Iraqi leaders, so he did his running and weight lifting right away. After that, he slept in the machine for three hours, arising fully refreshed. He had to leave at midnight to get to Nouri al-Maliki's conference room by 2 p.m.

Using the cloaking device he entered the room and waited as the others arrived. Because he had prepped them during his individual visits, they entered subdued, with none of the usual posturing and bluster. Once all the attendees took their seats, facing in the same direction, Nouri locked the doors from the inside, and they waited. Before he uncloaked, Joel took control of their minds and instructed them to see him as Muhammad. They didn't all see the same image; each one of them had a picture in his mind of what Muhammad looked like, and each man saw that image.

The room had a 30-foot ceiling. Joel sat, crosslegged, facing them, levitated to 20-feet, and slowly uncloaked. He did not speak to them, but planted the thoughts in their minds, using Arabic with a Mecca dialect. This way each man heard the voice he associated with Muhammad.

"I am greatly disappointed in all of you." His voice boomed in their minds. "You have all interpreted the teachings of the Qur'an for your own personal purposes. I demand that the killing stops immediately. Once peace is restored, I will drive the foreign forces from your lands. You will stop fighting among yourselves. Democracy is a good thing; I want suffrage for all my people, including women. Those who do not obey me will suffer pains at the hands of Allah. Your only mission in life from now on, is to bring peace and prosperity to all of my people, especially the lowest among you. Over the next few days, I will appear at mosques across Iraq, repeating this message to the masses. You will endorse it, and lead in carrying out my wishes. Remember, thoughts that oppose my wishes will bring pain. Now go home and start the work of Allah."

Joel recloaked, and sat there for a while, listening for reactions. The Iraqi leaders sat there stunned for a few moments, then gradually drifted out of the room. The press besieged them, but nobody had anything to say. Joel followed them out. He had a few hours before evening prayers and he planned to visit Dahr Sabah and Abu Tabil before going to the mosques.

That evening Joel visited the major mosques in Bagdad, Mosul, Fallujah, Kirkuk, and Al Basrah. He controlled the minds of the congregations and appeared to them as Muhammad. He delivered the same speech he had given to the leaders, leaving out the greatly disappointed part. The newspapers picked up the stories, but their still and video cameras could not pick up any sounds or images. The reporters saw and heard the message, but the cameras didn't.

Joel repeated this performance the next day, at all the prayer sessions, at numerous mosques across Iraq, exposing eighty percent of the population to his message. The terrorists, by definition, being devout Moslems, attended prayers at mosques near where they were located. So the message got to the right people. Terrorist activities ground to a halt.

On his way home Joel stopped in Washington. He visited the President, to tell him not to worry about the reports of sightings of Muhammad. "It is just my way of bringing the message of peace to a troubled nation, Iraq."

"How did you create the appearance of Muhammad?"

"I used mass hypnosis; I appeared to them as their personal image of Muhammad."

"I could use that to sway Congress."

"Don't worry. I had already set that plan in motion. You will read about it in the newspapers in the next few days."

Joel left the President to visit Nancy Pelosi next. "Have you set up my meetings yet?"

"I'm glad you dropped by; I was getting worried. The meetings begin tomorrow at seven thirty as you requested."

"Did you have any problems?"

"Yes a lot of complaints, some illnesses, and a few outright refusals."

"Give me a list of the refusals."

"I thought you might want that, so I have it here." She handed a sheet of paper with some names on it. It included both Democrat, and Republican congressmen.

"How about security?"

"I had problems with the press; they got wind of the meetings, and want to attend. They're crying freedom of the press."

"Let one news crew of two people attend each meeting; choose a different network for each meeting. That should satisfy them."

Joel visited all the congressmen on the list, and by the time he returned to his compound, they had all agreed to attend the meetings. He called Elena, and after a lengthy conversation with her, started his workout. Following that, he spent three hours in the machine, at eighty percent power. His mind still expanded more after each session on the machine. He found everything easier: cloaking, mind control, levitation, and travel. He no longer needed to switch on the transporter for short trips in town, he just cloaked, levitated to forty feet, the moved horizontally at up to thirty miles an hour.

The next morning he entered the congressional hearing chamber at 7:20, and watched the legislators arrive. At 7:30 Nancy Pelosi closed and locked the doors. Everybody waited in anticipation. First Joel controlled the minds of the newspeople, told them to go to sleep, remember nothing, and wake up when he told them to. Next he uncloaked and used mass hypnosis to control all the people in the room, and delivered his speech.

"As of today you will all work to a new code of ethics. You will sever all ties with lobbyists, take no money from them, and never consider their needs when voting on a bill. Your major concern will NOT be reelection or pork projects. Your only concern, with any bill, will be, 'Is it the right thing to do, and does it benefit the citizens of the United States?' You will abstain from voting on any bill that provides disproportional benefits to you, your family, or your friends. You will vote for a bill that rescinds the congressional pensions and puts legislators on social security. You will get severe stomach pains if you willfully violate the intent of this code or lie to your constituency. For those of you who do not have a conscience, I will be your conscience, and you do not want a visit from me."

He called an end to the meeting, cloaked, and then awoke the newspeople. They were bewildered, wondering why everyone left before the meeting started.

Joel repeated this scenario five more times, until the entire House and Senate had received his message. That evening the media, reported that nothing had happened at any of the meetings, but also reported that numerous legislators complained of severe stomach pains.

From Washington, Joel transported to Colombia to visit Elena. They were very comfortable with one another now. She told him of the frustrations of her previous life and the satisfaction she got from what she accomplished now. She had made contact with surrounding villages to build a school and a clinic in each one. Joel added 1,000,000,000 pesos to her bank account, about $600,000, for these new activities. He told her about his activities and what he wanted to do next. He found it wonderful to have someone to confide in.

He stayed for dinner. The villagers put on a feast for him and entertained him with their native dancing. Joel felt completely at peace with Elena and her people. For the first time in years, Joel experienced happiness. After dinner they walked along the riverbank. Joel switched off his suit, and they embraced. She pulled her head back to look into his eyes and he kissed her gently. He asked her if she would come visit him again, and received a quick emphatic yes.

"Would you like to see some of the United States?"

"Hey, could we do that?"

"We could go to a lot of places and just stay a short time, or we could go to a few places and stay longer at each."

"Why don't we do both? I'll come for two days. We can do the short trips the first day then stay longer the second day."

"What do you want to see?"

"I'll leave that up to you, but I would like to see New York, Las Vegas, and the Grand Canyon."

"Okay, I'll work on an itinerary. Be sure to wear something comfortable."

They arranged for him to come pick her up in two days. He left at about 10 o'clock, which got him home at 9 California time.

The next two days he spent consolidating his achievements so far. He visited all the U.S. cities, Iraq, and Afghanistan. During his twice daily machine sessions, he planned future projects. Next on his list was Sudan.

Chapter Nine

oel arrived in the village by 7:30 Colombian time. Elena was waiting for him, with a gift of a large blanket made by the Indians. "This will look good on your recliner."

He hugged her, thanked her, and told her how beautiful she looked. He gave her a spare force field belt. "Put this on. I leave it switched off unless we need climate protection."

They folded the blanket, laid it on the air cushion, got into the transporter, activated the cloaking device, and left on their adventure. Joel's plan was to fly fast at high altitude some of the time, but to descend and slow down when they passed over places of interest. Of course, there was no way anyone could see even a small percent of the interesting sights in two days, so he could only hit a few highlights.

He started out due north towards Florida. He descended as they approached Jamaica, flew over the Couples Hotel with it's offshore island for nude bathing. Then then hovered over the sleepy tourist town of Ocho Rios, where they could see tourists climbing Dunns Waterfall. Continuing inland, they crossed the Blue Mountains, to Kingston on the north shore. Soon they were crossing Santa Clara on Cuba, and could see Havana off to the west.

Next stop, the Florida Keys, 1,700 islands that run southwest and separate the Atlantic from the Gulf of Mexico. They hovered over the island city of Key West, and watched the people stream off the cruise liners, maybe heading for the Ernest Hemmingway Museum. Key West, the farthest inhabited Key, is one hundred and twenty-nine miles southwest of Miami. Heading along the Keys, they passed over Key Largo, the largest of the Keys, into mainland Florida. Reaching Miami, Joel flew slowly over South Beach, then along Collins Avenue, looking at the luxury hotels. Turning east, they crossed the Julia Tuttle Causeway, over Miami to the Everglades. Going north again, over Lake Okeechobee, they came to Orlando, and took a slow cruise around the different theme parks: Magic Kingdom, Epcot, Hollywood Studios, Animal Kingdom, and the two water parks. Elena was enthralled by all the sights. She said, "It would be nice to spend a week at each of these places."

Picking up speed again, they followed the coast to Savannah, where Joel picked up Highway 95, all the way to Washington, D.C. Joel moved very slowly down the National Mall, at three hundred feet altitude. Starting at the Capitol Building at the east end, they passed all the Museums of the Smithsonian, then hovered beside the Washington Monument, with the reflecting pool and the Lincoln Memorial ahead of them and the White House to the right.

"It's noon. Are you feeling hungry yet? I know a good restaurant that has great seafood," said Joel.

"That sounds great. Do they have crab? I love king crabs legs."

"That's one of their specialties."

Joel landed on Water Street, in a far corner of the parking lot of Hogate's. He uncloaked, they got out of the transporter, he recloaked the transporter, and left it in behind some bushes. Then wearing their belts with the force field turned off, they entered the restaurant. The dining room was crowded, but the short line to the reservations desk moved quickly and the maitred' asked them, "Do you have a reservation?"

Elena felt disappointed, until Joel answered, "Yes I called yesterday. The name is Sampson." Elena hadn't known Joel's surname before.

"Yes Mr. Sampson. You requested a window table." He handed two menus to his assistant. "Table 23, Joanne."

"Please follow me."

Joanne sat them at a table for four, against the window, with a beautiful view across the Washington Channel to the East Potomac Park and Golf Course.

"I was going to say this is like a fairy tale, a dream come true, but it's not like that. It *is* that."

Joel laughed, and took her hand in his. "All we have seen pales before you beauty. You're the loveliest woman I have ever seen."

"Thank you, sir." Her eyes glowed as she looked at him.

"Now! How about those crab legs?"

The waiter approached, bringing rolls and butter, and Joel, knowing Elena preferred a slightly sweeter wine, ordered two glasses of Kendall Jackson Riesling; then they turned their attention to the menus. Elena selected the house salad with a light Italian dressing, plus the full portion of king crab legs. Joel went for the French onion soup, with the Dover sole stuffed with crab meat.

"What do you have planned for me next?"

"Well, I'm saving New York for tomorrow night, and we need to be at the compound by 4, so with the time change that gives us six hours, I thought we could crisscross the country looking at some of the national monuments, both man-made and natural."

"What a great idea! Let's do it."

They both declined dessert but had coffee. Joel paid the check, they both used the restrooms, and they left the restaurant at one. Retrieving the transporter, they headed north toward Niagara Falls. Joel hovered in front of the larger Horseshoe Falls, and they hung there as 6 million cubic feet of water per minute dropped 173 feet from Lake Erie to Lake Ontario.

Heading southwest along Lake Erie, then across Indianapolis, they arrived in St. Louis, and Joel alit on the top of the Gateway Arch, 630 feet above the ground. The top of the Arch is 17 feet wide and the wind velocity was low, so Joel activated both of their personal force fields, with the cloaking on, and turned off the transporter. Elena clung to him at first, but soon let go and moved around a bit. The view was spectacular. Below them stood The Edward Jones football dome, The Scottrade ice hockey center, Busch baseball stadium, and in the distance, Forest Park and the third largest zoo in America. Elena looked at the vista in silence for a while, then turned to Joel and asked, "Can we go to the Alamo next?"

Joel laughed. "Are you reading my mind now? That is next on the itinerary."

From St. Louis, they flew southwest to San Antonio, home of the Mission San Antonio de Valero, or "the Alamo," where in February 1836, under siege, one hundred eighty-seven Americans died defying six thousand Mexicans soldiers for 13 days. Joel slowly circled the mission building at a height of ten feet, then after a slow cruise down The River Walk he headed for the Petrified Forest National Park in Arizona and the Painted Desert.

The colorful stratified layers of minerals and organic matter have hardened into dunes, mesas, and buttes of exquisite beauty, especially at dawn or sunset. At the southern end of the park lie the fossilized remains of the Triassic era coniferous forest where the 225-million-year-old bones of "Gertie" the Staurikosaur were found.

The next stop was the Grand Canyon, where Joel, after hovering above for a panoramic view, descended to the canyon floor and slowly followed the Colorado River, from North Rim to Lake Mead. Then passing over Las Vegas and The Strip, saying they'd return to see this at night, Joel headed for home.

Back in the compound Joel suggested that they take a nap to refresh them for the night's entertainment. When Elena agreed, he persuade her to lay back in his recliner/machine; setting the controls at fifty percent, he left her there for an hour. At the same time, Joel went down into his basement and used the machine there himself. One hour later he woke Elena.

"Has it been an hour? I can't believe how rested I feel." She stood up. "It's amazing; I'm ready for anything."

"Good. Pack a suitcase. We're gonna to stay at the Beverly Hilton tonight. We'll shower and change at the hotel, then go to the Hollywood Bowl."

She looked at him with her eyes glowing, then came into his arms and hugged him. Then peering into his eyes, she said, "That's wonderful. What's on tonight?"

"Tchaikovsky by the Los Angeles Philharmonic Orchestra, complete with a fireworks display."

"Will they play the 1812 Overture?"

"That's the highlight of the evening."

"Where are the suitcases?" She grabbed his arm, and he led her to her room, took a suitcase out of the closet, and placed it on her bed. "Go and pack yours. I can't wait to see the Beverly Hilton." She soon came out, wheeling the suitcase and wearing a plain white blouse with tight-fitting light-blue Jeans. She looked so lovely that a shiver of anticipation rippled through his body.

Thirty minutes later, with the transporter on his back like a backpack, Joel registered at the hotel. Of course he had a reservation for a suite in the Wilshire Tower. Once the bellhop had placed their luggage on the bed and left with a generous tip, Elena toured the suite. The large sitting room had a custom-built office area, a sofa, a coffee table, and two easy chairs. On the coffee table stood a vase of red roses and on the desk a vase of gladiolas both ordered by Joel. She oohed and aahed at the balcony's expansive view of Beverly Hills, the 42" plasma HDTV, the ergonomic chairs, the California king-sized pillow-top mattress, the L'Occitane bath products, and the spacious spa-like bathroom with a large stall shower.

Joel asked, "Do you want to shower first?"

"Why don't we shower together?"

She moved into his arms and he kissed her, long, slow, and passionately. Parting slightly, Joel unbuttoned her blouse, pushed it back over her shoulders, and let it fall to the bathroom floor. Her skin was silky smooth as he moved his hands down her back to unfasten her bra. Meanwhile, Elena had removed Joel's shirt, and as they pressed their upper bodies together, Joel felt a surge of happiness flow through his very core. He had never felt anything like this before, even with Beth. They laughed gently as they each struggled with the other's pants zipper. With their jeans around their ankles, they stepped out of them and each removed their own undergarment. The perfection of her body filled him with desire. Her breasts were firm, upright and full without being too big, her stomach flat, and her sparse pubic hair dark and silky.

Coming back together, they felt the warm contact of the whole length of their bodies. Joel placed his hands on her buttocks, pulling her tight against him and kissed her deeply several times, as they both reveled in the giddy headiness of their passion.

Joel reached out with his right hand, opened the shower door, and turned on the water. When the temperature reached a comfortable level, he lifted Elena off her feet and carried her into the shower. Gently standing her down, he reached for the L'Occitane soap, and as he lathered her wet body the lavender fragrance filled his nostrils. He handed the soap to her and as he cleansed her body, she returned the favor, with special attention to his large erection.

Returning his hands to her buttocks, he lifted her off her feet, turned his back to the shower water, felt her guide him inside of her. Then very slowly he moved her back and forth over his huge manhood. Gradually Joel increased the pace. He knew that they had waited for this a long time and neither of them would hold out very long. The thrust increased to a crescendo and she came as he exploded inside her.

Joel held Elena close in a bear hug for a long time; he could feel her heart pounding as loudly as his. After kissing her deeply, he resumed washing her body, enjoying every crevice. They dried off, then, lay on the bed entwined in each others arms.

"That was the most wonderful experience of my life," said Elena.

"I feel the same. Elena, I love you."

The silence stretched out between them. "I love you too, but I'm afraid it won't last and I will be hurt again."

"I will never intentionally hurt you. I want to be with you for the rest of my life."

They lay there snuggling and kissing for about fifteen minutes, before Joel said, "We must get ready; we have a show to go see."

Joel dressed in a pale blue shirt, grey flannel pants, navy blue blazer, and black leather loafers. Elena wore a simple black sheath dress with spaghetti straps, sheer black panty hose, and black pumps. Her jewelry consisted of large diamond stud earrings, a simple pearl necklace, a black diamond solitaire ring, and a gold pinky ring.

At precisely 7 o'clock a knock on the door revealed a bellhop with an ice bucket containing a bottle of Dom Perignon and two champagne flutes. They sat on the balcony, holding hands, enjoying the view and the warm night air, and toasted each other with tiny sips of champagne. At 7:30 the phone rang. Joel answered with the portable hotel phone. He hung up and said, "Let's go. Our chariot awaits."

They descended to the lobby, and exiting the main entrance of the hotel, found a limousine waiting for them at the curb. The driver held the door open for them as they entered the backseat. He then proceeded east on Wilshire Boulevard, north and east on Santa Monica Boulevard, and north on Highland Avenue. Turning left on Pat Moore Way, he circled the parking lot and dropped them off one hundred and forty feet from the Hollywood Bowl entrance.

The driver opened the door for them letting them out, then, from the front passenger seat retrieved a picnic basket, which he handed to Joel. Walking up the slight slope to the entrance, they proceeded to their seats, Box 543 in the Garden section, arriving there at 8:15. The box gave them a dead-center, eye-level view of the stage, thirty feet away. They had a 360 degree view of the Hollywood Hills and behind them the natural amphitheatre rose to a height where, to a lot of the 17,376 attendees, the stage was a tiny shell.

They turned their attention to the picnic basket, which had three separate compartments. On one side in a cooler they found two salads, a variety of dressings, a bottle of Kendal Jackson Riesling wine, and two bottles of Perrier. The other side held separately wrapped, oven-roasted potatoes, cauliflower au gratin, slices of prime rib, and pieces of chicken, all placed in a warming blanket. The middle contained wine glasses, cutlery, a cork screw, and a generous supply of napkins.

They had just started on their meal when the concert started. They were treated to a selection of some of the most beautiful music ever written. This included the Fantasy Overture from *Romeo and Juliet*, The First Piano Concerto, selections from three ballets, *Swan Lake*, *Nutcracker*, and *Sleeping Beauty*, the sixth symphony (Pathetique), and culminated with the 1812 Overture, and at the music crescendo the fireworks display started. They sat quietly enjoying the atmosphere as the audience started to leave. Neither off them wanted the night to end.

When the crowd had thinned, they walked slowly down to the parking lot where the limousine awaited them. The driver took the picnic basket from Joel, opened the back door, and they entered their chariot. The driver skillfully maneuvered through the congested traffic, but it still took forty-five minutes to reach the hotel.

Back in their room, Elena said, "It's been a long day but I still don't feel tired, do you?"

Joel thought of telling her about the recuperative powers of the machine, but decided he would keep that secret to himself. "No, how about a night cap?"

"That would be lovely. Is there any champagne left?"

They went out onto the balcony, and on the table they found an unopened bottle of Dom Perignon and two flutes in fresh ice. Elena laughed.

"You really planned this evening to the nth degree. I think it's wonderful that you are so thoughtful."

They sat on the balcony for about fifteen minutes, drinking champagne and talking about the things they had seen today. Suddenly Elena shivered, and Joel said, "Let's take the champagne inside; the late night air is getting chilly."

They went into the bedroom and placed the ice bucket on the bureau. Joel unzipped the back of Elena's dress and she walked over to the bed, turned, slipped the spaghetti straps off her shoulders, stepped out of her dress and placed it over the back of a chair. Joel began to undress without taking his eyes off her. She sat on the bed to take her panty hose off, then, standing again, undid her bra, letting it fall to the floor.

By now Joel was naked and his erection showed the effect she had on him. He walked over to her, pulled her panties down, and picked her up with her panties hanging around one ankle. Laying her in the middle of the bed, he lay beside her on his side, kissed her tenderly while he caressed her breast. Then, sliding his hand across her flat stomach and down between her legs, he parted her vulva and touched her clitoris. She moaned in his ear, "Don't wait any longer or I will come before you enter."

Joel rolled on top of her and entered her well-lubricated channel. The union didn't last very long, but they still both came together. They snuggled, falling asleep in each other's arms. Twice during the night, they woke up for a repeat performance.

The next morning they ordered room service breakfast, and ate on the balcony. Leaving the hotel at 10 o'clock, they spent the morning touring places of interest in the western states, spending about ten minutes at each location. With their force field suits on, they transported to the Mojave Desert and Scotties Castle. Then, after hovering over the top of Mount Whitney, they crossed Yosemite, Lake Tahoe, and Reno, on the way to Yellowstone Park. They headed south, across the Grand Tetons, The Great Salt Lake, to Salt Lake City and the Mormon Tabernacle, then on to Bryce Canyon. Finally heading west, they landed at Fisherman's Wharf at 2 p.m.

"Are you ready for lunch?" asked Joel.

"Yes. Could we have seafood again?"

"You're still reading my mind."

This time Joel had reservations at McCormick and Kuleto's, in Ghirardelli Square, with panoramic views of the San Francisco Bay, Angel Island, and Alcatraz. After lunch they returned to the compound to prepare for the evening. Joel had tickets to the Broadway musical *Mamma Mia*, which started at 8 o'clock. It would take an hour to get there, so with a three-hour time difference they needed to leave at 4:30. He persuaded Elena to nap in the recliner for an hour, set the controls at fifty percent power, then did the same himself.

By 4:15 they were dressed and having a light snack. Joel had reservations after the show at Club 21, a Prohibition-era speakeasy downstairs, with an elegant salon-style dining room upstairs. The menu included Speakeasy steak, roast saddle of rabbit, and sautéed Dover sole. The evening was a total success: the musical exceeded expectations, with the songs of Abba, delighting a new generation, and Club 21 had great atmosphere and excellent food.

On the way home Joel slowed down to cruise the Strip in Las Vegas, where the lights outshined those of Broadway. They hovered in front of the Bellagio hotel to watch the water fountains, which reached almost to the top of the hotel. He hung for a minute inside the top of the fountain with the water all around them. Then after going downtown to see the light show on Fremont Street, he headed back to the compound.

Elena shared Joel's bed that night and they expressed their love for each other, committing to a long-term relationship and sealing it with a night of lovemaking. The next morning Joel reluctantly took Elena home. He had to get back to business. Elena understood, and he promised to call often and visit her again soon.

Chapter Ten

The Republic of Sudan is the largest country in Africa by size, and the tenth largest in the world. The population of thirtynine million, even after the Darfur genocide of 2003/2004, is seventy percent Muslim. The country is ruled by President Omar al-Bashir and his National Unity party. Because of corruption, inefficiency, and fighting between rebels and government troops, very little of the relief supplies sent to the Sudan get to the people who need them.

To begin to resolve all the problems facing Sudan, Joel decided to assemble all the leading players he could find, get them moving in the right direction, and then work on any other people who tried to interfere. The eight regions, five in the north and three in the south, each have a military governor. Joel would start with these governors; plus President Omar al-Bashir; Vice Presidents Salva Kiir and Osman Taha; rebel leaders, Ahmed Haroum and Ali Kosheib; and United Nations representative Ashraf Jehangir Qazi.

Finding the eleven officials would be easy, the two rebels a more difficult problem. Joel decided to find them first. Sudan uses two languages, English and Arabic, two of Joel's proficiencies. He transported to the North Darfur region, cloaked, and cruised around reading thought patterns until he connected with someone thinking about Ahmed Haroum.

Probing this man's mind led him through two others men's minds, until he learned of Haroum's location.

The encampment nestled in the upper reaches of the Jebel Marra (Bad Mountains) range of dormant volcanoes, not far from the Deriba Crater, near a small village. The climate there was temperate, with sufficient rainfall and permanent water springs. Joel estimated a force of five hundred rebels camped there, with armored vehicles, mortars, and rocket launchers. Ahmed's headquarters occupied the largest structure in the village. Joel entered cloaked, but could not get the leader alone.

Finally he controlled Ahmed's mind, while still cloaked, and had him tell everyone to leave. He instructed him to be in the town of Abyei by noon the day after next. Aybei was recently destroyed in a battle between government and rebel forces. He could bring fifty unarmed men with him, with no weapons of any kind. Ahmed struggled with this order, but could not resist Joel's will.

He then had all the rebels assembled on the edge of the village, and did a mass mind control, so that Ahmed would not have a problem when he wanted to leave camp without any weapons.

Joel used the same method to find the second rebel leader, Ali Kosheib, giving him the same instructions. The eight governors, the three federal officials, and the U.N. representative presented no problem; he knew where to find them. He told them all to be in Abyei at noon two days hence. He ordered the governor of South Kurdufan to pull all his troops out of the area and to arrange for a conference room big enough for twenty people for the meeting. The fourteen participants now had their instructions. Joel went home to wait for two days.

Joel spent the next day visiting abusive people. He convinced fifty men in the New York area that beating their wives would only lead to severe stomach pains.

At 11:40 the next day, Joel hovered over the town of Abyei and watched all the participants arrive for his meeting. The South Kurdufan governor had instructed the general of his militia to clean up the only decent meeting room left in the severely damaged hotel, and guard it with a few unarmed troops. The principles and all their unarmed entourages milled around outside the hotel, as Joel landed in their midst. The fourteen attendees followed him into the meeting room.

Once everyone took their seats, Joel called the meeting to order. He took deep control of all the minds in the room. "First," he said, "all internal fighting will cease immediately; the civil war is over. Peace talks will begin between all the key parties. The only consideration will be what is the best way to help all the poor people. Food and medical treatment will be top priorities. All supplies from foreign sources will be delivered to the needy immediately. You will root out corruption at every level; the punishment for self-serving corruption will be so severe that nobody will want to risk it.

"A coalition government will be set up to serve the people. Agricultural tools will be given to anyone willing to grow their own food; everyone will be given a free education: secondary, high school, college and trade schools."

"How are we going to pay for all this?" asked President Omar al-Bashir.

"Each one of you will place all the money you have stolen from the people, to line your own pockets, in an account that will be used to fund these programs. Then you will borrow from the World Bank to cover what your illicit fortunes do not pay for. Once you remove all the corruption from your activities, the World Bank will be happy to lend you the money to keep the Sudan stable.

"Anyone disobeying these orders will suffer from stomach pains so severe that they will be incapacitated, and repeated violations will lead to a terrible agonizing death. I am tired of your wanton disregard for the suffering of the people entrusted to your care."

"What if we try to follow your instructions but people, not in this room, interfere and stop us from succeeding?"

"Call me and I will deal with them. But if you call me and I think you are dragging your feet and looking for excuses not to succeed, you will suffer dreadful consequences."

Joel spent a couple of days visiting abusers, attacking the ones at the top of his list identified as the most dangerous. The headlines in the newspapers shouted about the uncommon cooperation between the two political parties in both the Senate and the House. Another major story covered an epidemic of stomach pains that doctors could not diagnose. This virus seemed to hit a large number of politicians.

The most astonishing story covered the new bill in both chambers to rescind the retirement benefits for all federal politicians. The new bill would put them on the social security system along with all other citizens. This amazing bill had moved through Congress with record speed and arrived on the President's desk in record time. It had passed with a unanimous vote, so even in the unlikely case of a presidential veto, the veto would be overridden easily.

Joel decided to pay visits to each state legislature. He figured he could handle two a week and still keep up his other activities. That would mean in twenty-five weeks, all state legislatures would be working for the benefit of the voters and not for themselves.

Chapter Eleven

oel decided to upgrade his force field protection before he went to China. He had conceived an improvement that allowed him to move the force field away from his body to a 10-foot radius and to strengthen the force field to resist weapons of much greater capability. He incorporated the electrical field and cloaking devices into the new belt. Placing the belt on his mannequin and with the mannequin on his back, he transported to the Yuma Proving Grounds, where the United States Army tests new weapons.

The 20-ton Stryker Robot vehicle currently being tested here would suit his purposes. He intended to place his mannequin in front of one of the infantry carriers. He didn't want a manned vehicle, in case the collision injured the occupants. Arriving cloaked at the vast facility, Joel searched until he found the test area for the Stryker. He infiltrated the briefing for the day's activities, which included a map of the route to be driven, when, and at what speeds. A separate vehicle followed the tank using a remote control device to vary the speed and guide it. Joel went to a spot where the tank would be travelling at its maximum speed of forty miles per hour and placed the cloaked mannequin in its path. He extended the force field to a 10-foot diameter around the dummy, and increased the nuclear engine to maximum power.

He moved a half-mile away, to a position where he could observe what happened. About forty minutes later the tank reached the test position, collided with the mannequin, and came to an immediate halt. The front of the tank sustained severe damage, but the engine still worked. It kept pushing against the force field but didn't move an inch. Finally, the tank backed up; the controllers got out of the control vehicle, walked up to the obstacle, and started feeling their way around it.

Joel returned to the site and switched off the force field, causing two men, pushing against it, to fall over. Still cloaked, Joel retrieved his mannequin and transported to five hundred feet above the test grounds. He figured they would have a hard time explaining the damage to the tank.

Next, Joel searched for the Armory to see the latest rocket launcher weapons they were testing. He found two launchers being tested, both conventional, the largest with a fire power equivalent to a 105-mm bore tank gun. This block buster exploded with the equivalent of one ton of TNT. Taking one launcher and two rockets, he moved to a remote area of the test range. He conducted two tests, one with the force field expanded to the maximum ten feet, the other with the force field fully retracted. With the first test, the rocket exploded without any effect on the mannequin, the second explosion knocked the dummy over, but did no harm.

As Joel packed the mannequin on his back, he noticed four personnel carriers approaching his position, he had been detected. He activated his cloaking device and climbed to five hundred feet above the area. The vehicles stopped, mystified by the sudden disappearance of their quarry. They examined the only evidence of Joel's tests, a scorch mark on the earth where the rocket had exploded, and the rocket launcher he had left behind.

Joel returned home to spend time evaluating his capabilities. It seemed he could withstand all conventional weapons. Did he want to face up to nuclear weapons? The smallest tactical nuclear device in the latest United States nuclear weapons stockpile is the B61 MOD 14; it comes in a .3 kiloton size. That is the equivalent of 300 tons of TNT. The original atom bomb was 15 kilotons. Did he really need to prove he could withstand a .3 kiloton blast, or had his ego taken over? He decided that, before he went to China, he had to answer this question.

If Joel acquired two small nuclear bombs, he would need a way of transporting them. For the next few days, in between visiting pedophiles, other abusers, and state legislators, an interesting trio, he worked on the design and construction of a cargo box to tow behind the transporter. He made it 2 feet in diameter and 10-feet long with a 7-foot cargo area and a 3-foot tubular section at the front, attached to the belt by an umbilical cord. He could rise 20 feet off the ground, maneuver his feet into the tubular section by pulling on the umbilical cord, and then attach the tube to the belt. The force field and cloaking device enveloped everything. He still had his laser gun folded up against his chest.

Joel transported to Kirkland Air force Base, New Mexico, a nuclear storage facility. He landed undetected in a remote area of the base, unfastened the cargo container, and left it there. He then proceeded, cloaked, to the main facilities. Walking around undetected, he examined the minds of the people he encountered, until he found one, a captain, who knew the locations of the nuclear weapons. He learned that the bombs and their triggering devices were stored separately. The size of the triggers would enable him to carry them inside his cloaking device, so he decided to get them first.

Controlling the captain's mind, Joel found the name of Colonel Brackwood, a man who had authority to enter the storage buildings. Finding the colonel in his office, Joel controlled his mind, ordered him to go to the trigger storage building, and once inside, show Joel the location of the triggers. With two triggers inside his cloaking device, Joel then had the colonel take him to the bombs. This building had guards outside the entrance who checked Brackwood's identity, then inside he passed through a metal detector into an anteroom, where he was searched. Because of the limited space, Joel had a hard time keeping out of everybody's way.

Inside, the building consisted of a large hangar, with an aisle down the center. On each side of the aisle a chain-link fence reached twelve feet into the air. Additional chain-linked fences divided each side into five sections, to provide ten compartments for different types of nuclear weapons. Joel could see bombs, ranging from 10 to 350 kilotons; Trident submarine missiles, both 100 and 475 kilotons; intercontinental ballistic missiles, from170 to 335 kilotons; air launched cruise missiles, 5 and 150 kilotons; and tactical bombs, from .3 to 170 kilotons. Although the compartment walls were chain-link fence, the air-conditioning and cleanliness told Joel that whole hangar was a clean room.

The Kid looked at the array of video monitors that filled the wall in front of him. His name, William Bonney, got him the nickname of "The

Kid" at an early age, and now at 29, he even thought of himself that way, Billy the Kid. Colonel Brackwood had the authority to enter the weapons storage building, but why this morning? The Kid had not been informed of any activity today and it should be on his daily plan. He watched him walk down the center aisle and stop in front of the tactical weapons; this he had to watch.

Normally he would sit staring at the screens, bored to tears. To ensure constant survey of the screens, two men remained in the room at all times. They worked two-hour shifts, with one man changing every hour. The Air Force knew all about fatigue; if a problem occurred with a nuclear weapon, it could not be because every precaution hadn't been taken. Only well-trained staff sergeants or higher watched the screens; as a technical sergeant The Kid had seniority. He was in the middle of his shift. Rod had just come on and Jack hadn't left yet. "What do you think of this?" he said. "Blackie's in the weapons bay."

"He's cleared, so what's the problem?" said Rod.

"I know, but why is he there? we'd better put this in the log."

"Okay, I'll check all the sensors too, now, and again when he leaves."

The weapons bay had sensors across the surfaces of every wall, as well as the roof; any breech would be instantly detected. There were also cameras on the roof. Nobody had succeeded in getting anything out of this facility since it had opened. If a penetration occurred, a silent alarm would alert the guards at the front entrance showing the location of the problem. Armed military police would be immediately dispatched to that area.

Joel found the weapons he needed; he rose to the ceiling to examine the roof. He would not get two bombs past the guards at the door; he would have to go through the roof. Above the rafters he saw wooden boards supporting solid slate tiles. He noticed the extractor fans in the roof, directly above the bombs he needed; he would have to avoid those. A plan formed in his mind. He would cut through the roof with his laser gun, descend to the floor, load the weapons into his cargo container, and transport back out through the roof. He would have to uncloak to load the weapons, but it should only take a few minutes. His force field would be active all the time.

He instructed Brackwood to leave the building, and followed closely behind him. He had to stop the outer door from closing so that he could exit, but nobody seemed to notice the door hesitate before it closed.

Outside he instructed Brackwood to go back to his office, then he transported to where he had left the cargo container.

Retrieving the container, Joel activated the cloaking, and then returned to hover above the roof, just to the side of the extractor fan. He had to turn off the cloaking to use the laser. Quickly cutting a ten-foot diameter hole in the roof, he descended to the floor. He had just finished loading the bombs into the cargo container when four armed men approached the outside of the wire mesh fence.

"Raise your hands and don't move," instructed their leader.

Joel rose ten feet, and they fired at him. Luckily the bullets were aimed at him, not the container, and bounced off his shield. He went out through the roof with the container still dangling from the umbilical cord. Outside he hovered while he hauled the container up by the umbilical cord, placed his legs in the tubular end, and clamped it to his belt. Looking up he noticed a helicopter hovering about a hundred yards away. Joel activated the transporter force field just as the helicopter fired a rocket at him. The rocket exploded against the force field, but Joel felt no effect. Quickly activating the cloaker, he made it seem like the rocket had destroyed him.

The Kid had watched the whole incident on his monitors, from the moment Joel came through the roof until he disappeared in the rocket explosion, and everything was recorded into the computer. The recording would be useful, because nobody would believe what he had just seen. He ordered the military police to go preserve the wreckage; the two bombs should be there. Their casings could withstand the rocket blast. Only the nuclear blast triggered electronically from inside should shatter the casing. All the police found were fragments from the rocket. The intruder and the bombs had left no trace.

Back home Joel thought about the experience; at no time had he been in danger, but his existence was now a recorded fact. Would they somehow tie this incident in with the previous siege of his compound and come looking for him here? He would face that problem when it arose. For now he had to think about where to test the bomb on his force field.

Joel first thought Siberia would suit his purposes. He transported to the Republic of Sakha in Russia, which has forty percent of its territory above the arctic circle covered in permafrost. He surveyed the area between Noril'sk and Tiksi, south of the Laptev Sea, and to his surprise he found numerous towns. He could not find an area remote enough from any civilization. He tried the Chukotka Republic with the same result. He could not risk causing damage that might affect human life; he had to find somewhere else. Where would he find a place more remote than Siberia—not Alaska, or the Yukon Territories? Then it came to him, Greenland.

Greenland's inland ice cap is 1000 miles wide by 1500 miles long, and 3 miles thick at the center. His first trip to Greenland had to be aborted because of blowing snow in gale force winds. Finally, the storm passed and he could perform his survey. He traveled back and forth across this vast wasteland, and all he saw were polar bears. In the center he found absolutely nothing. The nuclear bombs were small enough that all they would do was melt an area of ice, which would soon freeze over again. The radiation would be negligible and soon dissipate.

Returning home, Joel began his preparations. He needed to replace the electronic switch in one of the triggers to operate with one of his mind-controlled switches, if he had to explode the bomb from inside the protection of his suit. Once he had done this, he loaded the two bombs; the two trigger devices; his latest belt design, with the expandable force field; a pair of very dark wraparound glasses; and a Geiger counter all into the cargo container. Everything was clamped in place so that they would not move during flight. He then fitted the mannequin into the passenger compartment of his transporter and set out for Greenland.

The weather remained clear and cold as he arrived in the center of the ice cap. He flew in circles covering a ten mile radius, but did not encounter any life forms, so while keeping comfortable inside the protection of his force field, Joel got out of the cargo container and landed. He unloaded the mannequin, attached the belt around its waist, and stood it on the ice with the force field at the maximum of ten feet diameter. He placed the bomb two feet away from the edge of the force field. Taking every thing else with him, Joel retired to a safe distance of ten miles. He used the remote triggering device to explod the nuclear bomb.

Joel heard the explosion, did not feel the blast, but could see a small cloud in the distance. After an hour's wait, and holding the Geiger counter in front of him, he slowly returned to the site of the experiment. The National Radiation alert level is 130 CPM (counts per minute), normal background levels are 5 to 60 CPM. Joel had obtained a reading of 10 CPM before he exploded the bomb. At ten miles away that level had not changed. At five miles the readings slowly climbed to a peak of 85 CPM at one mile, and then they started to decline. The radiation cloud had drifted away and the levels at ground zero now read 20 CPM.

The bomb had formed a hollow, where a lot of snow had been sucked up into the nuclear cloud. In the middle, the ice had melted the ice around the mannequin, and it had sunk into the shallow lake created. The ice had refrozen, leaving the mannequin buried up to its waist in ice. Joel activated the electrical current on the surface of the mannequin's force field, to re-melt the ice. Then hovering above, he switched off its force field and pulled the mannequin out of the lake. Joel examined it. He could find no damage of any kind; the Geiger counter readings did not increase. He took it back to where he had left the cargo container.

Now came the moment of truth. Did he really want to do this? He had come too far to back out now. Joel carried the second bomb and the modified trigger to ground zero. He placed the bomb on the ice, with the trigger beside it, moved fifteen feet away, and expanded the force field to a 10-foot diameter. He put on the dark glasses, faced away from the bomb, closed his eyes, and activated the mind-controlled trigger.

He sensed more than saw the bright light behind him, and he sank about ten feet. Apart from this, he felt no other sensations. Then he found himself in a dense cloud, swirling around and upwards. Joel lifted himself up about fifty feet, transported half a mile away, then turned and looked back. The cloud was rising rapidly, sucking the snow in from about a half a mile diameter. He continued on to the cargo container, retrieved the Geiger counter, and returned to ground zero. The CPM read 500, but started to decline right away; within half an hour it had reduced to 130 at the ice surface.

Joel gathered all his equipment at the ten-mile location, and transported back to California. Once in his compound he switched off the force field protecting him and took a Geiger counter reading. It showed 35 CPM. He now had the confidence to face any weapon any nation could use on him and easily survive.

Chapter Twelve

oel finished his preparation for his visit to China; he had attained fluency in Mandarin and Cantonese, the two official Chinese languages, and had studied the Chinese geographical, political, and religious status quo. He finalized the approach he would take. The size, advanced development, and stability of China made it a different proposition to Sudan. He must not upset the balance of power, too much and too quickly, or he might create chaos among a population of 1.3 billion. He would hypnotize the leaders, but he would also give them a demonstration of his powers, to reinforce the need for them to follow his orders.

The General Secretary, President, and Chairman of the Armed Forces Leadership, was Hu Jintao, but to make it possible for him to make the changes Joel wanted, he would need the cooperation of many other leaders, at least the following: Vice President Zeng Qinghong; Chairman of Congress Wu Bangguo; Premier Wen Jiabao; Chairman Political Consultative Conference Jia Qinglin; Members of Political Bureau Xi Jinping, Zhou Yongkang, Li Changchun, Li Keqiang, He Guoqiang; President of the Supreme Court Xiao Yang; Procurator General of the Supreme People's Procuratorate Jia Chunwang. He would let Hu Jintao add others to the group watching the demonstration of powers.

He found the home and office addresses of the twelve leaders he had chosen. Allowing a half hour with each and travelling time, it would take him a full day. Most of them lived in or around Beijing, so he would start there. Maybe he could get them to come to him. He would go to Hu Jintao's office at Zhongnanhai, the former imperial garden that is now the site of the Communist Party's Government offices, and have Hu invite them to his office.

Beijing's time zone was eight hours west of California, about an hour and a half in the transporter. To arrive in Beijing before 7 a.m. he would have to leave at 1 p.m. Joel put on his latest belt, the one with force field expander, laser weaponry, cloaking, and electrical shocking. Over this he wore the transporter belt, with its own force field and cloaking capabilities. At 1 p.m. he transported to Beijing, arriving at Zhongnanhai, at a 7:15. Zhongnanhai was part of the extended imperial palace of the later Ching Dynasty. He hovered over the Zhong Hai and Nanhai lakes, and could see the Xinhua Men, the Gate of New China, where the lowering of the Chinese flag ceremony takes place every day at sundown. The gate has two regular Beijing police officers patrolling out side the gate, but like the other gates to Zhongnanhai, is heavily guarded on the inside.

The exact location of Hu Jintao's office was not public knowledge, so Joel landed cloaked in the northwest area of compound. Very few people walked around this area, but he probed the minds of the few he saw until he found one who knew Hu's office location. Controlling his mind, he instructed him to go to Hu's office. Still cloaked, Joel entered the three-room office complex that consisted of the secretary's anteroom, a large conference room to the left and Hu's office behind the secretary. Joel entered Hu's office and stood in one corner, surveying the scene. The large, ostentatious room had all the trappings of power: the oversized desk, the voluptuous chair, the small conference table and four comfortable chairs, the communication center with multiple screens, and the computer complex. Today even the President of China was computer literate.

Joel looked into Hu's mind, and was surprised by what he saw. He had expected a cruel, vicious, uncaring person; instead he found a dedicated man who believed that all his actions benefited his people and the suffering he cause could not be avoided to achieve the greater good. The strength of this mind forced Joel to work harder than with any previous mind to gain control. Once in control, Joel had Hu instruct his secretary to arrange a meeting with the other eleven leaders, for today, as soon as possible in his office.

It seemed they all had offices in Zhongnanhai, but two were elsewhere in Beijing and could be there by ten. Joel settled for that, it would give him two hours to look around Beijing.

The obvious place to spend this time was at the Palace Museum of the Imperial Palace in the Forbidden City. From the middle of the Ming Dynasty, for five centuries, it has been the residence of the emperor and the ceremonial and political center of Chinese government.

Joel transported to Tiananmen Square and the Gate of Heavenly Peace that leads to the Forbidden City. In two hours it is impossible to do justice to a tour of the city; after visiting the Hall of Preserving Harmony, the Palace of Heavenly Purity, and the Palace of Earthly Tranquility, the two hours had passed.

Joel returned to Hu's conference room to find the eleven men seated around the table, waiting for Hu to enter. He looked into each man's mind, and this time he found some of the evil he had expected in Hu. All the minds showed a high level of intelligence, but some showed confidence and secure feelings, while others showed jealousy, doubt, and fear. By the time Hu arrived, Joel had deep control of all the minds in the room.

He told them that the time for political change in China has arrived; the chains of authority would gradually be loosened until China becomes a democracy. This would not happen overnight. They would be left as the leaders of China, but must begin granting freedoms that would lead to free and open elections to be completed in two years. They will start by granting freedom of speech, including freedom of the press, freedom of assembly, and the right to protest peacefully. This will include freedom of religion. There must be a free and open plebiscite in Tibet within six months, and if the vote was for separation, then they would grant Tibet autonomy.

Next, they will cease depriving people of their lives, liberty, and property without the due process of law. This will include discontinuing the practices of unreasonable search and seizure, cruel and unusual punishment, and compelled self-incrimination. They will be sensitive to all human rights.

They will instill these practices immediately and begin enacting laws to make them part of China's constitution, to be completed in three months. Then they must begin plans for elections. The two-year time period will allow the population to adjust to the new freedoms before the elections.

They will continue the good works they have started in the areas of education and public health, but they will reduce the expenditure for the military. The reduction in military spending will be slow so that it will not cause unemployment. The money will be spent to increase the standard of living of the poorest sections of your society. Theys will not need a large military, because Joel's powers would protect them. In the future, any country threatening another will have all its weaponry destroyed. To show them and the people they need to convince in order to make the changes Joel decreed, he will give a secret demonstration at a place of their choice in three days. They will decide who the attendees will be. He will face their forces alone, and defeat them.

Joel didn't waste the three days. The first day he spent twenty-two hours in New York, most of the time visiting pedophiles, and a few hours convincing the state legislature that the people's welfare came before their personal agendas. The third day he did the same thing in Texas. The second day he devoted to Elena.

When he transported to Colombia, he noticed that Elena seemed preoccupied and worried. When he questioned her, she told him there was another Cartel doing the same thing her family had. She met a man named Jorge Lehder, son of Carlos Lehder, a key member of the Medellin Cartel. Like Elena, Jorge didn't like what the cartel had done, and even though its size had diminished, the peasants still grew the coca plants as slaves of the drug lords. This region was to the south of the Norte Del Valle Cartel territory in the Department of Cauca. Carlos had heard rumors of the situation in Cauca Valley, and had plans to move in and take over their operation.

Joel told Elena not to worry; he would pay them a visit. Elena told him the location of the Lehder Villa, so Joel transported there, gave the principles of this Cartel the same brain control treatment he had given to the Ramirez family, and transferred the half a billion dollars in their overseas account to his own. He established the same arrangement with the villagers there, with Jorge Lehder as their patron doing Elena's job. He wiped out the Coca crops, then established a fund to provide for the farmers while they switched crops. He also instructed Jorge to build a school and a clinic.

Back with Elena, Joel told her what he had done and asked her to monitor Jorge's progress. He put $10,000,000 in Elena's bank account, to be used for both projects.

"Have you ever been snorkeling?" Joel asked Elena.

"Yes, I went to Cancun once and I tried it."

"Did you like it?"

"It was wonderful! Can we do some today?"

"Get your swim suit; I have towels and snorkeling equipment."

They loaded the transporter and Joel set a course for Blanquilla. This tiny island in the southeastern Caribbean has beautiful white sand beaches, for which it was named, a haven for scuba divers. Finding a remote beach, they put on their bathing suits and snorkeled the black coral reefs. The fish were abundant in numbers, variety, and color. They snorkeled for an hour, and then lay in the warm shallow water at the beaches edge, wrapped in each other's arms. Joel felt like Burt Lancaster in *From Here to Eternity,* his bliss encompassed his whole being.

"Are you ready for lunch?"

I'm famished. Do you know a good place nearby?"

"Everywhere is nearby with the transporter."

They dressed, and within minutes they entered Le Domaine De Lonvilliers resort hotel in St. Martin, heading for the La Veranda beach front restaurant. The buffet lunch had a large variety of French and Caribbean dishes, and the sommelier brought them a bottle of Kendall Jackson Riesling.

After lunch they went to Marigot, the capital of St. Martin, and walked down the waterfront to the open air market. The colorful tables featured bags of pepper, nutmeg, vanilla, and bananas. At the Octaedre shop, Joel saw a display of authentic St. Martin garnets. One necklace, with four large garnets, caught Elena's attention, so Joel purchased it for her. At the Vie en Rose restaurant, they sat on the balcony of the upstairs dining room, and could only manage a salad after their large lunch at La Veranda.

When sunset approached, they returned to Blanquilla, and as they strolled along a beach on the west side of the island, they watched the sun give a memorable display of colors as it sank into the sea. In the twilight from a sun below the horizon, they lay on the sand and made love, first gently, then with a passion that took their breath away. The twilight ended and an inky darkness descended upon them. They lay on their backs and looked up at a sky so full of stars that it seemed like they were in a planetarium.

Joel returned Elena to Chibcha, and they spent an hour with Esteban and Maria, who told them of their wedding plans. Back in California, Joel spent two hours in the machine, mentally working on preparation for the demonstration in China.

The site that Hu Jintao had selected for the demonstration of Joel's capabilities was in the Gobi Desert on the Ala Shan Plateau. The Chinese army has a secret weapons-testing facility there, with all the latest in weapons technology. The group of attendees had grown considerably. Hu wanted to make sure he had very little opposition to Joel's new ethics. All the senior officers of the armed forces had been invited, plus leading politicians. Joel wandered among them, taking control of the minds of all the new participants and giving them the stomach pain treatment.

Although the fourth largest desert in the world, only the western portion of the Gobi is sandy; the rest is mainly rock, and at an altitude of three- to five-thousand feet, has a cold climate. In July the daily high is the midsixties, and in January close to zero, almost the opposite environment to the American test grounds at Yuma.

Joel had told Hu to start attacking him at a low level and work up to major weapons. A bleacher-like viewing stand had been erected and all the dignitaries were seated there. Joel moved a hundred yards away from this structure to an open flat area.

The assault started with snipers firing high-powered rifles using high-explosive armor-piercing bullets. They had been ordered to aim for his head, assuming he wore body armor, so a dozen bullets exploded in front of Joel's face before they gave up on this attack. Next, ten infantrymen came out to him, attacking him with fixed bayonets. After enduring their attempts to stab him, Joel disarmed all ten men and left them unconscious on the ground.

After retrieving the groggy infantrymen, a tank came out to do battle. Joel extended his force field out to ten feet diameter, while keeping the inner field close to his body. The tank fired its 125-mm gun, capable of penetrating the armor of an enemy tank. The missile exploded at Joel's outer force field without causing any damage. The tank then tried to run over him, resulting in a sudden halt to the tank's progress and severe damage to the front.

Hu asked Joel to move a half-mile away from the viewing stand, and he complied. Then an attack aircraft flew over slowly and dropped a 500 kilo block buster bomb directly on top of Joel. After the dust settled and Joel emerged unscathed, the Chinese military hierarchy went into a huddle. Joel walked back to the grandstand and waited with Hu until they made their decision.

"Have you started making the changes I want?"

"No, I needed to have this demonstration first, to eliminate all opposition."

"Well, later today I want to see the first edict issued to initiate the changes."

"I will do that."

"I will be checking and if you don't I will replace you with someone who will."

"How do you travel between here and your home? I checked and there is no record of you entering or leaving China."

"I have a transportation system similar to the one on *Star Trek*."

"What is *Star Trek?*"

"An American television show. Get a copy and it will show you." Joel felt a little lie would do no harm.

Finally, the Chinese brass made their decision; they wanted a nuclear demonstration.

"What size bomb do they want to use?" asked Joel.

"A .5 kiloton—that would not cause a large radiation cloud, and if you can withstand that, they will be convinced."

"Where are you going to do it?"

"We have a facility ten miles east of here. It will take two hours to set it up; they didn't think you would survive this long, so they haven't prepared the site for a blast."

"Okay, I will go have some lunch and meet you there."

Joel transported to Beijing, and the Hongbinlou Beijing-style restaurant at 82 West Chang'an Ave. Beijing-style food is a collection of varieties from several regions of northern China. He ordered a selection, including Beijing Roast Duck; Bifengtang Prawns fried in oil and garlic; Gong Bao Ji Ding, a spicy chicken dish with peanuts; and To Doe Zi, stir-fried potatoes with green peppers and seasoning. After lunch he went for a stroll through the streets, and the exercise helped digest the large spicy meal.

Returning to the Gobi Desert, Joel found that preparations were complete. A small building had been constructed with the bomb inside. They asked Joel to stand beside it so that they could see him when the denotation took place. The main data-gathering facility was five miles away, but they had personnel in protective suits inside a bunker only half a mile from the blast.

Joel expanded his outer force field and did as they requested. No sooner did he approach the small building than detonation took place; they made sure he had no time to pull a disappearing act. The building turned to dust, a small depression formed in the rocky ground, and a mushroom cloud rose into the air. Standing in the depression, Joel waited for the visibility to clear, then waved to the observers as he walked towards the bunker.

One hour later Joel stood on the stage of a small theater back at the main base. Before him sat the Chinese leaders who had spent the day witnessing his demonstration of power.

"Any individual in the room who does not give Hu Jintao his fullest co-operation will suffer swift and harsh retribution from me personally. You will also be responsible for the support of the personnel under your command, and any negative action by them will place you in jeopardy. Is there anybody who feels he cannot comply with my edicts?"

A senior general, General Chang, in the front row stood up, saying, "I refuse to support the destruction of our way of life." He immediately fell to the floor clutching his stomach, obviously in severe pain. At the same time, several other members of the audience clutched their stomachs. Chang stopped writhing on the floor, then got back on his feet. "Your tricks will not stop me; I will fight you to the death."

"Then I must make an example of you." Joel pointed his laser weapon at the general and a beam hit the man, vaporizing him immediately and leaving an empty space where he had stood. "Anybody else have anything to say?" The audience sat stunned; they could not believe what they had just witnessed. When nobody answered, Joel continued. "If you think you can oppose me in secret you will suffer the same fate as your General Chang. Now I expect your full co-operation in implementing my reforms."

With this statement, Joel concluded his business with the Chinese hierarchy. He bade goodbye to Hu Jintao and returned to his compound in California.

Chapter Thirteen

Joel lay in the machine with the power at one hundred percent, thinking about his next moves. He had substantial activities going in the United States. Aid and education centers for the poor in all major cities, the federal government working for the benefit of the people, and a start on the state governments and abuse reduction. Abroad, he had major initiatives going in Colombia, Iraq, Afghanistan, Sudan, and China. And above all, he had Elena.

He felt that Anton Kelbeck would be very pleased, but as he tackled a few new projects he needed to consolidate the ones he had going now, and he wanted to spend some time with Elena. He worked twenty hours a day, and by taking advantage of time zone differences, always managed to be somewhere where it was daylight. Maybe he could find time to visit a few countries with tyrannical leaders and apply stomach ache treatment to help them mend their ways.

So Joel planned his schedule. Each weekday he would start work on the legislature of a different state. After visiting the leaders of the state Democratic and Republican parties, he would have them arrange group meetings with the members of both legislatures for a few days later. At these meetings he would apply the stomach treatment and convince them to put the needs of their constituencies first in all matters. Dealing with five states a week, he could handle all the states in less than three months.

This would give him plenty of time each day to visit pedophiles and convince them to mend their ways or suffer the consequences. During the hours of darkness in the United States, Joel could visit dictators in countries around the world that were still in daylight.

He would visit Elena every other day, arriving in Colombia at 6 p.m. in time for dinner and leave at midnight. He called Elena and told her of his plans; he made a habit of calling her twice a day.

She said, "Don't you think that schedule is too exhausting?"

"No, I'll be okay. I only need three hours sleep in the machine each night."

"Well, I'll be waiting for you with open arms; you can rest while you are here, at least part of the time."

"I take that as a promise," Joel said with a laugh. "I'll see you in two days, goodbye, my love."

"Goodbye my heart."

Joel decided to visit the states in order of population, covering the most populous first. He would start with California, then continue with Florida, Illinois, Pennsylvania, Ohio, Michigan, and Georgia, in that order. Along with Texas and New York, the two states he had already converted, these nine states accounted for more than half the population of the United States. The next morning he arrived in Sacramento early to talk to the legislature leaders. He had John Garamendi, Gloria Romero, and Dave Cogdill call a meeting of all the members of the Senate, and Karen Bass, Alberto Torrico, and Michael Villines, do the same for the Assembly. He gave them three days to set up the meetings. The rest of the day he worked on pedophiles in northern California. As darkness fell, he turned his attention to foreign trouble spots.

He started with the Middle East. Transporting to Ramallah he remained cloaked as he entered the office of Mahmoud Abbas, President of Palestine Authority. Joel took control of Abbas's mind and instructed him to call a meeting for 9 a.m. in two days in his office, and to ensure the attendance of the Fatah, Hamas, Third Western, and Islamic Jihad political faction leaders. From Fatah, Joel wanted Ahmad Qurei, Sakr Habash, Abu Shbak, Mohammed Dahlan, Rawhi Fattuh, Jibril Rajoub, and Salim Al-Zaanoun; from Hamas, Khaled Marshal Ishmail Haniveh and Mahmoud

Zahar; from Islamic Jihad, Ramadan Abdullah Shallah, Imad Abu Diab, and Muhammad Saadi; from the Third Way party, Salam Fayyad. In addition Joel wanted Nayef Hawatmah Secretary General of the Democratic front for the Liberation of Palestine to attend.

Abbas told Joel, "Some of those people will not come to my office for a meeting, especially at such short notice."

"You just invite them; I will see that they attend."

Joel then visited all the men invited to the meeting. Taking control of their minds and using the stomach pain persuasion technique, he instructed them to be in the office of Mahmoud Abbas, two days hence at 9 a.m. For those who were hard to track down, he used his technique of reading the thoughts of people he encountered until he found someone with information he needed; this way he found the leaders of Hamas and the Palestinian Islamic Jihad.

Joel transported to Jerusalem, where he entered the office of Ehud Olmert, the Prime Minister, and instructed him to follow him to the office of Shimon Peres, the President. Once he had the two of them alone in a conference room, Joel told them of the peace initiative he had in progress and instructed them to withdraw all their troops from the Ramallah region and to call a one-day complete cease-fire. He could tell that they were skeptical and didn't want to do it, but his will prevailed and the orders were given directly from that conference room. Joel then ordered Shimon Peres to call a meeting of the twenty most influential politicians in Israel, for noon the same day as the Palestinian meeting.

The next day after three hours of sleep in the machine, Joel transported to Florida. He followed the same routine as in California: arrange legislature meetings first then work on abusers. At 6 p.m. he arrived in Chibcha to a warm welcome from all the villagers. They had prepared a feast in his honor. Afterwards he spent some time talking to Maria and Esteban; they talked about their plans to get married, and Joel promised to attend the wedding.

Joel and Elena retired at 10, and she fulfilled her promise of an open arm welcome. She knew he would be leaving at midnight, but they slept entangled and he hated to wake her. It was 1 o'clock before he untwined, awaking her in the process, and after brief goodbyes he finally left.

He returned to the compound for some time on the machine, then, at

7 a.m., he started work in Illinois. Using the same routine there as in California, he put in a full day of work before he left for Israel. Arriving early for the meeting, he spent some time looking around Ramallah. He visited the wall Israel had constructed around the West Bank; the yellow-domed mosque, a distinctive landmark; sampled the Rukab's ice cream; and ended up at the courtyard of the Mukataa, the site of Arafat's tomb. The Mukataa is the location of Mahmoud Abbas's office.

All the attendee's he had requested sat patiently in Abbas's large conference room. Joel decided to use the same speech he had made in Iraq, with just a few changes. He entered cloaked, re-established control of their minds, and instructed them to see him as Muhammad. They didn't all see the same image; each one of them had a picture in his mind of what Muhammad looked like, and each man saw that image. Joel sat cross-legged, facing them, levitated to ten feet, and slowly uncloaked. There followed a shocked silence that Joel stretched out for two full minutes. He did not speak to them, but planted the thoughts in their minds, using the Palestinian form of Levantine Arabic. This way each man heard the voice he associated with Muhammad.

"I am greatly disappointed in all of you. You have all interpreted the teachings of the Qur'an for your own personal purposes. I demand that the killing stops immediately and peace be restored at once. You will stop fighting among yourselves. Democracy is a good thing; I want suffrage for all my people, including women. Those who do not obey me will suffer pains at the hands of Allah. Your only mission in life from now on, is to bring peace and prosperity to all of my people, especially the lowest among them. Over the next few days, I will appear at mosques across Palestine, repeating this message to the masses. You will endorse it, and lead in carrying out my wishes. Remember, thoughts that oppose my wishes will bring pain."

As he said that all the men in the room doubled up in pain, some sliding to the floor in agony. As the bad thoughts were pushed out of their minds by the pain's severity subsided. Once they were all back in their seats, Joel continued. "You will feel those pains every time you oppose my wishes; they will be more severe each time until the pains kill you."

"You will no longer oppose the state of Israel. It will be the land between Lebanon to the north, Egypt to the south, and Jordan to the west, including the Golan Heights and the Gaza Strip. The Palestine state will consist of the West Bank, including the Jewish settlements. The city of Jerusalem will be divided by the Wailing Wall, with an open border, allowing free passage to anyone. There will be free elections in both states with all Moslems, Hebrews, Christians, and persons of any other religion having equal votes in the state they live in. All peoples will live in peace and harmony in whichever state they live in now. Israel will agree to this division of lands. You will hold productive reconciliatory talks with Israel."

"Now go home and start the work of Allah."

Joel transported to Jerusalem for his meeting with the Israelis. He arrived early, and as in Ramallah, took the opportunity to see something of the city. As he approached, he could see a mass of white buildings spread over the hilltops with the old walled city as its center. The Old City is divided into four quarters: Moslem, Jewish, Christian, and Armenian.

He landed at the Temple Mount where Abraham prepared to sacrifice his son and where Mohammed ascended to heaven. The gold-topped Dome of the Rock stands in this compound, as does the Wailing Wall, the only remaining wall of the Temple that separates the Muslim and Jewish sections of Jerusalem. He could see many people kneeling at the wall praying and sticking written prayers in the cracks between the ancient bricks.

If not for the presence of a large number of armed security personnel, the scene would have had the appearance of quiet, everyday life in any big city. He passed through the Jaffa Gate into the Armenian quarter hidden behind high walls and the Christian quarter location of the Holy Sepulchre, where Jesus was crucified.

At 9, in a cloaked condition, he entered the office of Shimon Peres, and twenty-two men awaited him. He could feel the tension in the room. These men all had their own agenda and their body language said, "We will not compromise." Concentrating on each man individually, Joel took control of their minds and using telepathy told them the must obey his instructions or suffer the severe stomach pains. He gave them the same speech he had given to the Palestinians.

"You will not oppose the state of Palestine. It will consist of the West Bank including the Jewish settlements. The state of Israel will be the land between Lebanon to the north, Egypt to the south, and Jordan to the west, including the Golan Heights and the Gaza Strip. The city of Jerusalem will be divided by the Wailing Wall, with an open border, allowing free passage to anyone. There will be free elections in both states with all Moslems,

Hebrews, Christians, and persons of any other religion having equal votes in the state they live in. All peoples will live in peace and harmony in whichever state they live in now. The Palestinians will agree to this division of lands. You will hold productive reconciliatory talks with Palestine."

Joel could see that most of the attendees were having problems with intense pain. He waited until they had all regained their composure, then he continued.

"There will be no discussion of this division of lands. No new Jewish settlement will be started in the West Bank; the existing settlements can remain in peace or the settlers can move back to Israel. If you have problems convincing other factions to agree to these terms, I will come back and speak to them. If you oppose me the stomach pains will increase in intensity until you submit, or they completely incapacitate you."

As if to prove his point, one man dressed as a Hasidic Jews rose to his feet in protest, then collapsed on the floor. His neighbor checked his pulse and announced that he was dead. This brought the meeting to a close, but before he left, Joel took Shimon Peres aside and instructed him to call a meeting with Mahmoud Abbas immediately.

For the next few days he worked in different states during the day and in the evening he transported to Palestine to visit as many mosques as time allowed. He appeared as Mohammad and delivered the speech he used with their leaders, gaining tremendous support for the new Palestine state. After covering Palestine, he concentrated on Israel, visiting synagogues throughout the land, appearing as Jehovah, and delivering the speech he gave to the Jewish leaders. In the West Bank territory he spent time with the rabbis and other leaders, and prevailed upon them to support the land division.

Chapter Fourteen

oel lay in the machine plotting the strategy he would use against the world's worst dictators. To kill them or just remove them from power would create a battle for control that could result in civil war and the deaths of many people, a lot of them innocent citizens. He must control the dictators and their supporters and use them to make the changes he wanted.

This approach seemed to let them off lightly and not punish them for their crimes against humanity, but in a way they were being punished. Joel would make them do things they didn't want to do, and their opposition would cause them great pain.

Myanmar or Burma had a military dictatorship headed by Senior General Than Shwe. In May 1990, the government held free elections for the first time in almost thirty years. The National League for Democracy (NLD), the party of Aung San Suu Kyi, won 392 out of 489 seats, but the election results were annulled by the State Law and Order Restoration Council (SLORC), the military rulers, who refused to step down. Led by Than Shwe since 1992, the SLORC oppressed the people of Burma and suppressed any attempt to make changes. Kyi was imprisoned, and his first cousin Dr. Sein Win led a government-in-exile since December 1990.

Joel visited Than Shwe. The general seemed very old, and his mind seemed to wander at times. Shwe had the current Prime Minister, General Thein Sein, visiting him. Joel took control of both their minds. He ordered Shwe to assemble all the members of the SLORC, now called the State Peace and Development Council, (SPDC), and to bring the imprisoned Aung San Suu Kyi to the meeting. Next he had Shwe issue an edict outlawing the practice of slave labor, and ordering the immediate execution of soldiers committing rape.

Joel transported to a number of army installations and brainwashed officers at all levels, from lieutenant to general, into obeying the Senior General's edict. This served to start easing the plight of the oppressed masses as soon as possible while he worked on the leaders.

At the meeting the next morning, Joel took control of the minds of all attendees, and ordered Than Shwe to retire and appoint Aung San Suu Kyi Senior General, Prime Minister, and head of the SLORC. He then ordered the members of the SLORC to obey all Kyi's orders. Joel could see the pain on the faces of the SLORC members as they struggled with this order, but eventually they all came around, except former Prime Minister, General Thein Sein. "I will not obey," he shouted through his pain. Joel decided an example would reinforce Kyi's power.

"I will show you what will happen to you if you disobey me." He pointed his finger at the general and vaporized him. From the looks on the faces of the rest of the SLORC, he knew Kyi would have no more problems with them.

In North Korea 65-year-old Kim Jong Il had been in power since 1994 and ranked number two in the list of world's worse dictators. The Ministry of People's Security placed spies in workplaces and neighborhoods to inform on anyone who criticized the regime, even in their own homes. All radios and TV sets were fixed to receive only government stations. Disloyalty to Kim Jong Il and his late father Kim Il Sung was a punishable crime. Offenses included allowing pictures of either leader to gather dust, be torn, or be folded. The population was divided into "loyalty groups." One-third belonged to the "hostile class." These people received the worst jobs and housing and could not live in the capital, Pyongyang. Below the hostiles were the estimated two hundred fifty thousand held in prison camps, some for crimes allegedly committed by relatives. Executione were performed in public.

Using his cloaking device and mind control ability, Joel assembled the

President of North Korea, Kim Yong-nam, the Premier, Kim Yong Il, and Kim Jong Il in the dictator's office. These three men alone could change the politics of North Korea, so Joel gave them strict instructions on the way the country would be run going forward.

He could not resist giving them a severe example of the stomach pains, and he let it last long enough so that all three men were incapacitated when he left. He now had no doubt that North Korea would soon be a democratic country.

Over the next week, Joel visited King Abdullah of Saudi Arabia, Robert Mugabe of Zimbabwe, Sayyid Ali Khamenei of Iran, Islam Karimov of Uzbekistan, and Isayas Afewerki of Eritrea. The process he used was the same in each country. He assembled the men who held the power, took control of their minds, and ordered them to change to a democratic society. In each case Joel eliminated the man who gave the leader the most trouble. This brought the rest into line.

PART SIX
THE END

Chapter One

Joel returned to his compound and lay in the machine for three hours at one hundred percent. As the session came to an end, he heard a voice in his head speak his name. He got out of the machine and searched his basement, but found nobody. Am I going crazy? he thought.

"No Joel," said the voice in his head. "I have decided that you have interfered too much in my creation. Joel, I am going to appear to you in human form, to facilitate our conversation." A man appeared before Joel. If you thought of an average man, this would be it. Six feet tall, 180 pounds, well proportioned, Caucasian, dressed in a sports shirt, Dockers, and casual tan shoes.

"So God is male Caucasian," said Joel

"If you want I can be female, Black African, Asian, American Indian, Semitic, or Hispanic, take your pick." As he spoke, the figure changed its appearance to match the ethnicity, both male and female, as he mentioned it.

Joel stood there in a state of shock, unable to bring himself to speak. He tried to penetrate the apparition's mind and found it impossible.

"You cannot read my thoughts, my mind is far stronger than yours, but I can read yours. I know you have never believed in me, but now I am here.

What do you have to say for yourself?"

"You're right. I have not been a believer; as a scientist I saw no evidence of your existence. I found it hard to have blind faith. I guess I was wrong. It seems inadequate to say I'm sorry."

"In spite of your non-religious upbringing, you have led a good life. I am not angry with you. You have used the power at your disposal for good purposes, but you have interfered too much with my plans. In the past men have acquired far less power than you and always used it for evil purposes, but because you have tried to do good works, I decided to converse with you."

"Have you talked to other people in the past?"

"I normally do not answer questions, but you are an exceptional person. Even in the most advanced worlds entities perform good deeds for two reasons: one, they fear reprisals from authorities or from their deity, or two, they see some benefit to themselves. Your power far exceeds anything anyone else has achieved, yet you are performing good deeds for no other reason than it is the right thing to do. I have never encountered this before. This could be a benefit from your sessions on the machine or a quality inherently in your genes. Anyway, I will answer your questions.

"About once every millennium I find a reason to contact a human. I waited four billion years for the species to reach a reasonable level of intelligence. I first contacted Abraham in about two thousand B.C., basically to let people know that I existed. Then I spoke to Moses in fifteen hundred B.C., to give you the Ten Commandments. In five hundred B.C., because the populations of India and China grew so rapidly and religion moved eastward so slowly, I appeared to Buddha and Confucius. Then there came Jesus. I visited him at the end of his twenty-ninth year and told him to preach my gospel. He lasted three years before the corruptors of Abraham's religion killed him to protect their power. Finally in six hundred A.D. I talked to Muhammad."

"What purpose did you have for contacting these men?"

"I wanted each of these men to teach their people to love thy God, love thy neighbor, and lead a life of good works."

"Why didn't it work?"

"Each one of them was a great man, and each created a religion with God at its center, but once they died, lesser men took over. The basic c oncept became corrupted, too restrictive, and full of pomp and circumstance. The religions oppressed the people they were supposed to save, broke into sects, and spent their energy squabbling among themselves. I sadly watched the world go through the dark ages, crusades and inquisitions, holy wars, one religion fighting another, even one sect of a religion fighting another sect. Then came the world wars of the twentieth century.

"The only bright spot I saw occurred in the Americas, with religious freedom. It produced a shining, but slightly tarnished, glimmer of hope, trying, by example, to spread freedom throughout the world. This vanished when they tried to use force, to spread their version of democracy."

"Then what is wrong with what I'm trying to do?"

"Because you are trying to do good things, I am going to take the time to explain it to you, although you might not understand. I have an overall evolution plan and you are interfering with it.

"There are one hundred and twenty million galaxies' in the universe, ranging from one thousand to one hundred thousand parsecs (a parsec being nineteen trillion miles) in diameter, and they are millions of parsecs apart. There are between a billion and a trillion stars in each galaxy. Each star has between five and twelve planets. There is life on one planet in each galaxy, and only one. That's one hundred and twenty million planets with life.

"The life on each planet is at different period of evolution, from amoebae, to the ultimate life form living in peace and harmony. The life forms with high levels of intelligence travel within their own galaxy, but because of the great distances, never succeed in traveling to another galaxy. That is why one life form never meets another life form. If a star becomes a nova, before the life form can move to another planet within its galaxy, I start a new planet in that galaxy, on the first step of evolution.

"Sixty percent of these life forms are more advanced than Earth's humans. When an individual life form dies, regardless of its religion, it is judged according to how it led its life, in accordance with the commandment to do unto others as you would have done unto you. If good, their soul is reborn on a planet up the chain of evolution, depending on how good it was, or down the chain depending on how bad it was. A very good person could move up to a much better life on a planet a lot farther up the evolutionary chain. Inversely, a very bad person could move way down the chain. For example Anton Kelbeck, Jr., moved up one percent, which is over a million planets higher.

"Joel, you are upsetting the balance. Each world must follow the slow evolution plan. Your activities have moved the Earth forward at too fast a pace; a planet must evolve due to the efforts of the majority of its inhabitants, not just one of that life form."

"You are telling me I must stop helping people?"

"Stopping is not enough. I cannot leave you here. The temptation to help people will be too great."

"What can I do to reverse the damage I have done?"

"You cannot reverse it, but here is what I want you to do. You will go to everybody you have interfaced with and erase any memory they have of you. Then destroy all the machines you've built and any technology advancements, such as your transporter, and this compound. I will give you one month, then I will move you up the chain five percent; that will put you on a planet far in advance of Earth, giving you a good life."

"Then there is no Heaven, Purgatory, and Hell?"

"Should all good people, no matter how good, get the same reward? Should all bad people, no matter how bad, get the same punishment? Heaven is moving up to a more advanced life form; the more good you do the farther you advance. Hell is moving down to lower level life form; the worse you perform the farther down you go. Purgatory would be when I don't have the right place for a person; I hold their soul in abeyance until the right spot opens up. That could be soon, or a long time."

"Can I take Elena with me?"

"Joel, you don't understand. You will be reborn on the advanced planet. You will not remember anything about this life or me."

"You're going to kill me? Do I deserve that?"

"Death is not an ending, but a new beginning. You are getting what you deserve, an advancement of five million planets. If you disobey me, the best you can hope for is to be reborn on Earth."

Joel used all his inner strength to suppress his disappointment. He knew God was aware of this. "I thank you for the month. I see that is generous. I could do it in a lot less. This will give me time to spend with Elena."

"I will return in thirty days to conclude our business." The figure in Joel's basement disappeared, leaving him sad and lonely.

Chapter Two

Joel decided to spend six days eliminating all trace of his activities, then spend three weeks with Elena, and on the final day destroy his compound. He called Sandra Lee and asked if he could visit her for a couple of hours. She said she could take a long lunch the next day and arranged to meet him at 11.

That evening at Elena's home, he asked her to go on vacation with him.

"I would love that. Where would we go?"

"You choose. I want to please you."

"I've always wanted to go on a cruise."

"Okay. Where to and how long?"

"I think I would like more than a week; how about two weeks?"

"Good. How about the Mediterranean? We haven't been there yet."

"You must be a mind reader, that's exactly where I would choose, preferably the eastern Mediterranean."

Joel then made love to her gently. He made her climax twice during the foreplay and a third time when he finally entered her. At midnight he left her and transported back to his compound.

The next morning Joel left for Oakland, arrived at the Restoration

Corporate building before the workers, and removed all the working parts from the machine in his room. He talked to the leaders as they came in, removing memories of himself from their minds and promoting Brian Jefferson to the leader of the corporation. Flying five hundred miles off the coast, Joel dropped the machine parts in the ocean.

He then called a travel agent and found that the Holland America Line's Prinsendam left Athens in a week on a two-week cruise and the Owner suite could be obtained at $17,000 per person. He called Elena, discussed the itinerary with her, obtained her approval, and booked it.

For his next stop, Joel picked the Freedom Ranch. He could not leave without saying goodbye to Rachel and the girls. He landed in front of the main building. John and Pete came out to greet him. They went inside and Rachel hugged him, saying, "How long will you be with us?"

"Only a couple of hours. Where are all the girls?"

"You're a little early, they don't rise before noon, but I'll have Pete tell them you are here."

"I see you have some new guards."

"Yes, four of them; two are sleeping and two on the gate. We also have three new girls, and I hired a cook."

They went into the lounge, and Rachel had the cook bring them some coffee.

"Have the old guards given you any problems?" asked Joel.

"Lennie died in a bar fight, six months ago; he finally picked on the wrong guy. Wade moved back east and Ron and Mitch work as security guards at the Silver Slipper. They held a big investigation when Cy Richards disappeared, but nobody came here, and after a while it all blew over."

"Do you hear from Lacie, Laura, or June?"

"They call occasionally, and we see them at the annual meeting. With the income they get from the Ranch they all decided they could afford to go to college and get a degree. They seem to be very happy with their new lives."

"How about you? Are you happy?"

"Oh yes. I feel like I have been released from prison, I even have a man in my life. He's a pit boss at the Bellagio."

As they talked the girls he knew entered one at a time. They had taken time to make themselves look their best, and their best caught Joel's eye for each one was a beauty in her own right. Belle entered first, then Pat, Rita, Mary, Cate, and lastly Susan. Each girl expressed delight at seeing him, and after a big hug and a kiss from each one, his face glowed with several different shades of lipstick.

When they asked him about himself and what he had been doing, he had to be evasive, but he did admit that he had a significant other, and told them a little about Elena.

"How are things going here?" he asked, to change the subject from himself. They all started to talk at once in an excited manner.

"Whoa, one at a time. Rachel, tell me about the business side. Are you making a profit?"

"We're doing very well. Because we own the Ranch we don't have an owner draining off the profits. We have added some new things that are siphoning business away from the competition. We now include a buffet that is as good as any Las Vegas casino, and we supply transportation to and from the Ranch."

"Can you do this at the same price?"

"No, but once word got around, we found the class of men we want to cater to were willing to pay extra, and business is booming."

"And we sure like the better class of clientele, except the really fat ones." said Belle.

"We make good money, and with the annual profits and the money you gave us, our bank accounts are getting fat," said Mary.

They talked for another hour, then Joel said, "I've got to go. I have a luncheon engagement with Sandra."

"In Spokane?" said Susan. "How can you get there in time?"

Joel realized he had screwed up, but he laughed it off, saying, "Ah, that's my secret."

He hugged them all goodbye, went to the bathroom to clean up, then went outside. They all followed him, and as they saw him transport out of the compound, they knew how he was going to be on time for his lunch with Sandra.

Joel arrived in Spokane just in time to stow his transporter and walk into Sandra's dance studio exactly at 11. Sandra had just finished a class and waved him into her office while she freshened up in the little vanity at the back. When she completed the repairs, they walked down the road a block to a nice family-style restaurant that had just opened for the day.

Once seated, Joel told the waitress. "Bring us two glasses of the house white wine, and we will order later." The waitress left and Joel took a long look at Sandra. "You look wonderful, glowing with health and happiness."

"Thank you, sir, I do feel good. Things are going well."

"Tell me about it."

"Well, the dance studio is very successful. I have all the students I can handle. I had to hire two teachers to help me. I have no financial problems because of the money I got from the ranch, and to top it all I'm seeing a man who has replaced you as the man of my dreams."

"That's wonderful. Who is he?"

"I went steady with him at high school, but left him to go to Las Vegas. Now that's all out of my system, we're back together and talking of marriage. How about you?"

Joel hesitated. He could not tell Sandra the truth, but he hated to lie. "I've met a woman from Colombia named Elena. We love each other very much. I'm going to leave the United States soon."

"Will you be back?"

"No, that's why I came to see you to say goodbye. I also went to the Ranch to see our friends there."

They talked some about Elena, and he filled Sandra in on the news he had heard at the Ranch.

The waitress returned and they ordered lunch. While they ate the conversation flowed naturally. She talked about Charlie, her husband-to-be, and the dance studio. He told her more about Elena and the work they were doing with the farmers in Colombia. They reminisced and laughed about their adventure with Cy Richards.

After lunch, Joel walked Sandra back to the dance studio. With a hug and a kiss on the cheek he left.

Joel visited two more cities and repeated what he had done in Oakland. He began to feel low, so deciding he had done enough for one day, he headed for Chibcha. Later that night as he lay in bed snuggling with Elena, she said, "What's wrong, Joel? You seem miles away."

He realized he must throw off this feeling or he would spoil their last few weeks.

"Nothing, my darling. I'm just thinking about one of my projects that isn't going too well."

"Is there anything I can do to help?"

"Yes. Just hold me tight and tell me you love me."

At midnight Joel left Colombia and transported to Iraq, arriving in the midafternoon. He visited Dahr Sabah in Fallujah first. Dahr could not contain his pleasure at seeing Joel. He began telling him of all the success they had had and insisted in showing him a whole neighborhood in the Muallimin district that they had rebuilt. The results were astounding. The houses looked sturdy and modern, with the latest appliances. The people smiled all the time, showing their happiness. Work in progress could be seen in all the streets surrounding this neighborhood.

"How much activity do you have going on in the Jotan, Shurta, Muhandisin districts?"

"We have completed several homes in each district and are working on many more."

Dahr went quiet and Joel could tell some thing bothered him. "What is it, Dahr?"

Dahr did not speak for a while, then said, "You have done so much for us that I hate to ask for more, but we are almost out of money."

Joel laughed and said, "Let's go to the bank."

At the bank Joel deposited 1,200,000,000 Dinar ($1,000,000) in Dahr's account. When Dahr saw the amount he said, "Words cannot express our gratitude to you."

"No, Dahr, you deserve the credit. You did all the hard work. Now I must tell you why I came to see you." To make it easier for Dahr, Joel took command of his mind and told him that after today he would deal with a man named Brian Jefferson. He gave him Brian's phone number and told him not to hesitate to call him when he needed money. Brian would be expecting the calls.

"It will help if you send weekly reports to him showing progress and expenditures. He will visit you every few months. Please make him welcome. By the way, how is Salam doing? Has he mended his ways?"

"He works for us now. He oversees all activities in the Shurta district. We have made a new man of him. Will you stay and eat with us? My wife would be honored."

"Well, just a light snack. I have to visit Abu Tabil in Mosul next."

Joel finished his snack, then transported to the Al-Hadbaa' district of Mosul for his meeting with Abu Talib. It seemed like déjà vu. Abu delighted in seeing him, showed Joel the houses they had build, and had put Abula Shayma the cell leader and Abdallah Husayn, the battalion commander to work, leading construction teams. Abu didn't have to ask Joel for more money. Joel explained to him about Brian Jefferson and put 1,200,000,000 Dinar in his bank account.

All Abu could say was, "Is Brian related to Thomas Jefferson, who wrote your constitution?"

"I don't think so," replied Joel.

Chapter Three

eaving Iraq, Joel transported to Chicago to meet with Brian Jefferson at the Chicago corporation offices. He invited Brian up to his room, hypnotized him, placed him in the machine at eighty power, and planted this story in his head. He had been hired by a charity to manage all its activities. Each year on this date they would place approximately $150,000,000 in a corporate account for him to manage.

He would start at a salary of $200,000 a year, with a five percent raise each year. He could spend another $250,000 a year on travel expenses and salaries for a staff to support him, also with an increase of five percent a year. The rest must be spent on the corporation's charities, or carried over to the next year. He would send money to the established corporate offices in other cities and countries as they requested it. Elena's requests must be met without question.

He then planted in Brian's mind knowledge of all the charitable activities Joel had initiated in the last two years. He must expand to other United States cities, using local people, and to other areas of Iraq, Afghanistan, Sudan, and Colombia. He would find the leaders of Myanmar, North Korea, Saudi Arabia, Zimbabwe, Iran, Pakistan, Uzbekistani, and Eritrea receptive to him working in their countries.

Joel left Chicago convinced that Brian had the capability and integrity to carry out his instructions. He next stopped in the Cayman Islands and visited the bank that held the corporation money. The account had over $5,200,000,000 in it, so as soon as he identified himself, the manager came out to greet him and show him into his office.

He instructed the bank to invest the money in ten-year United States Treasury Bills, which paid over five percent. This would generate over $150,000,000 a year in interest. He gave the bank manager Brian Jefferson's phone number and the corporate bank account wire transfer information, and authorized him to transfer the interest to this account every year on this date.

The next day Joel visited the other United States cities, except Watts, that had corporate offices. In each city he replaced their memories of himself with memories of Brian Jefferson and disabled all the age-retarding machines. He left Watts until a day later, because next to Elena, this was going to be his most difficult task.

He arrived at the converted fourplex at 9 a.m. A year had passed since his first visit to this building and numerous changes had taken place. Cubicles filled the lounge and activity filled the cubicles. The hubbub of phones ringing, people talking, and computers humming filled the air. A line of people sat waiting along one wall.

Tywanna sat in one cubicle interviewing applicants for college funding for the next semester. The only requirement for funding was the ability to get accepted by a college, and if they couldn't do that they were assigned to the classes they needed to qualify.

In another cubicle Rashid interviewed men for jobs with large corporations made available by the Restoration Corporation subsidizing their salaries, and a girl he did not know performed the same task for women in the next cubicle.

Kory worked on obtaining facilities and instructors for the next round of trade classes. Tanisha had Parson Branch, who managed all their soup kitchens in southern California, in her office discussing expanding the size of two of them by moving to larger buildings in the same area.

Even the kitchen was being used. Four women had been hired to provide food and coffee for everyone, including the people waiting in line. Some of them looked like they could use a good meal.

One at a time he had the people who knew him take a fifteen-minute break and took them up to his room. He talked to each one for ten minutes about their lives and how they enjoyed the activities. He took great pleasure from the fact that they led happy, meaningful lives that gave them a sense of self-worth. Using hypnosis, he spent the last five minutes softening their memory of him, painting himself as a representative of a large charity that funded them through Brian Jefferson.

He found that the treatments he had given Kory and Tanisha made them highly intelligent and more than capable of continuing the work he had started. Joel left feeling that his legacy would live on even if his name didn't, and he knew that was the most important thing.

Two days before the cruise, Joel transported Elena to his compound. They spent a day buying three large suitcases and all the clothes they would need for a two-week cruise. Joel hired a limousine to take them to the Los Angeles airport, where they boarded the 6:30 a.m. Delta flight to Athens, changing planes in New York. They arrived in Athens at 8:50 a.m., where another limousine drove them to Piraeus, Athens' port. They spent two hours in the luxury waiting room for suite passengers and by noon they were in their suite.

The cruise made their senses reel. They visited Egypt, Israel, Turkey, Rhodes, Ephesus, Tunisia, Malta, Sicily, and ended up in Rome. They took shore tours by day, watched fabulous shows at night, gambled, danced, ate food that made your juices flow, and still found time to make love. On the days at sea, they would lounge around the pool and catch up on their sleep.

The vacation ended all too soon, and before they knew it they stood in the living room of Joel's house wondering how it all passed so fast.

"I want this to never end," said Elena.

"So do I. Why don't we go to Blanquilla for a few of days? Remember how beautiful it was there?"

"Yes, that would be wonderful."

"There's a sailboat that goes out of Isla Margarita for three nights. It holds six passengers, but we could charter it just for us. We can fish off the Los Hermanos islands, snorkel from the white sand beach at the Port Playa Yaque, and scuba dive the walls that the Isla Blanquilla is famous for. Captain Marc and his crew will supply everything we need, including Caribbean-style food and an open bar."

"Do you think it will be available?"

"I booked it three weeks ago just in case you wanted to go. They expect us tomorrow."

Elena flung her arms around his neck and hugged him.

"No wonder I love you so."

"We won't need much luggage, so we will use the transporter."

At 10 a.m. the next morning the forty-foot sloop *Audrey* left the Isla Margarita Yachting Marina with the captain, a cook, and two passengers on board, bound for La Blanquilla, sixty-two miles away. On the way out they did some deep sea fishing. They saw marlin and swordfish, but could not hook one. Joel caught a four-foot wahoo, and Elena a five-foot billfish. Jarba the cook said they had caught the two best eating fish in these waters, and they would have them for supper.

Five miles from La Blanquilla they passed the Islands of Los Hermanos just before dawn. While Elena still slept, Joel fished for a while in the shallow waters and caught some tarpon, pompano, and a large barracuda. They arrived as the sun rose over La Blanquilla and anchored in a beautiful solitary bay in front of a beach of singular beauty. The very fine white sand sloped down to a submarine paradise within easy reach of snorkelers.

They spent the morning snorkeling, and in the afternoon Joel taught Elena the basics of scuba diving. She learned fast and by late afternoon Joel took her to the edge of the wall, which started sixty-five feet from the shore and plummeted straight down more that three thousand feet. The wall is also rich with black corals, which were increasingly hard to find throughout the world.

Elena said, "This has been the best day of my life, although some of the nights have been better."

Joel laughed. "We'll walk the beach tonight and see if we can have our best night ever."

The next morning after breakfast the captain moved to another bay. The Playa El Americano was different but equally beautiful, with a spectacular natural bridge over a small inlet. The bay was home to numerous iguanas and small eagles called "Cachicares." They spent time exploring the island, snorkeling, scuba diving, and relaxing on the beach. That night they fell asleep in each other's arms to the gentle rhythm of the sea. The last day they moved to a bay called Las Tres Playas to spend another idyllic day of water, beaches, and sun. In the late afternoon they weighed anchor and headed back to Isla Margarita. Apart from soft drinks and a little wine with the delicious meals, they had made little use of the open bar.

From Isla Margarita, Joel took Elena directly home to Chibcha. He knew this would be his last night with her. It took all his willpower to keep from showing his sorrow. They made love for the last time, and when they finished he gently hypnotized her. To just disappear would be extremely cruel, so he had to change her memories of him. He became the man from a wealth charity, and her source of funds became Brian Jefferson. All the wonderful experiences they had shared became dreams that she could recall at will. He even planted the thought in her head that Jorge Lehder from Cauca could be a possible love interest for her.

Chapter Four

A rriving home, he proceeded to demolish all the equipment in his workshop, take apart all the atomic engines, dismantle all the age-retarding machines, and eliminate any trace of his existence. He kept one transporter. Then he sat in the living room waiting for God and thinking of Elena.

Finally, God appeared. Without saying a word he transmitted this thought, "I like your choice of a way to die so I will leave it up to you." With this, God disappeared.

Joel had procured a drug that would take ten hours to kill him painlessly. It would be five hours before he felt any effects. He went outside, took the drug, climbed into his transporter, took off heading for the moon, and set the controls at full power. This would propel him to a speed of over fifty thousand miles an hour and get him to the moon in five hours. The five hours passed rapidly.

Once outside the earth's atmosphere, the whole universe lay before him. First the beauty of earth filled his senses. He studied the land masses and oceans, tracing the courses of rivers, and marveling at the mountain ranges. Next he turned his attention to the solar system. He could see each planet that faced away from the blinding glare of the sun. He hadn't accounted for the heat and his air-conditioning system struggled to keep him cool.

Finally, Joel turned his attention to the stars. The constellations laid out before him in vivid clarity, and the stars of the Milky Way shone brightly as he struggled to identify them. By the time he reached the moon, he was suffocating in the heat, so he landed on the side away from the sun. The intense heat turned to frigid cold, once again straining his air-conditioning.

Leaving the moon, he set a path for Saturn, with Mars off to his left and Jupiter way over to the right.

Joel once again marveled at the beauty of it all as he slowly drifted off to sleep.

See 1stWorld Books at:

www.1stWorldPublishing.com

See our classic collection at:

www.1stWorldLibrary.com